Wife to
Charles II

About the author

Hilda Lewis was one of the best-known and best-loved of all historical novelists, known for her authentic application of period detail to all her books. She was born in London and lived for much of her life in Nottingham. She wrote over 20 novels and died in 1974.

Wife to Charles II

HILDA LEWIS

TORC

Cover Illustration: Catherine of Braganza by Jacob Huysmans.
Courtesy of the National Portrait Gallery, London.

This edition first published 2006

Torc, an imprint of
Tempus Publishing Limited
The Mill, Brimscombe Port,
Stroud, Gloucestershire, GL5 2QG
www.tempus-publishing.com

British Library Cataloguing in Publication Data.
A catalogue record for this book is available from the British Library.

ISBN 0 7524 3948 0

Typesetting and origination by Tempus Publishing Limited
Printed and bound in Great Britain

I

She had always known that she was destined to be Queen of England. But it made no difference either to herself or to her upbringing. She had accepted her destiny as a child does—a romantic tale; for she was to marry the most romantic prince in the world. It never occurred to her that life and romance are, for princes at least, poles apart.

She had been two years old when her father, Dom John Duke of Braganza of the royal house of Portugal, had been offered the crown... if he could take it. The country lay beneath the armed heel of Spain; the land dispossessed, its farms burnt, its daughters raped; and Philip of Spain flaunted a double crown. Would Dom John, the whole nation implored—high fidalgo to simple peasant—send the invader packing, wrest the crown from the usurper's head and put it upon his own? He had accepted; he'd had no choice. Already he had been summoned to Madrid—and death; the part he had already played in resistance and his royal blood made death certain. When the choice lies between certain death and the choice of a crown, what man could refuse? Certainly not Dom John, urged on by a wife that had no mind to be a widow and every mind to be a Queen.

So he took his choice and won his crown. The little Catherine left the country villa where she was born and came to the royal palace of Lisbon. That she was now a royal princess she did not know.

When she was seven—and an engaging little creature—her father sent an embassy to the friendly King of England, the first Charles, to negotiate a marriage with the fifteen-year-old Prince of Wales. But it had come to nothing. There were tensions between Charles and his people; and the English were not so much in love with his foreign Queen Henrietta Maria, that flouted their religion and had refused to be crowned. They had no mind for another foreigner—and a Papist at that!

A few years later the King of England went to the block and the son for whom Catherine had been destined became a wanderer—homeless and penniless; and her father put the idea aside—forgotten. Not so her mother. Donna Luisa was never one to put anything aside that might serve her country.

But meanwhile Catherine must be educated; at eight she was sent away to the convent that stood within the gate of Alacantra—a famous school that accepted only the noblest in the land. It suited the child well; truly religious, she delighted in the beauty, the order and the spirit of *The Sacred Heart*.

'She has a vocation,' Mother Superior said—and only one eye on a handsome dowry, 'one day she will make a great abbess.'

'My daughter's vocation is to be a wife and mother!' Donna Luisa said, a little sharp. 'I know my child. One day she will love a man as deeply as she now loves God.'

And the good Mother crossing herself; Luisa added, 'And, moreover, it is a child that loves dancing and music and fine clothes. She loves God enough to thank Him with a true heart; but she would not make a good nun. And that is as well; for her vocation is to serve her country. And that, Reverend Mother, is also a way of serving God.'

In the quiet of the convent the child grew to a girl. It was an education well suited to a lady whose life must be spent within the walls of her husband's estate—to carry herself with propriety towards God and her fellows; to order a great house and everything that pertains thereto—the properties of herbs and the making of simples; and the use of her needle both in plain and fine work. But for a royal princess who is destined to be a Queen, who must go out into a strange, free world to hold her own with the most accomplished women in the courts of Christendom, it was not enough; not nearly enough.

So Catherine grew up in a world that had little to do with the world outside the convent. Like her companions she never saw a man save a priest, or her father or a brother; but, like all the others, as she grew up, she joined in the talk young girls will indulge in anywhere—the man they should marry and the children they meant to have. Nor was it to be wondered at. They were high-born Portuguese and most of them betrothed from infancy; yet it did not stop them from whispering of lovers—romantic and handsome. But for all of them the hero of heroes, the most desired lover in the world was the young, uncrowned King of England—with scarce a pillow to rest his handsome head.

Even to Portugal came tales of his charms. He was handsome, he was gay, he was witty, he was kind. He had the most exquisite manners; and, when he danced, the whole court—whether in Paris or the Hague—would stop to watch him. 'You must be patient and wait for your prince—he is worth waiting for!' they would say, half-teasing. And, indeed, for her alone, no match had been arranged. There were suitors aplenty; she was a princess of a royal house and a pretty thing with a rich dowry—her father's only daughter. But Donna Luisa refused them all. The girl was meant for the English prince. So when her schoolfellows teased her she said nothing; a girl does not jest about her destined husband... but she dreamed of him at night.

She was eighteen when the death of her father came crashing into her gentle paradise. She had not known he was ill, had not seen him sink day by day into death; she had, indeed, seen little of him at all. Now she would see him never again. Weeping she treasured her memories of babyhood. How he would throw her into the air and catch her again on his strong arms; how, all-unknowing she had persuaded him to his crown. Her second birthday when the messengers came; and while he sat, troubled, Donna Luisa had put the baby into his arms. And he, melted by her infant charms, had declared her worthy of a royal sire. The little story made her weep yet more bitterly—for all she was grown-up and must take her place in the world.

Home again she saw almost as little of her mother as before. Donna Luisa was Regent now; Alphonso, the King, was not fit to rule. Childhood illness had left him a vicious, violent weakling, sick in mind and body. Donna Luisa had been a devoted wife, she remained a loving, anxious mother; she was to become known as the wisest ruler in Europe.

Catherine's life now was even more enclosed than that of the convent, where there had been, at least, playfellows in plenty. Here, even married women came seldom into court and unmarried girls almost never. She had, for company, her ladies and her duenna, beloved Maria de Penalva, that had guarded her infancy. It was the secluded life of a Portuguese noblewoman and Catherine did not quarrel with it.

So one year went by and then another; and, though she was for the most part content, one thing grieved her. The girls that had been her friends at school were married; they would come bringing their babies for her to see and her heart would turn over; she loved children.

When her friends had gone carrying away their babies, she would go to her chamber sighing because she was twenty and unwed. She would look at herself in the glass and wonder if she could be thought pretty. The glass showed her a small, neatly-shaped young woman with large brown eyes and dark formal curls framing a fine-featured face. But was she truly pretty? What of her mouth? The two front teeth projecting a little, gave a small pout to the upper lip. Sometimes she deplored it; sometimes it pleased her. It lent character to the neat pretty face. Yes... she *was* pretty. But how long would prettiness last? Portuguese women ripened all too soon.

She need not have troubled her head. It was a very young face. Save for her father's death she had known little grief and less experience. It was, moreover, a face that must always keep something of youth, so innocent the eyes; they mirrored a desire to be good, an essential purity no experience would entirely dim.

So although suitors offered for her hand, they were refused. Donna Luisa never lost sight of her ambition—her daughter should be Queen of England. One must, of course, wait with patience till the time came; but come it would—of that Donna Luisa had not the slightest doubt. This most passionate ambition was only partly for the girl herself; it was even more for love of her country. England would strengthen Portugal against hated Spain; and Portugal would make good return with gold and lands... and the beloved Infanta.

Donna Luisa was the first to recognise the changing wind; to understand that the English had tired of their dreary Commonwealth and wanted their King again. And, Cromwell being dead, and no-one strong enough to say them nay, their King they meant to have. But the time to realise her ambition was not yet. For how can a King with no pillow to his head share his bed with a wife? So again she must wait upon her dearest hope; and her daughter remained unwed.

When Charles came home again Catherine was twenty-two and looked younger. Charles was thirty now, and not a young thirty. Adventures—in love as well as in war—had left their mark. Now that he was a King the question of his marriage loomed at once.

The people wanted a settled peace; they had had enough unrest. They had their King; now they wanted their heir. No more trouble. And especially no trouble with the King's brother James, heir to the crown till Charles should beget him a son. James, they suspected, had leanings to the Catholic faith.

Donna Luisa had long angled for the English King; now was the time to bait the hook. She was the more encouraged to hear from her ambassador in Paris that King Louis was much inclined to the match; and, more. Henrietta-Maria was already in England to whisper on the matter—a whisper big with offers of friendship and a vast sum of money for the groom's private purse. Of course Louis favoured the match; Donna Luisa could well understand it. England and Portugal allied in marriage against hated and hateful Spain would suit his game well.

The Portuguese ambassador to England, Dom Francisco de Mello, moved cautiously in the matter. He was Catherine's godfather and stood firm by his princess's dignity.

His first approach was to my lord Manchester the King's chamberlain. 'It is good to be back in England,' Dom Francisco said, in his careful English, 'my country's joy is great that the son of Portugal's old friend wears his crown again.'

'We thank God for it!' Manchester said.

'God gives; but we must learn to keep His gifts. Your King must grasp his crown with a firm hand. He must marry and beget an heir. All Christendom waits upon his choice.'

'The choice is the King's!' my lord reminded him, a little stiff.

'But naturally. Now! We have in Portugal a princess very fit for your King. In beauty, in age and virtue, none fitter. And we should give a dowry equal to her merits. Were your King to search throughout Christendom he could find none fitter.'

'She is a Catholic,' my lord objected and added with quick courtesy, 'For myself, I have nothing against Catholics; nor the King, neither. But our English people!' He shrugged. 'A Catholic bride would cause some anger. The times are unsettled; we cannot afford it.'

'She is firm in her faith but she would make no trouble. She has been bred by a wise mother never to meddle in State affairs; nor, indeed, would she know how. She would be well content to enjoy her own worship and not concern herself with others.' He paused; he said weightily, 'I have authority to open negotiations with your King; and to offer such advantages as, I believe, no other power in Europe can offer.'

'But *I* have no such authority,' my lord reminded him.

Their eyes met; it was clear without words that the proposal would be carried to the King.

'...if you are interested, sir,' my lord Manchester finished.

'I *am* interested; very.' Charles pulled his pocket inside out; it flapped emptily. 'The exact state of my treasury! I'm at my wits' ends. Let's hear the offer again.'

'De Mello's right,' he said when he had listened for the second time. 'There isn't another country in Christendom could make such an offer. Half-a-million sterling!'

'More than any Queen of England has ever brought; or so I believe, sir. And with it the Isle of Bombay—all its bays and castles...'

'It's more than bays and castles, more than the island itself,' Charles said softly. 'Trade. Freedom to trade with India.'

Manchester nodded. 'They offer Tangier, also.'

'A fine harbour; good in all weather. It opens up new trade in the Mediterranean.'

'And they offer us further freedom to trade,' Manchester reminded him. 'Trade with Brazil; trade with the Indies.'

'And that's the richest gift of all,' Charles said. 'So many powers—ourselves included—have tried for that. Yet one and all, we've been denied. Now it's offered freely. Portugal's offer could bring great wealth to this poor country of ours, that needs it, God knows! But, tell me again, what Portugal asks in return.'

'Very little. Freedom for the Infanta to worship in her own faith; and to set up a chapel in any house where she may live. And, for your part, sir, you undertake to stand by Portugal against Spain—if need be.'

'To keep Spain down is the duty of wise rulers and good Christians. Yes, I know, I know! We've sworn a peace with Spain. But I trust Philip no more than a mad dog. The offer tempts me; it tempts me!'

He was silent for a while; then he said, loud and clear, 'I'll not touch it if an ugly wife be thrown into the bargain. Is she well-favoured, this Infanta?'

'Pretty and gentle—so de Mello says.'

'He's like to be prejudiced—her country's ambassador and her godfather to boot. I'll not touch an ugly wife to save my crown. But... pretty; gentle? I note there's naught said about wits. Well, so much the better; a woman's aye best in her proper place. No need of wits in bed. Yes, I'll consider of the matter; but first I must talk to Hyde.'

My lord Chancellor Sir Edward Hyde heard his King in troubled silence. Before he gave an opinion he must consider the matter with care; he had many enemies. But his first duty was to his King. He loved Charles better than he loved his own children—so they said. He had served his King in exile, sharing poverty hard to a man of full habit. And it had left its mark; scarce fifty, he looked past sixty. The King had shown himself grateful; but there were plenty to bespatter a man's most honest acts. Nor had his daughter's marriage eased his position; it had added to his glory— and with it, to the number of his enemies.

Anne Hyde had married the King's brother James, next in succession. This amazing thing she had done by wit and will. She was well enough to look at but not half so handsome as a dozen others. She'd caught young James when she'd been maid-of-honour to his sister Mary of Orange. There had been a secret betrothal—Anne had sworn it. And good reason! Her swelling belly proclaimed it. Their marriage had been secret, too—in Hyde's own house. He, good man, had not been able to withstand his girl's tears and lamentations, though afterwards he swore he'd known nothing about it. He'd been afraid; very much afraid. What had the daughter of a simple lawyer to do with the heir to the throne? For his own sake he'd wished Anne at the devil. A chancellor has sufficient enemies without raising up more; enemies that said boldly he'd engineered the whole thing himself, enemies eaten up with jealousy because of his greatness. Lord Chancellor of England; father to Madam the duchess of York—that might one day be a Queen.

Marriage of the King's heir. It should have been used to bargain with; all Christendom would have been eager with offers, one outbidding the other. Anne's marriage had been plain treason. He remembered Charles' kindness in the matter.

'I had rather, as God hears me, sir, have seen my girl the Duke's whore than his wife!' Hyde had said, screwing his face against the tears and, in that moment, almost believing it. 'I'd not complain if you took off her head.'

Charles had laughed outright. 'Destroy a little Stuart in the making; there's treason indeed! Come now, no more nonsense. The thing's done and can't be undone. We must make the best of it.'

Now Hyde's eye followed the tall figure of the King as he strode about the room. Charles was but new-come home—not yet crowned, indeed—and there was trouble enough already. There were cavaliers who had staked their all upon the King and whom the King without injustice could not always restore to their own; could not offer, even, fitting recompense. There were Catholics to whom a grateful King had promised freedom to worship—and an affronted Church of England demanding obedience of all; there were sour Puritans stirring up mischief everywhere. Trouble aplenty—without adding of it by a Catholic marriage.

'Sir,' he said, 'the King's marriage must please the people.'

'I'll please my people every way I can; but the woman in my bed must please me, first!'

'Sir, it must please the people first.'

'The woman in my bed is my own affair,' Charles said obstinate.

'True—if the woman be not your wife,' Hyde said, irritating the King with his bluntness. 'But a wife's a different matter. Sir, you are but lately come home. There's joy in your return but it has not yet settled to a firm love. It will settle—give it time and favour.'

Charles made no answer. He strode about the great room examining the dozen or so clocks that ticked away; he had a passion for clocks. Drawing a dial from his pocket, checking it against another and yet another, as was his fashion when bored, he reminded Hyde, without rudeness, that the good man was overlong in talk.

'Sir,' and Hyde was not to be hurried, 'choose a Protestant lady; choose one beautiful and well-endowed—so you please both the people and yourself.'

'And which lady do you recommend?' Charles was dangerously quiet. He had already made up his mind in favour of the Infanta and her irresistible dowry. He was in no mind to be crossed.

'The Princess Henrietta,' Hyde began tactless, earnest.

The King's face darkened. Just like the blundering old fool to remind him he'd been madly in love with the girl; but her mother the old dragon of Orange had rejected a penniless King. That refusal and the manner of it still burned. Now, with all Europe waiting upon his choice he'd ally himself only with a house that appreciated the honour.

He was about to say so in no uncertain terms; but the old fellow loved him and had served him well; and no amount of annoyance, however just, should be allowed to obscure the fact. He said now, with the smile that won men's hearts as well as women's, 'I'll not take Henrietta of Orange. But find me a well-favoured Protestant Princess—and why not?' And answered himself. 'Oddsfish there are none. Why man, they're foggy all. No, I'm for the little girl from Portugal. Pretty I hear and amiable... and well gilded. The little Catherine it shall be!'

II

Charles was disturbed. He had sent Dom Francisco home with full power to complete the marriage treaty. He had sent gracious letters to Donna Luisa and to Dom Alphonso the King. He had written to the Infanta—as charming a letter as bride ever received; it was enough to make a woman much more experienced than Catherine inclined to love him. There was joy aplenty in Lisbon. Dom Francisco had been raised to the dignity of Count—the Conde da Ponte. The treaty had been signed and here was the new count back again in England with the document that awaited only the groom's signature.

And now Charles was not at all sure he wanted the match. He'd been on the point of signing when Bristol, his ambassador, arrived hurrying from Spain. 'Hold your hand, sir,' he said at once, still out of breath one might say. 'You cannot wed the Portuguese Infanta, not though they hang her with gold, head to foot. She is not for England; and she is not for you.'

Charles said nothing. He knew Bristol for a mischief-maker and suspected that, for this particular mischief, Spain was paying well.

Bristol went on urging. 'It is not only that she's ugly; it is not only that she's unhealthy. It is worse, far worse. Sir, she is so deformed she can never bear a child. It is well-known. And Hyde, if he speak the truth must admit it.'

'If that were true Hyde would have told me.'

'Would he, sir? Might he not have reasons of his own for keeping dumb?'

Charles might be impatient, often, with Hyde but never did he doubt his honesty nor would he allow any other to question it.

'Hyde knows his duty,' he said very stiff.

'But does he do it?' Bristol asked pale and anxious. 'Speak with de Vatteville. He'll bear me out.'

'I have no doubt of it—he's Spain's ambassador. And Spain, I gather, is anxious to break the match. Portugal strengthened by England is an other matter from Portugal standing alone—not that she's done badly till now.'

Bristol being gone, Charles strode restless about the room. If this were true it altered things; altered them considerably. He must consider with the greatest care—before he was irrevocably bound.

De Vatteville came all eager to bear out Bristol's news.

'Sir, the Infanta is ugly beyond any word; she is black as a dried olive. She is sickly and ill-tempered. Never in a thousand years could she bear a child. For such a bride would you court your people's displeasure in a Catholic marriage? There are Protestant brides worthy of the King of England. My King will give any Protestant bride you may choose, a dowry to equal whatever Portugal offers.'

'We thank you for your thought of us and shall consider the matter,' Charles said and sent for Hyde.

'Spain, it seems is frenzied, lest we ally ourselves with Portugal. And that seems reason enough, almost, for the match! Philip's so alarmed he offers me a dowry equal to anything Portugal would give... *if* I marry a Protestant bride.'

Hyde laughed himself red in the face.

'You may well laugh!' Charles said. 'Spain offering to dower a Protestant bride! But then there's no Catholic marriage that wouldn't upset Spain's balance of power. The idea of Spain so warmly espousing our heretic cause! I laugh with you!'

'The Portuguese match would bring us advantages Spain would raise heaven and hell to prevent—that, sir, is clear. As you say, for that, alone, we should go on with it.'

'But, if the girl's deformed; if she cannot bear children?'

'Sir, I have made my enquiries. Small she is; but perfectly made. In shape she's like Madam your mother; and she, God be thanked, had children aplenty! As for the Infanta being barren—there's no man can know it; she's a virgin. Sir, you have gone so far, your honour's in it. Would you, for a spiteful lie, hold an innocent lady up to shame? Sir, think! Being refused by you—and for such a reason—who would ask her hand in marriage? She is forever ruined.'

'You are right.' Charles was contrite. 'And yet I know not what to do.'

'You are best not seeing the Portuguese ambassador until you *do* know, sir.'

Hyde had spoken from a true heart. He was not to know that, in the near future, tongues would wag against him, accusing him of urging a childless marriage that his own grandchild might wear the crown. He had never seriously considered such a thing. Of the King's virility there was proof enough; and, in a young virgin, one assumed fertility.

A humiliated Dom Francisco retired to his bed. But not for long.

Travellers into Portugal came with a quite different tale. The Infanta was the prettiest of princesses and the sweetest of ladies—not that she was all sugar-water, neither; she had a high spirit. She was charming and altogether fit to be a great King's wife.

And then to crown it, Louis wrote from France. The Infanta was a princess of great beauty and admirable endowments; but for obligations of State he would have married her himself. He offered his brother of England three hundred thousand golden crowns to buy a bridegroom's fallals, together with a secret promise that should there be trouble with Spain, France would stand shoulder-to-shoulder with England.

A bride, pretty, wealthy and amiable. New and great opportunities for trade; French gold and a French blessing; and support against Spain. Charles was inclined to hesitate no longer. And then, Donna Luisa who knew well that the affair halted, sent a miniature of her daughter.

Charles and Hyde studied it together.

The picture showed a pretty brunette with chestnut curls dressed in the Portuguese manner. The little face was set between two stiff triangles of transverse curls that hung in ever-widening fall to the young shoulders. And, to add to the strange style, a top-knot sweeping to the back of the head left the smooth forehead bare. It was a quaint and altogether charming picture.

Charles laughed aloud. 'She will scarce set the fashion here! Yet the forehead's good. And those eyes! They could hold me captive for ever and a day.'

'God grant it!' Hyde said. 'The mouth I fancy shows self-will. See how it pouts.'

'I like spirit in a woman—so long as it is not directed against me!' Charles sighed, thinking of his fierce mistress Barbara Palmer.

Dom Francisco recovered his health; the negotiations came to a happy end. The half-million sterling stood ready in sealed bags; the governor of Bombay had received Donna Luisa's orders. The governor of Tangier had received his also; and the Fleet that was to carry the bride into England would first take possession of the town.

For his part Charles promised his bride freedom of worship together with a chapel in whatsoever house she might choose to live. She was to receive an income of forty thousand pounds, to be paid even should she become a widow and choose to return to her own country. There was clear agreement for mutual help against Spain; and, finally, if either side broke any part of the conditions before the marriage the contract should be null and void.

There was one more thing; and Dom Francisco made a virtue of necessity. 'Sir,' he told the King, 'as a mark of our trust in you and of our great friendship, we shall send the Infanta to England, unwed. It is a thing, I believe, that has never happened to a royal bride before.'

'I believe it, also. Always there's been a marriage first. But—' and Charles spoke drily, 'let us be plain with each other. There's another reason—and a good one; Donna Luisa isn't called the wisest ruler in Christendom for nothing! The Pope has never recognised Portugal as an independent kingdom; he still considers it part of the kingdom of Spain. For the Infanta to marry a heretic—and for that marriage to take place in her own country—you would need a papal dispensation. And you would get it. But it would be a dispensation for the daughter of the Duke of Braganza; not for the daughter and sister of a King. Such a slight Donna Luisa would not endure; nor, indeed, should I care for it myself. It would not add to the value of my bride. So she shall be married here.'

The King was to be married. England should have its heir—its Protestant heir. True the lady was a Papist, but the children should be brought up in the Protestant faith—the King had sworn it. Rejoicings everywhere—fireworks and feasting. Only in her house in King Street Mistress Barbara Palmer paced the floor and twisted her fine lace kerchief to shreds... and wished she could get her hands upon the bride.

Now Dom Francisco had no reason to complain of his treatment; he took precedence over every other ambassador. Chancellor Hyde paid a state visit, two gentlemen going before bearing the mace and a purse full of gold. Mistress Palmer raged when she heard it. Hyde should pay for this; Hyde, insufferable puritan, that would not allow his wife to visit the King's mistress, Hyde that could have stopped the marriage.

A wise Charles hurried his coronation.

'I'll have no such trouble as our father had,' he declared.

James nodded. 'Mam was never crowned; she'd have no truck, she said, with the ceremonies of a heretic church.'

'And thereby caused great anger. No. I'll be crowned here and now.'

St. George's Day, in the year of grace sixteen hundred and sixty-one, Charles was crowned with greater ceremony than any King ever before. Among the new-made peers shone Edward Hyde, first earl of Clarendon... which did not endear him to his enemies.

A day of greatest splendour—ribands and arches and garlands and tapestries; and all of them wetted by rain and dried again in the sunshine; and wetted and dried again, in true April weather; while, joybells pealing and fountains of wine sprang, the crowd shouted itself hoarse as their King debonair and handsome beneath a canopy of blue silk went to his crowning.

And, at night, the great ceremonies and the feasting being done, the King went secretly—yet not so secretly but that he might not be marked—out of Whitehall and into a certain house in King Street and into the bed of a certain Mistress Palmer.

III

VIVA IL REY DI GRAN BRITANNIA! They cried it everywhere in the streets of Lisbon where above ribands and flowers floated the royal standard of England. For Dom Francisco was home again; home with the marriage treaty complete. He had brought with him a letter for Catherine; and a little packet besides.

When she could escape to her own chamber she opened her letter.

To the Queen of Great Britain my lady and wife whom God preserve...

She could read no more. Her future was drawing all too near. She was leaving her own land with its sunshine and its warmth and its kind hearts for the damp, the fogs of England. She was going to a strange land whose language she could not speak; where her religion was hated and, at best, despised. The English were a cold nation; cut off in their little island, proud and ignorant. They disliked foreigners. How should she fare among them? What should she do in this strange land, living with an unknown man, sleeping in his bed, bearing his children?

She could not do it. The old romantic dream fell to pieces.

She picked up the letter again. It was written in Spanish, and her eye moved slowly. Spanish was her mother's native tongue; Catherine could both read and speak it—but not with ease.

The signing of the marriage contract had given him great happiness, Charles wrote. But he was restless; she and she, alone, could bring him content. He recommended Dom Francisco, *who has served me in what I regard as the greatest good in the world*, to the good graces of Donna Luisa, *our Queen and mother*. He signed himself *the very faithful husband of your majesty whose hand he kisses*.

A most sweet letter; yet bringing her marriage so close, it must add to her fears. She sat there, letter fallen to the floor, packet unopened upon her knee. At the lifting of a latch she started; Donna Luisa stood in the doorway. Catherine rose to make her curtsey; with a gesture, Donna Luisa forbade it. They must talk now, Queen to Queen. She motioned to Catherine to sit and to pick up the letter.

Madam the Queen Regent said, brisk and cheerful, 'The King of England has written me a very proper letter. He has written, also to you,' and held out a hand for Catherine's letter. Queen and Queen they might be; but they were still mother and child. She ran a quick glance over the paper.

'Very proper, also. He has good manners this King of England. But what is here?' She picked the packet from the girl's lap. 'I have your permission?' It was the first time she had ever asked her daughter's permission for anything; she did not, however wait for an answer. With the silver knife she wore at her waist she cut the wrappings through.

She looked; she smiled; she handed the contents to Catherine.

It was a miniature of the King of England. The face between the long dark curls was older than they had expected; but the wide mobile mouth gave him a laughing look. Yet there was sadness behind the laughter; it was clear in the eyes. He looked kindly, he looked debonair; he looked both grave and gay. This was no prince out of an old tale; this was a *man*. Catherine's heart went out to him.

Now that the contract was signed she was no longer the Infanta; she was Madam the Queen of England. And, as a Queen was treated by all. With freedom to arrange her own life she found little to alter save that, for the first time, she arranged her own little journeys. Except for the convent she had not left the palace above ten times in her life; now she paid her devotions to shrines outside the city praying for happiness in her marriage.

In this, her first taste of freedom, the sun had never shone so bright, the winds blown so gentle. Delightful days when, with all the honours of a reigning Queen, she moved freely among a people that openly showed their love. As for her new life, her deepest fear was gone; she had seen her husband's pictured face; she was already a woman half in love. Now she longed to see the man himself. But even at her happiest a shadow remained—grief at leaving her own land—so that she would wake in the night to find the Queen of England's pillow wet with tears.

Summer was passing. The English ships had not yet arrived, they were still about their business in Tangier; but she would not have hurried these last days balanced so delicately between fearful joy and joyful fear.

The King of England—and even to herself she dared not name him Charles—had sent her an English tailor that she might be dressed in English fashion; for the ladies of Portugal wore still the hooped skirts of Charles' grandmother. Donna Luisa would not admit them.

'It is not fitting that a man's hand should touch the body of the Infanta of Portugal,' she said.

'I am the Queen of England,' Catherine said, very quick.

'The Queen of England shall decide—when she is in England. But, indeed, daughter, I care not at all for the shameless garments of the English court... so flowing, so thin, to show the shape beneath. And the bosom bare for all to see; and the hair hanging loose in wanton curls! I trust my daughter will show a seemlier fashion. The Queen of England should set the mode.'

'If the English fashion is shameless I shall, indeed, prefer our own,' Catherine said. *But...* That doubt she kept to herself.

Charles laughed when he heard the tale and sent his bride two English gowns—one of white and silver damask; the other of rose silk; and with them the promise of a chestful of such gowns.

'Then you can keep them for England!' Donna Luisa said.

In the privacy of her chamber, Maria de Penalva her godfather's sister on guard, she tried on the rose gown.

It was charming; the colour cast a warm glow upon the pretty olive cheeks; a glow deepened by the lowness of the neck—she was all unused to the display of small, high breasts.

'It is not decent,' the duenna cried and proceeded to spoil the shape by pinning up the neck with brooches. 'As for the skirts! I can see the shape of your leg quite plain. No wonder Madam your mother objects. Yes, here or in England, you must wear the *guarda*.'

'The *guarda*!' Catherine said admiring the delicate movement outlined in silk. 'It hasn't been seen in England or in France—oh for years! Madam Henrietta Maria sent it out of fashion when she went to England, a bride—more than thirty years.'

'Forty!' Penalva corrected. 'But—forty, fifty, a hundred even! Your mother will not allow you to wear that gown!'

Catherine said, enjoying the freedom, the lightness of the English fashion, 'My lord the King of England would never send me what is not decent.'

Penalva sniffed, forgetting herself.

'I speak of my husband,' Catherine reminded her. 'You may go, Penalva.'

She was learning English but very slowly. Her godfather came, often, to practise with her but she had little patience; it was too slow a way to learn about her new country and the man who was to be her husband.

'Talk to her in her own tongue, brother,' Penalva said. 'She'll hear little enough of it where she's going. Soon she'll forget it altogether.'

'Never!' Catherine cried out and was surprised at her own passion.

Dom Francisco told her about the King of England—how he had the gift to charm a bird off a tree. There were other things of which he might have spoken; but they were not the things even a godfather could discuss with a young girl. There was a tale that filled her with pride; she remembered it all her life.

'When the English sentenced their King to death,' Dom Francisco said, 'the young Charles—he would be seventeen or so—wrote to the Parliament begging for his father's life. Whatever the cost to himself, he would pay it. And he enclosed a blank sheet; nothing upon it but his own signature sealed with his own seal. And this blank sheet? For the Parliament to write its own terms. The Prince's death-warrant it could have been... had it been used. It never was used. But, on the back, so I am told, someone has written, *Prince Charles. His carte-blanche to save his father's life.*'

She listened and the tears ran down her cheeks. She had loved her own father; but could she have shown so much courage, so much love?

'You will hear much about the King of England,' her godfather said, 'and some of it not to his credit—he's a man like any other! But there's a wisdom in him and a great compassion.'

She could never be done asking about the King of England; and always there was something new. He had a quick wit, a merry tongue; and a mind for sciences and arts alike. He had gathered about him a group of leaned men—famous, some of them. They were engaged in studying the universe—the properties of air and water; minerals, and, indeed, everything in the world of nature. It was called *the Royal Society*. It was, one might say, the King's plaything—save that there was no play but dedicated work.

And, besides, he loved fine pictures and good craft-work; and fine gardens, Dom Francisco said. Even now he was making the gardens at Whitehall and Hampton Court beautiful for his Queen. And he loved animals; not only horses and dogs but foxes and all wild creatures. But he did not tell her that he loved all women—if they were handsome enough.

Autumn passed and winter; and it was spring again. Lord Sandwich had garrisoned Tangier and stayed to see all safe; now he was on his way. On a golden day of spring when peach and almond stood rosy against a deep blue sky, the watchman from his tower sighted the English ships. And now—the voice of the guns rolling across the water welcoming and returning welcome—Donna Luisa bade her daughter to the Regent's chamber.

In the royal palace there were furnishings of great beauty; but Donna Luisa's rooms were as sparse as a convent cell. Catherine would have sat at her feet but two equal chairs stood waiting.

Donna Luisa said, when they had seated themselves, 'There are two things about which I must speak. The first is less important; yet it is important, too. It is the English gown. It is not fitting men should see a woman's shape. I beg that you will respect your country's custom and wear *the Guarda Infanta*. The Infanta needs no guard to her virtue. But men—and English men! You go, I fear, to an unvirtuous court. But it may be—since queens set the fashion—that your example may bring the English ladies to copy you and so to protect their virtue—which God knows they need.'

Catherine said nothing. She could not believe that, after their light and easy gowns, English ladies would go back to the hampering weight of the great wired skirts.

Donna Luisa fell to silence. This second was something she did not find it easy to say. At last, 'It is an unvirtuous court,' she said again.

And now Catherine must listen; she could not dismiss the Queen Regent of Portugal as she had dismissed Maria de Penalva.

'The King of England is not chaste. He has already two sons; the one a priest in the Jesuit school in Rome, begot—' and her mouth was wry, 'when his father was not above fifteen. And the other—a boy that lives now in Paris; God send he remain there! From his boyhood, the King, I think, has never lacked a mistress.

'I have thought long and prayed much, asking God whether I should send you to such a husband. And, always I find the same answer. This is no private marriage. It is not Catherine marrying Charles. It is Portugal marrying England. It is a marriage to protect our hard-won freedom. You are Portugal, my child.'

She paused. She said, very slow, 'This marriage—I believe I am right; but if I am wrong then I ask God and you to forgive me.' Her sigh was deep. 'The King of England has a mistress—had, perhaps I should say. Your godfather tells me all is over between them; that the King of England, having good principles, vows to lead a virtuous life. I trust to God that is true. But men! Your father was virtuous but there are few like him. You know your brothers...'

Yes, she knew about her brothers!

'If the King has truly broken with her, then all is well. But, if not...' she sighed again. 'There's little you can do; but that little must be done. You must never allow that woman into your presence; nor to be mentioned in your hearing. I tell you her name that you may remember it. It is Palmer.' Donna Luisa's nose pinched as at a bad smell. 'She has a good husband, so I am told. Such women should be whipped. But she has another name now. The King has raised

23

her—the slut! He has made her a countess. The name is Castlemaine. *Castlemaine*. Remember it. The husband, they say, tried to refuse the title—and who can blame him—a title that descends to the heirs of her body. *Hers!* It says enough, I think. Still—a parting gift, maybe. Let us pray for it!

'Now,' she said slow and unwilling, 'the King's women—those he has had in the past—they are not your concern...'

'Yet still they must trouble my heart.'

'Then keep that trouble where it belongs—in your heart; let none see it, least of all the King. But, daughter, if there should be a woman now, *after* your marriage...'

'There will not be. The King of England is good—my godfather has told me. He'll not see me wronged.'

'God grant it.' Donna Luisa fetched a sigh from the bottom of her heart. She rose; the talk was over.

IV

From her high window Catherine watched the procession ride in and sighed that her father had not lived to see this day. First to greet England's ambassador came the open coaches carrying fidalgoes dressed in their proudest; and after them the mounted heralds, their trumpets glittering in the sunshine. Now, with a cheering to waken the dead, my lord Sandwich himself, riding, six white horses to his open coach, with postilions and outriders in scarlet and gold. On either side the great, gilded coach walked an escort of Portuguese gentlemen, feathered hat in hand and sword by side. Portugal had put on her most gorgeous show.

She was still at her window when Donna Luisa came into the room. She said, 'My child, you know well how I have asked myself whether I have chosen aright for you; asked and asked! Today I have my answer. My lord Sandwich was delayed on his way back from Tangier. He came up with Spanish ships all armed and making in our direction. He asked no question; he attacked and sent them flying. Now the whole city sings England's praises.'

Catherine said, 'Praise be to God that makes my duty so clear.'

For two whole days nothing but rejoicing. Bullfights and bonfires; fireworks and fountains of wine; dancing in the streets of Lisbon and in its palaces.

On the third day Donna Luisa and the Infanta received my lord ambassador in audience. For the first time he was to set eyes on his Queen. Thereafter he would report to his King; she knew it and was frightened a little. But, though she died for it, no-one should guess at her fear.

At the sight of her in so outmoded a costume, and crowned by the fantastic hair, Lord Sandwich gave no sign of surprise; but he was none the less startled. Yet, in spite of himself he was charmed; she looked so young, so gentle. He marked her good points for the benefit of his King—the clear skin, the great dark eyes, the richness of that tormented hair. Charles favoured brunettes; he would be pleased.

Joybells everywhere. And then a jarring note that might well put an end to their ringing.

The half-million sterling, the precious gold gilding the bride no longer existed.

It was Donna Luisa's misfortune rather than her fault. The money had truly been put aside; but she had been forced to use some of it to keep back the Spanish invaders. 'I can pay half,' she told Lord Sandwich, 'it stands ready in sacks. If his Majesty will content himself with that, I will pay the rest within a year; and that I swear.'

Only half the gold promised to a poverty-stricken husband; the gold that made the bride acceptable to a country that did not welcome a queen of her faith!

The treaty had been broken. There need be no marriage. But the Infanta, so innocent, so gentle, so gracious? To refuse her now would make her the scorn of Europe. And there was one other matter, also, to be considered.

'Madam,' he said at length, 'the lady is of more value than all her dowry put together.' And did not add that, Tangier already garrisoned, England withdrawing her soldiers would look foolish, indeed.

She understood him without words; had indeed banked upon it. Now she said, 'I thank you, my lord. And one more kindness your good heart will not refuse. Let not my daughter hear of this affair Keep it secret for this one year and there's no need she should ever know. The money shall be paid.'

The sacks stood ready upon the quay; Sandwich, idly poking with his cane, found them soft and yielding. He poked more fiercely and out trickled... sugar. He bade a fellow untie the next and the next. Sugar, sugar also; sugar and spices instead of gold. Anger drove him hot-foot to the palace. Twice, twice his King had been cheated!

Donna Luisa met him with an abject air that sat ill upon her. She had not told the whole truth—she confessed it. Driven by her country's needs she had spent not half the gold; but all. Now she was frantic with her offers. She would beg, she would borrow; she would strip herself of all she could lay hands upon—the crown jewels even. A pretty state of affairs! My lord was deeply perplexed. Here he was with the bride on his hands—and all England waiting. Refuse her now—and who could blame him? Not a soul in England; not a crowned head in Europe, not even the arch-deceiver herself. But what of the girl; the girl blameless and gentle and young? Would Charles wish to humiliate her, Charles so chivalrous towards women?

He said, at last, 'I will take the sacks; but not in part payment. Let that be clear. My King is no huckster to peddle your wares. Your Jew da Silva shall come with the goods and dispose of them as he can. The money shall be handed to us in part payment.'

Donna Luisa bowed; she asked, humble still, 'And your promise... not to tell my daughter.'

'My promise stands.'

St. George's Day sixteen hundred-and-sixty-two; a good day for a royal bride to depart into England. Already she had made her Farewells to the nuns of the Sacred Heart and to all those that had known her from childhood. Now it remained to make her last Farewell to the mother that had planned for her, guided her, looked to her interests. Just how Donna Luisa had looked to those interests,

Catherine, fortunately, did not know. Farewell to the brothers that had shared her childhood; farewell to the land of her birth forever to be left behind.

She came from her chamber this lovely April day; and it was as though she must carry each single thing she saw engraved upon her heart for ever. She walked slowly beneath the weight of the great ceremonial court-dress, six maids of honour carried the train; the ostrich feathers of her head-dress, precariously perched, added to her discomfort.

At the door of her chamber her two brothers waited. They took her each by the hand, they moved, all three, down the great staircase. The train of ladies and fidalgoes followed.

Where the staircase led to the chapel, Donna Luisa waited.

And now was the moment of parting. Catherine bent to kiss her mother's hand; but this Donna Luisa would by no means allow. She put both arms about the girl and kissed her, smiling the stiff smile that mirrored Catherine's own. To show grief in this moment must shame them both.

Her brothers took her again by the hand and down into the great hall they went and left Donna Luisa standing. As Catherine went through the grand entrance door she turned to catch a last sight of the mother she was never to see again; and down to the ground she went in her deepest curtsey. Donna Luisa lifted a hand in blessing; and Catherine went out into the sunshine and left her there in the dim palace.

She took her place in the coach; it was open to the sky and the curtains drawn back so that the crowds might take their last Farewell. She sat upright between her two brothers, not daring to move her head lest the high feathers or her court-dress strike one or other in the eye, her face stiff with the effort not to weep. As they moved slowly through the narrow streets she caught sight of her godfather in the first coach; he was Marquez de Sande now, honoured still further for his share in this great occasion. He was going with her—ambassador-extraordinary—to England. At the sight of this kind familiar face her heart a little lifted.

Behind travelled the coaches with her household train, both English and Portuguese—a very large household as befits a Queen. Among them would be riding the English gentleman Edward Montague, cousin to my lord Sandwich. Charles had chosen him to be her grand equerry and Master of the Horse. He was young; and she thought frivolous—light-hearted, perhaps was the kinder word. She smiled, remembering his laughter; and the way his eyes would look straight into her own, showing an admiration Portuguese custom considered it seemlier to disguise. She might a little disapprove; but she found it pleasing. With him travelled three almoners chosen by her mother; chief of them was l'Abbé Ludovic Stuart, lord of Aubigny and cousin to the King. He was her chief confessor also; together with Richard Russell he would take care of her conscience. In addition there were six Portuguese chaplains, and everywhere lesser priests in their dark robes. Plenty to care for her soul! And, for her body, physicians, a perfumer and a barber—the last very needful; for who, in England, would otherwise dress her hair? And, lest she find food unpalatable in a strange land, four bakers, two cooks and two confectioners.

Of personal attendants there were six maids of honour together with their governess—and all chosen less for beauty than for rank. The Queen's two duennas rode alone; ladies of the highest rank—her dear familiar Donna Maria de Portugal, countess of Penalva; and Donna Elvira de Vilpena, countess of Ponteval, wife to the new accredited ambassador. They were middle-aged both, as duennas should be, and stiff with etiquette.

Through streets hung with cloth of gold, with flowers, with playing fountains, the coaches took their slow way. Every bell pealing, every gun booming, they drove to the cathedral. There she listened to the mass and thought of the cold religion of her new land; and wondered whether God might use her, all unworthy, an instrument of His Grace, to bring the heretics back to the fold. But, seeing no milord present—since they walked in the cloisters during the service—she thought it unlikely; and sighed a little.

Out of the dim church and into the light of the April day came the procession; and, with boys and girls dancing to flutes before the royal coach they came upon the quay, to the blue waters of the bay where the tall ships waited to carry her away.

The coaches stopped. Her brother, the King, alighted to hand her into the royal barge; and, as it moved towards the *Royal Charles*, she stood watching the ever-widening riband of water divide her from the country of her birth.

The admiral's ship towered above her; a very great ship; six hundred her crew, and eight brass cannon sending out blinding arrows of light. She stood upon the deck, having climbed with some difficulty; for though she was light in movement, the great farthingale—the *guarda infanta*—was no help. Her brother the King took her hand and placed it within that of Sandwich; and now she was in his care. And, though she stood surrounded by her ladies and her chief officers, she felt desolate and alone.

It was my lord that conducted her to her cabin, her brothers following. It was fit for any Queen in Christendom—the walls hung with cloth-of-gold, the curtains and cushions of red satin, the bedcovering of red satin and white; the appointments all of gold. Catherine had no eyes for this richness. This was the moment of last Farewell. Her brothers took her in their arms and blessed her—lewd young men upon whose tongues the solemn words sounded strange. Now those ladies that were to leave kissed her hand, made their reverences and stepped back. She was alone.

Penalva came hurrying to comfort her dearest child. Catherine sat there, secluded from all eyes; etiquette demanded it. But they were leaving; her brothers were leaving. She was being carried out of their lives forever. She could endure it no longer. She was up, and lifting the heavy skirts, went hurrying up the narrow stairs, the *guarda infanta* sticking and wedging. Behind her Penalva hastened, crying out her protests... *Madam, it is not correct, it is not seemly*. Her brothers were descending into the barge as she came upon the deck; the King turned and, seeing her there, in defiance of all convention, with gesture commanded her below. Sadly she obeyed; and the wretched *guarda* blocking the narrow stairs, she vowed she would change, at once, into an English gown; and—her first gesture of defiance—tore the absurd feather from her hair and trod upon it with small determined feet.

There was a grinding and a jarring throughout the great ship. 'They weigh anchor, Madam,' Penalva said, cheerful. But, instead of forward movement, the ship moved towards land. Donna Elvira de Vilpena came in. 'The wind's against us, Madam. They're casting anchor again.'

Torn between joy of not yet leaving Portugal utterly behind, and the awkwardness of remaining after the ceremonious leave-taking, she asked for her godfather. 'He sails in the *Gloucester*, Madam, with the English milords,' Vilpena said.

She need not have feared an anti-climax. As evening fell, there came the sharp crack of fireworks. Hooded—as was seemly for an unmarried girl—she came on deck to see the world ablossom with coloured lights. Across the bay the city was ablaze with light, and all the English ships were hung with lanterns. There was no darkness anywhere; not in the bay where the water ran in ribands of coloured light, nor in the city, nor in the night sky that blossomed in showers and flowers of light. On the deck her ladies stood, hooded everyone; they laughed and clapped their hands under the watchful eyes of the two duennas and the correct and stern governess of the maids of honour.

Against the forecastle young Edward Montague stood smiling at this guilelessness; and wondering what the court would make of these ridiculous women in their ridiculous clothes... A sad disappointment; no amorous adventures here! Yet, put them in Christian clothing—or better still no clothing at all—and who could say? At present, the only comely one was the new Queen; she was, in her own way, charming. Would she learn to play her part in the lewd games of the court? She would find him a willing partner.

Looking at her face uplifted to the sky he thought such games were not for her. There was an innocence about her, a... purity; he boggled at the word but could find none better. He found her absurdly touching. He was a harum-scarum young man, not over-virtuous; but now he was taken with a sudden sentiment of chivalry. He vowed to serve her to the best of his endeavour.

V

The wind changed; the water was calm as they put out to sea. Standing to catch a last glimpse of the land she loved, Catherine did not notice the wind had changed again. They were in for a rough journey. Wind turned to gale; waves swept the ships that pitched and tossed. The whole convoy, English and Portuguese alike, the very sailors were sick. Catherine's ladies lay upon their beds and prayed endlessly for abatement of the storm. Catherine longed to do the same; but she must set an example. She would crawl from her bed and go from one to another with words of good cheer; then back she would crawl to fling herself upon the bed—from which she had prudently ordered the red-and-white satin to be removed—and, as the cabin rose and fell, tried to hold in the sickness.

Through storm and stress the ship held course. In the second week of May they sighted the Isle of Wight; and, a message being signalled that His Royal Highness, James, Duke of York, meant to come aboard, they cast anchor within a mile or so of Portsmouth.

And now Catherine found herself trembling. What would this new brother think of her? She picked up a looking-glass. A small green face stared back. Storm and sickness had not added to her charms. Her ladies must do their best for her; he would be here within the hour. Certainly he would write to the King of this first meeting, and, looks apart, he might find it hard to like her that must take from him the hope of a crown. She prayed he would not find her too easy to dislike.

In the stateroom all was ready. My lord Sandwich had transformed it into a presence-chamber; a great chair beneath a canopy stood together with a smaller one without a canopy. She sat in the great chair wearing the English gown of white-and-silver; she was pale as the gown itself. And, since there was no-one to dress her hair in

31

English style, she wore it, tortured still, in Portuguese fashion. She looked anxious; and, in spite of her dignity, a little forlorn. But good Penalva, though not full-recovered from the monstrous journey, had schooled her well. It would take death itself to make Donna Maria forget the smallest detail of court etiquette.

So sitting, Catherine heard the ring of footsteps, heard my lord Duke announced. She rose and made three steps—three and no more— towards this new brother that knelt before her. And, still kneeling, he would have kissed her hands; but she, defying the strict etiquette of her mother's court, stretched out two impulsive hands to help him to his feet. He stood before her tall and heavy, fair and florid—a comely man, save that he was somewhat pockmarked. He did not wear the fashionable periwig but his own red-brown hair falling in curls to his shoulders. She noted, with a down-dropping heart, the unsmiling eyes, the stubborn chin. He had, she thought, a cold and formal look; yet, if one dealt gently with him, one might, perhaps, win him for a friend.

He kissed her hand but not her cheek. 'It was my right and my pleasure,' he told her later, 'but I left the first kiss for your husband.' Which when she thought about it, showed him to be neither cold nor formal.

She seated herself in the great chair; and, since she had so little English, waved towards the second chair that he might also sit. And, when he would not, she pointed to the tabouret at her feet and there he seated himself. And now he began to speak in Spanish though the interpreter stood by. He stammered more than a little, and she thought it must be because the tongue was strange to him; she was to learn that, embarrassed, he stammered always.

Now, stammering and halting, he said, 'Madam, my sister and my Queen, I desire to serve you as your brother and most humble subject.' He asked her about her journey, regretting the foul storms. 'But,' he told her and he was smiling—a smile that made his heavy face attractive—'there's no mark of the storm upon you!' which was gallant rather than true. And now, seeing her so little and so kind, he was stammering less; and she, her fears calmed, was smiling also, gracious, and in spite of dark-ringed eyes, pretty.

He told her why the King was not himself come to meet her.

'It is the Parliament,' he said in his halting Spanish, and stammering still. 'Two months ago he besought Parliament to hasten its business that he might be free in time. But—' he shrugged, 'Parliament is the mother of talkers; a breeder of words, for the most part, useless. But, believe me, Madam, he can no longer support himself in patience, so great his desire to see you,' and found himself wondering whether Charles dallied still with his Castlemaine. 'Rest assured, Madam, he will be in Portsmouth as soon as Parliament shall release him.'

So reasonable the explanation she could not be sorry for the delay. She looked peaked and pale; her own mother could not have complimented her upon her looks.

James asked if he might present the gentlemen that waited to kiss her hand. He brought, first, the Master of the King's Household, my lord Duke of Ormonde, who recommended himself to her the more since he had brought her a letter from the King. Later, when she learned of his long and faithful service to his master, she was to love him with more cause. Next James presented my lord Chesterfield that was to be her Chamberlain, thereafter the rest were presented, each in his degree; and each she received with a smiling grace.

The first meeting had come to an end. James bowed very deep; Catherine stood up to go with him to the door. 'It is not for the Queen,' he said.

'It is my pleasure to do so out of love!' she told him and had her way.

The *Royal Charles* lay outside Portsmouth till news should come that the King was on his way. Every day James came aboard; and every day Catherine found him more kind. He asked to see her in the dress of her own country; and next day, there she was in her finest Portuguese gown. Even to her it looked odd and felt odder. But for all that he did not smile. 'I like it well,' he said, 'but I like you best as an Englishwoman.' It was as near a compliment as he could get, this silent man that seemed older than his brother the King.

'Have a care of him,' Penalva said. 'It is a man that, this way or that, means to have his own way. His marriage—'

'It honours him!' Catherine said, very quick.

'If he had been content to abide by his bargain, yes, but—' Penalva had long had the tale from her brother, 'He is capricious where women are concerned; lecherous, too, I hear. And his wife is one to hold the whip—and that suits him not at all. So when the first babe was born and when, alas, it died—the babe for which he'd married her—he tried to rid himself of his encumbrance. He swore that the child was none of his; nor could one say, rightly, *whose* child. She'd been over-free, he said, with her favours. And the King's friends said so, too.'

'And the King?'

'He'd have none of it. Had there been truth in the tale they should have told him before—and *would* have told him, he said. Nor did he think the lady one to imperil her future for a light pleasure. No! York was married. He'd made his bed and must lie therein. There must be no more such talk, the King said. And he paid even greater respect than before to his brother's wife, and to her father.'

She sent later to Montague, and he, having a little Spanish, confirmed the tale. And when she asked the names of those that had so spitefully used a woman, all unwilling he gave them.

'Berkeley; he swore he'd enjoyed her favours. And Buckingham's that a known liar; and Rochester, a most lewd man.'

She repeated their names. 'I shall remember them.'

'Madam,' he cried out, 'it is not wise to set yourself against the King's friends.' And, when she made no answer save by the setting of her chin, 'Handle them with care,' he advised. 'And, most of all, my lord duke of York. A good friend but a bad enemy.'

So, although York's kindness continued, Catherine could neither like nor trust him; but she remembered Montague's warning and behaved with all courtesy. And that was as well for it was true—a good friend he could be, but the worst of enemies.

On a fine morning, they heard the guns thundering that the King was on his way. Catherine sent for the Master of the ship and, thanking him for his care of her and hers, gave him a collar of pure gold, for which he thanked her with all his heart. 'It is less for the collar of gold,' he said, 'than for your golden words.' She sent him, also, gold sufficient to speak her thanks to all, down to the smallest cabin-boy.

There are some to say she had a closed hand; but those that knew her, knew also that she scorned meanness in any shape. When money was scarce—as it was during her years in England—she must, indeed give less than she desired. There were times, indeed, when she must count each penny; but she had rather gone without bread than scant her thanks.

Now, as land came nearer, Catherine that had, for the most part, stayed in her stateroom in obedience to her country's etiquette, came now on deck to watch; she was in England now, and here it was proper to show her face.

In Portsmouth harbour the mayor and aldermen were gathered, all very fine in new scarlet and fur, with gold chains about their necks. When James, stepping ashore, handed her from the barge, the great guns spoke again and again; and young and gracious and small and pretty she looked, smiling her thanks so that the sky rang with the cries of joy. So, into the State coach, with the curtains put aside that all might see her; and with a cheering and a crying of blessings upon her head; with the booming of guns and the music of pipe and tabor, the coach moved slowly through the cobbled streets till she came, at last, to the King's House, there to await her unknown groom.

VI

Charles, the coach swaying and bumping along the Portsmouth Road, was troubled. It was late; each in his corner his cousin Rupert and Buckingham slept. Rupert preserved his dignity even in sleep; Buckingham, wig awry, snored a little—as usual he had taken overmuch to drink. The ring of hooves as the troops rode with him, and Buckingham's snores kept him from sleep. He gave himself up to his thoughts.

After all his adventuring with women he was about to settle down at last. The women he had slept with, whether of high birth or low, had been beauties; quick of wit and full of charm. Now he was to take a wife—and God alone knew whether she were black as a dried plum or fresh as plum-blossom. He'd heard she was black as a bat; that she had a long back and short legs so that when she sat she seemed to be tall and when she stood she was clearly a dwarf. But

James had written that she was a pretty thing; and Chesterfield, that judge of women, had said that she was exactly shaped.

Well, whatever she was like he'd wed her tomorrow; and he'd do his best to make her a good husband. He'd said as much to Clarendon when the old boy had lectured him like a father. Clarendon was faithful but tedious... tedious; Barbara detested him.

Rupert stirred and sat up. He pulled down the window and took in a deep breath of the summer night air. Wide-awake now he had no mind for Buckingham's snores; he aimed a sharp kick and the snores ceased.

'Not asleep, Charles?' Rupert grinned across at his cousin. 'All night vigil; asking a blessing upon your sword?' There was a suggestion of lewdness that the King did not miss. He said, very earnest, 'I mean to start a fresh page, cousin. A virgin page with a virgin bride.'

'In the night all cats are grey,' Rupert said.

'Are you saying all women are alike in bed?' Buckingham spoke suddenly from his corner. 'Nothing further from the truth!' And he let out a great laugh.

'They're all alike in one thing! There's not one of them all that's ever refused our Charles. I cannot think this new little creature should be different from the rest. But suppose, sir, you cannot love her,' Rupert asked, a trifle waspish.

'Then still I'll cherish her as a good husband should. I'll be faithful; I swear it!'

'No woman's bed but your wife's!' Again Buckingham neighed his great laugh. 'It's not only yourself you must reckon with—there's my cousin; have you forgot Barbara? You know well the night the bride landed there were bonfires before every house—save hers.'

'You could not expect it,' Charles said, reasonable.

'You could expect it. And you should expect it!' Rupert was sharp. 'Your mistress should show respect to your Queen. You're too easy, Charles.'

'It is no time to cross her now,' Charles said, curt.

'Was there ever a time?' Rupert's voice was dry.

Charles flushed. Even at the best of times she was uncertain in temper; when roused—a fury; the whole world knew it. Now, pregnant as she was, she could—if sufficiently roused—do herself, or the child, or the King himself, some mischief. But she was beautiful in her furies and he loved the fire of her spirit. They said of him, he knew it, that on occasion, he knelt, asking her pardon. That was nonsense. He knelt in spirit before her beauty. He'd been foolish enough to say so once to Buckingham and had been misunderstood... or perhaps not misunderstood. Buckingham, tongue in cheek, playing his pranks.

Barbara was so beautiful just now. A beautiful woman near her time is a noble sight, he thought. A richness in the body, a delicacy in the face; a dusting of fatigue through which her beauty cries aloud. There's a pull upon the heart of the man that has filled her with his child that makes him long to put his heart beneath her heel.

Did she sleep now, bright hair spread upon the pillow; or did she pace her chamber restless in her rage? Last night—a wild cat—she'd refused to come into bed. Yet she had little cause to complain. He'd slept with her every night until now. No need to reform till the key was actually turned in wedlock.

Rupert's voice cut across his thoughts. 'She says she's to be made a lady of the Bedchamber; that you promised. But that's a piece of nonsense...'

'It is not nonsense. I did promise. And, why not?'

'You know very well why not—your voice gives you away!'

Charles said nothing. He did know; none better. And he'd refused at first; he'd gone on refusing while she went through the usual perform-ance—fire to tears... *You cannot so shame me; leaving me out you make me the laughing-stock of the whole court. I rather die... I and the child together.* And that not immediately moving him she had thrown her arms about his neck reminding him that the appointment would give her the right to lodgings in Whitehall, near, very near the King... *You could come to my bed and no eye to see, no tongue to wag...* Did she, he wondered, truly believe that possible? And then, seeing him determined still, she'd reminded him—for the hundredth time—of the debt he owed her; of her father killed in his cause; her own good name sullied.

He'd almost laughed in her face at that last. Everyone knew her capers with Buckingham, with Chesterfield... and others. But then she'd wept, her lovely face a flower bedewed with tears; and that—though he'd seen it often enough—he hadn't been able to resist. Meet him with anger, meet him with pride and he'd know how to answer; but beseech him with tears and the heart melted within him.

He said now, 'Yes, I have promised; and whatever you or anyone may think, the promise shall be kept. From my wife I fear no difficulty.' And since there was no reply from Rupert, said, a little anxious, 'She's amiable, I hear.'

'She's a woman!' Buckingham shrugged.

'She has a high spirit,' his cousin reminded him.

'Then she must learn to bend it to her husband's will!' Buckingham, persuader to folly, put in, very sharp.

Charles' smile was wry. He was alive to the nonsense of submitting to his mistress in this matter and expecting obedience from his wife.

Buckingham said, watching his face, 'It will be a curious pleasure to feel virtuous when you do your duty in bed! But then—when pleasure becomes duty it's no longer a pleasure.'

Charles said nothing. He was looking forward to his marriage with something of dread. He had slept with women a-plenty; but he'd never wived before. Buckingham's jest rankled. Women were a delight; but they were a damned nuisance! Certainly Barbara was; and possibly, that untried virgin his wife.

Well, he'd done his best to make things pleasant for his little foreign bride. He'd seen to it that Hampton Court, where they were to spend their honeymoon, was looking its best. The grass was brilliant and velvet-soft; the clipped hedges curious and perfect; the trees in young leaf and blossom. The freshness of the year must be over in Lisbon; she should have the delight of an early English summer when the sun is gentle and the breezes light. Portugal was a paradise, he'd heard—pomegranate and peach and almond all a-flower. But the great park at Hampton Court with its honey-sweet limes and the great chestnuts bright with pyramids of flowers, must be hard to beat. England, he thought now—as he had throughout his wandering years—there's no place so lovely!

And inside the great house matched the outside in beauty. There were tapestries worked from Raphael cartoons brought from Italy in his grandfather's time; there were pictures famous throughout Christendom and furniture finer than could be found anywhere outside Paris—and perhaps not even there.

And surely the little girl from Portugal must be overjoyed with her bedroom with its bedcurtains of crimson velvet worked with pure silver. They had cost eight thousand pounds—though he had not paid for them; they were a wedding-gift from the States of Holland and they held a certain melancholy pleasure. They had graced the bridal chamber of his sister Mary when she'd married Orange. Now she, poor girl was dead; and her son had lost no time selling them back to the States of Holland—twelve-year-old William, already showing himself devoid of graceful sentiment, the close-fisted young prig. Now they hung in the bride's room at Hampton Court. If Mary could know it would, he hoped, give her pleasure.

He thought, saddened, how Mary and their youngest brother Gloucester, smitten down by the dread small-pox, had died here in England within a few days of each other. They'd come to celebrate his homecoming... two years ago. A glorious year saddened by their deaths. He found himself praying that his bridal year would be unmarred but he was not hopeful. There were already troubles a-plenty. Trouble over freedom for worship, which he alone, so it seemed, desired; trouble over money, trouble with some that truly deserved more of him than he was able to give. And the endless struggle with Parliament. He had truly hoped to be in Portsmouth himself to welcome his bride; but Parliament, with no consideration, had kept him. Let him be never so brisk he had not been able to stay the spate of words Parliament had spewed forth. And that business done at long last, he'd sat with his Council till midnight to deal with more private business. That had been last night. All this day he'd been involved and, not until nine o'clock tonight had he been free at last. Weary, and not at all looking forward to meeting his bride, he had had to fight with himself not to sleep with Barbara once more. But his farewell as a bachelor had been made; a sense of fitness kept him away.

Now, deep in his thoughts, he spoke neither to Rupert nor to Buckingham. There was silence except for the beat of hooves from the troops riding with him. It was midnight before they reached Guildford and yawning mightily, changed into my lord Chesterfield's coach. 'You're in a mighty hurry, Charles,' Rupert said peevish. 'God save us, man, we're not all hastening to our brides!'

'And if we were,' Buckingham added, 'it would be wise to take a night's sleep first. She'll keep I hope!'

'You speak of your queen,' Charles said a little sharp.

Bumped unmercifully in the springless coach, his thoughts dwelt upon the girl committed to his care. Girl! She was past her twenty-third birthday; older by a year-and-a-half than Barbara. But she must seem younger; everyone spoke of her girlish looks. And, indeed, a woman is as old as her experience. And she—from convent to the closed etiquette of her mother's court—what experience had she? Now she was in a strange country awaiting her unknown husband. If he, with all his experience, found the meeting disturbing, what of her? He swore he would be good to her.

And she would need it. The business of bedding! To a man a necessary and pleasant affair; to some women—like Barbara—even more necessary, even more pleasant. But there were others, virgin and chaste; to them their first bedding could be difficult, repugnant even. Such women must be won. If he wanted his heir he must first win his wife. Well, it had never been hard for him to win a woman. They dropped into his hand like a ripe plum—and not because he was a king; it had been so with the wandering prince.

He began to think now of the women that had loved him. The first woman in his bed—older than he by some years; and kind. She'd given him his first child—the boy he'd all-but forgotten; just as he'd forgotten her—her face, her name, remembering only her kindness. And then Lucy; Lucy Walter the overblown beauty that had given him his beloved son... Jamie, under Mam's care in Paris. Mam was coming to England to meet his bride; he'd asked her to bring the boy with him... the lad was past his thirteenth year; time to be home in England, where he belonged. Handsome they said; bonnie Jamie.

Casting up the long list of ladies in his bed his head nodded; he was asleep at last.

Catherine awaited her lord in the King's House; it was a hard time for her. She delighted in the things she had heard about him... most of the things; she wore his portrait about her neck. But reality is a quite other thing; and a picture in words or paint may be false. She was very much afraid.

She had met her five ladies of the Bedchamber, the chief of them my lady Suffolk—aunt to the new-made countess Castlemaine—though, as yet, Catherine did not know it. She had thought there were to be six of them; she asked d'Aubigny to enquire of my lady Suffolk; but he, looking a little sideways, said my lady knew nothing of the matter and she put it from her mind.

Now, with every moment bringing her groom nearer, she sat within her bedchamber while her five new ladies stood about her and the maids brought forth the rich gowns her mother had commanded. It was well that Penalva had been left aboard with a putrid throat, for the ladies lifted their hands at the sight of the old-fashioned skirts. And when a maid brought forth a *guarda infanta* they could not restrain their titters, so she bade the woman carry it away. Yet she was ashamed, a little. This was the dress of her own country and her mother had bade her honour it.

Now the gowns the King had sent were brought out—the rose and the white. 'The rose gown,' my lady of Suffolk said. 'You will look like a rose and the King will love you in it.' Catherine understood not a word; but my lady smiled; so she smiled back and nodded. But alas for the rose gown. She went to bed with a feverish cold and there the King found her.

It was broad daylight when his coach thundered into Portsmouth town. He was dishevelled and yawning; but he was not to escape to his bed. In the courtyard Dom Francisco de Mello, de Vilpena the ambassador and the fidalgoes waited to greet him; and travel-stained as he was and half-asleep, he must show all courtesy, enquiring of their health and of their journey and all those things politeness required.

It was over-late now to seek his bed and his bride had waited long enough. While he was being shaved and clothed afresh, he thought of the unknown girl whose life was irrevocably to be bound up with his own. Toby Rustat, his valet, arranging the lace at the neck, arranging the long dark curls to fall, exact as a periwig, each side of the wide, troubled forehead, sent up a prayer of happiness for this so-loved master.

Standing outside her door, his heart beating like that of a young lad, Charles found it strange that, for all the formalities of two courts, he was to meet his bride, this first time, in her bed. He must tread delicately. Though she must know Queens held levees in their beds, he doubted Donna Luisa had ever formed the habit—Donna Luisa that talked to men, ambassadors, even, from behind a curtain; as for the girl herself, her whole upbringing forbade it. How would she welcome a strange man whose right it must soon be to enter not only her bed-chamber but her bed? And what of the retinue of gentlemen at his back whose entry both court and courtesy permitted? He tuned himself about and bade then wait outside. He saw amusement flash between Rupert and Buckingham; between Chesterfield and Sandwich.

He took a deep breath and went inside.

His first feeling was one of relief. He had nothing to fear from this small, gentle girl. He liked her looks; she was pretty—they had not lied there. He liked her large dark eyes and the rich curling hair, charming even in the ridiculous style she affected. He liked the lively look in those dark eyes and the sweetness upon the mouth; he even liked the way her upper lip lifted above the two small but prominent teeth; it gave her a little proud look not unbecoming in a Queen. Bending to salute the hand that lay upon the counterpane, he saw that it was small and delicate; it gave him the pleasure he derived from any perfect thing. A sweet little creature; there'd not be much fight in her over Barbara!

He had missed the firmness of the small chin.

He spoke to her in his halting Spanish cursing her mother that had not had her taught English. He said, 'Madam, my Queen and wife, it gives me great joy to see you in my country—which is now your own. There is but one thing lacking; when I see you restored to health my happiness will be complete.'

She answered—and she had the soft and charming voice such as he loved in women, and which Barbara, alas, did not have, 'I thank you, sir, for your kindness. Your majesty's wish must always be my pleasure. I shall be well tomorrow.'

When they had talked a little, he said if she should be well enough, they should be wed tomorrow; and, since she was tired, as her dark-ringed eyes showed, and he had much to arrange, he bade her Goodnight and left her to her rest.

It had been a long day but now all was finished, every last arrange-ment made. He found himself looking forward to the morrow; he was glad, though, he was not to play husband tonight. Clarendon, he knew, would be anxious about this day's meeting; and, late though it was, he must set the old man's fears at rest. Dawn was already breaking when he sat down to write.

I am happy for the honour of the nation that I was not put to the consummation of the marriage last night, for I was so sleepy, having slept but two hours on my journey, I am afraid matters would have gone sleepily. I can only now give an account of what I have seen in bed; which is, in short—her face is not so exact as to be called a beauty, though her eyes are excellent good...

And, remembering the cruel things they had said about her, how she was as black as a bat and squat as a dwarf, he added,

...she has as much agreeableness in her looks as ever I saw. Her conversation, as much as I can perceive, is good; for she has wit enough and a most agreeable voice. You would wonder to see how well we are acquainted already. In a word I think myself very happy.

And that was no more than truth. Had he not liked her he was free to send her home again, she being unwed and the contract broken in the all-important matter of the dowry—a sharp disappointment. But he liked her well enough even without the gold and he had never humiliated a lady in his life.

He had left her to rest but her happiness was too great. She lay still, hands crossed upon the rosary at her breast and thought of him. When she had first lifted her eyes to his she had, for the moment, been taken aback. He looked older than even his portrait had shown. There was grey in the dark flow of his curls; the eyes too looked sadder, wiser than she had expected. But there was a great kindness in them; and when he smiled, then merriment danced. His high and handsome look, his whole kingly carriage, drew the heart that had been fluttering, flying from her breast straight towards him. In that moment she lost her heart forever. She lay there, thanking Mary, sweet mother of Jesus, for her great happiness.

The King was her best physician; for though she slept but little for the singing of joy in her breast, yet she awoke in the early morning free from fever and bright with health.

VII

May twenty-first and a glorious morning; the sky very clear and a warmth to the air—promise of the flowering season very proper to a bridal day.

She was to be married according to the service of the English church—that, she conceded, was only right; for, if she would not have others offend against her church she must not offend against theirs. One thing, alone, troubled her happiness. If at the beginning of this new life she must not offend this country of hers, still less dared she offend God. She must be married first in her own faith.

She had not said so yesterday; she had taken it for granted. Now she found she had been mistaken. But, every arrangement made, the King—and she had no courage as yet to call him Charles—might well be angered at a last-minute change. Well, she must, however unwilling, risk his anger rather than God's. So when he appeared to ask how she fixed, she said—as urgent as she could in her careful Spanish, 'Beseech you, sir, let me be married first by the rites of my own church; without that I could not consider myself truly wed.'

Never was so easy a man! He made no trouble at all. 'I should be sorry if my wife felt herself no wife,' he answered, very cheerful. 'My lord bishop of London was to have married us this morning. Well, he must wait till after dinner. This morning we'll be wed in true Catholic fashion.'

How could she help but love him the more for his kindness?

So there in her bedchamber they were wed by d'Aubigny her chaplain-in-chief, with none but the Duke of York and her second chaplain Russell for witnesses. And, if she had loved Charles before, now that he was her husband given to her by God, it was hard to remember that God came first. And so it was to be with her all her life.

She asked for a prayer-book of the church of England and Charles, in his halting Spanish, explained the strange marriage-service. 'Oh, she said, 'how shall I remember it all? How shall I know when I must speak?'

'You will not I trust say *No!* And though his face was grave his eyes twinkled. 'As for the rest—when I press your hand you must say *Yes.*'

When he was gone she asked d'Aubigny to explain the service again that she might, with an understanding heart, marry the King according to his own rites. She approved the service; she had not expected heretics to be so outspoken. She thought, smiling, of the carved cradle that had once rocked the infant Catherine; at her own request it had accompanied her wedding-gifts.

And now, her ladies coming to dress her, she sent one of her own women to bring tea—the curious drink she had brought from home. They drank out of small china dishes, not at all sure that they cared for the taste; but it had, they declared, put a pretty colour into her Majesty's pale cheeks. And pretty she certainly looked in the rose silk gown set off with blue love-knots—for something blue a bride must wear for a wedding, they declared; but her hair she wore still in stiff cannon curls either side of the small face. And though such a fashion did not suit with such a gown, the courage was not in her to face an English gown, an English head-dress and an English marriage at the same time.

Her ladies following—and how she longed for her mother!—she went down into the presence-chamber; and there the King, already waiting, took her by the hand and led her to a dais where, beneath a canopy, stood two thrones. A step below stood the Portuguese ambassadors—de Vilpena and her godfather together with Sir Richard Fanshawe the groomsman and the bishop of London—these four and no other. Behind a barrier stood the great assembly—James duke of York and Prince Rupert in advance of the rest. Three paces behind stood the King's friends, the Queen's ladies and chief officers of both households, together with the Mayor of Portsmouth and his aldermen.

Still holding the King's hand she listened carefully to the service of this heretic church; feeling, herself, something of a heretic, she was yet painfully anxious to acquit herself, with respect. So when Charles pressed her hand she nodded, not trusting the English word upon her halting tongue—which was a pity; for afterwards they cast it against her that she was over-proud to soil her tongue with the English service.

But all that was to come. Now she was happy to be wed in the English custom since already she had been secured in her own. And, the ceremony being over and they two pronounced man and wife, the company cried out three times *God save them both!* And she felt truly the wife of her beloved husband.

The sun was still high, for it was not yet above four of the clock; but she was so weary having risen from a bed of sickness, that Charles led her to her bedchamber and bade my lady Suffolk look well to the Queen. So they put her to bed, Donna Vilpena assisting, since dear Penalva lay sick aboard. But first of all my lady Suffolk took the blue ribands from the bridal gown and cut them into small pieces and gave one to those present, as far as they would go—a bringer of good luck—so that there was not one piece left for the bride. It troubled her a little; for when one is happy, a little luck-to-come is a good insurance.

When the company had gone Charles asked for a brush and, with his own hands, brushed out the stiff curls that nobody liked except herself and there she lay high upon the pillows, the soft hair framing her pretty face. Full of her happiness, her thoughts turned again to her mother... Donna Luisa would be praying a blessing upon the marriage. But my lady of Suffolk remembered her niece awaiting her confinement; Barbara, she thought, had a better right in the bride-bed.

Catherine was glad to be back in bed; Charles sat beside her like any husband who is not a King; and the servants came bringing food and wine and those two ate and drank and were happy together.

Of her wedding-night and the first giving of herself she would never speak; nor could not—her whole upbringing forbade it. But... had she thought to have loved him before this? Now her love was enriched by his gentleness, his patience, his loving-kindness. She understood now what the nuns had tried to teach her and what she had never understood. Marriage was a sacrament or a degradation. Hers was a sacrament. That she thought so was something of a pity; Charles was not given to sacraments in his bedding with women.

Charles was in love with his wife; not with passion but with a tenderness lacking in all other affairs. All his life he had enjoyed the pleasure women gave him, in bed and out. A lovely woman was more precious than a fine marble or a noble picture; but her beauty did not last. It was her clear duty, therefore, to leave a copy to the world. Of the score of women who had been kind, he had loved none. One woman alone had taken his heart and held it; Minette, the little sister in France.

The years of his wandering had separated them throughout her childhood; when at last he had come upon her, he had not known her. He was a wanderer still, a young man in his mid-twenties; and she a child of thirteen. There she was in his mother's rooms in the Louvre, curtseying to herself in the looking-glass. She had worn—the memory was in his heart for ever—a shabby gown protected by an apron, so poor they were. He had thought her a little serving-maid and his heart had melted at her childlike innocence. She had, he saw, a little lame foot, which she seemed determined to ignore. Down she went in her curtsey, the foot carefully placed, the whole thin body bent to preserve her balance. It was the little lame foot and her valiant ignoring of it that had shaken him. And then, catching sight of him in the mirror, she had turned about; and there she was—his other self, but fair and gay and innocent; his own dark picture in bright colours. Even while she came running into his arms, the lame foot a little dragging, it had been something of a shock to know that this was his sister... already he had vowed to take her for a sweetheart.

But she was his sister. He had learned, in some degree, to transmute his love; though even now his heart leaped at the sight of her. Did she feel the same love for him? It was a thing they never spoke of.

And now there was a new woman in his life... and forever. His wife. She was utterly different from Minette; from any woman he had known. She had no blinding gift of wit and beauty; but she had a candour Minette had lost in the court of France. And she had a purity; Minette had lost that, too. How could she not, married to vicious Orléans? A wise man, could he choose, would take this wife of his rather than the rarest beauty, to breed his children. To bed with her was not only a duty, it was, in its piquante way, a pleasure. *At night all cats are grey...* He was wrong there, Rupert; and Buckingham right. She took the business of bedding with a gentle obedience. She never refused him; but she never made an advance. Beyond the yielding of her body—no sign of pleasure. That she did experience pleasure he was too knowledgeable in women to doubt. The prudery with which she had been bred inflamed him.

In these first days when he was entirely taken by her sweetness, her smallness, her prudery even, he wrote to Donna Luisa,

> I am the happiest man in the world... I cannot sufficiently look at her or talk to her.

Before ever he'd set eyes upon her he had promised himself to be a good husband; he'd said as much to Clarendon and that promise he meant to keep. The good old man would be anxious to know how these early days were going; he must set Clarendon's mind at rest.

> I cannot easily tell you how happy I think myself. I must be the worst man in the world—which I hope I am not—if I be not a good husband.

He thought, himself surprised, Oddsfish—I mean it! Let that, at least, stand to my credit.

Towards the end of this first week of their marriage, they set out for Hampton Court. A great procession as befits the wedding-journey of a King. Gilded coaches, matched horses, outriders in royal scarlet and gentlemen riding with feathered hats and flowing curls; and all along the road soldiers with pikes standing to attention. And, finest sight of all, the King in his Garter robes than which there are none grander, sitting there in the open coach and making much of his Queen—she, very pretty in her English dress. Looking at her happy face he swore he would make her happier still so that she would turn to him in passion as well as obedience.

Some of her Portuguese ladies, in charge of my lord Chesterfield, her chamberlain, had gone ahead to prepare for the Queen's coming. Their gowns, a century out of fashion, and hideous hair set the crowds on the streets in a roar. My lord Chesterfield wished his charges at the devil. He was to wish it more intensely before journey's end. Nothing it seemed would satisfy them. Their ridiculous wire cages took up more room than the carts could afford; and they were such prudes they'd not sleep in any bed no matter how new the linen, that had been slept in by a man. There they stood, eyes downcast and mimmed up mouths, till he longed to tell them that unless they altered their ways, these beds were all of a man they were like to get.

Catherine enjoyed the journey. The country was all agog to see her; everywhere, even to remote villages, there had spread strange tales of her looks. Now when the people saw her—no flaming beauty it is true, but no monster neither—a young girl sufficiently pretty with her delicate air, they let themselves go in cheering. And certainly, in her English gown and hair loose upon her shoulders, though still she wore the swept-back top-knot, she was sweet enough to win all hearts.

That night they rested at Windsor; early next morning saw the procession on its way. Everywhere cheers and blessings rained upon them. It was Charles' birthday, May twenty-ninth. A new year... a new life. Again he vowed to be a good and faithful husband; he was, he reminded himself, thirty-two; time to settle down! Yet he could not entirely keep his mind from Barbara and wonder whether their child was born... he hoped it would be another son. Nor could he keep his mind from the promise to make Barbara a lady of the Queen's Bedchamber. Looking at the gentle little creature at his side he was certain there'd be no difficulty.

Hampton Court at last; they passed along the great lime avenue where soldiers stood to attention. She sat upright, smiling her pleasure from right to left; when the house came into view she took in her breath at its magnificence.

'Fifteen hundred rooms,' Charles said with seeming nonchalance, 'and each more beautiful than the one before!'

In the courtyard, all England it seemed, stood to honour them—Clarendon with his councillors and the members of both Houses; my lords the archbishops with the princes of the Church, the princes of the State; the judges, the high officials and the foreign ambassadors. It was the King himself that handed her from the coach; my lady of Suffolk in court dress carried the train; behind her walked the Queen's duennas, the ladies Penalva and Ponteval, looking like ghosts of a hundred years since.

Within doors waited those others privileged to kiss the Queen's hand—the lesser nobility, the lesser officials, and the gentry each with his lady grouped in rooms according to rank. Catherine received them with such grace that Charles, watching, thought everything about her—even the funny little smile lifted upon her front teeth—utterly charming.

At length he took her away that she might not be over-tired, and that he might see for himself her first delight in the Queen's bedchamber. When she cried aloud her pleasure at the velvet and silver bedcurtains, he did not tell her their history lest it sadden her. She looked into the great mirror set in beaten gold that his mother had sent and made a little face at her own reflexion; she took up the golden toilet articles as though wondering what to make of them. He promised himself to be her teacher.

Later in the evening she rose and James brought his wife to pay her respects. Catherine thought she might be handsome had she not so proud a look—the lawyer's daughter that was now second lady in the land. Certainly Anne had a proud, cold air; she understood perfectly the meaning of *render unto Caesar*. She would scant no tittle of honour due to the Queen—and she would forgo no hairsbreadth of honour due to herself.

So now, Charles leading her forward, she curtseyed to the ground; but Catherine, with that impulsive way of hers, raised her and kissed her upon both cheeks. Anne, cold as ever and hiding her pleasure, went to her place about the Queen.

Catherine was never to win her friendship—a foreigner come to oust the Yorks from the throne. She was always to regard the Queen with jealousy but never with distrust. The Queen's honesty shone clear.

VIII

The morning sun shining through the wide windows awoke her with promise of yet another golden day... seventh golden honeymoon day. She rose gently lest she disturb Charles and slipped on the pretty cotton wrapper he admired; she looked sweet as a sugar rose, he said. She knelt upon the window-seat and looked out upon the wide view—the river running blue, and the fountains, even at this early hour springing white into the cloudless sky, and the close velvet of bright lawns. From beneath her window came the smell of hyacinths Mary had brought from Holland. The flowers should stay there forever, Catherine told herself—reminder of the sweet sister that was dead—for Charles had, after all, told her the story. She sighed, a little, for Mary dead this lovely day.

She glanced at Charles in the great bed wishing he could wake up. He had promised to take her walking in the green gloom of the hornbeam drive where the close foliage made a secret walk, casting so dense a shadow there was no need for the great green shading fans she had brought from home. In this secret place no-one walked without invitation. She cast another impatient look upon the sleeping Charles; to walk alone with him was her great joy.

She had never thought life could hold so much joy. She meant to please and to be pleased; and both were easy. Charles showered her with attentions; she felt cherished. Her prettiness flowered; the golden mirror sent back a picture worthy of its own beauty. These days she wore nothing but her English gowns; and, to please Charles, since his lightest wish was her delightful law, she dispensed with the top-knot. The soft-flowing curls, the graceful gown, gave elegance to her small figure. Charles was delighted; not so the two duennas. 'Bare breasts; stays cast aside!' Vilpena said. 'Were a man to press close he would feel the whole of a woman's body. It is far from proper.' Penalva said, quick to defend her darling, 'Donna Luisa has a saying—in Rome do as the Romans do!' and added, hastily, 'But not everything they do!' Catherine, a little pricked in conscience, went on wearing her English gowns. She was prettier even than the pretty portrait Lely made of her that year.

No end to the festivities. There were balls that began with stately court-dances and ended in country romps. There were feasts with strange exotic foods; once she saw Charles turn to the grave gentleman behind his chair—Mr. Evelyn his curious name—and offer from his own dish a piece of delicious vegetable. It was called pineapple and smelled sweet as a fruit; it came from far Barbados, Charles said. Such a thing she had never seen; at home food was simpler. There were river-picnics at night, the barges lantern-hung and sweet music sang out over the river, music plucked upon a guitar—an instrument she knew well, but new-arrived in England and very fashionable. And there were fêtes-champêtres, graced in the French style by satin-clad shepherdesses and be-ribanded swains.

Those days they were both so happy. It was a virtue to love one's wife; Charles enjoyed the rare feeling of virtue. His happiness was pricked now and again by thoughts of Barbara. True she was out of mischief at present; but any day now would see the birth of his child. And, when she should be sufficiently recovered—what then? No need to trouble his heart over much. So perfect Catherine's desire to please him, so quick, so smiling her obedience to his lightest word, he did not doubt but that she would receive Barbara into the Bedchamber. He doubted, indeed, that she had ever heard of Barbara; certainly she had let no word fall on the subject. Meanwhile Barbara was well employed; he was content to take things as they came.

That the number of Bedchamber ladies was still incomplete troubled Catherine not at all. She liked them all, except my lady of Suffolk—that elderly high-coloured beauty. Behind her perfection in the Queen's service, Catherine sensed a coldness, a dislike, even. Her Maids of Honour she found charming; she liked best the tall thin Stuart child Minette had sent from France to serve her *dearest sister. The prettiest little girl in the world*, Minette had written; but her promise of beauty was certainly hidden. Childish and immature she lacked all fashionable charms. But Minette had sent her. And because of this; and because the girl was young and innocent and poor—and a Stuart kinswoman besides, Catherine made much of the girl.

It was easy for Catherine to be happy these days; her life had burst into blossom. She had come from the cloistered etiquette of a court where women walked, modest, within the cage of their clothing, arms and breast covered. Now she showed her pretty bosom and lovely arms—and enjoyed the admiration in her husband's eyes. She had spoken little with men; now poems were written in her praises, songs sung, compliments paid. The court of England was all light and easy... too light, too easy? She wondered at times; but Charles approved and she was bound to obey him. But was there not a higher judgment than his? She was disturbed, too, by the scant attention paid to God. Church, young Montague told her laughing, was a fashionable rendez-vous where ladies and gentlemen ogled and flirted. Nor could she acquit herself of a certain carelessness in her own praying. She was taking God's gifts too lightly. She must spend more time—much more time—in her own chapel. But Charles did not approve of over-much praying; and her godfather, devout though he was, supported Charles.

'It is a wife's duty to obey her husband in all things. Your husband desires you to take your full share in every pleasure.'

'And, if my pleasure is to thank God?'

'That, too, in measure.'

'Can we measure your thanks to God?'

'Not in the heart. But we must order our lives in due proportion. If we live aright, doing our duty—that is another way to pray. And, to love the husband God has given you is a way of thanking Him. You cannot turn the King's house into a convent; but every house may be a house of God.'

'You make it too easy,' she said.

These days she obeyed her mother, also; the name of Castlemaine never passed her lips, not even to Penalva. The woman could not be important; one neither saw nor heard of her. Penalva longed to utter her warning but dared not, of herself, speak the hated name. Once she did venture. 'You live in golden clouds, Madam my darling; but I fear one day you will see too clearly... and what you see you may not like.'

Catherine said, a little stiff, 'What my husband approves cannot give me cause for dislike.'

God send it! Peanalva made no answer.

The lady had borne her second child—the King's child. About the first—the one-year-old Anne, she herself could not have said *whose* child... her husband's? Chesterfield's? Buckingham's? The King's? But of this one there could be no question. She had not slept with her husband nor with any man but Charles for a year.

The King's child; and a son.

The husband, hiding his shame, and perhaps to cover her with some rag of honour had—poor, good cuckold—declared the child his heir and had it baptised in the Catholic faith. But to grant her a shred of honour was laughable. She was prouder to bear the King's bastard than her husband's lawful heir.

Catherine first heard about it from Penalva. Young Montague, pitying his Queen with that pity which is near to love, deemed it his duty—her grand equerry—to warn Penalva. At first the duenna said nothing; she went about teeth caught upon her lower lip, hand lifted as though to wipe trouble from her brow. Catherine knew the signs and asked the cause of her distress.

Penalva said, unwilling, stumbling upon the words, 'Madam my dear my darling... *that woman*... she has given the King a son.'

The colour left Catherine's cheeks; she put out a hand to prevent herself from falling. She had not known the woman was expecting a child; her mother had said nothing. And here, in England, she had heard no word of the woman—her very name had not been mentioned; or if it had, the sense had escaped her scant English.

Now the news struck her—a bitter, unexpected blow. *That woman* had given the King a son. He had known his wife was coming but he had not cared enough to wait. She was crushed beneath a sense of betrayal, of grief and shame. She was filled with anger top-to-toe.

Penalva knew the signs of Catherine's anger; though it was an anger so schooled that, since childhood, she had shown but little. She came now and stood beside the girl. 'It is bad,' Penalva said, 'but not so bad. It was before ever he set eyes on you.'

'Nine months; nine little months! The marriage contract was signed. I was acknowledged Queen here, in this country; they prayed for me in every church. And,' she added, bitter, 'they had need to pray!' She took in her breath so that it sounded like a sob. 'He was writing to me, writing to me as his *wife*...'

'But you were not his wife. And a man's a man!'

'I was coming... I was *coming*!'

'You did not come in time.'

'I am no more than yet another woman in his bed!' Catherine cried out, distracted.

'You are his wife—and there's the difference. The King loves you...'

'Love!' her voice was fierce about the word.

'...as a man loves his wife; a gentle love, a lasting love. But between a man and his mistress, it is a different thing. It is hotter; it is shorter.'

'Shorter? And what of the child; what of his son? With such a bond it is not possible all should ever be over between them!'

'Yet it will happen if you are patient; and if you are kind. What's done is done....'

'Yes it is done,' Catherine said in an odd flat voice. And then, with sudden passion, 'And what must I do now—a woman alone in a strange land?'

'You are not alone, Madam my darling. What of my brother and myself? We would die, both of us, to make you happy. And most of all—there's your husband. You shall make your bond with him, not once but many times; a better, truer bond than *that woman* or any other could make—the bond of lawful children. These are such early days. Madam, you must be patient—though patience comes hard with you. And you must be kind—and that at least comes easy. Patience and kindness are everything with him.' Penalva stopped; she said, her very slowness driving home each word, 'And, above all, you must ignore the matter; you must know nothing of it. That would be your mother's advice; and it is my brother's advice; and my advice, also. And here's one thing, at least, for your comfort. The King has not set eyes upon that woman since you came. It could be the habit is broken; it could be she is finished and done with!'

'Done with—and the child to hold them fast? Done with? I wish I might believe it.'

Gossip went flying about the court; even the Queen's scant English must grasp it.

My lady Castlemaine was boasting everywhere that her child was the King's. Let her husband so much as look at the babe and she would rush—a veritable fury—to snatch it from the nurse. It was a wonder, they said that, as in the old tale, the child was not torn in two.

She had broken her marriage. Husband and wife forever parted. So much dishonour the poor cuckold had endured; he could take no more; no more. He was leaving England; an arrangement to suit my lady perfectly.

The next news—worse still. To those that knew *the lady* not unexpected; to the Queen, humiliating, unbelievable.

The woman was within a few miles of Hampton Court; she and her bastard with her. She had emptied her husband's house in King Street; plate, furniture, pictures, carpets—everything of value, gone. She was living now with her uncle Villiers in Richmond palace.

Catherine paced her chamber like a wild thing.

Near. So near. You could cast a stone! *Cast a stone!* She began to laugh drearily and not all Penalva's endearments could comfort her.

And still gossip flew hot-foot... the King visited *the lady* every night. Not till morning did he come to his own bed! And it was true; gossip, she found, had a frightening way of being true. When he came to her at last he was loving, he was tender... but he was already spent. She made him no reproaches; but she importuned God that she might bear a son—his true-born son, his heir. Only then could she cast off her humiliation; cast *that woman* and her bastard out of his heart. She was only half-right. Her humiliation she could cast away; but never his kindness for an old love nor passion for his children however begot.

Not even to Penalva could she speak the full measure of her grief; nor did anyone dare to speak to her face the name of her tormentor. She lost her pretty looks; she went about white with misery. There were some to pity her; but more to smile. Let her find a lover—if she could; it was the way of the court, they said, not caring one jot for the whey-faced papist Queen. She no longer pleased the King; she had lost her brief popularity.

So short a time of happiness; so long the misery. Now when Charles came to her bed, her modesty, no longer obedient to her will, stiffened against him. She could not, though she agonised, give herself; she loved him, desired him, but anger and pride kept her rigid—he had turned the sacrament of marriage into sacrilege. She tried to fight her anger, her pride; she prayed for humility that she might give him the old loving obedience so that she might conceive; but the modesty with which she had been bred and her own high spirit betrayed her. And the modesty that had, at first, intrigued him, angered him now. He came to her bed—it was his duty. But he came untender, and he came late... but however early he might have come, it was too late now; too late.

Unhappiness was a thorn forever festering; she was never free of its pain. The long nights were bad; but the day brought its own sorrows. The King's coldness and her own unpopularity; and above all the fear that somehow, somewhere, *that woman* would shame the Queen with her shameless presence haunted her day and night. Above the sound of music her ear would strain for the sound of a name, her eyes look sideways for the sight of a face. She did not know what to look for; yet she knew well enough. She had but to look for the handsomest piece of flesh in England.

She might have spared herself her pains. The time, when it came, came with a flourish of trumpets.

'I have been patient long and long enough!' my lady Castlemaine cried out. 'I'll wait no longer. You must see that I am named for the Bedchamber. At once; at once! You hear me, Charles? I'll brook no delay.' And his friends besought him also. Buckingham her cousin that had enjoyed her favours and hoped for more to come; and Berkeley, new-made Earl of Falmouth, that had behaved so basely in the matter of Anne Hyde—Berkeley whom the King loved. And dissolute Rochester besought him also; and Lauderdale whom the King trusted—all, all knowing that the lady could spread butter upon their bread, and honey, too. But the Queen's empty hands could scarce provide dry bread.

But still Charles hesitated. Buckingham the dissolute, charming fellow that was forever the King's evil genius, laughed outright.

'Does Charles, beloved of all ladies fear... his *wife*?'

Charles that feared his Barbara more than he feared God or the Devil, lifted an angry face. 'Fear? Fear my obedient little Queen?'

Buckingham and Berkeley said nothing; their lifted brow said all.

Catherine was dressed for riding when Charles came into her closet. Beneath the gay feathered hat her face was pale and listless. And, seeing her so, his heart smote him. But—and he remembered his friends—she had none but her obstinate self to blame. Let her but give way on this one thing to which his word was pledged and he'd have both roses and smiles back again.

He said, and he spoke still in Spanish, though by now she had a little English, 'A small matter... an appointment or two in your household. If you would oblige me in the matter...' and held out a paper.

'But, yes!' And she was glad to pleasure him in this, at least. And, no quill at hand, she took a pin from her hat.

She pricked the first name, she pricked the second and the third. At the fourth her head went up with a jerk; she looked at Charles. His jaw was set; but his eye entreated.

She refused him. For the first time and last time in her life, refused him. Her fingers tightened upon the pin. With a vicious stroke she scratched the paper through. A long tear stood where the name had been.

The colour—even the sallowness—left his cheeks, he lifted a grey face; his mobile mouth was drawn to a thin line. He was angrier than he could remember, ever, in all his life. It was not only anger at the double insult to her husband and her king; he was angered most of all because he was taken completely aback. He had thought he knew her; yet here she stood, the quiet and gentle creature, crimson in the face and stiff with her anger. A virago. She could outdo Barbara herself!

He knew her as yet, as little as she knew him. Penalva could have warned him of angers rare but deep that moved her whole being; could have warned him, also that, for a principle Catherine would lay down her life... but not his love. It was a thing Catherine, herself, did not know. But Penalva knew and would never tell.

He made her his courtier's bow and left; his morals might fail but never his manners.

That night he did not come to her bed; and the next morning, seeing him dark and stiff she knew that nothing would satisfy him but complete surrender. And that she would never give.

The next day and the next it was no better. She could endure it no longer; could no longer live in this cold England where, lacking his kindness, all was dark. She sought him in the King's Side since he came no longer to the Queen's. She spoke with grave respect and her courteous Spanish added weight to her request, 'Sir, since I am so unhappy as to offend you, I beg you will allow me to return home.'

In spite of her respect it was less entreaty than command. Again she had surprised him, his quiet little wife. He was about to answer in no uncertain terms; but, at the misery in her face, his heart misgave him. He said, 'If you return home shall you offend me less?' and kissed her hand. That night he went to her bed. But something between them was gone... a trustfulness? A kindliness? The sweet cherishing? She could not name it; but it was gone. She prayed that she might find it again.

She had thought that, tearing out *that woman's* name from her service, she had torn out the woman herself—made an end of the matter. She had, instead, made the affair more public. But, she comforted herself, surely, for very shame, Charles must give way. So little did she know him! Because of the publicity he would die rather than give way. And, indeed, had he wanted to, he would scarce have found it possible. If Catherine went on refusing, he must reckon with Barbara. She knew no reticences—a tiger when roused. Between two angry women the King of England would cut a fine figure! And his friends gave him no rest. To keep a mistress—or three or four, or as many as should please him, was right and proper in a King. Let him remember his grandfather great Henri Quatre of France. He'd commanded the Queen herself to bow before his mistresses; yes, even the Queen his wife. He'd thought nothing of making her, proud Medici, to ride in the same coach not with one mistress but with four! And my lord Sandwich that was old enough to know better, 'Sir, you have separated *the lady* from her husband; her father died in your father's cause. Shall you leave her, now, to be the scorn of Europe?'

All, all pleading the cause of *the lady* that could make or mar a man. And why, indeed, should any man neglect his own good for the sake of a Queen with nothing to give?

Catherine, young and new to love, took no counsel save that of her own heart; and that heart burned with anger. What use to speak with Penalva? Penalva was old; she was forty at the least. What could she remember of the anguish of love? So she walked stiff in her pride; yet however gentle she might have shown herself now, it was too late. For now it was not only a question of soothing his mistress or pleasing his friends; it was his own obstinacy driving him; an obstinacy his friends were pleased to call his honour. Nothing would serve now but surrender; surrender open and complete.

There were times when, knowing the whole court set against her that dare set herself against the King, against Queen Castlemaine, she must, for very weariness, give way. But Penalva that by her office of duenna felt responsible to Donna Luisa, Penalva that loved Catherine, sought to stiffen her courage. 'You are Queen of England; you are of the royal house of Portugal. You may ignore the insult—indeed you must ignore it; but you cannot encourage it.' And Catherine, remembering suddenly that her mother had advised her in any difficulty to consult Clarendon and to follow his counsel, and remembering, also, his fatherly look, asked, 'What does my lord Chancellor say in the matter?'

'He says nothing. He trusts it will blow over. But, if he should be pushed to it, I think he will stand by what is right. He's one, so my brother says, that's not afraid to speak his mind to the King.'

Catherine said on a deep sigh, 'It is good to know there's one man, at least, that knows right from wrong and will stand by his duty.'

Charles said no more on the subject. Save for a coolness that, she thought, must soon pass, he gave no sign of anger. She thought the matter over and done with.

IX

They had been at Hampton Court two months; and now there was no joy between them. Though Charles said no more, he had neither forgotten nor forgiven the matter. His obstinacy stiffened her own. Penalva advised a gentler bearing. 'Madam, my darling, you are right; but to be right, alas, is no guarantee of victory. You cannot, of course, accept *that woman* into the Bedchamber; but—if Madam the Queen will forgive me—you could refuse with more kindliness.'

'What! Wheedle and smile to keep that harlot from my sight!' Catherine cried out, 'I'll not have her. It is enough!'

These days Charles visited her but rarely; and then showed himself courteous but cold. His coldness cut her to the heart. She longed that he would show himself kind. She prayed with passion that she might find herself with child... *Sweet mother of Jesus, grant it!* Surely then he could not refuse to send the woman away. Let him hang the creature with gold, head-to-foot—if he could afford it; but let her name offend his wife's ears no more.

And now it was August. The days were hot, even for her that loved the sun; here there was no wind from the bay to temper the dusty heat. She drooped; she walked no more in the hornbeam grove—she could not endure to walk there alone. Undone with heat and fatigue, she kept within her chamber and importuned God and the Virgin with prayers for a child.

She leaned back in the great chair, eyes closed. On either side the duennas sat over their needlework; her younger ladies practised the new dance from France to a tune young Montague plucked from his guitar. They looked very English, her Portuguese ladies; it was not easy now to pick them out from the others. Their governess, indeed, complained that they had slipped not only into English dress but into English manners—looking boldly through curled lashes and smiling; yes and kissing, too.

The door from the anteroom opened; and, unannounced, Buckingham came in, at his heels, Berkeley, Rochester and my lord Sandwich; unwilling, she gave them her hand to kiss. And now followed a dozen or so of ladies and gentlemen, that, these past days, had ignored her existence. Her court had not been so honoured for weeks. What might this mean? Had the King at last relented? It seemed that he had; for the company were forming a lane from the door to the Queen's chair.

She was smiling her welcome, glad to be once more accepted, when Charles himself entered; he was leading a lady by the hand. She was handsome, she was tall, she was more richly dressed than the Queen herself. But, for all its beauty, Catherine disliked the face; the curled lips, the proud eye, the arrogant carriage she found distasteful. Still, Charles had brought her; it was enough.

They stood before the Queen; the King murmured a name Catherine's foreign ear did not catch... and was, perhaps, not meant to catch. The lady sank into a graceful, careless curtsey. And now Catherine could see how truly handsome she was, with her dark blue eyes and the dark red curls that the sun lit to a shining gold.

The Queen held out a gracious hand. It was at this moment Penalva bent to whisper in her ear.

Catherine's hand dropped; she stiffened in her chair. She caught sight of young Montague; he was white. But Sandwich, his cousin, carried himself, she thought, with an air of triumph.

She was here, the woman she had sworn never to see, whose name she had forbidden in her hearing. In this very room, the lovely witch and everyone gathered to see the harlot's triumph and the Queen's shame.

Catherine tried to speak. Her mouth opened; she could not utter a sound, could not breathe, even; her lungs were choked. She struggled for breath. She felt something stream upon her chin, upon her bare bosom. She put up a hand. She looked at her hand. It was blood; blood that flowed from her nose. Had it flowed from her heart she had been less surprised. She lifted a face bathed in blood and tears. Penalva caught her as she slipped sideways from the chair.

Charles did not send to enquire of her. He was grey with mortification... A Queen of England, her face all tears and blood, testifying against his cruelty! He was angry with himself that had forced the situation; angrier still with her that with her tears and blood had forced him to withdraw *the lady* before the eyes of the court.

But for all that no-one had the least doubt as to how this must end. The little foreigner could never stay the course; and, though some might pity her, not one would show pity for the vanquished.

She had outfaced the King; dared more than any person at the court—man or woman—this obscure princess, this quiet little nobody he had raised to the throne. And his friends fed his anger, pricking, pricking at him, flicking at him, did anger show the least sign of failing, reminding him that he was England's King—not that he needed reminding; he had more than his share of Stuart pride.

He sent his peremptory command. The Queen had offered *the lady* public insult; and that insult must be made good. My lady Castlemaine must be received at once—lady of the Bedchamber. Catherine refused; she went on refusing. She showed a calm, proud face; not even the watchful Penalva knew the full weight of her grief and fear.

She thought herself friendless; yet one person lifted his voice in her defence, though she did not know it then. Clarendon bluff and rough spoke his mind and continued to speak it.

'Sir,' he told the King, 'you lay upon Madam the Queen more than flesh and blood can endure. And when flesh rebels and blood flows, you turn about and blame the victim.' And, undeterred by the King's flashing eye, went boldly on. 'In France a man may thrust his mistress into the presence of his wife and it will pass; but in this country it is not so. Here a King's mistress is hateful to good folk; and shameful as any slut that sells herself in the gutter. Your court laughs at the situation—it follows the manners of the French court. But let not that blind you to the truth. This tale will spread beyond the court. And then? If you persist, you will lose the goodwill of many; you will please only those that long to see, once more, the downfall of the crown. Sir, I am warning you!'

'Hold your tongue, Clarendon. I've made a promise and that promise I shall keep. Go, talk to the Queen; see if you can persuade that stubborn mind of hers. Tell her if she give way on this one thing she shall find me a kind and faithful husband.'

You haven't it in you to be faithful to any woman, least of all a wife. I love you, Charles, but God knows that's true.

'I like *the lady*; I like her company and I'll not be kept from it,' Charles said. 'If the Queen is reasonable I'll enjoy it in innocence. If not, oddsfish, I'll seek my lady's company where and when and how I choose. Warn her. Warn her, Clarendon!'

And when the good man, unwilling to undertake so distasteful a task, would have protested, the King cut him short.

'My honour's in the matter. Would you have men say that I obey my wife as a pupil his master? No! This one thing she must do! Tell her, if she agree, it is the only hard thing I shall ever ask of her. Nor it shall not be so hard, neither! Barbara shall behave herself. I swear it. Let her show but the slightest disrespect to the Queen and I'll never see her face again!'

'Sir, if I must take your message, why then I must. But I do it with a most unwilling heart.'

'I command not your heart in this but your tongue.'

Embarrassment sent the good man stiff and blunt to the Queen; impossible to guess at the good heart beneath the severe manner.

She received him, with Penalva at a respectful distance; and d'Aubigny to interpret.

'I regret, Madam,' he said when he had made his salutations, 'the disagreement between the King and yourself. The King is not a man to be driven; the Queen's anger, the Queen's stubborn temper sets him more surely in his own direction.'

The Queen's anger! The Queen's stubborn temper!

She took in her breath. No need to justify herself to this common red-faced man, she the wronged one! Did he not, of himself, know the law of God? She opened her mouth to tell him as much, caught Penalva's warning eye and sat biting upon her lips. She tried to thrust down her anger, to answer him reasonably, kindly; but his manner had overthrown her. To her mortification tears poured down her cheeks; she sat weeping like a four-year-old.

She was fully as shocked as he. She could not blame him when he said, 'I shall call upon you again, Madam, when you are more able to receive the humble advice of your servant that wishes you well.' And so was gone.

Penalva, distressed at such tears, unseemly both in a Queen and in a princess of Portugal, though provocation had been severe, said, 'The Queen is right to be firm; but, forgive me, Madam my darling, you should be more kind. The good man does his best.'

And d'Aubigny, 'I speak as your ghostly adviser. Under that harshness there's a good heart. Treat him with courtesy—it is his due. So he will continue, as already he has shown himself—believe it, Madam—your friend.'

When Clarendon asked for audience next day she granted it at once. She was contrite, asking him to forgive her anger and her tears. 'I have few to wish me well, and among those few I do count yourself. From you, sir, I shall always be glad to hear advice; yes and to take it... if it be possible. But do not blame me if sometimes I give way to the misery that breaks my heart.'

And, that being translated, he said kindly enough, 'I am your very humble servant, Madam; and it may be my duty to tell you things we had both rather leave unsaid.'

'Sir, I beg you will tell me those things I should hear.'

He was touched by the sweetness in her face; but his duty both to her and to the King drove him to plain speech.

'You are little beholden to your education, Madam; it has taught you nothing of the follies of men.'

She answered, very downcast, 'I did not think to find the King's affections already engaged.'

'Come now, Madam! Did you imagine the King had kept his heart all these years for a wife he had never seen? Do you believe that, when it shall please God to send the King of Portugal a wife she shall find the court so virtuous?' And sent her a sharp look from beneath shaggy brows.

Yes. Almost she had said it. Her brothers were unchaste, so much was true; but neither would allow his women anywhere near the court. Nor would they load their harlots with riches they couldn't afford and undeserved honours. Least of all would they expect virtuous men and women to treat their creatures with respect.

To say all this would not help. Other words crowded upon her tongue, words that surely he must understand. *Even did I not love my husband I could not endure his woman thrust beneath my eyes—self-respect*

65

forbids it. But I do love him, with every beat of my heart. It is torment to me that he sleeps with another. When I think of that woman's child—my husband's child—I run mad with grief and pain.

But he did not look a man to understand a woman's heart. She said, instead, stung by injustice, 'The King must hate me to put such insult upon me. And, if I submitted in patience the world would say I deserve it... and I should deserve it. No, sir!' And again anger overthrew her, 'Put me aboard a ship, and send me home again.'

He was taken aback, she could see. When he answered it was with something of his old coldness. 'It is not a case of what you will or what you will not. Let me remind you, Madam, you have not the disposal of your own person to go where you will. If the King does not desire it, you may not stir, even, from your own rooms. As for returning to your own country—here are plenty to wish you there! But, ask yourself, what welcome you would receive from your mother. You would do well, Madam, to hold your peace.'

And when she stood silent, shaken by the truth of this, he said, more gentle, 'Let me advise you—Madam, I speak as a friend. Do not show such passion to the King. If you think it proper to deny him anything, do it as though you consider rather than refuse. Provoke him to anger—and you'll get the worst of it. Madam, I know the King.'

He was right and she knew it; knew it by the way d'Aubigny translated with such earnestness as he might be speaking from his own heart; and by the way Penalva, seemingly without knowing, nodded; knew it most of all by her own commonsense. Yet it was hard to stomach his blunt words. Yet there was nothing for it but to thank him and agree. When he was gone d'Aubigny said, 'Madam the Queen, forgive me if I speak out of turn but I am your priest. Clarendon's heart is with you in this—and not only because he knows right from wrong. But also because he would be glad to see *that woman* bested—there's no love between them. But he does his duty to the King; and it makes him blunt and boorish; and that you must forgive because of his true heart.'

Charles said, 'Were the Queen as gentle as a dove, still I'd not give way. My word has been passed. And—' he spoke from a darkened face, 'let her beware how she anger me!'

'Sir, the Queen acts out of a loving heart and not a peevish one. Have patience. I have hopes to bring her to it.'

'See to it, Clarendon—though I have waited long enough. My friends are amazed I have not yet had my way. If I do not get it now—so they warn me—I shall never get it so long as the Queen lives.'

'They are not friends that so counsel the King.'

'Oddsfish, man! They are right. A man must be master in his own house.'

'I beseech you, sir, do not rub upon the raw place.'

Clarendon left him to his troubled thoughts.

A man must be master in his own house—true! But this wife of his—she was honest and showed some courage. And she was gentle with it; and, save in this one thing, obliging. For all his anger he had a kindness for her... she was a pretty thing and she loved him.

That night he came to her bedchamber—a thing he had not done for weeks. He had done better to stay away. She was already in her bedgown reading a book of devotion. She kept her head down lest he surprise the joy in her eyes. He had intended to speak her fair; but no sooner had he set eyes upon her than anger took him at the sight of this small, pale, *obstinate* thing. Before he could stop his tongue he had called her stubborn and wanting in duty; and she had taxed him with being a tyrant regardless of her honour. And, in spite of his lame Spanish, she made everything clear. She ended with, 'Sir, you treat me very ill. I shall go back to my own country.'

The threat uttered for the second time filled him with hotter rage. 'Ask first if your mother will have you back!' he advised.

She raised a troubled face; Clarendon had said this same thing.

'Well, Madam, you shall soon have a chance to find out! I mean to send away all those servants of yours, those hangers-on that encourage your obstinacy.'

He saw in her face that she did not believe such unkindness to be in him. 'Rest assured,' he cried out, 'I shall do as I say!'

He was shouting now at the top of his voice, shouting her down; and that was easy enough—her voice was low. But also he was shouting down the voice of his own conscience; and that was not so easy. He would regret the noise later; but nothing could stay him now.

The whole court, it seemed, had heard the noise of their quarrelling. He felt the smiles at his back; and *the lady* spared him no bed-time lecture upon an ill-governed wife—which, he could not but think, came oddly from her! Between them—Catherine with her dumb obstinacy and Barbara with her unbridled tongue—they kept his temper in a constant rub. It was their honeymoon; yet husband and wife avoided each other; they spoke only when they must. He would do well to send his Barbara packing; he knew it. There were plenty as handsome and all of them better-tempered. But she had just given him a son. And she knew how to alternate the passion of her anger with the passion of her flesh—so sweet, so yielding she could be, his own flesh melted.

And then, too, he smarted still at Catherine's threat to leave him. All unknowing she had struck a shrewd blow there! So obstinate she was, she might, he believed, attempt it. And what a fool should he look, Charles that great lover—with his wife leaving him in the middle of the honeymoon! He must break her pride now, before it was too late; rid himself, as he had sworn, of those that so spitefully supported her; so his father had done with an obstinate wife.

He sent for Clarendon again.

'Sir,' Clarendon was troubled, 'must she lose all her friends, now when she is so unhappy?'

'If she have no others, the fault is hers! Out they go, lock, stock and barrel!'

Now Catherine must believe it was no idle threat. She sent for Clarendon; thereafter he reported their conversation to the King.

'She said, sir, she has been too angry and is heartily sorry. She implores your pardon; she would ask it on her knees if that would please you. But, she said, "the way the King has treated me most shockingly surprises me, it shakes me to the heart." And then, sir, she said, "I pray that whatsoever provocation he shall put upon me, God will give me patience so that anger shall not carry me away." And then, sir, she asked, "Who should choose my servants; the King or myself?" I told her, sir, she had the *right*... but it was a right no wife should use once her husband has recommended a servant. I advised her to give way lest she repent too late.'

'And then?'

The red face went purple. 'She said, sir, she could not understand how you or I, or anyone with a good conscience, should ask her to give consent to what could only be an occasion to sin.'

The absurd, strait-laced, *obstinate* little creature! Charles felt unwilling respect but no kindness that she so stubbornly upheld her principles. Well, driving her was useless; he must try another way.

'Tell her,' he said, 'that if she give way I will end the affair with my lady.'

Clarendon gave him a long look. *So you swore before ever you set eyes on the Queen. Do you truly mean to free yourself from your witch? Can you free yourself?*

'Yes, I will finish the business!' Charles said and could not meet the good man's eye.

Catherine was learning too fast to be convinced.

'The King must do as he pleases,' she told Clarendon. 'But I will never consent to do as he asks.'

'Oddsfish, she has been well-primed by those hags of hers; nor do I exempt the meddling godfather!' Charles exploded into anger when Clarendon brought his answer. 'By God, I'll teach her better!' And he actually called upon the name of God—a thing rare with him.

He went storming into her chamber. 'You rate yourself too dear!' he cried out. 'And well you may—for dear enough you cost me! Yes, you play innocent; but you know well the trick your lady mother played upon me!' He saw by her bewildered eyes that she knew nothing; but anger drove him. He told her, very plain, the tale of her dowry—of sugar instead of gold. He spoke with contempt; and that was bad enough. He spoke as though she had been privy to the deceit; and that was worse.

He saw her proud air crumple; she was white now as a fresh-laundered sheet. He did not believe her anything but innocent; yet he cared nothing for that. Any weapon at all to end the intolerable situation.

He pressed his advantage while he had it. He sent away the Portuguese *family*; yet, when it came to it, he had not the heart to leave her utterly forlorn. The ladies Penalva and Ponteval, were, indeed, bound to remain—the one with her brother, the other with her husband; he could not offend the Portuguese ambassadors. He kept also the least number of priests to honour the marriage contract; as for the rest, out they went, bag and baggage, old and young—and no thanks nor any gift. Afterwards he was sorry for his ruthless behaviour. To clear them out had been right and proper; but he should have done it with more courtesy.

'I promised them advancement, I *promised*; and now that promise is broken!' Catherine cried out, white and wild. 'They were sent back without a gift... I had nothing to give. I have had no penny of my allowance. Nor could I stoop to ask!' And, indeed, had things been loving and easy between them, still she would not have asked, being bowed with shame at the tale of her dowry. 'I did not believe he would do so. I did not believe he would send away those that loved me—my own people, penniless and disgraced.'

She shook, head to foot, with the violence of her weeping. Penalva, arms about her, tried to comfort her beloved child; but she was beyond all comfort.

'He is good to all, he is generous, he is kind; but to me, most hard, most bitter. Had my mother known how I must fare in this unkind, unvirtuous country, she had not sent me to be a most unhappy wife!'

'For your unhappiness she must grieve; but not for sending you here. She weighed Portugal in one hand and you in the other—the happiness of many against the happiness of one. And which weighed heavier do you think?'

A stranger in a strange land. A prisoner of her own making. She shut herself within her own apartments while outside the world pursued its pleasures regardless of the sad Queen. There were no more quarrels; now she might almost welcome them. Then, at least, she had seen her husband; now, it seemed, he could do very well without her; she rarely saw him. It seemed also that pleasure filled his days and his nights, too. Now and again he would come late and briefly to her bed—he must, after all, present the country with its heir. He performed his task without love and without tenderness.

X

That woman had left Richmond. She was lodged beneath the same roof as the Queen; in Hampton Court itself. When Catherine heard it the blood left her cheeks; so pale she was, Penalva thought she must fall. She said no word; she turned and went into her inner chamber. *You must never allow that woman into your presence; nor her name to be mentioned within your hearing.* And how was she to prevent it save by keeping fast within the prison of her rooms?

Her heart burned against Charles; yet, when young Montague told her that, outside the court, there were plenty to pity her and blame Charles, it did but add to her distress. Dare to blame their King! Dare to pity their Queen! Humiliation upon humiliation.

Charles, himself, was not finding things easy. Though fawning friends urged him to stand fast and courtiers smiled approval, he could not acquit himself of ill-behaviour to the Queen. And always he carried in his heart the fear that the quarrel continuing, would make trouble not only with Portugal—which was bad enough; but worse still with France that had smiled upon the marriage; that, because of it, had sworn a secret treaty of friendship.

And there were other difficulties of which Catherine knew nothing. He was always pinched for money and it was not due to his own extravagance. The country was all-but bankrupt; Cromwell's armies, Cromwell's navies, had drained it dry. He himself had never received anything like the revenue Parliament had promised—one million two hundred thousand pounds; the smallest possible sum to cover every need—the country's and his own; they had all agreed to that! Cromwell had spent twice that sum—and left crippling debts behind. But he, himself! The first year of his reign he'd received no more than seventy thousand pounds. Seventy thousand pounds to support the army and the navy and to pay his officers of State; to say nothing of Dunkirk—Cromwell's baby that! A greedy little monster that alone swallowed one hundred thousand pounds a year! Better sell it back to the French; they'd pay a good price—Clarendon was right there! And there were a thousand other public expenses. Last year the revenue had fallen short of four hundred thousand pounds—one third of his income meagre as it was; and this year looked to be no better.

And there were private debts—for the most part, not of his own making. First and foremost those his father had left. Repudiate them; his friends advised it. But that he would not do. They were debts of honour and must be paid; somehow paid, were it shilling by shilling.

And, in addition to his money troubles—religious troubles. The country was torn by strife—in the King's opinion, unnecessary strife.

'I'm a simple fellow,' he told Clarendon. 'I thank God for all His mercies; and so should every man. But must we all address Him in the selfsame words? If we have a grateful heart, though we use different words, shall He not listen?'

'Sir, it is well to keep such thoughts to yourself; else you will offend everyone—Papists, Protestants and Non-conformists alike. And especially you will offend your Parliament that means to tighten the law against all, of whatever sect, that will not conform to our church services.'

'There are many, and especially Papists, that lost their all in serving me. I promised them freedom to worship—all I had to give. Must I go back upon my word? And those others that dissent from the actual words of the Prayer-book, good men that would choose to suffer in the flesh rather than in the spirit—must these, too, come to grief for conscience' sake?'

'Sir, they must. It is politic. Parliament has taken its measure and passed its act. Any minister of religion that does not pray in the approved form shall lose his living... if nothing worse.' He saw the pain in the King's face and said quickly, 'Sir, you must put tolerance from your mind; the country is not ready. You have spoken of an act that shall allow those of tender conscience not to conform; it lies in your desk already drafted. Keep it there. For the House will refuse and go on refusing... and you must put up with it. You cannot afford to offend your Parliament. You must bide your time, lad!' The word slipped out in spite of himself.

'Yet I shall go on trying!' the King said.

With all his troubles upon him there were times when his good spirits deserted him; then, oppressed by melancholy, he must indulge in pleasures—at the play which he loved above all pleasures, in the dance; and, since his wife was withdrawn, pleasures less innocent.

Clarendon was forever at him to make his peace with the Queen; it was a thing my lady Castlemaine would not forget.

'Sir, the people look to you for an heir; there can be no child while the Queen is so troubled. Remember the kingfisher; he can breed only in gentle weather. Take your lesson from him.'

A man must be master in his own house! Remembering the strictures of his friends, Charles shook a fierce head. Clarendon said, 'There is talk everywhere! The court, sir—I must say it—is not virtuous; but the common folk respect the moral laws. Quarrel with Madam the Queen over... *the lady,*' and his mouth was wry, 'and you are bound to lose many hearts. Can you afford to lose even one heart, you that are but late come home?'

'Have done!' Charles broke in impatient. The old man deserved well by him—Charles would be the first to admit it; but he was growing restive under the fatherly tones; and *the lady* had not ceased to rub annoyance raw.

Madam Queen Henrietta Maria was coming to England to greet her new daughter. Catherine said, 'Now the King must make up the quarrel. He will not let his mother know the trouble between us.'

'Such a thing cannot be kept secret,' Penalva said. 'It could be the reason for her coming.'

It added terror to the meeting. That the Queen-mother was formidable everyone knew; Charles, himself, feared rather than loved her.

'You need not fear, Madam my darling,' Penalva said. 'She will understand. She came, like you, a foreign bride, to this country—and she had troubles aplenty! There is, besides, much you share with her. There is first of all our blessed religion; she is so strong in the faith, she refused to be crowned or even to watch the crowning of her husband. She would attend no heretic ceremony, she said.'

Catherine said, on a sigh, 'There's no word about my crowning. I think there never will be; or why was the King crowned before I came? A crowning is a great thing...'

'Peace in a household is better. The King was wise.'

'What peace? There's none—'

Penalva said, 'If I speak out of turn it is for love of you. Make no complaint to the Queen-mother. She has wit to see the truth for herself.'

'I trust she will prove a friend; for that I do pray.'

'Amen to that!' Penalva said.

In mid-July, pelted by rain and driven by wind, Charles and James set out to meet their mother. Henrietta Maria, sick from her tempestuous journey—*Mam's ill-luck at sea*, her children said—was escorted with royal honours to Greenwich palace, there to rest until recovered. It was a fortnight later when, attended by a great company, the King and Queen set out from Hampton Court; it was the first journey they had made together for weeks. Catherine sat within the coach pale with anticipation; no bride can meet her mother-in-law for the first time with equanimity—still less a bride notably at odds with a beloved son. And the formidable Henrietta could mend or make more trouble. Catherine prayed it might be mended; she was sick to the heart of quarrels. Yet she herself could not end them—she was in the right. What would this frightening mother-in-law have to say?

Catherine found courage to raise her eyes to the figure that stood at the top of the great staircase to greet them. She was taken by a deep sense of disappointment.

So this was the enchanting Henrietta that had her lovers still—so they said. She was dark, she was old; she was shrouded head-to-foot, in black; she was a symbol of death. Catherine thought in something of panic, *Life goes by. How soon before I look like that?* She was taken with anguish to make all loving again between Charles and herself.

They had reached the top of the staircase before she remembered that she must show respect to this mother of her husband. She made then to kneel to kiss the withered hand, but the old Queen would not allow it. She raised Catherine in her arms and they looked one at the other; it was not hard since they were both of a height. Madam the Queen-mother knew the signs of unhappiness. She kissed the girl on both cheeks with such kindness that Catherine's heart warmed towards her; she vowed to be an obedient daughter... whenever in honesty she might.

An arm about Catherine, Madam Henrietta Maria said, 'Let us put aside all ceremony. I am come to this country to love you as a daughter and to serve you as a Queen.'

It was so long since she had been called *daughter*, Catherine was deeply moved. Now, in her very halting English she made her long-prepared speech. 'I al-so have ver-y great joy in this meet-ing as nev-er wom-an had. Not an-y one of your children shall ex-ceed me in love and o-bedience to my new moth-er.'

The Queen-mother's arms still about her they went into the presence-chamber. She made Catherine sit in an equal chair at her side; but Charles sat in unwonted humility at her feet. James was announced now, and she kept him standing—a sign of her displeas-ure; but his wife that had been Anne Hyde was permitted a footstool. Not long since the old Queen had said, *If my son's wife come in at one door, I go out of the other. I will never forgive James his disgraceful marriage.* But the thing was done; she must endure it with what grace she might.

Charles' first enquiries were about the beloved little sister. The news was not good—her husband was a vicious brute; yet it was not all bad—she stood in high favour with his brother the King. When they had drunk tea in honour of the bride, Madam Henrietta Maria drew Charles aside. What they whispered about Catherine could guess; for, on their return, Charles was kind again. That night they supped together in public—a thing they had not done for weeks; and, when she looked about her, there was no sign of the handsome, hateful Castlemaine.

Madam Mother-in-law came in state to return the visit; she was to stay with them for a while. Again the two Queens met with affection; as Penalva said, they had much in common. For two weeks Catherine knew the taste of happiness; Charles behaved well and not once did *that woman* show her lovely brazen face. 'We are finished with her!' Catherine stretched herself all languorous with joy.

Penalva said nothing.

London was preparing to greet its new Queen. Catherine was a little frightened. When she compared herself with the court beau-ties—Frances Jennings a flower of a girl; with Lady Chesterfield that flaming beauty; with la Belle Hamilton—a true queen of loveliness; with half-a-dozen others, she felt herself small, insignificant. Then she would remind herself of the Queen-mother—the immense dignity, the intense force of that personality—and take heart again.

In the last week of August and a golden summer day, they embarked for London. Everything perfect; save that Penalva had been left behind; she was having trouble with her eyes. Catherine missed her—the one person to whom she could speak her heart.

Charles liked her looks; and rose upon her cheeks, the dark eyes wide with excitement—it was hard to believe this charming Queen was the pale, sulking moppet of a short while ago. 'Our English fashions give you height; your own fashion robs you... so.' He brought a hand close to the floor and laughed to think it had been spread about that she was a dwarf: 'And your hair... the charming curls. They give you back the pretty look that hideous top-knot filched from you. I like my wife very well.'

How should she not enjoy a day so well begun?

She continued to enjoy it. All along the river-banks soldiers stood to attention; and, behind them, crowds pressed for the sight of the unknown Queen. They must have liked what they saw; for all the way to London there went with them one unbroken cheer. Within a few miles of the city they changed barges for the great entry.

The State barge was all scarlet-and-gold; the canopy, decked with plumes at each corner, was set upon Greek pillars banded with rib-ands and flowers; upon the sides and at the bow hung the royal arms of Portugal and England entwined. Four-and-twenty water-men, picked for looks no less than for skill, and handsome in royal scarlet-and-gold, bent to the oars.

The royal barge leading—and Cleopatra herself could boast no finer—there followed the long procession of gilded and garlanded boats carrying the royalty and high nobility of England.

Catherine was happy. Charles admired her; and, more than that, he was kind. He must have given his orders, for, though she cast about beneath her eyelids among the following boats, she caught not a glimpse of *that woman*. Now, as they drew near Whitehall she caught sight of my lady standing with others to see the procession. There she stood voluptuous, elegant. Bright curls flowed from beneath a large black hat with yellow plumes; a man's hat that enhanced—as was meant—the femininity of that lovely face. She looked enchanting; Catherine's self must own it. She knew the moment's sick envy. As the royal barge passed, *the lady* sank to her curtsey. There was, Catherine thought, mockery in its depth.

My lady had risen from the ground when the thing happened.

A child came running forward to see better; he ran to where a piece of scaffolding trembled, about to fall. But she was there first, the lady in the plumed hat, skirts held high above the lovely legs, running, running towards the child. She had scarce pulled it—and herself—back to safety when the great plank fell.

Acknowledging the greetings of those upon the river, Charles had not marked the incident; and Catherine, herself, might have missed it, save that the woman's beauty must always draw her jealous eye. Now she tried to tell herself there had been no real danger, that the thing had been done for effect—to catch the King's eye. But she could not believe it. There had been danger; and in all the crowd, *that woman* alone had marked it... and dared it. She had saved the life of a child. In spite of herself Catherine must remember it.

And now she must put my lady from her thoughts. For there came my lord Mayor of London and his aldermen all in scarlet and gold and rich fur—and their barge as fine as the King's. And with him came the city guilds in their richest livery, all in gilded barges; and following them, yet other barges where pretty boys gay in holiday finery stood and threw flowers upon the water while music sounded from river and shore. And now the booming of guns and the roaring of crowds drowned the music while the royal barge made its slow way upon a river so crowded there was scarce a piece of water as large as a crown to be seen.

It was full six of the evening and the sun bright still and the sky blue when they tied up at last, and there, amid the thunder of cannon, standing upon the flower-decked landing-stage, the Queen-mother stood to greet them. It was the crown of Catherine's pleasure; here, in the whole thoughtless, unfriendly court, the one true heart. She was rejoiced to hear that this kindly friend would remain with them at Whitehall while Somerset House, the dowager's palace, was made fit for her residence.

XI

Her first days in London where all was set for her delight, were poisoned by my lady Castlemaine. Since that one appearance at Hampton Court where the Queen had wept—tears of blood you might truly say—*the lady* had more or less kept out of the way. But here in Whitehall there was no escaping her presence—the flaming beauty, the high and noisy laughter, the heavy perfume that announced her presence and lingered to mark her absence. Eye and ear and nose, all assailed. Her rooms adjoining the King's advertised his freedom in her bed. She received homage like a Queen; she behaved, indeed, as though she were the Queen. She granted audiences, granted favours—at a price; she refused favours and chose her favourites. Among the men, Buckingham was chief—he was her cousin and the Queen's avowed enemy; among the women, Frances Stuart—it was pleasant to take her from the Queen. The girl was thin and scarcely pretty—no competition to be feared; she was, besides, kinswoman to the King, a useful addition to my lady's court. She kept the girl for ever at her side. And the girl, seeing in such favour the road to success and being, besides, very poor, obeyed my lady with blind adoration. Catherine had no mind to compete with such a benefactress; she withdrew her kindness.

The matter of the Bedchamber had not yet been settled. Charles, anxious to placate Catherine, swore that his mistress should never live in the same house as his wife. But she was already there! To turn her out would be worse insult, even, than the Queen's refusal; in spite of his promise he did not see how it could be done. He was disturbed and he was vexed. He wished, more than ever, he had never set eyes on his Barbara. She was too tempestuous, too domineering and too damnably expensive; her gaming-debts were a scandal. He could wish himself well-rid of her. At such times he was not sorry—in spite of all discomfort—that his wife stood firm.

Catherine, too, was vexed and disturbed. Besides the constant sight of her triumphant rival, besides the estrangement from the King, she had yet another cross to bear. There was a pretty lad about the court come in the train of the Queen-mother. He was fourteen or so; young Mr. Crofts. No need to guess who his father might be. He had the King's charm and a true Stuart face; Charles' bastard by Lucy Walter. Charles had been scarce eighteen at the time of the boy's begetting; and a young man cannot be expected to remain virgin for the sake of some far-distant, mythical wife—so much she had, with sorrow, learned. But all the same she did not take it kindly that the boy was thrust beneath her nose. He'd been well enough in France; he should have stayed there.

Henrietta Maria's shrewd eyes missed nothing.

You think me unkind that I bring the boy? Tactless, perhaps? Believe me, daughter, it is neither. I know my son's joy in Jamie Crofts. A wise wife studies her husband's pleasure.'

'But what, Madam, if a hus-band shall take too much of pleas-ure?'

'A wise wife knows when to stand—and when to give way... and your English advances nicely! Now, listen, daughter; I speak not as the mother of my son but as your own mother might speak; and, as very like, she did speak. Royal marriages are not between one man and one woman; they are between country and country, for the good of both.' She waited to see whether the girl, with her scant English, had understood; and, Catherine nodding, went on. 'You married England to help Portugal—at need. In the quarrel with my son you are in the right. But, anger him—and what becomes of your country then? The King has little obligation there; the terms of the marriage-contract were not, all of them, honoured.'

She saw crimson fire the girl's pale cheeks and said more kindly, 'My child, men are but men. My husband was the chastest of men; the most devoted of husbands. But while he was in prison, while he was in Carisbrooke, do you think he never slept with a woman? Of course he did! And I did not love him the less. Rather I was glad... a little, he should find some comfort.'

'It is not the same. You had his children; there were no... no...'

'Bastards?' Henrietta Maria supplied the word.

She nodded. 'I have no son... not yet; and this bast-ard, he do... does walk like a Prince of the blood.'

'Then you should pity him; yes and his father, also. Jamie is handsome and charming—gifted to win all hearts. But he can never wear the crown—and the fault not his own. Be kind because he is your husband's son and because he can never wear the crown.'

It was good sense. And since Charles doted upon the boy and nothing in the world could alter his birth; and because he was debonair in every degree, and because Catherine was just, she showed herself friendly. And because of his charm and her own good heart, she found herself growing to love him. And that was another knife in her heart; for he paid her courtesy due to the Queen and no more; and sometimes, not even that. But to *the lady* he showed the devotion of a troubadour; he was forever at her side. There was no escaping the sight of the handsome creatures.

Catherine could not forget the warning thrice given—by the King, by Clarendon and now by Madame Henrietta Maria. Should Portugal need help against Spain... and should Charles refuse? She had thought it her own private quarrel; she saw now, with fear, that it might affect her country's good; perhaps her brother's crown. Her high and stubborn spirit gave way.

She was cold as ice when she told the King that she would accept *that woman* into the Bedchamber. Charles kissed her hand and then her cheek. She accepted the salute; there was no warmth in her.

Her acceptance did little good. She could not guess at his disappointment that she had thrown away her just cause; he had not guessed it himself. He had admired her honesty and her courage; he had found himself respecting her as he had respected no other women—not his mother, not Minette. Expedience had set them both juggling with honesty; but his wife's honesty shone like the sun—so he had thought. Now he saw her as obstinate, merely; perverse, light and fickle. And it did not occur to him that he had wanted the impossible. He had wanted her to give way and to stand firm. Unyielding she must yet yield. And it did not occur to him, either, that she had been moved by love of her country; that and that alone.

She had given way. It was, she thought, enough. She could not bring herself to any show of kindness—neither to him nor to the mistress he had thrust upon her. And this lack of kindness *the lady* repaid with interest.

'She flaunts her infant within Whitehall itself!' Catherine cried out, her own language hot upon her tongue. 'She invites everyone to mark its likeness to the King; and the husband, poor, good cuckold, no longer pretends the child's his own. He'll endure it no longer; he goes abroad, they say, to forget his troubles; Would God it were so easy for me!'

'He may easily cast off his duty to his country and his King; not so you, Madam, my darling. You have given way; but it is not enough. You must show yourself gracious.'

'*To that woman*! Strange advice from my Penalva!'

'Circumstances have changed; yourself have changed them. You have admitted the woman; if now you do not show yourself gracious—you play her game. When you refuse to look at her, then the King must look at her with added kindness. When she comes into the Queen's presence, because you give no welcome, he must hasten to her side. And the others, seeing it, flock about her, also; Madam, my darling, you have seen it for yourself. There she stands, holding her court at one end of the room—the Queen's own room; and there you sit alone save for Ponteval and me and a handful of others. But it could be worse. She could hold court in her own lodgings. Take care you do not drive her to it—for where would you be then?'

'Is there no justice, no right?'

'I begin to doubt it. But the wisdom of showing oneself kind—in the right time and place—that I never doubt.'

Charles was friendly again. Catherine had, after all, saved his face. He waited for her now to change her manner to his mistress. She felt the pressure of his will. Yet, in spite of it, in spite of Penalva's advice, she could give way no further.

Early in September he took her to visit his mother installed now in Somerset House. Henrietta Maria received her with especial kindness, seating her, as always, in a chair equal to her own. There were some half-dozen people present; York stood behind his mother's chair, his duchess, as usual, sat upon a stool. Again Catherine found herself wondering if ever she could come to like her. Anne's coldness in public never altered, not even to her husband. She never spoke of him, even to the King, save by his title; nor had Catherine ever heard her address him save as *duke*. Hard to believe, Catherine thought, that anyone at all could have seduced this cold, proud woman. It must surely have been the other way about—her strong will beating him down. Now she strove to make up for her irregular marriage by behaving in public with excessive propriety. Edward Montague said that in private life it was quite other. So shortly married each pursued his cold lusts. Well, Anne's private life was her own affair...

She was shocked from her thoughts by the sound of a name.

My lady Castlemaine—young Mr. Crofts in attendance and both sure of a welcome—was curtseying to the Queen-mother. The mistress was graciously received; the bastard with affection. Anger possessed the wife. She sat aloof, unseeing; she did not, could not, acknowledge *that woman's* presence.

Charles did not mark it. He was talking to a gentleman with a shrewd eye and a full laughing mouth; a gentleman finely, almost foppishly dressed. The Queen had never seen him before but he had seen the Queen, often; he had marked it in his private journal.

Charles brought him up to be presented. 'Here is Mr. Pepys—our walking news-sheet. He sets down every word he hears, so have a care what you say before him!' And then, forgetting his own advice, proceeded to comment upon Catherine's looks. 'She is fatter than when she came. I believe she's already with child!' he told his mother laughing and cast a look upon *the lady* to prick her a little that had pricked him so much. 'Come now, Kate, tell us!'

It was not a thing she could take lightly. To bear the King's child was a sacred hope. And, besides, she had been married scarce four months. That he should discuss her condition before this strange, tattling gentleman and her hateful rival, offended her over-bred decorum. 'You lie!' she cried out.

She had meant, only, that it was not so. She saw the King rock with laughter, guessed by the mischief in his eye and the startled look of Mr. Pepys that her halting tongue had betrayed her. The pleased look of *that woman* and the blank look of the Queen-mother confirmed her guess.

'Come, now,' Charles was laughing still, 'tell us again!' But for all his coaxing she would not be drawn. 'Oh Kate, be not mealy-mouthed.

If I lie—tell me so like an honest lass. Bid me *Confess and be hanged!*' But she knew the meaning of those two words; it did not need the slight shake of the Queen-mother's head to seal her lips.

Nor was she better pleased when later, Charles handed her into the coach and then—and no by your leave—handed in his mistress. Nor was that all. He followed himself with his pretty lad, young Mr. Crofts. She sat withdrawn; the laughter of the others fell upon her outraged ears. It was not right, it was not seemly—the King, his wife, his mistress and his bastard by another woman, travelling in close company. Nor did the sight of Mr. Pepys' surprised eyes and full lips drawn to a whistle make things better—the man was a walking news-sheet.

She said no word. She was learning to discipline her tongue—a long, hard lesson. She said no word; but the anger in her eyes she could not hide.

If she could not receive her husband's mistress with courtesy, she had done better not to give way at all, she thought, bitter. Then, at least, she had preserved her dignity. Now things were worse than ever. Charles pursued his mistress with ever-increasing ardour. He was gay with all—herself excepted; gayer than she had ever seen him.

'He playacts,' Penalva said. 'They say he tires of the woman and her angers.'

'Never believe it. He sups with her every night; he stays with her till daylight. They say everywhere she's with child again!'

The days dragged on. Daylong Charles went never near his Queen; evening and night found her alone. Now it was no longer his mistress holding her court at one end of the Queen's presence-chamber; that presence-chamber was altogether deserted—Penalva had proved a true prophet. My lady held her own court in the splendid rooms so convenient to the King's; and there the flatterers swarmed about her. 'Some of my own household!' the Queen cried out to Penalva. 'Licking her feet in hope of favour.'

'They'll get no good of it; she gives nothing away. Madam, my darling, life goes hard with you, now. But, show a little kindness and things will right themselves. And take this for your comfort. For all the King's displeasure, he'll not allow one word of disrespect against you—so Ned Montague says. No! And least of all from *that woman!*'

But there was little comfort in that. The empty room mocked her so that she cried aloud, 'Even the humblest suitor knows there's no good asking; the Queen of England has no power to grant the smallest favour. No influence; no money. My promised revenues—the forty thousand pounds—I've never had; nor am like to have. They dole me a pittance; not enough to pay the wages of my household, or the bills for meat and drink, I say nothing about clothes for my servants or myself, or the upkeep of my houses; Chesterfield says some fall in ruin for lack of repair. There's money enough to hang *that woman* with jewels, to pay her gambling debts, to fill that bottomless purse of hers! She gets revenues higher than those promised to the Queen—fifty thousand a year, and more; more. The good God alone knows how much more! But to keep the Queen in decency—nothing!'

'Should you not, Madam, speak to the King?'

'No. That trick—over the dowry; it seals my tongue.'

For all his show of gaiety, Charles was far from gay. He knew—sensitive as he was to public opinion—that he was losing something of the country's goodwill. It needed no Clarendon to remind him how slippery his seat upon the throne. He had allowed himself to be blinded by the joy with which he had been received. Now there was a general disappointment because the land did not flow with milk and honey, and every man did not—and could not—receive his just reward; and every day was not a coronation day. The joy with which he had been welcomed home—he saw it now—was but the swinging of the pendulum; revulsion from Cromwell and his joyless Protectorate. But... might not disappointment send it swinging back again? For money was shorter now than at any time in the two years since he had come home; and more painful the pinching to make ends meet. Since Cromwell's death—all of four years ago—the army had not been paid. The men had been long-suffering; but now there were clear signs of revolt. For them money must be found; for the navy even more. *My sailors go hungry, my ships fall into ruin*—his brother James, High Admiral of the Fleet, continually urging. Not that a man needed much urging. The army and the navy—the lifeblood of the country. The trouble was a man didn't know where to turn first!

And he'd been in too much of a hurry to give every man freedom to worship. While an unwilling Parliament were still considering the matter, he had, this last week, actually released those that lay in prison for conscience' sake. Result? He'd gained nothing and lost much favour. Every man, it seemed, wanted freedom for himself; for his neighbour, none at all. Now unrest and whispering and sedition was openly preached; and they were saying everywhere—since most of those released were Catholics—that the King himself was a Papist; how could it be otherwise with a papist wife and a brother that was as near a papist as made no matter and a papist mother ruling from Somerset House? Soon, they said, all England would lie beneath the heel of the bishop of Rome. No, he hadn't done himself much good; but for all that he had been right. Right... but not clever, to rush at it like that! Freedom to worship—he must let it rest awhile; but he'd not forget it, ever.

And he had not been clever about Catherine, either. To add to his troubles they were saying, and saying it everywhere—he had it from Clarendon—that the King cared only for his whore and not at all for his true wife—who, for all she was a Papist, was a good enough woman. Unclever, utterly unclever—he saw it now—to make the Queen ride with his mistress and his bastard. Others besides Pepys had seen it... and Pepys, himself, was not known for discretion. So now there was Clarendon buzzling again like an old hornet, *You cannot expect the Queen to give you a child all troubled as she is... you must set her mind at rest...* He'd sent Clarendon off, a flea in his ear. But for all that the old man was right. Yet what else could he do? Barbara was breeding again; he couldn't desert her... but he could deal more gently with Catherine. She had given way; it was enough. He would ask no more in the countenancing of his mistress.

Suddenly, without warning, the fortress surrendered.

XII

My lady Castlemaine came flaunting into the Queen's presence.
Charles, irritable at the display, longed to turn her out; it was one of
the times he wearied of his ill-bred mistress. How could he blame
the Queen for her coldness? Even as he asked himself the question
he saw—and could not believe his eyes—Catherine turn smiling
and gracious to the enemy. He should have been pleased; but he was
not pleased. He knew at once that, though himself had driven her
to this, she had lost yet more value in his eyes, as she would lose it
also, in the eyes of the court.

And now, the first step made, generous as she was and naive as she
was, Catherine must run, hands outstretched to the enemy.

'It is a debating point whether to freeze or burn is best!' the King
told Clarendon. 'I do not understand this turnabout at all!'

And that was true. He loved women, but he had no great opinion
of their honesty. He had known no woman capable of such humbling
of her pride; did not understand that, not for her own sake but for
the sake of her country, the fortress had surrendered. More than ever
he believed Catherine to be light and capricious, merely.

'A wife with principles is like a bed with prickles,' he told
Clarendon. 'The prickles prick; but the bed is there. Take away the
bed... and a man falls to the floor. I am disappointed and you may
tell her so.'

Clarendon, himself irritable at the discomforts her principles had
brought and angered because she showed kindness to his enemy, did
not spare the Queen.

'You have cast away your greatness to show humility to one you
have contemned—and justly contemned. Now men will say it is a
hard thing to know your mind since you do not know it yourself;
they will not be anxious to serve you. Nor will it help you with
the King. When he remembers the anguish you once expressed, he

86

must conclude it was all pretence acted to the life by a nature crafty, perverse and inconstant.'

She said nothing; she sat very still wondering how long she could endure his rudeness. And he himself; also wondering, was ruthless still. He had believed her honest, for her he had taken his stand against the King. She had made more than the King look foolish!

'Believe me,' he added with some satisfaction, 'the King will know, in future, how to deal with you. He has not the same value he once had for your honesty or your judgment.'

And still she made no answer.

When he had left she paced the room, unable to sit or stand. *Crafty. Perverse. Inconstant.* She that was simple and loving, and constant to please her husband. Why had she come to this hateful country, this hateful King?

She was too honest to believe her own question. Let him behave how he would, she still must love him; still must choose—were she to choose again—to be his wife. For all the unkindness, all the humiliation, without him she would not choose to live.

She had lost the King's respect—all, it seemed, he had to give. Had she stood firm he must have given way. Now, so far from keeping his promise to be done with his mistress did his wife yield, he sought *the lady* more than ever.

'And why not? The Queen's objections were perverse, merely!' Buckingham said.

'The Queen is not honest,' Berkeley said—he that had smeared the good name of Anne Hyde.

'The Queen confirms my low opinion of women,' Rochester said.

He would be gentle with his wife—Charles had promised himself; and this promise, too, he did not keep for, if she heard never a harsh word from him, she heard never a loving one, either. He treated her with the respect due to his Queen and exacted the same respect from everyone—*the lady* not least. Save for this show of respect and the genuine kindness he showed to all, she had nothing left. It was not possible, she thought, so to love a man and get so little in return. Penalva could have told her she had much to learn.

One thing, though, she was learning—to carry herself with patience; for her the hardest of lessons.

It was altogether a hard winter for Catherine, this year of 'sixty-two. Her first winter in England must always have been difficult; but this was the bitterest the country had known for many a year. Even Charles who enjoyed the cold welcomed a cloak of sables from the Muscovy ambassador—and handsome he looked in it. In the streets frozen mud hard as stone piled high. The Thames was solid ice. From her windows she could see the skaters and the booths and the braziers casting a ruddy light upon the ice. In Whitehall, for all the roaring fires, she could scarce keep her bones from rattling.

That November she was unwell. Twice she was taken with nausea and once she fainted. There were high hopes throughout the country; and in Charles' heart and her own, the greatest hope of all. She had Penalva bring out the cradle in which she herself had been rocked, and kneeling and smoothing the carving with a loving hand would make her prayer, *A son. Sweet Mother of Jesus* grant it. Charles showed himself kind again; her birthday, her first in England, was kept with high festival. There was a great ball; and a play-actress Moll Knight came to sing for the court. Catherine, who loved music with passion, noted not the singer but the lovely voice; Charles noted both. He would remember the singer; at the moment he was passionately involved... and not with the *lady alone*.

The girl Frances Stuart had grown, most suddenly, from a green girl into startling beauty. Mr. Pepys noted with some regret that now my lady Castlemaine must play second fiddle. And what a beauty the girl was! So slender, so delicately rounded, carrying her simple gowns with distinction. And how perfect the features, set off by the pure, pale skin! And above all the eyes—so heavenly-blue, so heavenly innocent. But... were they so innocent? Catherine was not alone in wondering.

Childlike innocence together with the elegance of one bred in Paris—dazzling combination to overthrow the King. Charles doted upon her. He kissed her in corners; he bestowed jewels upon her, he pursued her to her chamber-door; that it was no further, was scarcely his fault. Too late *the lady* saw what she had done; she had raised a younger, gentler, more beautiful rival against herself. Yet still she affected friendship—she dared not offend the King. Those two were seen everywhere together; now they shared the same bed... when my lady's was not otherwise engaged.

There was a tale going about the court. My lady and the girl had taken part in a lewd frolic. They had been married—bell, book and candle; they had been put to bed with all the marriage freedoms—stocking-throwing, hippocras wine and wafers.

Catherine heard the tale by accident. She was sitting in her closet with Penalva; in the next room her ladies chattered, between the rooms the door stood ajar. She heard them with distaste. Those two, *that woman* and the girl, nay those three—for the King had held his sides with laughing—had shamed their religion with low jests.

'Nothing but a trick put about by *the lady* and the King to get the so-virtuous Stuart into his bed!' It was the voice of Winifred Wells edged with spite. Jealous! Catherine knew it. Wells had had an affair with the King before his marriage; now he was heartily sick of her. 'The lady skipped out and the King skipped in!'

'Never believe it! Catherine knew the voice of Frances Weldon. 'Do you think *the lady* would, for any consideration, give up her place in the King's bed?'

'Not if she could help it; but she cannot help it!' and now it was the voice of Eliza Bagot. 'If she's not obliging about the girl she loses the King altogether. But if she *is* obliging—she'll be rid of the girl in no time. The Stuart's a beauty but she's a ninny; dull as ditchwater. *The lady* with all her faults amuses the King. She angers him to madness; but he always comes back for more. Let him sleep with the girl half-a-dozen times—and he'll have had enough!'

'A sly one, the Stuart!' Wells broke in spiteful. 'She plays virtuous; she knows she can only hold the King by keeping him off!'

'A useful lesson—if learned betimes!' Bagot said, remembering a dirty rhyme concerning this same Wells and the King.

Catherine was all for breaking in upon the speakers but Penalva held her back. 'The poison of spiteful tongues is below the Queen's notice. You are best to ask the Stuart outright; but, Madam my darling, let your anger cool first.'

Frances Stuart stood before the Queen.

'Yes, Madam, I did take part in the frolic; so much is true. It was wrong but I did not stop to think. The rest—as God hears me—is false. For let Madam the Queen think! Had I wanted to...' she faltered; desperation drove her on, 'to sleep with the King I had done it long since and no-one the wiser... and myself much richer.'

The childlike face seemed unaware of the enormity of the speech. Shaken with anger Catherine could yet almost believe in the girl's innocence.

'Madam the Queen does not know the difficulties that beset a woman in this court if she be young, if she be poor and with it not ill-favoured. I beseech the Queen's kindness...'

Catherine said, very quick for all her lame English, 'You are maid of honour—no? *Maid* and *honour*. On these words, think!' And then, in spite of herself, 'If you shall need help, to me you may come!'

'The Queen is so good!' Frances sank into a curtsey, so spontaneous, so graceful, it seemed a compliment fresh-made for the Queen. No wonder the King was infatuated! Catherine sighed. Was the girl truly innocent or a sly coquette? Catherine sighed again; she did not know.

The Queen's hope was false. Not pregnancy but ill-health had brought her low; grief working upon a frame never robust accounted for the nausea, the fainting. The cradle was carried away; never would she look at it again until she held a living child in her arms.

There was, it seemed, to be no end to her troubles. Charles, to sweeten his disappointment, announced his intention of creating young Jamie Crofts a duke. Bewildered anger drove her to the King's Side. And, her halting English unable to bear the weight of her grief, cried out in Spanish, 'Have I not endured enough, enough? Must your bastard, in this very moment of my sorrow, move to highest honours before my eyes?' And when he made no answer, cried out, 'Do it—and you shall never see my face again.' Charles smiled his mocking smile; he bowed and left her.

In both hearts disappointment and anger; but on the outside all was gay. There were balls and supper-parties; there were picnics on the ice; there were games and bogle-tales told by the roaring fire. And above all—the play. Charles had always loved the play; in his wandering days it had helped him to forget his troubles. Now he made it the fashionable diversion. The old-style theatre was gone; the new-style, copied from France, gave audiences the illusion of themselves taking part in the play's adventures—a pleasant illusion; for plays, free now of puritan restraint were robust and bawdy. And the illusion was the pleasanter since, for the first time, women were acting on the public stage; pretty women, witty and clever and trained in their art. The stage was glamorous as never before. For old and young, for those with learning and those without, for all that could afford it—the play was truly the thing.

In spite of her rigorous upbringing, Catherine might have come to enjoy the play; instead she must sit, cheeks burning behind the shading fan she had made so fashionable. And it was less because of the hussies on the stage than because of the hussies flaunting themselves in the King's box—*that woman*; and that seeming-innocent *la belle Stuart*. The King would flirt outrageously with them both... unless his eyes were fixed upon some brazen beauty upon the stage.

Clarendon was smitten with gout and could not walk; King and Council must come to his house. It was tiresome; and it was undignified, the King's friends told him. And above all, *the lady* rubbed him into continual irritation... the man was too old for public affairs; he was in his second childhood. But—and Charles could not forget it—Clarendon was not an old man; he had aged in the King's service. He had been faithful in exile; he had returned with his King's triumph and in that triumph had sought to guide his steps. Yet, for all that, Charles found it increasingly difficult to restrain his impatience. But Catherine forgot the rudeness to herself; she sent daily to enquire of him, sent kindly messages, sent gifts. But, lying there in his pain, Clarendon knew—as others knew—that it was but a matter of time before he must go. Already Nicholas, Secretary of State, his old friend and the King's most faithful servant, had been turned away like an old dog. Hardly that; Clarendon corrected himself. Charles would not treat a dog so; Charles loved dogs.

And always my lady Castlemaine worked against him; she had plenty to remember—himself must admit it. He had objected to her elevation to the peerage; he had refused—and still did refuse—to allow any friendship with his wife. And, above all, he was the known champion of the Queen. Take him all round, he was steady in pursuit of his master's good—which, she knew well, was not her own. She'd have his blood, she swore it.

Helpless in his bed he knew that not only his master's heart was turning against him but the country's also. He had persuaded a not unwilling Charles to sell Dunkirk to the French. 'The town does us no good, no good at all! It cost us untold wealth; we pour away our gold like water; we go deeper and deeper into debt. Five million golden livres the French offer. We need it; we need it badly!'

True. But it had bitterly offended the country's pride—hand over an English port to the French! It had offended the King's pride, also; though quite clearly he had seen the need. He was growing every day more weary of advice, of reproaches—Clarendon knew it well. How long before he gave way to his friends' persuasions, his mistress's vituperation and his own annoyance? How long before a faithful servant must fall?

Charles paced his closet where no-one might come uninvited save Chiffinch, his confidential servant, that kept the only other key; not the King's mistress, nor the Queen, nor his mother nor any friend however dear. Pacing restless, he dwelt upon his troubles—so many and come so soon. Private troubles; disappointment in the hope of an heir, his fierce mistress, the coy Frances and his disappointing wife. And all his public troubles. Well, he'd not think on them. The end of the year was come. Pray God for a pleasanter one. He shrugged away black thoughts; tonight was the New Year Ball.

When she came into the great ball-room Catherine saw *that woman* ablaze with jewels—like a crystal chandelier! She'd wheedled the King out of his own Christmas presents they said; he'd had nothing else to give. Looking at the display Catherine could believe it... that ring; surely the French ambassador had given it to Charles. And the diamond feather; she had herself seen the ambassador from Spain present it. She did not envy the woman her jewels; what she did envy was her peaked looks—the creature was breeding again; her second child by the King—the third, maybe! She'd been delivered of a son during the Queen's honeymoon; and, as if that weren't enough, here she was breeding again—and the Queen's hope gone.

Bitterness against Charles swelled in her throat. There he stood debonair and smiling between the achieved mistress and the desired one—Frances looking chaste as the moon. Pray God she prove so!

Catherine was not dancing; she had danced too little at home to expose herself to the unfriendly gaze of the court. The King opened the ball with his brother's wife, in the stately *Bransle*; thereafter he led Frances in the *Coranto*, the fashionable quick-step from Italy. While he danced the court stood and the Queen stood also. Charles whispered that, in view of her ill-health, she might sit; but she had been bred in the strictest court in Europe and to stand was correct. Unable to take her eyes from him she understood why, in Paris and the Hague, the whole court had stopped to watch him dance.

Charles, it seemed, could not weary; he outdanced them all—my lady Chesterfield, my lady Castlemaine, Frances Stuart, la Belle Hamilton, my lady Shrewsbury—bright beauties all. The ball was coming to an end; it had long been daylight. The candles were guttering when Charles, reluctant to bring gaiety to an end, called out, 'The dances of old England. Let's have *Cuckold's Awry*!'

Cuckold's Awry. He might well say it—Charles with his ladies and every courtier bound to the gallant game. He supped with *the lady* almost every night; he slept with her, returning in the small hours when the sentries saw their King snaking in at dawn to the bed of the Queen. And still he pursued Frances Stuart... and pursued in vain.

Catherine found it hard to keep cheerful these days. 'Madam, my darling,' Penalva besought her, 'time is young; you have been married scarce half-a-year. And, believe it, you'll never win the King with a dismal face.' And the Queen's godfather, Dom Francisco de Mello, remonstrating also, she set herself to learn not only the stately dances of the court but the old country romps. She found, to her surprise, that she loved dancing. She was small, and—in spite of malicious tongues—neat-made; and she had a pretty foot. In her own closet she practised the steps; d'Aubigny and Russell—chaplains both but bred to the court—practised with her.

But it was hard to show a cheerful face. For three months the King had not supped with her; and, when at last the came to her bed, he was already spent with love-making.

There was a pale gleam of hope. *That woman* had been reprimanded for the Queen's sake. She had taken advantage of her position as a Bedchamber lady to enter the dressing-room against the Queen's expressed wish.

Catherine, sitting patient beneath her woman's hands, looked up in surprise.

'I wonder your majesty has so much patience!' My lady, peaked looks gone and magnificent now in pregnancy, indicated clearly the uselessness of the Queen's efforts.

'I am being patient for so much,' Catherine said in her slow, pretty English, 'I shall be patient for yet a little.'

Ned Montague saw to it that the tale reached the King.

It came at the right moment. Charles was weary of my lady's violence. Fearing, at long last, lest she lose the King to Frances, she was quarrelling violently with her dearest friend. Frances answered never a word; but the clack of my lady's tongue was maddening. Charles seized his chance. He scolded her—and no word minced—for impertinence to the Queen. Off she flounced to Richmond and the court knew the blessing of peace. But Charles didn't know when he was well off. He went hunting—so he said. But he was the hunted when he brought her back again.

Catherine had need of whatever patience she might possess. Young Mr. Crofts was still behaving like a prince of the blood. In February, despite the Queen, he was created Duke of Monmouth; and, as if that were not enough, he was to take precedence of all dukes—except the King's brother. No end to the favours bestowed upon handsome Jamie. He was made a Garter knight; he was betrothed to the prettiest, sweetest, richest heiress in the land—little Anne Scott, one of the Queen's ladies and sole heir to her father the Duke of Buccleugh.

In the Spring they were wed. 'They are children!' Catherine was shocked.

'Jamie's no child in such matters!' And there was something of pride in Charles.

'But she... so small a girl!'

'To bed they shall go; but they'll not lie together. They must wait awhile for their pleasure!'

Sighing over the little bride, Catherine wondered whether the handsome lad would prove kind. When one caught sight of his face in repose, there was a certain shifty look. She took herself to task for jealousy. But all her life she was to have grief—and great grief—from Monmouth; charming, faithless, heartless Monmouth.

There was a coolness between the brothers on Monmouth's account. James was brave, he was faithful, he was honest; he was a fine soldier and a God-sent sailor. But he was blunt where soft words would serve and he leaned towards the old faith. His virtues went for nothing; he was disliked and distrusted.

If James were sour, his duchess was sourer; she carried herself with a hard, cold look. There were whispers everywhere that Charles meant to legitimise the boy; to make him heir.

It was all nonsense and Catherine knew it. Charles loved his son; but Charles would see him dead before Jamie took a true-born Stuart's place. Till her own son was born, York was the heir. And, moreover, she had been married scarce a year; she was young and she was healthy. Why should James or Monmouth or anyone at all count upon an heir other than the child the Queen should give?

It was St. George's Day. At Windsor there was a grand ball to celebrate the saint's day and Monmouth's recent marriage. Charles, temperate as a rule, had drunk more than usual; now, seated between his two ladies—Castlemaine and Stuart, he watched the dancing.

The Queen was dancing with Monmouth; the boy danced with elegance, holding his hat against his heart as was proper. *The lady* bent smiling to whisper in the King's ear.

The King rose; his lifted hand stopped the dance. He walked through the wondering dancers, straight to where the boy stood beside the Queen and kissed him upon both cheeks. Then, in a voice loud enough for all to hear, cried out, 'Jamie, put your hat on your head!'

Put his hat on his head when he danced with the Queen! It was to give him all the consequence of royalty. Catherine did not need *the lady's* smiling eye to tell her so. Charles had put his bastard on a level with the Queen....

Was there, could there be point in the rumours?

XIII

Midspring. And Catherine, though far from happy, was settling into the ways of the court. Her English was sufficient now to set her cheeks aflame at the sallies of the King and his friends. Her speech was less than her understanding, but her expressions were lively; and she was learning every day. When she saw others smiling—or trying to hide a smile—she would ask what she had said amiss and put it right.

'I do not care for this horse,' she said once when a groom had brought round the mettlesome creature for her ride, 'he does make too much vanity.'

'Then we have misjudged his sex!' Charles threw back his head in laughter.

'It is the gentlemen not the ladies that do make too much vanity,' she answered very quick; and then, sighing, 'This England tongue is hard to come by.'

'You do well enough!' he kissed her hand with his usual courtesy. 'Soon we shall all forget we have a little foreigner amongst us.'

'Never shall you forget it!' she flashed. 'Nor me, neither. One day, maybe, I learn to love this country; but my own, always best.'

'You can have too faithful a heart,' he said.

She said nothing; but her sigh was deep.

If she carried herself like the fashionable beauties, might she not win her husband's heart again? But for all her trying she could not do it. To be like them one must be impudent! Nor for all her pretty legs could she parade in man's dress; no, nor uncover her bosom as low as a wet-nurse. Nor did she like what she heard of behaviour in their churches.

'One must go to church—it is the fashion!' Ned Montague told her. 'How else shall we show off our new clothes? We flirt a little, we sleep a little... and time passes.'

She looked up shocked. He saw no harm in it, the charming, frivolous young man.

'It is the King himself sets the fashion for sleeping; but he, at least, has good excuse. He rises early, he works hard, he's up with the lark...' he stopped abruptly. He knew, as well as she that, at times, the King came straight to church from *that woman's* bed. He turned the conversation with a jest. 'Lauderdale was scolded from the pulpit yesterday. He snored so loud 'twas feared he'd wake the King.'

She could not find it a matter for jesting.

'I wonder they dare so behave!' she burst out later to Penalva. To Penalva she might speak with no consideration for tact, her own language quick and free upon her tongue.

'To attend regularly in the house of God—there are worse fashions!' Penalva said. 'Who knows when a chance word may not bring about a change of heart?'

'Change of heart? The King will never know it till he come into the true Faith. Then he would not so lightly treat his God. If I could be the means to bring him into the true Church, I would gladly die.'

'You would do better to live, Madam, my darling.'

'Please God!' She lifted a happy face. She had hopes again that she had conceived.

But for all that she was troubled about Charles. She loved him so utterly, she was as much concerned with his soul as with his body— and that soul stood in peril. She did not think it would be hard to bring him into the true Faith. His mother was devout; Minette, whom he so loved, belonged to the church of Rome. York was, at heart, a Catholic. But she had reckoned without Charles whose conscience in the matter was both slippery and subtle.

'The Catholic faith is the only faith for a gentleman... if he can afford it. I cannot afford it. I cannot afford to anger this people.'

'You can afford to anger God?'

'He will not be too harsh. He knows the difficulties!' Charles said, cheerful.

She was bewildered that a man should show himself indifferent to his soul's safety. Yet the root of the faith was in him. With time and guidance it would blossom in the sight of all men. She wrote to the Pope for advice; it was a pity. Her letters stood, damning testimony, when her need was sorest.

She had conceived. Thanks be to the sweet mother of Jesus! Charles was overjoyed; and some comfort he needed. Things were more difficult than ever. Clarendon had turned against him—faithful Clarendon. The King's bill allowing men freedom to worship as they would, had been thrown out. It had gone as far as the Lords; and there Clarendon had spoken against it—against the thing so near to the King's heart. Clarendon had scotched it for good and all. He had done it because he hoped to break the younger men the King was raising to power—Bennet that had Nicholas' place as Secretary, and the libertine Berkeley that the King loved; these and others. They had backed the bill; they backed the King in everything, good or bad, Clarendon said—and mostly bad.

Charles made his old friend no reproaches; not though Clarendon had known—none better—his master's heart in the matter; memory of faithful service kept the King silent. And when the law forced him to banish all Papist priests—except those allowed to the Queen by her marriage contract—still he said no word. But there were some that had risked their lives for him; and to them he had promised immunity—he'd had nothing else to give. Now he was shamed to the heart; his word had been broken for him. It was a thing he could not forget, still less forgive.

His friends were not slow to strike back.

Clarendon must go. In addition to all his misdeeds he had allowed the King and Queen to be married without proper form of ceremony—they spread it everywhere; a clever stroke. A Catholic Queen in England must be forever suspect. With one blow they struck at Chancellor and Queen together.

Charles came into the Queen's closet; he was grey with his anger. He said—and he spoke in Spanish so that there might be no misunderstanding, 'It is being spread abroad that we are not true-wed; that you refused our English marriage-service. They say we were wed by a Papist priest—and that's no marriage at all. They say that we have, thereby, put the succession in danger.'

She said, pale as ash, 'What of the witnesses that saw us wed in the King's house at Southampton?'

'They say you did not make the responses; that you stood dumb.'

'You know the truth of that!' she cried out heartbroken, remembering her trouble to learn the service. 'And so does the bishop that wed us; and so does Fanshawe your groomsman.'

'I have said all that need be said. You need trouble yourself no more.' For the first time Charles openly took his stand with his wife; and, in his anger against his friends, she felt herself cherished. Buckingham he castigated with his tongue, threatening dire punishment should he repeat his vile nonsense; but the man was his friend and his mistress' cousin—and he let it go at that, leaving Buckingham a thorn in the Queen's flesh to the end of his life. And Bristol that had spread his lies concerning the Queen's dwarfishness and inability to bear a child, he sent from the court. But Berkeley—whether he spoke a private word or no—Berkeley he kept still by his side.

Catherine was languid; the morning sickness left her weary. She besought the King's permission to take the waters at Tonbridge.

'With all my heart,' he said at once. 'If you will wait until Parliament finish its business we'll go together.'

He had offered his company! She could scarce believe her happiness—especially since *that woman* must remain at home. But when she remembered the reason, her happiness was riddled with bitterness; my lady's time was drawing near.

'It is not the King's child, so they say!' Penalva reminded her. 'Take comfort, Madam, his appetite for her is all-but done.'

'So you thought before; yet still it seems to linger. And, if it did not?' She shrugged despairing shoulders. 'He is mad for the little Stuart; and, this one or that—what matter?'

'All the matter in the world! She's a good child.'

'How long could any woman hold out against him, be she never so virtuous? This simple child least of all.'

'It is the marriage-bed for that one—or no bed at all!' Penalva said, cheerful.

Was Frances so simple... or so clever? Was she holding out for the highest price of all? And suppose the King should offer it?

'There are many would rejoice to see her in my place,' Catherine lifted a sick, white face.

'Another in your place! Are you crazy, Madam, my darling? You carry his child; his heir. And if you did not, never, at any time, would the King consider it; he has his own faithfulness... such faithfulness is not a little thing.'

'It is not enough... not enough. Oh!' she cried out with sudden passion, 'I would give my life had he written for me the verses he wrote for that girl... I live not the day when I see not my love... He wrote that!'

Those words are true of you, poor child! Penalva was stabbed by pity.

'And he says, in those same verses, there's no hell like loving too well. And he's right, right!' She cried out with shocking bitterness.

'You can never love too well,' Penalva said.

Parliament's business was tedious; but for all her impatience Catherine could not complain. A long discussion had ended with an agreement between England and France to help—at need—her own country against Spain. She was well paid for giving way to *that woman*. She thought so more strongly when, before the end of June, English soldiers fought in Portugal and sent the Spaniards flying.

But the meetings of Parliament were not always so pleasant. The House voted one half only of the sum so desperately needed to refit the navy; and not nearly enough to meet the debts Cromwell had left on the army alone. And, to add to the King's troubles, in Ireland and Scotland constant rebellion. Charles took it all with cheerful patience. He tried to economise; he and Catherine reduced their households. Once she had believed him inclined for pleasure, only; now she saw that no man worked harder. He would rise before five to ride; he would cheer himself with some small pleasure—to eat strawberries at Woolwich; and then, home he would come to his despatches, to his Council, to his endless arguments with Parliament; and always he showed a cheerful common sense, lit at times, by a most penetrating shrewdness.

The coldness between Charles and his Chancellor had deepened. Clarendon—the King thought angered and showing it—was at the bottom of those mean grants. Catherine was troubled; where else would Charles find so faithful a friend? She thought, too, with pity, of the old man himself. To be cast off by Charles; what fate more bitter?

She dared to raise the matter with the King.

Had one of his spaniels spoken Charles could scarce have been more surprised. He had little liking for women meddling in affairs. But because she carried his child he answered her kindly. 'He's honest and he's faithful; but he looks forever backward. Those that live in the past must be left in the past.'

She said no more but she worried no less. Like Clarendon she did not trust the King's new advisers—Bennet that lied to break her marriage; Berkeley that had lied to break York's. And worst of all, Buckingham—*that woman's* lover and her own bitter enemy. It had been to break the growing power of these young men that Clarendon had set himself against the King. But it had not helped. When Charles raised Bennet to the peerage—my lord Arlington; and Berkeley—my lord earl of Falmouth, the obstinate old man knew all was over. Yet still he held on, grim; he might yet serve his King. It was his nature.

These days, whatever Charles' difficulties, whatever his annoyances, his kindness to Catherine never failed. They were seen riding daily in the park laughing, and leaning one to the other. She had about her the bloom of a happy woman—Mr. Pepys noted it; noted, also, how now and again Charles would reach out so that they rode together hand-in-hand. *The lady* was riding, also. She was clearly near her time; it lent her added magnificence. In her yellow satin gown and the great beaver with sweeping yellow plumes, she was worth looking at. But, beyond a first bow, Charles took no notice—he was not at all sure whose child she carried. And, when she alighted, there was no gallant waiting—so quick was the court to learn its lesson; and her own servant must hand her down. She looked out of humour, as well she might. Mr. Pepys noted it with some regret; he admired my lady. But besides himself, there were few to grieve.

For all his kindness to the Queen Charles could not get over his passion for Frances Stuart. He could never be done looking at the lovely face with the small, fine roman nose; and the charming figure that was both slender and delicately rounded. Since the King admired her, she was courted by all; ladies and gentlemen alike hastened to shower her with favours, to join in the simple games in which she delighted, to assist in the building of her intricate houses of cards. She could have married well; her own cousin and the King's—Charles Stuart—offered to make her duchess of Lennox and Richmond. But to every offer she turned a deaf ear.

Did she truly love the King with a virtuous heart? Catherine wondered. Or—she was but sixteen—did that heart sleep still? Or beneath those innocent eyes did she wait to take the Queen's place?

Well, let her wait! The Queen was with child. There could be no divorce.

In July, under a blue sky, Catherine and Charles, the court for escort, rode out for Tonbridge.

Tonbridge was enchanting. And the life they lived, enchanting. Charles and Catherine lodged in the largest house the little town afforded—and it was not very large; the court lodged in cottages and delighted—so they said—in the simple life. They walked, they talked, they drank the waters; in the evening they danced upon the green to the tune of the guitar. When the King rode to London on business the Queen and the whole court would ride out to meet him on his return, to bring him into the little town with all the people crowding in to cheer. Catherine wished they might stay here for ever.

She was carrying the child badly. She was too often sick, too continually tired. Her joy began to be pricked with anxiety.

'Could we not go to Bourbon?' she asked Charles. 'The waters there could help our business on.'

'No money.' He shrugged, rueful.

So they went instead to Bath and they stayed at the Abbey House which belonged to the King's physician Pierce—which should be handy at need.

Charles was charming these days. She had won back his affection—of that she was sure. But—love? She must be patient still. When she put his child in his arms, he would, she was certain, love her again.

The King continued kind. They visited Bristol; a great city, she thought, with its busy river and its fine houses and gardens; and when the citizens presented her with a purse stuffed with one-hundred-and-thirty pieces of gold, it seemed finer than ever. Not enough to take them to Bourbon, alas; but one could find good use for the money.

At Bristol her happiness was shattered. *That woman* had been brought to bed of a fine boy—the King's, my lady declared, her second son by the King; and she would make him own it! But, though Charles was cool—he had no guarantee, he said, that the child was his; it brought little comfort to Catherine. *It might have been… and still might be.*

They took Oxford on their homeward way; and, in Oxford—*that woman* was waiting. Charles greeted her with as much coolness as his kindness would allow; but some kindness he must show; she was new-risen from her lying-in; she looked thin and pale.

'But for all that as brazen a piece as ever lived!' Penalva threw up her hands. 'That babe! Its father might be any one of half-a-dozen—the husband excepted—he's been abroad nigh on a year. It could be Buckingham's or Chesterfield's or Berkeley's.'

Catherine's nose pinched in disgust. 'Were it the King's son, it would break my heart; yet I could understand. It is hard not to love him. But this wanton cannot name the father! The King should send her from the court!'

The first of October saw them back in London. Catherine was still unwell. Four months gone with child, she felt—small-made as she was—the weight of her burden. She rested a good deal; her physician Prujean commanded it. Charles was as kind as he had time to be. He had come back to find rebellion in Yorkshire. He took it calmly—it was his way. He put it down thoroughly—that was also his way. He was merciful in punishment—that was most of all his way. Yet for all that he was troubled. It seemed to him that opposition to the Crown was strengthening... he had no mind to go on his travels again.

Now weary and troubled he felt the need of diversion. Frances was, as ever, elusive; but *the lady, the lady*, invited. He fell again into the old habit of supping with her and soon he was sleeping with her also.

Catherine was growing stronger; the Bath waters and the rest had been helpful. But *that woman* troubled her peace. She was restless with jealousy, and then, fallen asleep at last, was disturbed by the King at dawn; to share his wife's bed was, he considered, his duty. Between mind and body she found no rest by day or night.

In the early days of October, worn by weariness and distress, she stumbled upon a stair. She was more shocked than hurt. But it was enough. That night she had a miscarriage.

Never had her life seemed so pointless, so wretched. She fell into a melancholy and thence into a fever. She lay tossing and turning. She knew not what had happened; but that something dire had befallen that she did know, in the depths of her body's pain recognised and knew.

XIV

She lay without strength to move in the bed, save for the restless turning of her head upon the pillow. Her body, burned with fever, barely lifted the bedclothes. Her mouth was scorched as though with fire and bitter as gall. She was racked, every limb; her head was splitting as though the executioner stood by and hacked with a sword. Now and again her lids just lifted upon a room full of people; they were all in black; and the sound they made fell into a form she knew well... she knew then that she was dead and they mourning.

But for the most part she wandered in darkness, wailing weakly for home. And sometimes she would be home. She would be walking in the gardens of the Villa Viçosa. She walked up the garden path and came to the great door of the house. The door was shut. She was glad it was shut... behind that door—empty sockets, grinning jaw—Death waited. She turned; she ran. She chose a quite different path; it ran in the opposite direction. The path led her to that same door. Again she turned and ran; but whichever path she chose led her to the door.

The door began to open slowly. She turned about; this time she did not run, she flew; flew like an angel floating above the ground.

Her hair grew thick-tangled, matted with sweat; she could not endure its weight; still less the touch of the comb. The lightest touch, and she screamed with pain. Her hair. It troubled her. Between sleeping and waking she heard a voice. St. Catherine said, *You are overproud of your one poor beauty. God will find you fairer without it.* And though she tried to shut her ears, still the voice came clear. She was to offer her hair—a sacrifice.

The room bobbed up suddenly; she shut her eyes against the light. Her head felt strange... light... empty. She put up a hand. Her hair was gone. She let out a great cry. She opened her eyes again. Someone was sitting beside the bed. It was Charles. He said, 'You begged us to cut your hair; you *kept* begging. But, indeed, we could do no other, so heavy it was and tangled. It has begun to grow already; soon it will be as pretty as ever; you will see!'

She did not believe that; she put up her hand again as though to comfort the poor head; now she felt the little lace cap through which the hair-stubble pricked.

'A holy relic of St. Catherine, herself. The Pope sent it,' Charles said.

The door opened gently; Penalva came into the room. She took Charles' place by the bed. When he had gone Penalva said, 'He has scarce left your bedside but for business of State. Here he stayed and here he prayed; and here he slept and here he wept.'

Catherine began to weep, herself, all weak as she was, that her gay King should weep for her. But it was wonderful, also. She began to wonder how he found her in looks, hair shaved and—she looked down upon her hands—bone-thin. She was shocked to find her thoughts upon her looks; they should be elsewhere. But all the same she asked for a looking-glass; and though Penalva was not willing, still she had her way.

The skin stretched tight across the bones was grey with angry blotches from unhealed scars. 'Spotted fever,' Penalva said. 'Thank God you are well again.' But when she saw herself, shaven head beneath the lace cap, the livid spots the only colour in her sick face, she felt herself a figure for laughter, for disgust. She wondered that he, who loved beauty, should endure the sight of her.

Penalva said, 'The King did more than pray and weep. With his own hands he fed you. And, indeed, Madam my darling, though your wits wandered, you knew the touch of his hands; you would take no food save from him. Had it not been for him you must have died.'

She lay there, the slow tears running down her ruined face and thinking how much better for him had he let her die. So, when he came back she said in her slow English, 'Never grieve for me. I shall die and it is best. Then you shall marry some other to give you children and bring you happiness.' And then she said, 'I would leave the whole world with joy, save for you, for you alone.'

'I cannot live without you,' he said; and, for the moment, believed it. And now there came crowding back into the room the priests and nuns, all in black. Charles said, very stern, 'I have forbidden you this room. You burn up the air; you give Madam the Queen no peace with the noise of your praying and the noise of your weeping.' He turned to Penalva. 'Why have they come again?'

'Sir, it is to say their Farewell; and to give Extreme Unction.'

'Farewell? Extreme Unction? Madam the Queen is not going to die—not while I am here to keep her alive.' And with his own hands pushed out those that did not move fast enough for his liking.

When all had gone save the surgeon Prujean and Penalva, he flung the window wide. And when those two remonstrated against the flow of air, 'The room stinks of their bodies,' he said. He took his place again in the great chair where, nights on end, he had slept; and, in the cool and the quiet, she fell asleep.

She took her slow way to recovery. When she was a little restored, though weak still, d'Aubigny said, 'The Queen's recovery is a miracle from God. Madam, do you return thanks to Him?'

'Yes,' she said. 'And to the King that under Him worked the miracle.'

She was out of danger and Charles might go about his business both lawful and unlawful. *The King of England*, the French ambassador wrote home, *begins the day with tears for the Queen, and ends it laughing with Castlemaine and Stuart.* And, certainly, he sickened of the sickroom where she slept for hours on end; sleeping she did not need him.

But, even in sleep, she missed him. She would sigh and wake and ask where he had gone; and, in the shifting glances, read her answer. Grief took her afresh; she had mistaken his pity for love. In her weakness the disappointment was too much. She had lost her child; hatred for the woman that had borne Charles two children, three, perhaps, overcame her. She turned her face to the wall; weeping, she felt life slip from her.

The country waited to hear of her death; but with curiosity rather than pity. Who would be the next Queen? Mr. Pepys, that dressy gentleman, stopped the making of a gay cloak—unwearable if the Queen should die.

Day by day nearer to death.

She asked Charles that her body be sent home. She asked him to stand by Portugal against Spain when she was gone; and, weeping, he promised. She received the last rites and now he did not forbid them.

All was done; she lay waiting for death.

'She has no will to live,' her physician told the King. Charles looked down into her unheeding face; already she had gone far from him. She had been sweet and loving and full of hope. And now? Shame and grief overthrew him. *Kate... Kate!* Her name burst from his lips.

Across the border-line of death she heard his voice. Her eyelids fluttered; she made the faintest movement of the hand towards him. He took it in his own; her eyelids dropped. For five long hours she slept. And all the time he sat unmoving by her bed. When she awoke her feet were set firm in life.

His grief had been deep; but still there were bets made as to its endurance.

She was sitting up in bed weak but clear in mind. She looked at him; for the first time she saw that his hair—the fine dark hair was now completely grey... and he but thirty-three! She put up a hand to touch the once-dark curls; tears of weakness ran down her face.

He guessed the cause—himself had had a pricking on that score; he was not without his vanities. Now he laughed. 'A grey-haired husband! It will not do.' He twisted that mobile underlip to a grin. 'I have so longed to be a gentleman of fashion; but I have begrudged the money. Now with a good conscience I can get me a periwig!'

From that time he wore the fashionable wig and the court copied him—even James whose bright curls needed no addition; but for all that he had them cut. 'It is as I did say; men do make more vanities than women!' Catherine told Charles.

Her life was out of danger. The high fever was gone, the scarred face healed, the dark hair already ringing in tendrils. But she was more than ever a sick woman.

Always she had loved children. If a woman could not love her husband, she had thought, then marriage was worthwhile—so there were children. Now, loving her husband with so desperate a love, knowing what a child must mean to him and to England, knowing what the loss might mean to herself—divorce with all its griefs, all its humiliations, she could not endure to face what she had lost. And, it was the more unendurable that the same month of her loss, her enemy had borne a child that might well be the King's. *That woman* dropped her bastards as easily as an animal; but for the Queen, difficulty and danger... and loss.

When her anguish was no more to be borne she would lie back in her bed and, this unkind world slipping away she was in another world, blessed as paradise, a world in which her child lay at her breast.

It was a boy strong and lusty and dark like his father. But soon, in this heavenly world, a thorn began to prick. She told Charles her trouble. 'It is an ugly boy, not worth to be your son, dear love.'

He put his hand upon the small delicate curls of her head. He said, 'It is a very pretty boy!' And could not bring himself to look in her face childlike in her weakness. And she, seeing he could not look her in the face, never knowing how much she tormented him, persisted in self-torment. 'Nay, it is an ugly boy... an ugly boy!'

'Someone has been telling you the tale of Mam—how when I was born, she, being proud to death and not wishful to show it, wrote to her mother that she was ashamed of her little blackamoor. You have confused yourself in your poor head; ours is a pretty boy—he is like me.' And he was ashamed of so deceiving her; but Prujean had advised him.

'If he be like you then he is beautiful!' She thought of Vandyke's lovely picture of the little Charles with the dark eyes thoughtful and far-seeing, and the charming, graceful little body—promise of the man he was to be. She lifted his hand and kissed it.

And still she lived in her world of fantasy; it was her shield, lest, coming too soon into life, she died of grief. And, the fantasy strengthening, she believed she had borne yet another child; and another and another; three boys and a girl. 'The boys are like their father—every one of them!' she told Penalva happily. 'And my daughter—' she was tender over the word, 'a true Stuart with bright hair and all the Stuart charm—like Madam Minette, the King says.' And, always upon waking, her first words were, *How do the children?*

Now she had the will to get strong again. She submitted with patience to their hateful remedies—to the bloody pigeons still warm, applied to her feet, and the noxious physic so that she all-but heaved up her heart. But for the sake of the children she endured it all. In the joy of her children her body grew daily stronger; she did not know that, beyond her doors they whispered, nor that the whisper spread throughout the country, *The Queen is mad*.

Her sickness did not spare her the duties of a Queen. She was still confined to her bed; but she must receive a visitor new-come from France. She made no demur. She knew well that a prince must live and die in public; must dress and undress, eat and drink, sleep and wake beneath the public eye. The King of Spain, they said, could not ease himself unless two nobles held his chamber-pot.

Charles might not have asked it of her; but when a prince dies the first cry is poison. If she should die his enemies would be quick to say he had rid himself of a barren wife; he had not been—he was the first to admit it—a faithful husband.

Monsieur de Cateu knelt by the Queen's bed; kissing her limp hand, he brought greetings from his King and Queen; and from Minette, Madame of France. But so weary she was that, before he was finished, she was back in her private heaven. So sick she seemed, so loud the gossip that Monsieur wrote home,

the meanest among the courtiers takes the liberty of marrying his royal master... each according to his own inclination...

These hopes she spoiled by getting well again.

In November, her birthday month, she was strong enough for truth to thrust away fantasy. Then, knowing her dreams for what they were, tears ran down her wasted cheeks; she would sit unmoving, melancholy, withdrawn. Her life was bitter as gall.

Gentle Penalva, brutal with need, goaded her into some sort of action. 'You leave the King to *that woman*... and to any other that shall catch his wandering eye. And who shall blame him? He no longer has a wife!'

Even while the tears ran down her wasted cheeks she set her lips and called for her looking-glass. She was shocked by what she saw. Within the hour she had sent for her tailors, for her hair dressers, for her tiring-women and for the barber that concocted her lotions, her creams, her perfumes and her paints. She would welcome death... but she was not willing to die a fright!

She had taken her first steps about her room; she had left her bed-chamber to pray in her chapel; she made her first appearance at the court. Everyone—with the exception of *the lady* and her friends—welcomed her with kindness. James' wife overdoes her warmth, Catherine thought bitter; a barren Queen is no menace. But the rest pitied her frail air; she had been so near death. Waller, the court poet, made a verse for the occasion. It said how, in all his troubled life, Charles had never wept, save for her, alone.

> He that was never known to mourn
> So many kingdoms from him torn,
> His tears reserved for you, more dear,
> More prized than all his kingdoms were.
> For when no healing art prevail'd
> When cordials and elixirs fail'd,
> On your pale cheeks he dropped the shower,
> Revived you like a dying flower.

Rochester that was a poet himself did not think much of the verses. But Catherine thought them beautiful and they were true—his tears alone had brought her back to life! She kept them in her prayer-book along with her holy pictures.

On her birthday Charles gave a little ball in her private apartments so that she might sit and enjoy it. It was kindly meant; but there was small comfort in it. To look on while others danced! To know that neither paint nor powder could disguise her ravaged looks. And there they were, the beauties of the court—my lady Chesterfield, my lady Southesk; and *that woman* in all the splendour of motherhood. But, outshining them all, in her fresh youth, her untouched loveli-ness—Frances Stuart.

No, the ball was little comfort to a sick woman that had never been a beauty!

Charles tried to pleasure her in small ways. Minette, he wrote, was to send pictures of saints—the finest that might be got—to mark places in the Queen's prayer-book; they were not to be found in London. She spent too long on her knees, he thought; and told her so roundly. But she was seeking peace and not even in prayer could she find it.

She grew stronger. The new year of 'sixty-four saw her full-recovered, mind and body both. She had faced the truth about the children but without accepting it; in private she still wept her hopeless tears.

'You are young, Madam my darling,' Penalva would say. 'Madam Anne of Austria, when she was Queen of France, was full thirty-five before she was brought to bed of her first child. And, once, started—there was no stopping her.' And, looking into that downcast face added, a little sharp, 'However low your heart, show yourself cheerful. The whole world—and the King above all—loves a cheerful face!'

'Yes,' the Queen said, 'yes... But—' she flared into sudden anger, 'How? *How?*'

XV

She might well ask *How?* Ever more shameless, my lady Castlemaine thrust herself before the Queen; no escaping sight nor sound of her. For all his kindness for his wife, for all his passion for the little Stuart, Charles could not free himself from his enchantress. Let them quarrel, let her rage so that, half-jesting, he asked pardon upon his knees, she held him with her Medea spell.

The flaunting, fruitful mistress was unendurable to the barren wife. When the Queen thought of the friendship she had forced herself to show, she was sick with humiliation. Clarendon had been right; who could despise her more than she despised herself?

Yet in one thing she was richer; she had gained a friend, a true friend. Eliza was wife to my lord Duke of Ormonde, but lately lord Lieutenant of Ireland now lord Steward of the royal household—the King's faithful Ormonde. Wise and experienced, she possessed a delicacy rare in that court; a fit friend for the Queen. Old enough to be Catherine's mother, she was yet younger, every way, than Penalva ageing fast in the uncongenial climate of her new home. With this new friend Catherine's knowledge of the English tongue was growing fast.

But Eliza's friendship was worth more than that. With her unmatched knowledge of the English court she was invaluable. She listened to the Queen's complaints and she answered with truth. Though custom decreed one must flatter a Queen, she never lied to Catherine. To Maria Penalva and Eliza Ormonde the Queen could speak her heart.

That woman came sailing into the Queen's presence. She came, as always, uninvited and unwelcome; she came to press her right—Lady of the Bedchamber. She was aware of conversation cut off as with a knife; of the Queen's unseeing look, of my lady Ormonde, eyes not lifted from her needlework, and of Penalva stiff with distaste. She cast an amused glance round and sailed out again.

'*That woman!*' the Queen cried out. 'She vomits me!'

Eliza said, in her clear voice, 'Madam, she may be listening at the door. It is, I believe, her habit.'

'Then let her hear me what I say! She do disgust me... my blood cooks. Those great bosoms... all bare that every man shall see—the shameless one!'

There came to them the tap of heels moving away. My lady had heard enough!

'How long shall I carry it... so much pain here?' the Queen cried out and laid a hand upon her heart. 'It hurts me also, from the little Stuart. She is not to blame... I think it. A good child... so there is nothing to say.'

But there was a good deal to say; they knew it, all three.

'A child...' the Queen said again, her voice uncertain.

'Madam, someone must tell you!' Eliza said, troubled. 'You have been long from the court... too long. Do not trust the girl for all her childish ways. She takes everything from the King; gifts and kisses as much as he's pleased to give... and all the time she plays chaste. She runs... that he may run after. Madam, do not be deceived. She gives the King all—it's common knowledge—all save her maidenhood; and that she'll sell when the price is high enough!'

'You are wrong,' the Queen said. 'If she do not love she shall not sell herself... whatever will be the price. And, God be praised, she do not love the King.'

'I pray, Madam, you may be right!' Eliza sighed; Penalva echoed her sigh.

Charles was falling into the habit—when the press of affairs was troublesome—of talking to his wife in the privacy of her closet. Not that he did her the honour of listening to anything she might say; still less of following any advice she might presume to give; but it was good to speak freely to one he could trust. In spite of her quick temper she was gentle; she had a fine quality that set her apart... and she was his wife. She was his wife and she was in great grief; he did not deny to himself that the fault was less hers than his own. He did not love her; but, himself surprised, found himself enjoying her company—she rested him, he said. Had she not been there at his hand, he would have been surprised at the measure of his loss.

That year Lely painted her picture. In the black velvet gown slashed with white satin, the soft curls lifted from a wide forehead and the great dark eyes shadowed by the loss of her child, she was sweet enough to please Charles or any man. The Dutch painter Huysman painted her for the King's pleasure; thereafter he painted her for his own. He took her as a model for his madonna—which in the circumstances was ironical; and for his Venus—which was hardly less so. She was pretty, certainly—Mr. Pepys, that judge of women, thought so; but her prettiness paled beside the flaming beauties of the court. And loveliest of all—he noted it down—the little Stuart with her sweet shape and her perfect face.

Eliza Ormonde whispered in the Queen's ear and she cast aside her sober gowns. She and her ladies in silver lace that took the sunlight shimmered like butterflies. Now when she rode with the King she wore a short scarlet skirt with a white-laced waistcoat, and the dark curls flowing free beneath a feathered hat.

But in her bedchamber nothing was changed. The furnishings were of the simplest. The only beautiful thing it contained was an Indian cabinet inlaid with silver and ivory; she treasured it less for its beauty than because she had brought it from home. Its drawers held her prayer-books, her holy relics, her religious pictures. By her bed a stool held a flask of holy water together with a clock and a lamp that she might read her prayers when she awoke in the dark night.

Well enough for a nun, Charles thought; and, coming from my lady's bed found himself chilled—body and ardour, both.

'You should allow yourself some comforts,' Penalva said. 'This is no room...' The flush deep upon her old cheeks, she went on, '... for love.' It had cost her not a little to cast away the long habit of propriety; now nothing could stop her. '*That woman's* bedroom! I have heard, oh I have heard! Such a room! Such velvets, such brocades, such marbles, such pictures! Such furnishings—gold and silver, no less. And...' she paused, 'A fine gilt bed from Italy shaped like a swan.... A very bower of love!'

Catherine shrugged.

'Oh you may shrug, Madam; but must you give your husband away—both hands—to that shameless woman? And the little Stuart's bedchamber! That I have seen for myself. It is fine; not so fine, I daresay as *that woman's*... she does not give so much. Yet, even so, it is finer by far than your own. Madam, my darling, you are the Queen. Make your bedchamber fit for the King.'

'It *is* fit... for the King of Heaven.'

'I could wish at times...' and the old woman longed to shake her darling, 'you had not been convent-bred.'

'You would wish me bred like *that woman*?'

'God forbid!' Penalva said.

Charles was beginning to take his wife about with him. She drove with him to the opening of Parliament; she went robed and crowned—though there had never been a coronation. And more than once she went with him to see the House at work; she began to understand something of its pressures and its powers. He took her to see the Fleet where it lay upon the Thames; the sea, the ships, were at least, one thing they had in common. She was the daughter of a seafaring nation; the toughest of weather could not spoil her pleasure. When swashbuckling Buckingham turned green, there she was, the wind whipping her cheeks rosy, and alive with laughter. He was proud of her then, he loved in her this love of ships; it was a thing he shared with no other woman, a link that, sure as love, bound them together.

She would never forget the October day when he took her to Woolwich to see the launching of a new ship. Pett, that master-craftsman, had built her—a beauty, bow to stern. In spite of her elegance she was built for hard service; seventy brass guns flashed in the Autumn sunlight. The most beautiful ship in the world, Catherine thought.

'Her name, do you note it?' Charles passed his spyglass. He heard the intake of her breath; she was pale with pleasure.

'The name pleases you?' he asked.

She could not speak for delight. It was the finest compliment he could pay her—or anyone at all—this lover of ships. In spite of all his gifts to that woman he had never named a ship for her. That he had named a child for her, in that moment she forgot. His new, his most lovely ship bore the name Catherine. *The Royal Catherine.*

She wanted to tell him her thanks; the words were on her tongue. Buckingham spoke first.

'You love a ship, Charles, more than you love a woman!' he said quick with spite at this sign of affection between those two; he forever cherished the hope that the King would put the Queen away.

'You mistake me, George. I adore them equally... if they be delicate and fine!' He raised Catherine's hand and kissed it. She cherished his courtesies; but she would give them all for one hour of passion such as he had shown in the first days of their marriage.

His ships, she understood, were his symbol of power; as a woman must be fitly adorned, so with his ships. And—she pressed the analogy further—as every man must salute the King's mistress, so every ship of whatever nation, must dip her pennant in the narrow seas, salute his ships.

Well, she could understand it. She knew how he had found a ruined navy and of the pittance Parliament had doled out to restore it. When she saw his ships lying there fine and trim, her heart swelled. 'Every visitor to England,' she said, 'is to admire your ships.'

'Without ships we cannot live,' he told her. 'I build less for war than for peace. Oh we shall fight... if we must; but war! It drains a country of its blood. But trade; trade is the life-blood itself.'

She nodded. She was a daughter of Portugal; she knew the truth of it.

'Wherever the Dutch butter-boxes sail,' he said, 'we must follow—unless we get there first!'

But the Dutch were as alive as the English to the value of trade. Full as proud as the English and as stubborn, they fought in British home waters and in Dutch; Yarmouth and Enkhuisen bore the scars.

The whole country was aclamour for war. No need of pressgangs to man the ships; men freely offered their lives. And, more surprising, Parliament offered money—a generous sum. Mr. Pepys and his clerks at the Admiralty ran hither and thither buying in stores.

'Yet still I pray there'll be no war. I am no war-monger!' Charles told Catherine. 'I've sent Downing to the Hague with our most reasonable demands. But if we must fight...'

'There is no *if*. Never did I saw... see ... so great a hunger to fight as your English.'

'I'll not give way to brute appetite. I look only to what is just and right for the honour and good of this country.'

But he went on equipping his ships.

The Dutch had turned a deaf ear to Downing.

Excitement went to the head like strong wine; the English were drunk on it. They were fierce, they were quarrelsome; they were hawks before the hood is lifted. Only the King's desire for peace held war back and that could not be for long.

Catherine, too, was taken with the excitement. She longed, passionately, to see the Fleet ready for sailing. Charles took her down to Chatham and she stood amazed at the proud ships, their size and number as they lay upon the water. She said, all awonder, 'So many ships... so little money!'

'You must thank Sandwich and Pepys and all those good fellows at the Admiralty.'

'Yours was the head and the heart and the will!' She spoke in Spanish since, in English, she could not find the words.

The tall ships with their masts and sails blurred in tears of pride. She held out her hands to him. It was the first spontaneous gesture of friendship she had ever made; always she had feared rejection. Initiate a gesture—until this moment—she had not dared. Now his quick wits caught the implication. He took her hands in his. She felt his warmth, his nearness; the beating of her heart all-but overthrew her. He sent her his lazy smile.

'Why Kate, the wind brings colour to your cheeks; and very becoming it is!'

'It is not the wind,' she said very low.

'Then what might it be?' He cast a mocking glance. 'Shall I come and see for myself... tonight?'

That night he did not come. He had cast aside waistcoat and periwig in the summer heat and caught a heavy chill. It was a pity; for when he was well again more than his fever had cooled. And, indeed, there was more on his mind than the wooing of a wife. His hands were full with the coming war; its certainty no man could doubt.

'He do not... does not... give himself time to grow well,' Catherine told Eliza. 'From his bed he do come before it is light, though the fever be not gone; and so late he comes to his sleep...' she stopped. She did not care to say what everyone knew—that for all his kindness he slept every night with his mistress, returning to his wife in the small hours. And, when he came at last, it was to find her, as often as not, asleep; and sometimes her cheeks were wet. At his coming she would awake. But it was the old story. He was too spent to make love again.

The two Fleets faced each other in the North Sea. Deep in the business of war day and night, Charles had little time for pleasure. And in that brief time it was not *the lady* he pursued but the little Stuart. My lady could wait; but la belle Stuart might slip through his fingers. So open, so passionate his pursuit, my lady's lodgings were more deserted than the Queen's. The Queen's court was, indeed, surprisingly full; courtier's arithmetic is quick. The Queen was, it seemed, in the ascendant. To her the King was showing attention; to the lady—none.

My lady Castlemaine was not one to suffer in silence.

'She flings herself at the King's head before the whole court,' Eliza Ormonde told Maria Penalva, 'yet she wins nothing but a polite smile; and sometimes not even that. Or she berates him with a coarse tongue till we know not where to look. She embarrasses us all; herself not least!'

'For all her fine family she is low-bred,' the old woman said with some satisfaction. 'Why does the King allow her to stay and vex us all? He cares for her no longer.'

'I'd not be too sure of that!' Eliza said. 'He tires of her at times; but she's in his blood. Always he comes back to her.'

'Why does he not make her behave? In my country a man would know how to deal with such a mistress!'

'I think he fears her. She is forever threatening to make public his letters.'

'The letters he should seize and burn; and herself he should cast into prison!' the gentle Penalva said.

'It is not his way; he has principles of justice.'

'A fig for such justice when it hurts my mistress!'

My lady Castlemaine continued to behave as though there were no such thing as the King's displeasure; and Charles was too indifferent—or too occupied—to put an end to her arrogance. But for all that she did not always get her way. There was the tale of the French coach.

The Count de Grammont, banished from France, had been welcomed by Charles. In gratitude he sent to Paris for a gift—the most beautiful coach ever seen in England; a bubble of glass and gilt—a coach out of a fairy-tale. It was the glass that set it above all other coaches—the first closed coach in this country where those within could see and be seen.

The first to drive in the coach were, as was proper, the Queen with the duchess of York. It should have been—in my lady Castlemaine's opinion—herself. Well she had not been the first; but certainly she would be the next. Hurrying away to demand it of the King, she found another before her—Frances Stuart, the girl she herself had raised from nothing, on the same errand.

Charles not unamused let them fight it out.

'I carry your child,' my lady cried out; and, indeed she was breeding again. 'Disappoint me in this, and be sure I shall miscarry.'

Frances bent and whispered in the King's ear. What she said my lady did not catch; but one thing was clear—the girl was to have the coach. My lady, raging, put about a scandalous tale. *Disappoint me in this*, she reported Frances to have said, *and I shall never be with child by you!*

The tale flew all over Whitehall; the lady published it to the sound of her fury. There was no escaping that voice screaming at the girl for slyness, for lying, for whorish ways and an ungrateful heart.

Once more *that woman* was with child by the King! Catherine's heart took the shock—a shock more bitter since she, herself, showed no sign of pregnancy. And, moreover, the whole tale was degrading! From *that woman*, exactly what might be expected; but from the girl, the girl that played chaste—unspeakable; if it were true. Was it true? Catherine would not insult her dignity by any question.

It was the girl, herself, that sought the occasion.

'It is not true!' she said, childish eyes awash with tears. 'Trust me, Madam the Queen, it is not true.'

'You had the coach!' Catherine said and turned her back.

XVI

Catherine uttered no further word on the subject; not to Eliza, not even to Penalva. Nor did she condescend to dismiss the girl— the matter was beneath the Queen's notice. What she thought about it not even Charles could guess; by word or look she gave no sign.

Two things she had lacked when first she came into England—tact and patience. In a hard school she was learning both. These days she never entered her own dressing-room without some small warning noise lest she surprise the King together with Frances. Nor did she enter the King's own rooms without giving him time to bundle some fair frailty out of his bed and through the ruelle and down the back stairs. *That woman* he visited in her own bed; Frances Stuart he did not visit at all—she would not allow it. But there was often some stray pretty in the King's bed—a playactress, or a poor pastor's comely daughter, or a court lady; his tastes were generous. Once, seeking her husband in some urgency, she had caught sight of rose-coloured slippers beneath the bed-vallance. It was a lesson she did not choose to learn twice.

And she had other troubles, also. She was still so poor, so utterly pinched for money; the Queen's full revenue had never been paid.

The court said of her that she was mean; she knew it and her heart burned. *That woman* could cast away twenty thousand pounds in an evening at cards; but the Queen must count every penny! There were times when she could not pay her servants.

'Madam, my darling, you must speak to the King!' Penalva said.

'I cannot.' When she thought of her mother's trick she was dumb—it was a trick that had already cost her much. And dumb she remained however they miscalled her. *A close woman!* She that longed to give with both hands. It hit harder than anyone could guess.

She had so few friends she could not afford to lose one. Now she was to lose the Master of her Horse, devoted Montague. She knew him for a man careless in many things, and certainly with money—his own and other people's. But whatever his faults to others, to her he was a faithful servant; and in that service, perfect. And he was a charming companion. He shared her love of music; he played the guitar well and sang charmingly. He brought her news of the latest dances in Paris and together they practised the steps. She was grateful, too, for his kindness to Penalva. Cataracts were darkening both eyes; and, in the sickness for home that grew steadily with failing sight, he played, delightfully, the devoted son. He listened to her with patience; he ran to fetch and carry for her; he brought her small, charming surprises. And, best of all, he would sit by her describing this and that—Miss Price's ridiculous new gown or the fantastic coat the Count de Grammont had had sent from Paris. And always he spoke as though they were seeing these things together. For his kindness to Penalva, alone, the Queen must value him.

But above all, in a court that took everything at face-value, he was the one man to see through the shyness of the Queen to the bright spirit beneath. Dissolute in a dissolute court, he loved the Queen with a deep respect; in that court such love was rare.

She knew his love—she was a woman; but she gave no sign. That Charles amused himself with other women gave her no licence to amuse herself. Yet, to feel herself not utterly despised, that one man, at least, set her above the light beauties, saved her from humiliation. She was grateful for his devotion.

In the court, gossip spared the innocent less than the guilty. For the guilty there was fellow-feeling; for the innocent, laughter not unmixed with spite... *he holds the Queen's hand over-long; he whispers too often in her ear. These things in the public eye! What of those things where the public eye does not reach?* Charles heard the gossip; his friends saw to it. He heard all there was to know—and a good deal more. Because he said no word on the matter, Eliza that knew him well, advised the Queen to send the young man away.

'Shall a young man not look at me with favour?' she asked Eliza, asked Penalva. And then, with something of her old temper, 'Must I not be admirable?'

'Admired, Madam,' Eliza corrected her.

'Admired!' She was more than ever impatient. 'Am I not like other women?'

'The Queen is above all women!' Penalva said at once.

'And the King?'

'With the King it is different,' Eliza said.

'How so?' Catherine asked, cold; but she knew her answer. If the King had a bastard, it was expected. In the Queen it would be high treason.

'Madam, my darling,' Penalva wrung her hands. 'The court is talking. How it talks!'

'Who talks?' Catherine cried out, stung. 'The King's friends with their whores and their lusts! I'll not send my good friend away!'

Gossip swelled; but still she refused. Send away the one true heart that raised her to the level of women that are loved!

Look to your wife! Buckingham would urge the King; and Berkeley and Rochester and the rest. Charles would affect to laugh, would make a doubtful jest; but still they irked him. And still he said no word to Catherine; but once, in her hearing, careless and smiling, asked the young man, *How does your mistress?*

The play upon words stiffened her yet further. That he should dare, Charles with his sluts! Never would she send away the faithful heart that served her.

Edward Montague had decided for himself. A harum-scarum young man... and worse, some said; but his honour was delicate where it concerned his Queen.

'I beg the Queen's leave to resign my post,' he said very calm, as though it were not torment to leave his place about her.

'Your resignation... I cannot accept it.' Anger upheld her; and the foreshadowing of the emptiness his going must bring.

'Yet still I beseech the Queen. I am weary of soft living!'

'Where shall you go?' And she could not believe him, the penniless young man conditioned to comfort.

'If I leave the Queen—I care not!'

He was gone leaving his debts behind him; and, in the heart of the Queen, grief for the one man that loved her. She would, at first, put no-one in his place. She missed his warmth, his laughter, his kindness... she and old Penalva missing him unendurably.

She had lost not Edward alone. Chesterfield, her perfect chamberlain, resigned under pressure from my lady Castlemaine. She missed not only his kindness but his efficiency; in a country that was still so strange, she knew not which way to turn. But, greater than any trouble—*that woman.* Though still the King pursued Frances Stuart with unslaked passion, my lady was winning him back again.

Rigidly schooled though she was, to the etiquette of courts, the Queen had suffered overmuch; her long patience broke. It broke not upon those that deserved it but upon the blameless. She knew it; even while she behaved unqueenly, she knew it. But she could not help it; grief had made the breach. All she could say afterwards to Eliza, to Penalva—since Charles refused to listen—was that but for unhappiness she had not behaved so.

Spain's new ambassador had presented his credentials; after an audience with the King he asked audience of the Queen. She was in no mood for courtesies to Spain.

'No!' she cried out at once. 'He is of my country the enemy! Spain do ask for Tangier; or so I understand.'

Charles nodded. 'You may leave that to me!'

But that she could not; she had not learned, as yet, his shrewdness, his uncanny sense of knowing when to bow and when to defy.

'Tangier!' she cried out. 'It is of my dowry; it is mine, my own!'

'It is not yours; it is mine! I shall know what to do with it.'

To her it was no assurance. 'Insolent of Spain; insolent! Tangier was to my country from old days. Never could it be took from us; only could it be given; of ourselves, freely given.'

'You may leave it to me,' he said again. 'And you will receive Don Omeledio!' And he had no mind for meddling women; from a mistress, he must at times endure it; from a wife, never!

She was already angered when she sent to admit the ambassador to audience. And, her anger increasing, she requested him to address her not in Spanish but in French.

It was rude upon two counts. He had the right to speak in his own language; and she had no shadow of excuse to forbid him—she spoke Spanish well. In French she made poor showing; it suited her purpose. She was determined to understand little and to say less.

It was bad behaviour; she did not need Charles to tell her so. And he did not tell her; but he behaved with marked coolness. After their growing friendship they were back to the old misery. She longed to say *I was wrong... my one piece of deliberate bad behaviour. I will not offend again.*

She did not tell him so; he gave her no chance.

The year moved on. Charles thawed a little but the blossoming friendship had been frost-nipped. She tried to be gay, to be gracious even to those friends of his she counted—and rightly counted—her enemies; to win him every way she knew. But he was kind, merely, with the careless kindness he showed to those for whom he cared little. And all the time her jealousy gnawed. *That woman* had got him back. Save for Frances Stuart—and he was as far from his desire as ever—he was as completely my lady's as he had ever been. There were no more fair frailties in his bed; he slept the best part of every night with her, coming back spent with love... and all England repeating the old lie that the Queen could never have a child; all England blaming her because there was no heir.

My lady Castlemaine was one to thrive upon new sensations. Now she was proposing a flirtation with the Church—a new kind of flirtation indeed.

'Such a convert we can do without!' Catherine cried out goaded.

'God cannot do without. He cannot, I think, do without a single soul that may be saved,' Penalva said.

'*That* for her soul!' Catherine snapped finger and thumb. 'I am not deceived... and God is not deceived.' *It is to force the King's eyes from the Stuart girl where still it wanders, back to herself!* She could not say it, even to Penalva. She said instead, 'It is to thrust herself yet further forward lest she be overlooked; to make herself the centre of every eye, the subject of every tongue.'

'She may make her plans; but God, maybe, has others.'

The lady's friends besought Charles to make her stop her nonsense—in a troubled England, who knew where such nonsense might end? He took her conversion even less seriously than the Queen. 'I may interfere with a woman's body—if she be so kind,' he said; 'but never with her soul!' An answer that, brought to Catherine, stung her to further anger.

Life went on. A dutiful Charles went to his wife's bed; but still there was no sign of an heir. It was the old tale. He was already fatigued with love-play and she, too anxious. And, besides, she had been bred to show no pleasure in the marriage-bed. She loved him, longed for him... and was ashamed of her longing. Showing her own pleasure she might have pleasured him; might, even, have roused his passion. But she never did.

The Queen's court grew ever larger; larger than that of the Duchess of York whose cold pride kept courtiers at a distance; larger than that of the Queen-mother whose ardour for her faith frightened those that feared to be tarred with the Papist brush. And certainly it was gayer than either. English was easier upon her tongue; she might halt for the unfamiliar word, or use a foreign construction or a wrong tense, but she was quick to understand and to answer... and her answers were always to the point. There was dancing aplenty—for dancing she had a passion; and always there was music—light music and grave; old music and new. She had opera sent from Italy—the first ever heard in England; and she was the only one to enjoy it. Ned Montague, she thought, would have understood it, this formal, sweet Italian music. Even Charles thought it affected and odd. 'We like our own airs better,' he said, 'they are simple and charming.'

'You cannot bind... bound... music by the sea. It is being free as air,' she told him.

He gave her a searching look; her answer was unexpected as endearing. The court continued its diversions. Charles, too, diverted himself—but he worked harder than he played. The situation with the Dutch was fast coming to the boil; he must keep a wary eye upon Dutch and French, both. Louis was his own secret ally; but France had her open alliance with Holland. If war came France must stand by her ally; already Courtin, the French ambassador, had uttered his warning. Early and late Charles was at his despatches; he was in constant consultation with James, lord High Admiral; with my lord Sandwich of the Admiralty, a shrewd man; with Mr. Pepys—even shrewder.

So far there had been short, scattered sea fights; engagements at the discretion of the officers. Short of a miracle, England or the Dutch must declare war. Peacelover though he was, Charles was no longer sure he wanted the miracle.

By March he was certain he did not; a goaded England declared war. Early in May the Fleet sailed. Never in England so glorious a sight. A hundred men-of-war in perfect trim; and a royal admiral to share the dangers of common men. Stuart stock rose high.

The war began quietly enough; the news, it seemed, was much as usual—scattered action at sea; English and Dutch coast-towns shelled. So close it followed the old pattern, it scarce seemed war. The first month James, himself, took no part in these engagements; his, a more dangerous part. He was slyly cruising the Dutch coast to spy out the enemy's strength. It was stronger, even, than he had dreamed. Now he was home with his information; and since the Fleet needed overhauling—damage made good, refuelling and provisioning—he ordered it into quiet Solebay. There the ships lay at rest; and there the Dutch found them.

On the first day of June London heard the boom of guns. Mr. Pepys came rushing in upon the King at my lady Castlemaine's lodging with the news. The Dutch, under great Opdam, had attacked the ships in Solebay. James, for all his surprise, had, great seaman that he was, driven the enemy from the bay. The fleets were facing each other in the North Sea.

For three days the battle raged; the booming of the guns declared it... the sound of guns grew ever fainter. Who was on the run?

Once more Mr. Pepys came hurrying. It was the Dutch; the Dutch chased back to their own doorstep. Eighty of their battleships sent to the bottom of the sea. Great Opdam blown sky-high—a shot from the admiral's flag-ship, the *Royal Charles*, had finished him! Ten thousand Dutch seamen killed. Twenty standards taken to mark the victory.

Daylong, nightlong, throughout the country joybells pealed, bonfires flared. In London, the drunken crowds danced about the flames, madly fed the fires with furniture, with books, with clothing; with anything, anything at all to keep the joyful flames alight. Before one house, alone, no bonfire flamed—the house of the French ambassador. *God have mercy upon this poor house*, they chalked in great letters and signed it with the cross—mark of the plague; and continued their dancing. Daylight found them drunk and dancing still. James was the nation's darling, the nation's hero. With unbelievable personal courage—the very eyebrows singed in his blackened face and the hair from his head—he had wrested victory from the enemy. Every taphouse, alley and gutter echoed with his hiccoughed name.

The next day brought ampler news.

A great victory. But the sound of laughter changed to weeping. The list of the dead was appalling.

Catherine was with Charles in his own room at Whitehall; he was tracing the course of the battle upon the globe when they brought him the lists. She saw the paper drop from his hand.

Berkeley's name stood first. Berkeley, my lord Falmouth with so short a time to enjoy his new honours; Berkeley whom the King loved. A worthless sort of fellow in the opinion of many... but he had been faithful and loving, the King's heart's friend.

Appalled she watched his tears; she longed to say the words of comfort. She dared not.

But my lady Castlemaine knew no such delicacy. She wept copiously, she paraded her grief. Good reason; Berkeley had been her lover, the court said. True or not Charles enquired no more than he had ever done. If it were true he had no complaint—Barbara had loved Berkeley; Catherine had detested him. The chain had lengthened by so much to bring him closer to his mistress, to take him from his wife. He was more than ever at my lady's lodgings... and they did more than weep together.

That summer Catherine lost a third friend. The Queen-mother left for France; she made her Farewell to Catherine in the Queen's closet.

'I have said little but I have thought the more,' she said. 'Now I tell you there's no mistress can stand against a wife—if that wife have love; and if she have courage. You are such a wife.' And then she said, 'I am not well..' and, indeed, she had a gaunt and yellow look. 'I go to Bourbon to drink the waters. But, unless you promise me a thing—here in London I shall stay; and here, very like, I shall die.'

'I promise... if it shall be in my power.'

'It is in your power. My little chapel in Somerset House; I give it to you. It must remain open always; but *always*. It must open to everyone of our faith—but everyone, however humble. Do you promise, daughter?'

'I promise and am glad to promise.'

She was gone; and though, of late, Catherine had seen little of her mother-in-law, she had felt her friendship. Now she knew her loss. Henrietta Maria had understood what it meant to be a stranger in a strange land; she knew the heartbreak of serving her faith in the midst of enemies. She had borne mistrust, dislike, unkindness.

Catherine's grief must have been still deeper had she known she was never to set eyes upon this friend again.

XVII

A lull in the fighting; both Dutch and English licking their wounds. Impossible for either to put to sea just now. The Dutch fleet lay at the bottom of the ocean; the English, not shattered but badly battered, had much to make good. For the Dutch—gold aplenty to make all well; for the English—nothing but what Charles could spare from his own pocket. And he must waste no time. If Parliament, enthusiasm cooling, could vote nothing, then he, himself, must beg or borrow, sell or steal. The navy must be made good.

And now, with no time to draw breath, the country must face an enemy more remorseless than the Dutch; an enemy against whom ships and weapons, courage and strength were alike useless. So quiet an enemy they had, at first, scarce noticed. Now it was on them.

The plague.

In the first week of June between four and five thousand died. Never before had the plague struck at any but the poor; *poor man's sickness* they had called it. Never before had it struck at the comfortable, the well-fed. Now they, too, went down under the attack. And the sickness was showing itself in a new form; the stricken died with a horrifying speed.

For the first time Parliament acted in the matter. Where a man sickened, his door must be marked with a red cross a foot long—no missing it. And, writ large and clear, *Lord have mercy on us*. Before it had been custom merely; now it was the law. And the door of such house, and every window also, must be sealed up until the law gave permission for unsealing. There the poor creatures must stay, the living sealed up with the dead, until the last of the living laid himself down among putrefying corpses for his last sleep.

All that first week the dead carts could be heard, their sad bells ringing and the cry *Bring out your dead!* But the dead were too many and the living panic-stricken at the sight, the smell, the sound; now only in the dark hours were the carts allowed about their business. Then they would rattle upon the cobbles, the bell carrying their warning, a voice hoarse with repetition crying out the dreadful summons. Then, to the sound of weeping, or an oath maybe, off the cart would rattle again, piled high with corpses carelessly thrown—a stiff arm outflung as though for help, a stiff leg out-thrust as though to flee; or a body, perhaps, unknowingly dropped, so overcrowded the load.

But who cared? Not the dead-cart drivers; the plague was their daily business. The dead were tipped together into a common grave as quickly as might be; and, that grave full, another dug upon it... so many deaths, so many corpses. Even in the palace of Whitehall, isolated, so it seemed, in safety, they could hear the echo of the doleful bell, the dreadful invitation; could catch a whiff of the stench of corruption.

The unbelievable had happened. Within the royal palace itself, the first victim sickened and died... a servant, merely. But a warning. The

King commanded the court to Hampton Court; he would join them as soon as he could free himself from the press of business—business that must include an eye instant upon the Dutch.

And so began the journey from fear; a journey made in all the foolishness of fashionable travel. The ladies wore velvet coats caped and cuffed to the exact pattern of a man's, and cavalier hats with ribands and feathers; some of them had taken to the fashionable peri-wig. They looked—the younger ones—like skirted boys, charming and perverse. Gay and laughing and chattering as they went, it was hard to believe that they rode from the plague-stricken town where so many must fearfully die.

Catherine sat within the coach with Maria Penalva and Eliza Ormonde. She was quiet and sad—she had left Charles behind in Whitehall where already the plague had struck. She had besought him to let her remain behind; but No, he said; and *No!* The Queen was too precious. From the window she could see the long line of coaches before and behind. When they stopped to change horses there was *that woman* handsomer than ever in advanced pregnancy, lolling in her magnificent coach; and the little Stuart riding like a young Diana.

Ahead of the procession went the officers of the crown. They rode into the villages of Richmond and Kingston and, with a white cross, marked those houses fit to lodge the ambassadors; for these gentlemen—to their fury and their fear—must remain in London till lodgings be found.

London had become a desert; streets empty, shops shuttered, between the cobbles grass already growing. In four days, alone, thirty thousand had fled; thousands were leaving every day... and nowhere to go; no village, no house would receive them, no farmer allow their pitiful camps within his fields.

The King left London with his Council; and the ambassadors with him—ambassadors must follow the court. But, close on their heels, stalking its victims—the plague. Outward through the suburbs, taking toll as it went, the killer followed; and, out in the open country, came up with its advance guard—those that had fled already stricken.

Within a second royal palace the plague struck again. In Hampton Court a guard sickened and died. By August the villages about

Hampton Court were all infected. No longer did the courtiers walk outside the palace grounds; for, upon the road, one would surely find the rotting corpses of those that had died in vain escape; hedges and woods told the same grim story.

The court must move on. Surely Salisbury would be far enough. Easier to say than to do! There were not enough coaches, there were not enough carts. And, for any cart there might be, the price fantastically high—ludicrously high... if this were a laughing matter. Two pounds in gold, paid in advance, for every seven leagues, never mind how ramshackle the cart, how broken-winded the horse; and, making the most of their harvest, the owners saw to it that the carts were half-full only. And always there was the difficulty of finding lodgings on the way.

By mid-August the court reached Salisbury; they brought a visitor with them. The plague. One of the royal grooms sickened. He was sealed within one house together with his known contacts, but... what of the contacts unknown? Impossible to keep the plague out! In spite of roads and gates close-guarded, a man got into the city. For two days before he showed the fearful signs, he walked and talked freely. Two hundred paces from the royal lodgings he fell dead.

Salisbury lived with the plague, ate with the plague, slept with the plague, died with the plague. The court, surrounded by death, must contrive unending amusements; no time to think! Games out-of-doors and games indoors; and always, within and without—the game of love.

Bowls and archery and tennis; dancing and music, hide-and-seek and riddles; and above all a game much affected by the court, *I love my love*...

'I love my love with a *G*,' the little Stuart would begin in her turn, 'because he is good; I hate him because he is greedy; he comes from Greenwich and he is going to...' and someone would have to supply the pretty fool with her lover's destination. It was a game of which they never tired; one could load it with innuendoes.

And there was another favourite pastime—the recounting of dreams.

The little Stuart dreamed she was in bed with the French ambassadors; all three. She told it all blushes and giggles. 'I was on the side next to Monsieur de Verneuil; and he, happily, is a bishop...'

'A bishop's a man like the rest of us!' Charles roared with laughter.

So they played their games; and sometimes the Queen played with them. But more often Penalva found her on her knees beseeching St. Catherine to intercede that the plague stop. But St. Catherine was overbusy; that week in London, alone, eighty-two thousand died. In Salisbury, too, things grew yet worse; people dropped dead in the street like flies.

Catherine was always to remember Salisbury as an unhappy place. In spite of the constant diversions, the King was never well; the air did not agree with him; more than once shaken with dread, she feared the plague had marked him down.

It was here, too, that she had her own, sad news.

Montague had been killed before Bergen. Less than a year since he had been alive, the handsome young man, alive and loving. She made no show of grief. He had gone away to save her good name; she must not waste his sacrifice with a show of tears. But in the privacy of her closet she wept and would not be comforted. 'For the sake of a handclasp, a whispered word... such little things... for these he had to die!'

'It was not for the handclasp, Madam, my darling, nor yet for the whispered word. It was for love of you; and that is not a little thing.'

'A handclasp, a few words only...' she was deaf to Penalva's words.

'Madam, my darling, do not grieve overmuch, nor make of him a hero. He was charming... so charming. But not—Madam I must say it—very good.'

'He loved me!' the Queen cried out. 'And he was the only one! Now the world is shrinking!'

A sigh broke from the old woman. He had been like a son to her. Her world was shrunken, too.

The summer days went by. Charles was pale and listless; my lady Castlemaine, her condition aggravating her natural violence, spoiled his joy in the child she carried and emptied his pockets—and God knew they were lean enough. With his ever-ready compassion he was giving, from his own purse, a thousand pounds a week to sufferers from the plague. It was a constant cause of anger with his mistress;

she could not see that such vermin mattered at all. But the Queen added penny to penny, denying herself even small comforts... and for her it was the time for comforts.

She was pregnant; but she would not tell it, not yet. To Penalva, alone, would she speak of her hope.

'Madam, my darling,' the old woman urged, 'you must tell the King. In these sad times give him his joy.'

'No,' Catherine said, 'there has been disappointment enough!'

'You are my lady and I obey you... as long as I can. If you do not speak, then I must. I owe it to Madam your mother that put you in my charge.'

'I have said *No!* If you cannot obey then you had best go home!' And, seeing the grief in the old face, cried out, 'Forgive me. I did not mean it. I cannot do without you. But I am *driven*. I will speak in good time.'

But still she said no word. *That woman* carrying the King's child and flaunting her big belly, kept her dumb. The wife saw how the mistress moving lightly, moving proudly, beneath her burden made a triumph of shame.

In Salisbury the plague was bad as it could be. Charles moved the court to Oxford. Christchurch received him and his staff; Merton, the Queen and her ladies. At Merton the lodgings were simple. The Queen had no quarrel with that; but *the lady* troubled the air with her complaints. Impossible to escape sight or sound of her. It was an added burden upon Catherine.

But Charles was happy to be in Oxford, loyal Oxford that loved him. He worked with his Council, applied himself to his despatches, consulted with my lord Sandwich and Mr. Pepys upon the fleet, and dealt, as best he might, with the business of the country. Parliament did little to support him save to vote a sum—small enough—to carry on the Dutch wars.

To Catherine he was kinder; it was a kindness that did her little good since he did not neglect his ladies. Every morning, between prayers and breakfast and before he saw the Queen, he visited first one and then the other—Barbara Castlemaine languid and voluptuous with motherhood; Frances Stuart, lovely, virginal, untouched.

Still Catherine said no word. But so pale she was, so peaked that, Penalva whispering to Eliza and she, in turn to Charles, he sought the Queen in the privacy of her closet. It was the right moment. When she told him her news she saw in his eyes and the whitening of his mouth, a joy equal to her own. He said, 'My dearest dear, we must take all care. No grief nor annoyance shall come your way, I swear it!'

And he meant it. But, as long as *the lady* remained, grief and annoyance there must be. And how could he send her away; how disgrace Barbara that also carried his child?

Now it was my lady that, knowing the Queen's condition, and, in her turn, envying one whose child was the country's undoubted hope, must disguise her envy. She forced her Bedchamber duties upon the Queen; and more than ever flaunted herself and her burden; Catherine could scarce endure to look at her. More than her dislike, more than her disgust was the dread that the woman be brought to bed beneath the Queen's own roof. She was obsessed with the idea that such a birth threatened her own child. She tried to rationalise her dread; to pretend, even to herself, that it was the humiliation she feared; that and that alone.

'She must go; she must go at once!' she cried out more than once to Penalva. 'She must go before she give birth here, in my own lodgings. It is insult and humiliation she should be here; such insult, such humiliation I cannot, nor I shall not endure.'

'Humiliation?' Penalva was gentle. 'You cannot talk of humiliation now!

'Can I not? I tell you if she give birth here, in the Queen's lodgings, I shall die of shame.'

My lady was as determined to stay as the Queen that she should go. To be brought to bed beneath the Queen's roof was essential; only so could she triumph in this situation. She kept the King at her beck and call; let him delay her summons and the walls of Merton echoed with her rage.

And now it was autumn. More and more Catherine found life in Oxford unendurable. Again and again she besought Charles to leave for London—the plague was abating; the weekly figures showed it. But if it were not so—and now she was frantic, indeed—she would risk the plague, the plague itself, before that woman should lie-in under her roof.

But it was not yet safe in London. She must wait a little, Charles said; when the falling death rate was constant, then they should go. But the court said—and the town echoed it—that he dare not leave until his whore had cast her burden. They made a song about the King; they called him Old Rowley after his black stallion that had sired countless handsome foals. The streetboys whistled it everywhere.

My lady had won. Three days after Christmas she was brought to bed of her fourth bastard; and this child Charles did acknowledge. The baby was christened quite shamelessly George Fitzroy; George the King's son. Into the Queen's lodgings flowed gifts, flowed congratulations. Catherine said no word, not even to Penalva. The insult cut too deep; she bled inwardly. Her drawn face, her colourless lips tight-pressed above her grief spoke for her.

Charles was truly sorry. Less than ever could he, at this moment, turn his back upon Barbara; but this should be her last child by him; he swore it to himself. And more; as soon as she was strong again it would be Farewell. She had angered him by her behaviour to the Queen, she had exhausted him with her rages. Meanwhile he would put an end to his uncomfortable position. He would not turn *the lady* out; but he could go himself! Yes, he would move with Parliament and the Council to London; the plague, as Catherine said, was truly abating.

But still he dallied; he would see the New Year in. And still Oxford was agrin; more than ever in the streets they whistled the tune of Old Rowley.

The new year of 'sixty-six came in sharp and cold. Though Catherine had the frail look she always wore in pregnancy, she was well enough; at such times, though, she must always take care. Charles was tender, was cherishing; but for *that woman* her happiness was perfect. 'There was never a man like him to comfort a woman and to be her joy,' she told Penalva. Penalva smiled and nodded; and kept her opinion behind her dimming eyes... *He has experience enough.*

By the end of January Charles was ready for London.

By the end of January my lady was full-recovered; to the fastidious eye a little coarsened, perhaps, but glowing, vital, sleek and graceful. Childbearing agreed with her; it fulfilled her deepest need—female triumph over the male. And not over the male, alone; triumph over her rivals—and, most of all, triumph over the Queen.

Charles was to stop at Hampton Court for a few days to deal with business there. Catherine begged that she might go with him; she wore her white, frail look and he was afraid. He refused. She must remain in Oxford until Whitehall was ready to receive her. A few days, merely; then she should join him in London. But the nearness of *that woman*, female triumphant, disgusted her; without him she could not endure Oxford a day longer.

'I am *well*,' she said, 'I am well!' And gave her women orders to pack. She was to wish, with a most bitter regret, that she had listened to Charles.

Stepping into her coach all joy to be gone, she stopped unwilling, unable almost, to believe her eyes. She stumbled a little as she took her place within; she was white as a bleached bone. My lady, aglow with health and hateful with triumph, was stepping into her own coach; behind her the nurse carried an infant wrapped in sables. Charles, riding ahead, had not marked the incident; had not known, even, that my lady followed upon his heels.

Within the coach Catherine sat torn by anger and twisted by nausea. She turned her wild face from Eliza to Penalva. 'Never to know the quiet mind!' she cried out. 'Never, even at such a time, a little peace!' She cried out louder as pain took her; pain sharp, sudden, unexpected.

She lay in bed at Hampton Court weeping over her lost hope.

My lady Castlemaine had put it about the Queen had not been pregnant nor ever could be. Yet certainly she had been pregnant—her physician declared it. She had had a miscarriage. They could, had the King desired it, have named the sex of the child. My lady's voice drowned theirs.

'She knows well how to plant her poisoned darts; she will be the death of me!' Catherine said frail and pale in the bed.

'You must not say such a thing, no, nor think it!' Penalva said. 'Where is your courage Madam, my darling?'

And Eliza, 'The physicians have told the King the child was perfect. All of them agreed. Do you think he would believe anyone—anyone at all—that says different?'

But if the King did not believe my lady, the court did; and the country believed her also. Miscarriage after miscarriage—it was not possible! The Queen had never miscarried at all—for the simple reason that she had never conceived. And never could conceive. The King had been warned; before his marriage he had been warned; and that warning he had chosen to disregard. Best now to put the Queen away; never could she give the country its heir.

Bitterly disappointed both for himself and for her, Charles was gentle with Catherine. But something had gone from him; she thought it was hope. She knew it whenever he came to her bed.

XVIII

London after the plague. Grass thick between the cobbles, streets half-empty, shops, for the most part, shuttered still; houses fallen into decay, windows hanging crazily, upon doors the red cross, smudged and faded, echoed a warning still.

Whitehall palace was strange after months of absence. For all the great fires in the Queen's room the air struck cold; the wintry gardens, lacking autumn pruning and tidying, wore a neglected look. A weary indifference lay like dust everywhere. Catherine, not yet recovered from her miscarriage and grieving for her loss, drooped and cared little for her appearance. With her, looks depended upon health and spirits. Happiness was a charm to transform her into glowing prettiness; sad or ill, she was lacklustre, plain.

And she had more than her loss to trouble her. Charles had left her to sleep alone till she should be stronger; it was a kindness in him... but more than ever he was sleeping with the Castlemaine. He was, after all, a man without a wife. And he was pursuing the little Stuart with a more purposeful passion. It was his way of coming to terms with disappointment.

This same January France declared war.

It hit Charles hard. He had hoped that his secret understanding with Louis would prevent it.

'Now we must face the joined armies of Holland and France,' he told James.

'We are ready,' James said.

Ready? Lifted brows asked the question.

'As ready as we shall ever be... till Parliament puts its hand in its pocket.'

'Parliament has lost its appetite for war!' Charles sighed.

'Then we must whet it again!'

War with France hit Charles hard for another reason. It must cut him off from Minette. They wrote to each other every week, gossiping, loving little notes that bridged the sea between them. And he was the more troubled that Minette expected a child. Highly-strung, she would need cherishing care; and this, from a vicious husband forever concerned with his pretty boys, his mignons, she was not likely to get. Charles feared for her.

This trouble he did not discuss with his wife. Minette's hope bore too heavily upon their own loss. But Catherine needed no word; she knew his love for his sister, knew his fears. She knew, also, that it made his own loss no easier that James had already two little daughters—the four-year-old Mary and the baby Anne... James founding his line.

In March came news of Donna Luisa's death. Childless, Catherine was now motherless. She felt truly orphaned. She missed her mother more than at any time in her life. Always she had believed that they would meet again. Either she, herself, would go home for a visit; or her mother would become England's honoured guest. Now it was too late. Unwell and in low spirits, she was inclined to believe *that woman's* taunts; to give up hope of a child. Already ill-health and grief had stolen her looks, nor did the unrelieved black she wore add to them. But the mourning ordered for the court suited *that woman* to perfection; it threw up the fine red and white of her complexion so that my lady went about laughing and gay. Now Catherine did not trouble to hide her hostility; and my lady repaid her by forever thrusting herself in the Queen's way... but she was more careful of her tongue; the King had warned her.

Of Frances Stuart Catherine saw little. She demanded no service nor did the girl offer it. She behaved to the Queen with deep respect, longed for Catherine's countenance and did not dare approach her. These days Frances sat alone building her card houses. Once every man about the court would have run eager with help; they did it no longer—she was in the King's desire. She kept herself as distant from him as she could... but still she was the King's. No man dared approach her, these days no woman envied her. She was the loneliest creature in the court.

And now it was Spring; and—as Charles had feared—England must face the massed navies of France and Holland. As James had said—they were ready; as ready as, lacking gold, they were ever likely to be. Always Charles had given long hours to the country's affairs; now he worked both day and night upon the problems war must bring. His snatched moments of amusement he spent with *the lady* whose rages did not allow her to be so amusing after all. But he had fallen into his old habit; when he needed rest it was to Catherine he went. Love her he did not; but he took comfort from her gentleness—a comfort he found nowhere else.

James had been forced to divide the Fleet. Prince Rupert with thirty ships awaited the French in the narrow seas; Albermarle with sixty, watched for the Dutch in the North Sea. De Ruyter, that great admiral, had taken Opdam's place. It would, Charles thought troubled, need the full Fleet to stand against him alone.

As before, a year almost to the day, the booming of guns could be heard in London; but this time they came fainter. The engagement was being fought off the Dutch coast.

Charles paced the Queen's closet. 'We should not have divided the fleet—the Dutch are two to our one.' He was talking to himself rather than to her. She lifted her head from her needlework; she said, 'We must watch the French and the Dutch, both. We cannot risk to be attacked both sides. And Rupert is no fool. If he be needed he shall himself join Albermarle.'

She was right. On the fourth day Rupert joined the battle. Within a few hours the Dutch were on the run; their fleet shattered and scattered made for home.

Again all the bells in England pealing; again bonfires blackened the summer sky... and again, with ampler news, joy turned to sorrow. A long, long list of the dead; and the fleet—the glorious fleet Charles had pinched and pared to put to sea—broken as surely as the Dutch.

'The ships must be refitted, the seamen replaced,' Charles told Catherine. 'But how? God alone knows where the money's to come from.'

The people of England gave him his answer.

'They come in by the hundred', he told her, 'the common seamen, crying out for revenge upon their dead. And France's threat to invade has done us good service. The people flock in their thousands—gentle and simple alike—offering their lives and their gold to drive the French back to their own land. Oddsfish, how I love this people!'

But for all his victories, all the joy in his people, he had a lean and yellow look. Who can wonder? Catherine thought. Save with me he knows no rest. Always it is work; and work; and work. And *that woman* forever teasing him, offering herself and then withdrawing till he gives her the thing she must have—the jewel or the land or the gold he can ill afford. Between his work and that vulture he is worn out...

If she could save him from the annoyance of *that woman*, at least! But then she must put the hateful, humiliating situation into words; and words, she knew well, have a way of forcing facts out like the crystals she had seen once in Charles' laboratory. She spent hours imagining a conversation with my lady that should make the situation clear... and, at the same time, ignore it. The thing was beyond her. It was with less than her hard-learned tact that, anger betraying her, she spoke at last.

'I fear, my lady, the King does take cold staying so long in your apartments.'

She had done better to hold her peace. Laughing and spiteful my lady said, 'The King leaves me in good time, I do assure Madam the Queen. If he is late abed it is because he has stayed elsewhere.'

Fire flamed in the Queen's cheeks. The insinuation that the King honoured more than one bed before his wife's set her whole body shaking with anger. Hard-learned discipline broke; angry words crowded upon her tongue.

'You are a bold piece—' It was not the Queen's voice but the King's. He stood in the doorway eyeing his mistress with distaste, 'so to answer the Queen. Leave the court. When we require you we shall send.'

My lady made a deep curtsey to him; a light and mocking one to the Queen and so was gone.

My lady wrote, oh so humbly, to request the King that she might send for her furniture. Come and get it yourself! he answered—as she had known he would. And come she did; and with tears and smiles and a wanton exciting of him, peace was made.

Catherine wept with disappointment; she was still far from well.

'Dry your tears, Madam my child!' Since Donna Luisa's death Penalva had taken to this form of address; in her forlorn state Catherine welcomed it. 'With *that woman* it is the beginning of the end.'

'I think it, too!' Eliza said. 'The creature is worse than ever. She deafens him with her rages, she tears him with her jealousies, she stings at him like a hornet. She is vicious, she is greedy. She gives him nothing but her body—and that he must share with others. I cannot think he will suffer this for ever. Madam, be patient....'

'Patient?' the Queen cried out. 'How? How, patient? She has his children, his lovely children; and by them she holds him. And I? What of me?' She struck herself upon the belly.

Penalva caught at the wild hands. 'You have carried a babe more than once; but you have not borne a full-time child. Nor will you, Madam my child, as long as you eat out your heart. *That woman*—she'll not poison your life much longer. The King bides his time. As for the child she carries—he swears he'll own it never... he found the little Jermyn in her bed!'

'But still she cries out that the child is the King's?' Eliza said. 'Who has not heard her? *God damn you but you shall own it!* she screams aloud for all to hear. And then she threatens him. *If you'll not own it I shall bring it into the Stone gallery as soon as it is born and dash its brains out before your eyes.*'

Catherine's face pinched with disgust. 'Enough!' she said and wondered that any woman—even this one, wild and violent as she was—could bring her tongue to such vile words. She must get away from the foul air of scandal. She would take Penalva's advice. She would make herself strong; she would give Charles the child all England so ardently desired. She would try the waters of Tonbridge again. They had done little good before; but, at least, she had been happy there; she and Charles together.

Tonbridge was as delightful as ever; but though the court walked and talked and flirted, and brought pretty trifles in the gay shops; though once more they danced upon the green in the evenings, the old enchantment was gone. Catherine obeyed her physicians; she drank the waters faithfully; and, wet or fine, took her walks between tankards. And she obeyed her priests also; she offered masses, gave alms, wore her sacred relics. As for *that woman*, as before she stayed in London to bear her child. How many times, Catherine wondered wretched, must this piece of misery repeat itself?

But though the enchantment was gone she grew in health and looks. Charles would come and stay for a day or two; but always the press of work—or *that woman*—called him back. To tempt him to stay she sent for players from the King's theatre. Moll Davies came; a pretty creature with a voice like an angel. And with her Eleanor Gwynn. No beauty this one, with the small bright eyes that would disappear in the creases of her plump cheeks when she laughed—which was nearly always. Yet she had her charms this Nell Gwynn with her tumble of red curls and her cherry mouth; and her careless gown slipping from a white shoulder to reveal a sweet full bosom. A spiced piece, this, impudent; and gay as a wedding-tune. Charles' eyes, Catherine marked it well, gazed thoughtful upon both charmers. Thereafter Tonbridge afforded the Queen little good. The end of the month saw them all back in London.

XIX

Catherine twisted and moaned in the bed. In the dark hours of this September morning sleep was troubled by the smell of burning. She was in agony of fear for the children. The children of whom, waking, she never thought now, knowing them to be fantasy, in sadness or ill-health still troubled her dreams.

Now she saw them clearly. They were standing at the top of a staircase, she knew not where. Their faces were white with terror; yet rosy, too... painted with light, flickering light, flaming light.

Between them and herself a pit yawned; a pit of fire and smoke. There were no stairs left; the flames had eaten them. She tried to come to the children, to pluck them from danger. Her limbs were heavy as lead; she could not move.

She awoke to the sound of her own weeping; the room was full of the smell of burning. The children were still so real she could see the terror in their eyes. She cried aloud; and, even as she flung aside the bedclothes, Eliza came, candle in hand; and Penalva carrying a bedgown.

'I heard you stirring, Madam.' Eliza put down the candle and drew aside the bed-curtains. 'The smell of burning—it awoke me, also.'

Penalva put the gown about the Queen and pulled back the window-curtains. Red light rushed into the room, flickered upon their upturned faces.

'A fire. A great fire. It looks to be in the city,' Eliza said.

And now, full-awake, Catherine's first thought must be, as always, for the King.

Chiffinch opened to her knock; even in this anxious moment she was careful to give warning lest she catch some pretty playmate in the King's bed. But Charles was up and dressed; she thought he had just come in. He smiled when he saw her. 'It's nothing, I dare wager!' he said. 'This old city of ours; always here and there a house catches fire.'

'So much of wood—is there not danger?'

'There never has been, thank the Lord. God, I fancy, has His eye upon us—which is not to say He'll keep it there! We may flout Him once too often! How many hours we have spent, Wren and I, talking about this London of ours—that it should be rebuilt; and how, give us the chance, we should clear away the alleys where two men cannot walk abreast; and how we should make wide roads and squares with grass and trees; and fine houses of brick. But—' he shrugged, 'folk, for the most part, cannot stomach change. And besides—' he pulled out the pockets of his coat; the linings hung forlorn. 'There'll be no new London for me!' He sighed and grinned at Chiffinch. 'My throat's parched with the smell of burning. Fetch us a dish of Madam the Queen's brew; a thinnish drink but it clears the wits instead of clouding them.'

They were sipping at their tea when Chiffinch, very pale, announced Mr. Pepys. In he came, white dust powdering his fine buckled shoes and stockings; the dark curls of his wig, his lashes, even, thick-coated.

'Sir,' he cried out and all-but forgot his reverence. 'Sir...' his voice came out breathless. 'London. London burns!'

'Nonsense, man! In London there's always some fire or other.'

'Sir, this is not some fire; it is... *the* fire. It broke out in Pudding Lane—your own master baker's. Some dolt of a 'prentice forgot to rake out the ashes. And, as luck would have it, there's a storehouse next door... *was* a storehouse,' he corrected himself, 'piled high with pitch and wood. The wind blows from the east and a gale at that! It carries the fire right into the city; the houses go up like tinder... one house catches from another; whole streets are aflame.'

'What's being done? How are they fighting it?' And, at the look in Pepys' face, asked, 'Is nothing being done?'

'Nothing, sir. My lord mayor that should be foremost, stands and wrings his hands. And the people—each for himself; busy, one and all, to save what he may. And who shall blame them? As I came up the river I saw barges piled high with Clarendon's household stuff; nor was he the only one. He sets an example.'

'Then we must set another!'

James came into the room. He had forgotten his wig; the short reddish curls gave him a boyish look.

'It's worse than ever!' James said. 'There's but one way to stop it. We must blow up all the houses that stand in its path; across space fire cannot travel. Send at once, sir, to my lord mayor.'

'I doubt, sir, he can listen!' Pepys told him. 'Between wringing his hands and looking to his goods, he's in a frenzy. And, besides, I doubt he'd obey. He fears the mob. All they'd see is so much destruction the more. There'd be a riot. I swear it!'

'He must be made to listen. Bid him call out the trained bands. Tell him I come at once to see he has obeyed me. James, go with me.'

When the brothers rode down to the city the lord mayor had not ceased to wring his hands, nor the citizens to salvage what they might of their own; nor to lay sly hands upon the property of others. The fire was spreading throughout the city and towards the suburbs; street by street the flames ate their way.

It was James that commanded the gunpowder, that stood by to see it properly laid. It checked the fire for a little only; the flames had taken too firm a hold.

Night paled into morning; September sunlight saw the flames spring fiercer. All that day the fire raged; flames shamed the daylight. Dusk fell. By night the fire raged worse than ever. The dark sky flamed red and smoky over London... and beyond. Forty miles of smoked and reddened sky.

On the leads of Whitehall Catherine stood with Eliza. Lungs irritable with smoke, mouths parched, they watched the black figures running this way and that against the blood-smeared sky; wherever they looked the sky hung low and red. 'Can nothing stop it; nothing at all?' Catherine wrung her hands. 'One would say all England burns.'

On Tuesday—and the fire raging two whole nights and days—Mr. Pepys came in with the news. He was thick-coated with dust and grimed with soot—the fine gentleman; the plump, white hands blackened and blistered from grasping at buckets.

'St. Paul's,' he said; and it was almost as though he wept. 'So many churches gone; and now... *St. Paul's*! God has, indeed, turned away His eyes.'

Catherine turned her head to where the gothic towers of the great church still stood, an island in a rising sea of fire. The first flame leaped about the spire, about the great cross. She hid her face. When she looked again a waterfall of boiling lead—like blood in the red light—cascaded into the streets below. Pepys said, and could not control his voice, 'The heart of London burns.'

'The heart of London—is the King!' Catherine said at once. And then, '*the King?*' Her voice grew urgent. 'Since yesterday I did not see him. Yesterday he did ride out on the great mare, high, that all should mark him. Today I did not see him before he go. Where is the King?'

'Where most he is needed, there he will be! As for the mare, Madam— back in the stables. She could no longer endure the stink and the heat; she was trembling, Madam, head-to-foot. The King had pity...'

'For all but himself!' she cried out, a little wild. 'He does not come to sleep nor yet to eat. I do not know, even, where he shall be... save that where danger is most, there you shall find him!'

'A King, indeed! Madam, you have said true. He stands in the forefront of danger—and his brother with him. When he saw the fat aldermen that should be fathers to the city looking to their treasure rather than to the citizens; when he saw the people overwhelmed by disaster and not knowing which way to turn, he himself took charge. He cried out to the trained bands, *I am your captain*. Now, where the fire is fiercest, he heads the line and with his own hands passes the buckets. Though he is black with soot and his eyes red with smoke; though he works in his shirt sleeves and has cast away his wig, yet every man knows him for the King—every smoky inch of him! Never such a King, Madam, to stand with common men; not only to share the danger but to lead the way—his always the first risk. It is not a thing to be forgot.'

'God grant it!' she said and tore herself from the fire that held her with so hateful a fascination, and went to pray for the King's safety.

And still the dire news came in.

'Who can say what loss, what damage?' Mr. Pepys said. 'Ten thousand houses gone up in flames the first day alone. None but a blind man could know his way about London now; not though he'd lived there all his life! And the noise, Madam, the noise. The roaring of flames, the crashing of timber, the splitting of glass and the failing of stone... and beneath it all, like a tiny instrument that accompanies a great tune, the weeping of the old and young... a bedlam, Madam!'

'And the King? *The King?*'

'Stands knee-deep in water and does not mark it. As always he's the first to advance; he recks nothing of falling stone-work, or flaming timber, not he! And Madam, he has two men stand by him, holding, each, a bag of golden guineas. When reward is earned, 'tis paid upon the spot. When the bag is empty he sends for another...'

Bags of golden guineas... and he so poor he can not at times buy him a new cravat! Her eyes were blinded with tears.

The fire was slackening. On Thursday, having raged for four days, it halted at Smithfield and there died.

From her place upon the roof Catherine saw the brothers fight their way through the cheering crowd. Mr. Pepys was right. Blackened as they were, wigless and in rags, still all men might know them by their height and carriage.

Later, cleaned and rested, they stood with her upon the leads and looked over the ruined city. Soot hung heavy in the air; charred papers floated like dying blackbirds; blackened stumps of buildings stood like broken teeth in an empty mouth. Yet the round church of the Temple stood untouched; and the Tower foursquare within its walls; and Westminster lifting its spires to heaven. All that was left of the proud city.

Away to south and north where yesterday the sky hung low and black, they could see it high and clear and blue. Mr. Pepys joined them all agog with news—the suburbs, though knee-deep in flying papers and ash, had been saved. 'All that is saved is due to the King; they say it everywhere.'

'No, to my brother here,' Charles said, very quick. 'And you must tell them so. But for James and his gunpowder, all, all must have been destroyed. Well...' and his eyes twinkled, ringed though they were with fatigue and reddened by flame, 'now at last we can get to work, Wren and I. Now we can build the city as we dreamed.'

But still Charles could not rest but must post off to Moorfields where crouched the poor wretches that had lost all—men sitting head within their hands; and mothers some great with child, others suckling their little ones. And everywhere children crying; and everywhere men and women, young and old, shivering in the night air with naught but the clothes in which they stood; and of food—none.

Charles walked among the stricken creatures saying his words of comfort. 'Food and clothes are on their way; and money, also. And so it shall be as long as there's need. And more. Never shall there be such a fire again. We shall rebuild this city to a better pattern. And we start at once. I swear it!'

They knew of the great part he had played; now he was lifting some of their misery. They blessed him to his face; and to the sound of their blessing, broken and low, he rode away.

Catherine was beginning to learn this husband of hers. Compassion—it was the inner core of him. With his own eyes he had seen the homeless sheltered; from his own poor purse he gave and gave again. *If need be we must lay up our ships. The people must be fed.* So he had told Parliament; and she knew what it cost him to say it... lay up the navy he had built at the cost of so much hardship, his ships that were needed to bring the Dutch War to its victorious end! But the people came first.

Yet men called him uncaring, lazy, even. It was his easy grace that misled them. But when they were alone—he and she, then he would let the mask slip; would give himself up to his fatigue and the weight of his burdens. If, save for those first bridal nights, he had never turned to her with passion, he yet turned to her for comfort, for friendship... Charles that had taken no woman, ever, for friend.

The end of September. Already they were at work upon the ruined city; they were clearing away rubble, they were levelling, they were marking out new streets.

In her closet this fine autumn morning, Catherine was dressed for riding and waiting for Charles. She had picked up her gloves when he came in with Wren and Evelyn; and he was not dressed for riding. Wren she knew well; Evelyn scarce at all. But Charles esteemed him—a philosopher and a lover of fine buildings and noble gardens; she wished to know him better.

'The plans for our new London!' Charles threw a roll upon the table. 'And you, Kate, shall be the first to see them. One grain of commonsense from that little head of yours will outweigh a load of talk!'

Under his gaiety she thought he had a tired look. *That woman* had been quarrelling with the full violence of her spleen; her voice, loud enough to reach the public places in Whitehall, attacked him because he had no ready money to meet her whims. And then, fearing her boldness, made it up, no doubt, by the equal violence of her love-making. Now, once again, he had come to his wife for peace.

Greeting them, all three, she pulled off her feathered hat and laid her gloves upon the table. 'It is my great pleasure to see Mr. Evelyn,' she told him.

Charles unrolled the plans pointing out the wide streets, the square-built houses. 'No more gables leaning one to the other, to shut out air and light. No more houses of wood. Never again such a fire as we have just suffered.'

'This new London—it is a trust; and we are blessed to have our hands therein,' Mr. Wren said; and there was worship in his voice.

She stood intent upon the plans; she lifted a troubled face.

'Why shall you pull down streets the fire did not perfectly destroy? Yes, I know how you shall answer me. A good answer; but mine, better. A fair city; it is very well... if one should have the gold; if one should have the time. But those that lack a home shall they be content till your fine dream come true? And the merchants; shall they wait for your paradise while trade die?'

'There speaks the daughter of traders!' Charles said; and he was only half-laughing.

'Madam the Queen speaks good sense,' Evelyn said. 'We must do only what has to be done; and we must do it at once.'

'I'd give the rest of my life to build this city as we planned!' There was infinite regret in Wren's voice. 'But it would cost more—time and money—than even Madam the Queen could believe.' He ran a finger across the plan. 'Here. And here again, solid foundations are unharmed; whole lines of masonry. To dig them out would take more time than the homeless can afford—or our purses, either. Sir, the Queen is right. We must make use of what we can. London cannot wait and England cannot wait. Trade would surely die and we should be ruined.'

Evelyn said, above the King's downcast face, 'A dream is a good thing to have! And some of it, sir, we shall make come true.'

'Here, at least, it shall be fulfilled,' Wren said and laid a finger where St. Paul's had once stood. 'The old church was not worthy of our city. For years we've longed to build a new one; we had decided, even, upon the style. Not the old gothic—barbarous, we said. No; we should build in the noble style of ancient Rome. How they laughed, those fools with whom we discussed our plans... and some were angry. *Heathen style!* they said. *Such a church in England? Never!*'

'Oddsfish, they shall laugh the wrong side of their faces!' Charles cried out.

'Or for joy... perhaps,' Wren said.

It was not to be the London of the King's dream. Yet still it would be a good London, clean and spacious, with fine buildings of stone. And the great church, so lovely, so fit for worship, should rise rounding upon the skyline as no church in England ever before, a beacon to Londoner and a welcome to all travellers—homecoming or foreign—to the city.

Soon they would make good the damage to the city; damage to the human heart is not so easily made good. The homeless, the hungry, the workless gave tongue. Irresponsible with misery, only half-believing their own nonsense, they were content to bring danger to the most helpless, the most disliked, the most feared of their neighbours... the Catholics.

Rumours; evergrowing rumours. The fire had been started by foreigners; papist foreigners. Fireballs had been wickedly, wantonly thrown.

'There is no rest for those of my poor Faith,' Catherine told Charles. *And, when shall it reach to me? when shall it start again, the old, ugly whispering, because I am a foreigner, because in the four years of my marriage I have borne no child?*

'Patience, sweetheart. They are not yet healed of their burns, this poor people of mine. Pain looses a spiteful tongue; they care not whom they attack.'

'Not you... surely not you!'

'Myself, also.'

She stared at that. He that had stood daylong nightlong in danger; that had the skin scorched from his hands; that had emptied his pockets to feed the people!

'It makes no sense,' she said.

'Oddsfish, what's sense when the heart is sore? They do not say I burnt London with my own hands. But they do say I am glad of the fire that I may play at building... and, maybe, there's something in that! And—' his face twisted in distaste, 'they say I went down to the fire to rejoice over the ruined city that killed my father!'

'Oh!' and she wrung her hands, 'Ingrateful, wicked! I am finding... I find... no word.'

'There needs none from you!' And there was tenderness in his voice. 'I know your heart, Kate. If you had your way you'd see me enthroned among the angels.'

'Not yet, sir. One throne... it is enough!' She tried to laugh; she found herself crying instead upon his shoulder.

In moments like this, she thought, moments of trust, of tenderness, surely we build for the future. But what future? When shall it be? Shall it be when the flesh troubles us no more? Then he will not be this same Charles; nor I, myself neither! I am young and I love him now... *now!*

XX

Rumour thickened. The Papists were plotting the country's downfall; and now it was not only the foreigners, but Englishmen—Englishmen, if you could call them so! They meant to assassinate the high officials, to murder the King, to hand the country over to the Bishop of Rome. And it was not only the ignorant that believed the tales. There was fear everywhere and there was anger; anger, most of all against the King that, with foolish indulgence, had left the way open to such vile plotting.

Blame their King that had spent himself in their service! Catherine found it hard to bear.

'We must be patient,' Charles said. 'The people have suffered too much. First the plague and then the fire. And the result? Prices rising. Price of food—of flour, of meat. Price of wool, of wood; of every day-to-day need. And we are still at war with the Dutch and with the French. We are menaced; we are poor—no money. These things cannot make for a gentle humour.'

'But anger against you; you that work only for their good. Can they not *see?*'

'An empty belly clouds the eye!' Charles said.

An empty belly was, indeed, clouding many eyes.

Mutiny in the air.

Charles rode alone to the Strand to face the hungry mob. Its anger he could understand. It is hard to be patient when backside goes bare and children cry for bread. But for all that he must beseech their patience. Let them trust him. Let them go about their lawful business and they should be paid—every penny! He swore it; and he meant it—he with but three cravats to his name. If not punishment must follow; the only punishment for mutineers—the gallows.

So honest he looked, so debonair—and withal so set upon his will, they gave him three cheers and went their ways.

Lacking ships, fighting-men pinched with hunger, the Fleet set out to meet the Dutch—the Dutch in full fighting-trim, well ordered, ships and plenty of them; men well-fed, well-paid—fighting cocks. The Dutch sailed up the Thames. They stormed Sheerness; they sailed up the Medway. London shook to the thunder of their guns. They broke through the chains set to keep them out. They burned the English ships within the port. They sailed off again with—unendurable insult—the *Royal Charles* towed behind them.

Ships burnt in their own backyards! The English bowed their heads in shame. Not so their King. He was here, he was there, he was everywhere. He was looking to the forts, he was examining his ships, he was encouraging his men to fight and fight again. But it was not easy; the men were still unpaid.

In London preachers prophesied doom upon a wicked nation; naked men ran this way and that throughout the streets carrying fire of coal upon their heads. Londoners, fearing yet another raid, hid their wealth. Prudent Mr. Pepys buried his treasure within his garden. Charles had no treasure to bury.

And everywhere the rumours. *The King means to use the army to overthrow the government. The King puts the country's revenues into his own pocket. The King has fled the country....*

Charles spoke his mind in Parliament. 'I am too much of an Englishman to wish to govern by anything but law. As for my revenues—I have never received the sum you promised; and the little I had in my private purse I have poured into maintaining the army and the navy.'

Mr. Commissioner Pepys of the Admiralty, at his wits' ends for money and inspired by strong liquor, spoke eloquently in the House. He talked himself into tears and Parliament into a grant; 'a small grant but better than a kick in the backside,' Charles said.

In November Charles gave a ball in honour of the Queen's birthday. She was twenty-eight and looked younger; but it seemed to her a great age. She could not think she had given Charles or the country much cause for joy... there was, as yet, no sign of the longed-for child. She could not but wonder, also, whether in this time of hardship and unrest a ball should be given at all.

'Yes, it is wise,' Eliza said. 'It puts an end to the absurd rumour that the King has fled. And, moreover, he needs relaxation. He works himself to death upon the nation's business—though the people don't know it, so smiling he is, so easy. Surely, Madam, we'll not grudge him a little pleasure!'

'For eight months we have been in mourning for Madam your mother,' Maria Penalva said. 'Now it is time for a little joy.'

She was being laced into a new gown of white and silver—the King's present and heaven knew how he was to pay for it!—when Charles came in. He wore an old suit of black and white satin; it became him well. He looked debonair, he looked young; the periwig with its dark flowing curls gave him back the years he had lost. Her heart turned over with love; he smiled upon her with pleasure—he had chosen the gown well; she was in looks tonight.

Light streamed from crystal chandeliers upon black and white and silver; no other colour for a court in half-mourning. Yet the full court-dress a-glitter with jewels, with decorations, was as unlike mourning as one could imagine. It had almost a carnival air; it lifted the heart like wine.

Catherine sat smiling and gracious. She smiled upon James and his wife, heavy and handsome both and a little over-size in cloth of silver; she smiled with especial warmth upon Eliza and Ormonde. She smiled upon them all, the court ladies and their gallants; yes, even upon Buckingham and his wife—whom for all her trying she could not like. Yes, she thought, it is time for a little joy.

She had forgotten *that woman*... but for the moment, only.

Suddenly she was there, my lady Castlemaine, outfacing them all; the full breasts above the low white gown challenged the eye. And everywhere—head and breast, hand and arm, jewels flashed; her harvest over the years, filched, coaxed or shamelessly demanded from the King—a King so poor that some recognised their own gifts to him brazenly displayed. She poisoned the Queen's pleasure; nor did she appear to add to the King's.

He made no sign that he saw her. He had suffered over-much humiliation from this woman. The child she carried beneath her girdle was, very like, not his own. It might be Jermyn's or Buckingham's or Churchill's... or her own footman's even; she was not delicate when the flesh drove. He'd not own the child she carried, let her threaten as she would! At the memory of those wild threats he sickened.

And she stood unmoving. Skin yellow against her white gown, eyes set in stained skin proclaimed her pregnancy; that pregnancy she had always flaunted made more bitter her humiliation. She stiffened with pride. It will pass. *Soon I'll have him on his knees again. And then he shall pay for this. God damn him—how he shall pay!*

The red burning in her sallow cheeks, she moved backwards, found a place among the less notable ladies; the haggard dark-blue eyes shifted a little.

The Queen's eyes followed, rested upon Frances Stuart lovely and young; so young, scarce nineteen. In clouds of grey and white she moved like a goddess; and, like a goddess, was adorned with a crescent of stars. Charles was looking at the girl; he was hopelessly lost. James' touch upon his arm recalled him. Like a man in a dream he offered his hand to the Queen; and though he kept his eyes fixed upon the dance, she knew well where his heart wandered. *What use all his kindness? What use?*

Of all the beauties of the court Catherine feared Frances Stuart most; and with cause. The girl was young and lovely; she was virgin and gentle. She was a Stuart... and Minette had sent her.

Charles loved Minette above all living things—her wit, her courage, her gaiety, her beauty and her gentleness... but he could not marry Minette. Was this the cause of his hunger for women? *Is he forever seeking that which he can find in Minette, alone?* The question struck at her; struck and struck again.

Quiet above her fears she watched Frances. That the country would welcome the King's divorce from a barren Queen she had known ever since her last miscarriage. Now she was to learn— Mary Buckingham taking care not to lower her voice in the next room—that, especially, the country would welcome a Stuart Queen. If Charles could win the girl—then his wife had lost him for ever.

And what woman had held out, ever, against him? The wonder was that this young creature had held out so long.

Charles spoke no word of divorce though Buckingham was forever at his ear. But he burned with his passion. He was restless, he was melancholy. Once he had kissed Frances in corners; now he kissed her openly. Why not? She was his cousin. But it was not as a cousin that he kissed her. He issued new coins. The court said it was that he might have her forever under his hand; for he commissioned Rôtier, his royal medallist, to engrave her as Britannia. And there she sat with helmet and trident—a figure, Charles said, to hold Englishmen forever enchanted. He could not endure her out of his sight. He pursued her with offers. Her cousin and his, Lennox, had offered to make her his duchess—duchess of Richmond. But the King would make her duchess in her own right.

'A duchess; in her own right!' Catherine choked upon her anger.

'She'll not accept,' Penalva said.

As always, when alone, they spoke their own tongue, though Penalva, too, had some English. Catherine, indeed, now spoke well; but, though for the most correct, it came more slowly to her lips; and the pretty foreign accent must always proclaim her foreign birth. When deeply moved she found it hard to make this new language bear the full weight of her passion. With Penalva she did not have to try. It was a comfort to both to talk together in their own tongue.

'She'll not accept,' Penalva said again. 'She's ambitious, that one! She'll not rest till she be a Queen.'

'You do her wrong!' Catherine cried out sharp with fear. 'She'll not lie with any man save in the marriage-bed; no, not though it should make her a Queen... and that she can never be!'

Can she not? The question was instant in Penalva's mind. She said, slow and heavy, 'Buckingham works for her.'

'Yes,' the Queen said and there was no colour in her cheeks. They had heard, both of them, Buckingham's foul offer to kidnap the Queen and ship her off to the Indies. Then, she being safe out of the way, he would put it about that she had run from the King. So it would leave the way open to divorce.

'To run from my husband; who shall believe such a tale, shameful alike to the King and to me? And who should tell it but Buckingham that's known for a liar and my enemy? Who shall believe him?'

But they knew both of them that plenty would pretend to believe him—and not only his toadies; not only Rochester and Sedley and the rest of the King's dissolute friends, but men of greater weight that, for the good of the country, desired the divorce and would welcome any step to secure it.

'They do not know the King,' Catherine said. 'His fancy may lead him... will... will o' the wisp these English call it. But his good heart must always send him home. Divorce. To a Christian soul the very word is shame.'

Penalva said, very slow, 'Bristol, the wicked man that once tried to wreck your marriage, is now bent upon that same business. He has sent two friars home—yes, to Lisbon; they will bring back the news—these holy men, their tongues, well-greased—that your marriage was a cheat. They will say—Madam, my darling, forgive me—that you are barren and that you knew it; you and your mother, both. There are those, their tongue well-oiled, will swear to it.'

'The King shall give them the lie!' The scarlet ran swift in the Queen's cheeks. 'I have quickened three times and the King knows it. There is no reason, no reason at all, I should not bear a child. The King knows that also; the physicians have told him.'

'Yes,' Penalva said. 'Yes... but if the lie be repeated often enough?'

If it be repeated often enough... what then of Charles? Would he stand against the voice of the people? How long—let them speak loud enough—could he stand? Would he put his crown in danger? She could not think it. And more. Till she had borne a child there was no heir but York; he, too, leaned towards the blessed faith and the people knew it. If the King had no lawful child how long would the Stuart line endure?

But Frances is a Stuart and Frances is lovely and Frances is young... The thought rang in the Queen's head as clear as though someone had spoken in the room. She could endure it no longer; she dismissed Penalva and knelt once again importunate in prayer... *Sweet Mother of Jesus have pity; intercede with Him that He send me a child...*

For Charles she desired it because it must make safe the crown. For herself she desired it because the child would be his. The crown was well enough; to be his wife was better. Were he to be sent once more upon his travels she would follow him though her feet bled upon the stones.

The clamour against the Queen grew louder, angrier; it reached out against Clarendon—a powerless Clarendon that, by the King's kindness, sat yet in the place of honour. It reached out against his daughter and against York that had married her. *Clarendon arranged the King's marriage because he knew the Infanta was barren... because he meant his daughter to be the mother of Kings... maybe... a Queen herself.*

In vain Charles protested that he had married against the old man's advice; that he had married to further the trade of the country and to fill his own pockets... and because the Infanta had pleased him. Neither Parliament nor the country believed him; Clarendon must go.

'They'll never forgive the old man for selling Dunkirk. It was sound policy; yet still it sticks in the gullet,' Eliza said.

'No lie too... too... foul to beat a poor old man,' Catherine said in her careful English. 'Now it is Tangier... my Tangier. They are saying he does mean to sell it to Spain; but, poor man, he has no more the power. But at the same time they make complains of the cost.'

'The cost is high, Madam. Always we must defend it against pirates from Morocco.'

'I know. Better to give it back to my own country where it does belong. But no. Nothing shall please this ingrateful people!' And remembered how, everywhere, they bawled their filthy rhyme.

Three sights to be seen,
Dunikirk, Tangier... and a barren Queen.

It was cruel. It struck to the heart. It showed her where she stood—a disaster among disasters.

Eliza said, seeing the Queen's shadowed face, 'Madam, you take things too much to heart.'

'Do I? *Can* I—a foreigner of the hated faith... and childless?'

'The people do but bark, Madam. A barking dog, they say, never bites.'

'I cannot endure the noise of their barking.'

But still she must endure it.

And still Charles burned for Frances Stuart. He might, amidst public rejoicings, have cast off the Queen and married the girl. But he had a sense of justice; and he had an ever-growing value for his Queen. There were times when Catherine, weary to the heart and remembering the old sweet days of childhood, wondered whether it were not better to cast away the world, to enter a convent.

She asked Penalva. She asked Eliza.

'Offer to God what is not good enough for a man! That is not love of God but love of yourself; it is anger because you are not the only woman in your husband's bed!' For the first time Penalva spoke severely to her beloved child. 'To retire to a convent would mend nothing. I tell you, Madam, very clear—devout you are; but you have no vocation. The religious life is not for you.'

Eliza said, 'It would help nothing. The King would make the little Stuart a duchess but never a Queen; she is not the stuff of Queens and he knows it. You have more royalty in your little finger than she, in her whole body.'

'Yet it is a body that serves her well. What use a little finger in love?'

'You would not change places with her, Madam, if you could!' Penalva said. 'You are a Queen and you are a wife.'

But I am not a mother... I am not a mother.

Frances had refused the King's offer to make her a duchess.

'You are right; you are very right!' Buckingham said, forever at her ear. 'Who would be a duchess that might be a Queen?'

But Charles, for all he burned with passion, had breathed no word, ever, as to that. 'He would not so dishonour himself,' Frances said. 'Nor the Queen; nor me; nor me, neither.'

'Wait till you get into bed with him!' Buckingham said coarse and laughing.

She lifted her arm; she struck him full in the face.

When once again Charles sought her out she said—and the colour flooded her pale face, 'I ask the King's pardon; I have no mind to share my bed with half-a-dozen others.'

'To find a husband that shall be faithful—even to so lovely a creature as yourself!' He shrugged. 'You might as well seek the philosopher's stone—which never existed and never will! And, moreover, what would you do with a faithful husband? Stuarts have large appetites—you should know that for yourself. If not—' he shrugged again, 'our cousin Lennox must surely have taught you!'

Again the scarlet flamed in her face. A few nights ago Charles had come, unexpected to her chamber—*that woman*, she was sure, had sent him. He had all-but caught Lennox in her bed. Lennox, thank God, had been clothed again; but she'd had only a bedgown to cover her nakedness. Charles had turned on his heel; he was gone and not a word spoken... but, within the hour, Lennox had left the court.

She said—and she held out her two hands as though for pity, 'I am weary to the bone of loneliness, of poverty. Lennox would marry me tomorrow—let the King give the word.'

'Lennox—let me remind you—has buried two wives; he was faithful to neither. Have you a mind to meet that same fate?'

She said—and her little head was high, 'Were Lennox my husband, I'd keep him faithful, never doubt it... he, or some other good gentleman, so he have fifteen hundred a year.'

'A little sum to buy so much beauty.'

'Oh,' and she was desperate now, 'with all what you are pleased to call my beauty, there's no man but one will marry me. They fear you, sir.'

'Fear... *me*?' His eyebrows quirked.

'Yes,' she said. 'What man dare take the King's choice; what jackal feed on lion's meat?' Her eyes, her lovely childlike eyes were steady upon him. 'Buckingham's been whispering a thing I do not like.'

'And has been well-clipped for his pains—so I hear.'

'Was it not deserved? Hark you, sir, I'll take no woman's husband; that was never my game!' She looked at him standing there so debonair, so charming and so sad. In spite of herself the words burst forth. 'Would to God it were!'

He took a step forward; small hands against his breast, beat him back.

'You love me, Franchie,' he said. 'Can you deny it.' And caught at her frantic hands.

She leaned against his breast; she could fight no more. She took the kisses that fell upon forehead and cheek and mouth... they were the last she would ever take. After this she must go thirsting till her death.

'*Can* you deny it?' be asked between kisses.

How could she deny it, there against his heart? She pulled herself free. Now, now she could deny it! But the lying words would not be spoken. She lifted her white, childish face.

'What woman could not love you?' she said; and, when he would have taken her again in his arms said—and she was shivering a little, 'It is no use, no *use*! I'll take the first offer. A woman must marry; and most of all, I must marry. I am a Stuart; we have our appetites... yourself has said it.'

He looked at her. She meant what she said. Frail and young, she was yet firm with purpose.

He said, and there was wonder in his voice, 'So fair... and so unwilling.' Suddenly he was bitter. 'Would God I might see you ugly and willing! But—' and he laughed, 'the one's as likely as t'other!'

'Ugly and willing.' And there was the ghost of a smile on her lips. 'Well, I could wish it too... almost; if it gave you peace. Would it do that, sir? Would it give you peace?'

'Oddsfish, who knows? I never kissed a plain woman in my life! But you are not any woman; you are Franchie; and plain or beautiful, willing or unwilling, I love you!'

She said, 'They hold me for a fool because I laugh at little things. But is it better to weep for what I cannot have? We are not free to love, you and I; nor never shall be. They hold me for a fool, also, because I build my houses of cards. But it is good to hide one's heart somewhere, even in so frail a shelter. But you have broken into my house of cards... and I think you have broken my heart.'

And, when he could have come close again, once more beat him off. 'My heart you have broken but not my strength. Keep from me, Charles; keep from me and listen. The first good man that offers—be it Lennox or another—that man I'll take. And I'll be an honest wife; of that be sure!'

He cried out at that, harsh, as for all his kindness he could be. 'I'll not permit it. Without my permission no Stuart may wed.'

'Be not too sure of that!' she cried out frightened and defiant.

'No, I am not sure; I am not sure at all!' He sighed. 'I lack the will of my grandfather! He thrust our kinswoman Arbela Stuart into the Tower for marrying against his will... and there she died.'

'No, you are no such man!' In spite of herself she must laugh so that the small delightful sound rang in the room.

'You've will a-plenty,' she said when she was serious again. 'But it is all good-will; there's no cruelty in you!

'And now there's nothing more to say. I love you, Charles—and that I'll not deny; and, if I did, who would believe me? That you love me, maybe... for a little while. But were you so faithful to love me for ever, you are husband to another; a woman so good, so true, I'd not break her heart to ease my own. For make no mistake—her heart would break; she's not one to learn the trick of twice-loving. But I?' She lifted her lovely head; she was so exactly his Britannia that his heart turned over. 'I am over-young to have a broken heart... but not over-young to marry.'

'I'll not permit it,' he said again.

She looked at him; she could not doubt he meant it.

The Queen must help her. The Queen was good. In spite of all the scandal she had given no harsh word no cold look.

'Madam,' she entreated, 'I dare stay here no longer lest my honour be blown upon.'

'It is blown upon,' Catherine said.

'Yet still it is clean... I do not speak of Lennox, Madam.'

'Then of whom?'

'Madam the Queen knows.'

Catherine waited inimical.

'I speak, Madam... of the King.'

'Do you *dare*?' Catherine let herself go on a rare burst of anger. 'Oh you play your game; you keep the King aboil. You grant him everything... except your bed. You reap your harvest to cheat him at the last. And you do dare talk of honour! Better an honest whore than such a cheat!'

'To play such a game was never in my mind; Madam, believe it, I beseech you. I was pleased, I was flattered...' the bright head hung low. 'What woman would not be?

'Are you pleased to fancy yourself in love with him?'

'What woman would not be? Frances said again. And the Queen, pressing still for her answer, she said at last, 'I do love him... and it is no fancy... and will do till I die. Do you think it easy for me to go away? I could comfort him...'

'For a barren Queen?'

'Before God, *no*, madam!' Frances cried out white and shocked. 'But for his sister that sent me... for *Madame* he never sees and to whom now he cannot write... it is the war; for Minette he so loves. I can talk of her; I am like her... a little, they say...'

'I cannot think you waste your time in such a talk!' the Queen cried out stung. 'And you are not like her. She is virtuous; she has known no man, ever, save her husband. Shall you be able to say the same?'

'If Madam the Queen will help me.'

'How, help you?'

'My cousin Lennox... he would marry me.'

'No!' the Queen cried out, herself surprised. Lennox! That dull and drunken sot for this bright thing!

'Madam, he loves me... enough to dare the King's anger; that says enough, I think. And if I marry him *now*, I also shall say I have known no man, ever, but my husband. Give me the chance, Madam. Give us your countenance, your countenance, it's all I ask. You need not know our plans; but when I am gone intercede for the King's kindness towards us. Madam, will you do that?'

Again the Queen wanted to cry out *No!* The girl was delicate, was fine, by the King untouched. But if she remained here, at the court? She could not deny the King for ever. Already she had held out longer than any woman ever before. Let her go. But... to Lennox; to Lennox twice-widowed, Lennox drunk and lecherous?

'He will be good to me,' Frances said. 'And I will care for him—a faithful wife. So you help both him and me, Madam.'

And so I help myself! 'You do truly desire this?'

'Most truly, Madam.'

'Then I will stand your friend.'

When Frances had curtseyed and kissed the Queen's hand and gone, Catherine all-but called her back. Had it been wise to let the girl go? What new woman would Charles now pursue? Someone less true than Frances; so much was sure. So many women! What drove him? Did he, indeed, seek something he could find only in Minette? Her mind came back to Frances. How would he take the girl's flight; the girl that looked like Minette?

She was taken by a fearful jealousy of Minette. It wanted but that to add to her pain.

God help me to bear my love. Kneeling she made her prayer.

XXI

Frances had gone. She had fled to her cousin Lennox. They were married. Charles said nothing; only the yellow crept into his face and there remained. He had a jaundiced look.

A few days later he dismissed Clarendon.

It is because he had a hand in setting the King's lovebird free—they said it everywhere. It was not true. Clarendon had no finger in that matter and the King knew it. For five long years Charles had kept him against the advice of friends, of Parliament; against his own will and the will of the people. He had curbed the old man's power but still he had kept him in the seat of honour—Chancellor still.

Now the thing was beyond his power. Hatred against the old man had steadily grown. It was not only that he would not move with the times; it was not only Dunkirk and Tangier and the King's marriage. It was because he, a man of no birth, might yet see his grandchild, or—an accident, an illness—his daughter, even, a Queen. And that daughter had done nothing to win the people's love. She was cold, she was proud. Her husband was a secret Catholic—a secret everyone knew; and she, herself, as near one as made no matter. If the Queen bore no child then it looked as though a Catholic must reign over the country.

Nor had my lady Castlemaine ceased working against Clarendon. She was forever at the King, *Old… too old. He has failed in every task.*

He has set Parliament against you; through him they vote no money. Through him we suffer shame of defeat in war. Through him you will lose the love of your people. If he stay you will end in ruin... you and the country, both!

And she had the ear of the younger ministers; not that they needed much urging... the old man was a stumbling-block; shove him out of the way.

Too long you have taken upon your shoulders the burden of this old fool; now you must let him go. If you do not do it of yourself, Parliament will do it for you. Once they listened to him; now they have had enough. Parliament will impeach him; he will end in disgrace...

Disgrace for Ned Clarendon, the faithful old servant!

Charles sent for James. 'For his own honour Clarendon must resign. And the reason? Good enough. He's a sick man. Go, tell him so.'

The old man refused to listen.

'I have served my King with a most faithful love. Does he turn me off now like an old dog? Scarce that; he loves his dogs.'

There was some justice in that, Catherine thought; but she was the only one. She pleaded with the King, partly for love of justice; partly because *that woman* had set her heart on Clarendon's disgrace.

'Clarendon must go. I can protect him no longer!' Charles said. Yet still he did nothing; let the next move come from Clarendon himself. He waited patiently. At the end of the Summer he sent Mr. Secretary Morice to take away the Seal.

Clarendon would not leave London. Humiliated, heartbroken, he stayed in his fine house while great affairs went by him. Once only he came to Whitehall; came in grief and doubt where once he had come in certainty and pride. But even now pride did not fail.

'Let them bring their charges!' he cried out. 'I will face them all!' And, seeing by the grief in the King's eyes that he was not to be moved, flung himself out in anger. 'I was glad of his anger,' Charles told Catherine. 'I could not have borne his tears. But she... *she...*'

Catherine knew well whom he meant. That woman had seen the old man go by; she had run out into the privy garden in her shift and cried out good riddance; she had blessed herself that he had gone at last. How could she, even she, so hurt an old and broken man?

But it was the old man that had won—Eliza had told the tale. 'He said, *Madam, you too, will grow old*—that and no more. And he bowed and left her. She went white—like one stricken. Without another word she turned and went within.'

Charles could not get over the loss of Frances—he wore his lean and yellow look. But pride sustained him; pride and anger together. He would see her never again; she was a slut that had shot her bolt. Let her enjoy herself while she might—a third wife to that drunken sot! Let her enjoy her husband's titles, my lady Duchess of Lennox and Richmond; she wouldn't enjoy them long... the fellow was drinking himself to death. And the King would have made her a duchess in her own right!

In the spring they heard that Frances had gone down with the smallpox. *Pray God I live to see you ugly and willing...* he would give the world to unsay the hateful words. He had not himself known the depths of tenderness within him. He could not rest; he sent continually to ask how she did. She was very ill; they doubted she could recover... better, perhaps, that she did not. Her face, her lovely face; her eyes, her eyes, even closed beneath the cruel scabs... Franchie's sweet eyes...

'She may be blind. How shall she endure it, Kate?' *Or I; or I, either?*

'She has courage,' Catherine said.

Frances was out of danger. Charles went to see her; he was wild to bring her comfort, assurance of friendship; to ask forgiveness and to receive it. She refused to see him. She could not endure he should see her disfigured face. And, remorse still driving, he rowed himself alone down the Thames to Richmond House; this time he asked no question. He was over the wall and in at the door before any man could stop him.

Gentle he must have been; for when the scabs were healed, back she came to Whitehall. She was a pretty thing still—a candle where once she had been the sun. The unflawed beauty was gone; and with it the old childishness. Courage had taken its place. The old, quick gaiety had gone, too. She could laugh still; but laughter came slowly; for her eyes, her sweet eyes had not escaped. She had lost the sight of one; and, though the damage did not show, Charles could not forget it. His manner was different now; no longer the lover. He treated her with gentleness... so he might have treated Minette.

Catherine, pitying the girl and loving her courage, raised her, young as she was, to the high honour of a Bedchamber lady. Now she was forever about the Queen—old Maria, middle-aged Eliza and young Frances, sharing the Queen's love; Frances, the only one of the King's loves to give pleasure to the Queen... but then she was the only one that had never shared his bed.

Charles' prophecy came true; within two years her husband had drunk himself to death. Whether he had been good to her no-one could say; but never, now or afterwards, did any hear her speak anything but kindness of him for his love of her.

Frances was no longer in the King's desire; and *that woman's* day was, at last, coming to an end. The whole court knew it by his increased generosity. He bought property for her, he increased her revenue... but he gave her no personal presents.

'Now she is, indeed, finished!' Eliza said coming upon Frances and Penalva where they sat together. 'The King found her in bed with young Churchill.'

'I doubt he was surprised,' Frances said. 'But anger's another matter. Was it terrible?'

'Not at all. He laughed—a maid she slapped publishes the tale. *Poor fellow what a way to get his bread-and-butter!* he said, and went on laughing. Anger she could deal with; but ridicule—it must have been death to her!'

''Twas an answer much to the point!' Penalva said. 'We know, all of us, that she pays to get the young man into her bed.'

Eliza nodded. 'I cannot like her; yet I must pity her. There's a new song about her—*Allinda's growing old*. Old—at twenty-six!'

'You cannot lead the life she leads but it must leave its mark!' Penalva said.

'Soon she won't be able to afford John Churchill—he costs too much!' Eliza told them. 'He's squeezed a fortune out of her already. She'll have to look for something cheaper. The King, indeed, makes a recommendation—Jacob Hall.'

'The tight-rope dancer! Has she sunk so low? No. The King jests... but the jest is cruel,' Frances said.

'Good advice!' Eliza was brisk. 'Like herself he's a handsome animal.'

'She needed no such advice!' The Queen's voice broke in upon them. They sprang to their feet, all three dismayed; how much had she heard of the distasteful subject?

'Yes,' the Queen said and shrugged. 'Hall's no stranger to my lady! She has, indeed, sunk low. Well, we have talk... talked of *that woman* long enough!' Her nod dismissed them; she caught at Penalva's hand and drew her back.

'She's been the tight-rope walker's mistress for weeks!' The Queen found relief in her own tongue. 'That same maid she slapped tells all. But she—*that woman*—shameless! She'll hang about the court to plague us all. And the King will laugh and allow it. He's over-kind.'

'Would you have him less kind, Madam, my child?'

'Yes. To her and her like! And to me, to me also!' she cried out, passionate and wild. 'What use his *kindness*? Let him love me a little... only a little and I'd not care if kindness failed. Love is cruel; I know it, I! Well, cruelty and love—I'd welcome both. But six years married and his kindness never fails. I am sick to the bone of his kindness.'

'When kindness meets kindness, something precious is born... love, maybe, a wise love... rich. Such love needs time to grow; but, like a rock, it stands for ever.'

But I am hungry now; I starve. What use some distant doubtful feast? A crumb, it's all I ask... a crumb now... now.

Tears pricked Catherine's eyes; she did not brush them away—Penalva could not see them. The cataracts were thick; she looked frail; very old. She longed for her own land—though that she'd never admit. Of Penalva's own selfless kindness something precious had, indeed, been born—the love that may be between mother and child. Catherine would cherish this precious kindness for a little... a little yet; then she must make the sacrifice. Penalva must go home.

The King took no new mistress. No-one now the Queen need fear. Yet still she feared. He was much drawn to play-actresses; Moll Davies and Nell Gwynn—he was sleeping with them both; but he was not deeply involved with either. Moll had a fine house and a fine coach with gowns and jewels to match; but she was never received at

Whitehall as a guest; she was there only to entertain the court with her charming voice.

But Nell was another matter. Nell was always about the court. Ignorant folk said the Queen had made her a Bedchamber lady; but that was because they wished her well. Everyone knew Nell. The beggars knew her and the linkboys and those down on their luck—and all of them to their advantage. The gallants knew her, though—since the King had taken her up—not as well as they could wish. She was the toast of the town; even her rivals had a good word for Nell; all except *the lady* who jeered at *gutter-breeding*. But that didn't offend Nell; she never played the fine lady—though, when she chose, her manners were better by far than my lady Castlemaine's. She'd been born in a cellar, as a child she had hawked fish; she was ashamed of neither. She had served in a brothel and kept her virtue; she had sold oranges to the hot bloods at Covent garden and kept it still. She had become an actress... and lost it. She was not ashamed of that either. To be an actress you must be prepared to pay something! She was fresh, she was gay. She had a sweet, warm, slightly husky voice; she had a light foot and a shapely bosom. She excelled in comic roles and her laugh was lovely. She was the idol of audiences and a favourite wherever she went—a mighty, pretty soul, said Mr. Pepys that judge of women. She held Charles as much by her wit and kindness as by her charming body. A mistress so honest, so natural had never, till now, graced the court.

The court enjoyed her and the King needed her. When cares pressed hard she eased him with her wit and laughter. Catherine knew it and endured Nell with courtesy. It was a courtesy returned. Nell spared no-one else her jests, not even the King; but to the Queen she behaved with deep respect.

Nell bore the King a pretty boy. Catherine wept when she heard it. The King's women she could endure if she must! These Molls and Nells were thorns in the flesh; but the children, the children broke her heart.

Yet he trusts me a little, cares for me a little; and I am his wife. There was some comfort in that! For, however late the hour, he came every night to his wife's bed. Yet there was never a night but she lay awake envying the woman that kept him. And when he came at last, even in his arms, jealousy pricked still; but it was a pricking not a tearing jealousy.

The Queen was with child. She was unceasing with her thanks to Heaven; and not only upon her knees. At meat, at music, at cards—wherever she might be—she would stop to remember her thanks to Mary and to St. Catherine. She blossomed, she bloomed; she felt like Mary after the Annunciation. The joy of all England matched her own; only Buckingham scowled as she passed and wished her a miscarriage.

Charles was a reformed man; the court saw nothing of his mistresses. Even Nell had disappeared... into a pretty house close at hand. He was the most gentle, the most cherishing of husbands. Yet it was through him that he and she—and all England with them—lost this last hope.

He had a passion for animals; to him they were human—and more lovable than most humans. He allowed them more privileges. His horses he looked to with loving care; his bitches might whelp in his own bed and suckle their young wherever they chose. He had a fox, a pretty creature that lived in the King's closet... too wild for a pet, the Queen thought. The fox thought so too; it was frantic to escape.

The Queen came into her bedchamber on a quiet evening. She had dismissed her women—even Penalva; these days she had a need to be alone with her happiness. The bed stood ready; and she desired nothing but to get into it and dream of the time when she should hold all England in her arms.

She was about to step into bed when something sprang from beneath the sheets... a grinning mask and little wicked bared teeth.

She stood staring in terror; and the creature, sensing her fear, stared back. It was when she opened her mouth to scream that her own terror struck back upon the creature's heart. Mad to escape, it leaped from the bed; and so leaping, knocked against the Queen. Weak with her terror she fell to the floor.

That night she had a miscarriage. There was no hope of a child now.

She thought she should never recover from her grief. She lay abed and there was no comfort anywhere—not in her priest, nor in Penalva who would have died to bring a smile; and, for the first time, none in Charles himself. The very sight of him brought on paroxysms of weeping so that she wept heart and strength away. She never reproached him; but there were times when she must bite upon her tongue to keep back the bitter words.

But he could not sufficiently blame himself. So when Buckingham began once more to whisper of divorce, Charles turned upon him in anger. And once he cried out, 'If my conscience allowed me to put away the Queen, then it would allow me to put her out of the world altogether. I'll hear no word on the matter; never dare to mention it again!' And it was not only Buckingham that felt the weight of his anger. He would allow no-one to hint, even, that having no children was a fault in the Queen. Once she would have reddened at such public talk; now she must turn to hide the tears that there would be no child now nor perhaps—ever.

But it was not all conscience with him. He knew her love and her loyalty; he valued her wise head and her discreet tongue. And she was a pretty woman still... though sometimes he was inclined to forget it; then Huysmans his court painter that never tired of painting her must remind him. 'The perfect Madonna, sir. Those eyes—so dark and gentle; and the sweetness and the courage that can make sorrow into strength... a young face; yet all experience lies there.' And, 'My most charming Venus. Perfect the neck and shoulders; and the prettiest arms and feet in the world. As for the face—always it holds new delights for eyes that can see.' An exaggeration, perhaps; but a court painter is expected to flatter; he sent Charles looking from portrait to model and back again... yes, there was a charm! He would come more eager to her bed.

XXII

Too many problems pressing upon one man.

The shame of the Medway to be wiped out; the dragging Dutch war brought to a victorious conclusion. But how? There was no money. For ships, for arms, for men—no money. The country was slipping and sliding into bankruptcy; and because of it—always the threat of mutiny, of revolution. England's good name must be restored together with her prosperity... Hercules trying to carry the world on his shoulders! *I am no Hercules* Charles thought, rueful.

And his own personal troubles aggravated his difficulties.

No child of his would ever wear the crown—he knew it now. No heir but James; and for James he would have to fight. James had not yet declared his faith—no need; it was an open secret. Now the country looked upon him with a jaundiced eye; his superb courage, his unmatched seamanship, his victories—forgotten; forgotten, all, in dislike of his religious faith. How long before dislike hardened into hatred?

He would find himself, at times, playing with a thought. Were it not wiser to give up the struggle, to resign the crown before they took it from him... and his life, too, perhaps? Then he would be free—a free man; free to worship as he chose, to devote himself to the arts and sciences—above all the sciences. There a man could serve his country well. But even while he played with the pleasant thought, he knew it was impossible. He had been called to a King's work; and that work he would do. Every year should see things better; if only a little better—the Dutch war ended with honour, religious freedom coming ever nearer, the country growing into stable prosperity. With patience it could all be done. See how, inch by inch, London rose beautiful upon its ashes. It showed what a man could do, let him have courage.

But it needed more than courage, more than patience. Ever-changing politics abroad and never-changing disaffection at home; these things needed a clear and subtle mind. It meant the careful weighing of friendship with one country against another...

He smiled a little though the smile was wry.

Here he was a lazy, happy-go-lucky sort of man; and he must scheme and plan and plot to get his way.

France grows ever more powerful; she advances across the Spanish Netherlands. How does this affect us? He asked Clifford and Arlington; asked Buckingham and Ashley and Lauderdale—his ministers men called the Cabal. But it was, after all, an answer he must find for himself. He found it in the Queen's closet, talking not to her, but to himself; working it out step by step, finding peace in her quiet.

Peace with France—the only answer. But the people hate France. Then peace with Spain—the people would prefer it. But... if France beat Spain? Then we have an enemy instead of a friend across the Channel...

Spain was beaten in the Netherlands—and that settled Spain. Now the choice of friend lay between France and Holland.

Make peace with the Dutch against the French? But safety lies with France; the country's safety... and my own. The little matter of my secret friendship with Louis...

While he hesitated France and Holland might come to terms. And then?

They will share the Spanish Netherlands between them. France will be topdog on land, Holland on sea. And England, my poor England? Nowhere. Nowhere at all!

With doubt and misgiving he made his choice.

Peace with Holland; a pact of friendship to stand together, at need; and, to strengthen the alliance—Sweden. It marched well with Dutch plans—France was growing altogether too powerful, too close a neighbour. And it pleased the English, this triple alliance—Protestant against Catholic.

But for all that Charles was deeply troubled. He had sworn a secret friendship with France; he had taken French gold and spent French gold. Suppose Louis made known that secret friendship, that secret passing of gold?

Beset with difficulties he carried himself in public with his easy, smiling charm. No-one would guess, Catherine thought, of the weary hours pondering his problems, the sleepless nights.

Of all his difficulties, the most pressing was still money.

'So many hungry men demanding their wages! If Parliament doesn't open its hand there'll be mutiny. I quieted them once; I doubt I could do it again. *Mutiny.* That means hangings... and the poor devils not to blame!' His dark face was heavy with compassion.

What now? There was but one answer... the old answer. French gold... secret gold. And this new triple alliance? Louis and he would deal with that when the time came. He must go cap-in-hand to Louis once again.

Minette was coming. Charles was like a schoolboy; he could scarce contain himself until the beloved little sister should arrive.

'To all the world it's naught but a visit—natural enough between brother and sister that have not clapped eyes upon each other for nigh on ten years. But Kate, there's more to it than that!'

She nodded; she had guessed as much.

'It's a secret I dare whisper to none but you. Thank God for a wife I can trust.' He lifted her hand and kissed it. 'You—and one other. Arlington; a true friend. I lean upon his counsel.'

'My sister comes to seal a new friendship between Louis and me—and God knows we need it! I have been troubled—tormented's the better word—lest France stand with Holland against us. Lest they divide the Spanish Netherlands between them. It could leave us with out a friend.'

'And Louis... you trust him?'

He nodded. 'Louis gains also. He strengthens his own hand against the Dutch, and my weasel-faced nephew of Orange that leads them. Louis needs my friendship as much—almost—as I need his. And he's prepared to pay for it. A great sum; a very great sum. And God knows we need it! But let the breath of a whisper leak out—and finished; finished, England and me together.'

Yes, she knew that! The slightest suspicion would bring Spain and Holland—both, stinging about their ears. As for himself—let the country know that he twisted the slant from Catholic to Protestant— and it might well be the end of him altogether!

'Then you must go—how do you say it? on the point of the toes? Your people see you now at the head of a Protestant league; it does you much good. So you do grow in their love; that is a King's strongness.'

'Strength!' Charles smiled. 'This friendship with France—it is of the greatest good; not to me, alone, but to all England. Were it not so, oddsfish, I'd not touch it. It is a great design; my *grand design* I call it. We have agreed upon the terms; Minette brings them for me to sign. Wish me luck, Kate.'

'Your luck is my luck. But, indeed, I am pleased; France was always a good friend to my country and to me.'

'One thing troubles me. A promise to enter the Catholic faith. Louis demands it. And I—I should like it, also.'

And I! And I! She bit back the words. That he, her dear love, should share her faith was too great a happiness; his soul was dearer to her than her own. And more. Were he to come into the Church, she would be safe. There could be no question, ever, of divorce. But still she must say nothing. It was a matter between himself and his God.

'To rest in the Church!' His sigh was deep. 'I would welcome it with all my heart. But the people would not. It is not the time and I must wait upon their will; lacking good-will I am a useless King. But Louis bids me choose my time, Louis will wait.'

Will God wait?

'Oh but it would please me to enter now!' He sighed again. 'And it would please Minette...' Something in her face touched him. 'And you, too, it would please. Minette and you—my two dearest. I am a sad husband, Kate, but that much is true.' And then, surprising himself as much as her, 'I lean upon you, Kate; your wisdom and your kindness. In France the King consults his mistress; in England—his wife.'

From Charles that boasted he allowed no woman, ever, to meddle in his affairs, words to be cherished. Might such kindliness, such trust deepen to love? She began to hope again. There was, she thought, at this moment, some chance of it. He pursued no new love. Apart from sporting with his molls he was a good husband, looking always to her comfort. There was the night, a little while since, that she would never forget; and for which she forgave him every infidelity.

She had gone to bed with a chill; it was morning when he came and she had not slept. Now, taken with nausea and fearful lest she vomit, she lay stiff and cold. So different from this her usual welcoming that he raised himself upon the pillow. By the light that burned before her clock, he saw how it was with her. He was out of bed, not staying for the warmth of his bedgown, and, quick as a cat was back again, carrying a basin. Before she could lean towards it, the sickness had defeated her.

Fastidious as she was, she was overwhelmed with shame; she covered her face with her hands and could not look at him. He took them away gently; he said, very kind, 'Even the saints are human!' And brought a damp towel to sponge hands and face. That done, he sponged the soiled sheets and placed beneath them another towel,

173

clean and dry. It was odd to see him about such homely business. He lifted her gently and placed her on the clean side of the bed—his own side. Then, only, did he remember his bedgown and her women.

It was not until he had seen her comfortable and cared-for that he went to his own rooms; snuggled into his warmth she fell asleep at once. When she awoke Penalva told her that, before he allowed himself to sleep, the King had come three times to see how she fared.

How, Catherine wondered, could one help but love such a man?

May; and the year of Grace sixteen-hundred-and-seventy. And Minette come at last.

When Catherine saw this sister of Charles' she was conscious of both disappointment and a rather mean pleasure. The adored Minette was not as beautiful as they said; she was not beautiful at all. The Queen saw a thin, pale young woman who, at twenty-six, looked little younger than herself at thirty-two. Then Minette smiled.... *She is a crystal lamp when it is lit; she is a glass of golden wine set in the firelight; she is a jewel brought from a dark room...*

She tried to describe Minette to Penalva who could no longer see for herself. 'She has a look of Frances; the same eyes, the same bright curls. Not so beautiful as Frances you might think—Minette is pale and frail. And suddenly she is lit from within and Frances cannot hold a candle to her. She is eager, she is lovely; she is fire and air... all spirit. And I know why the King loves her with so deep a love. She is himself; she has his grace, his quickness—heart and mind. His better self—so he sees her; purged of every fault.'

Minette was to have four days in England; her unloving husband had grudgingly agreed. But the matter was delicate; she might stay a fortnight if need be—the King of France had said it. Carefree, it seemed, amidst all the gaiety, an anxious Charles weighed every word in the treaty.

'A good treaty,' he told Catherine at last. 'We are pledged to help each other. I stand with him against Spain—which should please you, Kate. He stands with me against the Dutch. If it should please him to declare war against the Dutch, then I declare war also. In that case he pays me three million gold crowns a year as long as the war lasts... but I doubt it will arise. Meanwhile we observe, in public, our present alliances—he with Spain; I with Holland and Sweden.'

She nodded. 'There is something else?'

'I am to make public confession of the Catholic faith; in that I cannot move him. And for that he gives me, myself, two million golden crowns at once.'

That he was to make profession of her faith at last, filled her with joy; yet it was spoiled that faith could be bought and sold.

He was quick to guess at the shadow on her face. 'I do not sell my soul,' he said. 'You know my heart in the matter.'

'But your people; how shall they take it?' she was anxious.

'I announce it at my pleasure. It cannot be my pleasure... yet.' He grinned. 'Come now, Kate, it's a good bargain. I am bound in open friendship with Holland and Sweden; in secret friendship with France. So I secure both Protestant and Catholic friendship. That makes this country strong; stronger than it has ever been... and it will be wonderful to have money in my pocket.'

'Minette has done well. Sharp wits hidden beneath those charms; your true sister!'

'And yours, also, I trust?'

'Mine also. We have come close, she and I.'

Their last speech together Catherine would treasure to the end of her days.

Minette was lying back in a great chair, bright head against the cushions, eyes closed. When Catherine came softly into the room, the eyelids flew open; Minette smiled. She smiled with her whole self—flesh and spirit; it was her chief charm.

'Catérine,' she spoke with the prettiest accent of France, 'I am glad; I am so glad you are wife to Charles. Once I thought no woman good enough; now I say you are, perhaps, too good.'

She caught at the Queen's hand; Catherine saw how thin Minette's hand, now lacking in strength.

'You are best in the world for him,' Minette said. 'He does not always know his true best but he will learn; he will learn! Have patience with him, sister—with women he is much to blame. But there is something within him that seeks and seeks... and what that is he does not know.'

He seeks you, Minette… his best self.

'Yet he will surely find it in you, Catérine—give him time. You are his sure refuge and he knows it. Never, but never would he let you go—oh yes, one hears the talk; such stupid, *stupid* talk! If you do not, of yourself leave him, he is yours now and for always.'

She lay back and the blue-veined lids fluttered down; like Christmas roses, Catherine thought.

Suddenly she sat up. 'Never let them part you, Catérine. *Promise!* It is for him I ask and not for you—though I value you with all my heart. You are strong and you are wise and you see life steady. He needs you—your wisdom, your strength and your truth. And your love… you love him, Catérine, so much.

'When we are green we ask to be loved; when we are wise we ask to be let to love. To be let to love—it is the reason for living—the greatest good thing in life. To love and to be loved—that is Paradise.' She was silent a little; then she said, 'Charles loves you—not so much as you deserve; but still it is love—though, I think, he does not, as yet know it himself. One day he will understand. You are his harbour and his home; and home he will come in the end.'

'In the *end*?' Catherine's smile was wry.

'It is worth the waiting. As for me—let me wait till Judgment Day—there's no hope nor never was. They married me to a monster.' A shudder took her slight frame. 'I have not spoken of this, ever, not even to my brother; but I speak of it to you, my sister. Orléans has no need of women. Like his father, like his grandfather, he loves boys. He and his boys! They teeter on high heels, they giggle like girls, they are forever at their kissing. Always there is one of them in his bed. And I and my household must pay them respect. For me he cares nothing—save to torment me and put me to shame. To leave him for four days, four little days—he would not allow it. Escape from him even for so short a time, never! But Louis commanded…'

She stopped. She said, slowly, 'Louis would make me his mistress—me, his brother's wife. It would add a flavour to his love-making; his palate's jaded. The English court, they say is over-free, *lewd*. Visitors have brought us word. But it is innocence and light compared with the court of France. Would God!' she cried out with sudden passion, 'I might stay at home forever—I count myself English; Exeter born, did you know that? I was carried into France a babe-in-arms; it was when the rabble took my father. And in France I have lived all my life. I speak French speech, have French manners, wear French fashions. I speak English like a foreigner... but I have an English heart. Home is where the heart is. When shall I come home again?'

She lay back. So worn she looked, so white, Catherine's heart misgave her. When Minette spoke again it was of something quite other.

'I love Charles the wrong side of worship... his smile, his eyes, his hand, his whole beloved body; but dearer still—his soul. I could endure to see him never again, could I be sure of one thing. If I could know him safe within the Church I'd die content.'

'Die?' Catherine said a little sharp. 'Who talks of dying? Not you—and all your life before you!'

'Did I say die? I did not mean it. A trick of speaking because I am tired... tired and troubled. Catérine, help him; help him to save his soul. When you win to heaven—as surely you will—shall you be happy knowing him forever lost? Win him; win him for God!'

'It is my heart's wish. But I dare not stand between the King and his people.'

'Dare you stand between a man and his God?'

'I do not; nor I could not. He must himself find God. And Charles shall find Him... has found Him, I think, though he does not say it aloud. It is not yet time.'

'That's my Charles!' Minette sighed from the heart. 'He leans towards God but cannot take hold of Him. He has tolerance towards all faiths—which is faithfulness to none. He will wait till great sorrow strike; then he will run to God. See that he run in time, Catérine; let him not run too late!'

'Never trouble your heart...' Catherine said and stopped. Minette's lids had dropped; surprisingly she was asleep. For a few minutes she slept quiet as a child; then she awoke, knowing at once the time and place.

'If I have troubled you, Catérine, forgive me... but do not forget me. As to my brother's soul—you are right. It is between himself and God; no man can mend or mar. But for the rest—there I am right. You are his home and his harbour—himself has told me; remember it.'

She rose from his chair with that quick grace of hers. 'A ball!' She flung her arms in a yawn above her head. 'Heigho, I must go dress! I *adore* a ball...' and now she was rosy and laughing as a child.

Catherine thought long of this astonishing Minette that, from her own ashes, could rise like a phoenix. She had seen Minette's heart as none ever before; not Charles, even. She was taken with love for the girl that was so like Charles; so loving and by him so loved.

The last, faint jealousy was gone.

XXIII

Minette had brought in her train a baby-faced blonde, small, rounded, and very young. Her golden hair curled prettily, her skin was apple-blossom. Her eyes were sea-blue; a slight cast in one added piquancy to her attractions; it lent the subtle, intriguing woman her childish look. Beneath that baby-face a cool brain worked—as Louis of France knew well. She had a gentle manner and a sweet voice; she was infinitely obliging. She carried herself with an elegant grace; but then she was of old and noble stock; yet so poor she was, the convent had seemed her only end. But friends had brought the girl to the notice of Minette and Minette had made the poor young thing a lady-in-waiting. Louise de Kérouaille had been mistress of the King of France, they said; but they said wrong—though the fault was not his. She was a virgin when she came to England—and that was not his fault, either.

Mid-June and a sweet summer's day when Minette sailed for France. There was some comfort in Catherine's grief; Minette would take her lady with her. For Charles, though discreet, had not been discreet enough. There had been glances and whispering in corners; but, Catherine thought, and rightly, not much harm done. She had taken her own Farewell of Minette; now she left brother and sister alone. Charles had a parting gift for his sister—a necklace finer than ever he had given to a mistress; or to the Queen, herself, for that matter. When she would have thanked him, he said, 'Give me in return one jewel; one simple jewel from your store.'

'With all my heart!' She had the endearing trick of using his very words; and called to Louise for her jewel-casket. Above Minette's head a sly glance flashed; Louise's hands still upon the casket, Charles covered them with his own. 'This is the jewel!' he said.

Troubled for Catherine, Minette said, 'I would give you anything but this. Her parents lent her to me; and—' her level glance held his, 'I must return her as I received her. Make another choice, brother.'

'This—or nothing!' And nothing it was.

And now it was time. Charles could not endure the parting. He took his sister in his arms and, between kisses, tore himself away to return again and again. And she, proud *Madame* of France, wept openly, forlorn as a child. At last, Charles turned and went within; and she, calling upon her courage, was once more, *Madame*.

Even then Charles could not let her go. Waving from the ramparts, Catherine saw the water widen between the harbour and the departing ships; saw a yacht put out, Charles' own yacht. Sails spread, the *Jenny* followed as close as she dared in the great ships' wake. And Minette? Did she, the Queen wondered, stand, eyes shaded against the Summer sun and watch that little boat that held all she loved? And when the *Jenny* turned again, did she stand watching until the cliffs of England faded... forever?

Catherine would never know; Minette would never come back to tell. The grief of parting had surely something of prophecy.

Two weeks; two little weeks—and Minette was dead.

Only once did Catherine speak of Charles' grief; and that was to Penalva. '*Stricken with grief*, these English say; and it was perfectly that. That moment, when he heard, the light went from his eyes, the colour from his mouth.' But she did not tell how he had turned upon his heel, and, speechless as though beneath a stroke, had gone to his closet; nor how she had dared follow him. No, nor how she had found him weeping bitterly—Charles the debonair, the gay; nor how all the melancholy in his nature, rising to the surface threatened to carry him away. Nor how he had turned, crying out, *He has poisoned her, Orléans, vicious Orléans has poisoned her... she was the flower of the world.*

Vicious Orléans undoubtedly was; but in this, at least, innocent. Minette had died of cholera. Yet still Charles continued his outcry. *This way or that—what does it matter? Inch by inch he murdered that sweet spirit!*

Catherine tried to hush his too-free speech. 'If you speak so, the French ambassador will go home... must, indeed, go home. So you make an end to friendship with France—and everything you hope to pluck therefrom. And it is not your hope, alone, you throw away. It was Minette's hope, her dearest; the thing that was in her heart when you said Goodbye.'

'Yes, you are right!' He sighed deeply. 'The work to which she set her hand must go on.'

His own hands were full of tricky policies. He must sign the secret treaty; yet he must appear to honour the triple alliance. He must satisfy, at one and the same time, Louis of France, Holland and his own people. Minette was dead; her work must not die with her.

Buckingham, that pernicious man, went to Versailles on the King's business—and did some on his own account. He coaxed Louise de Kérouaille to England. He did it for three reasons; and all of them, to himself, good.

Louis had made it worthwhile. But he would have done it in any case to punish his cousin—my lady Castlemaine was loud against the thing nearest his heart. Trying to wheedle herself back into the King's bed, she could see, beyond a doubt, a barren Queen was less to be feared than a new, lusty wife. My lady, the Queen's champion—no less!

And the third reason? Charles had been taken with the girl from the first; now she must be doubly dear. She had been close to Minette living, she had seen Minette die... and Minette had loved her. Buckingham meant to strengthen his waning influence with Charles through this young creature. He had forgotten the lesson Frances Stuart had taught him—that the young are not always to be led by the nose.

Charles wept when he saw Louise. Buckingham had been right on one count; for the King, the girl had a mystical tie with dead Minette.

Louise played her game well... played gentle, played quiet, played oh so grateful for notice; above all, played chaste; like ice she sparkled with chastity.

Catherine watched, troubled. Here was the strongest rival she had ever met, or was like to meet, cleverer than the Castlemaine, less honest than Frances—the little Louise so well-bred, so innocent, so chaste. She would, in the Queen's opinion, cost more than Castlemaine in happiness, in good will, in hard cash... unless she made a slip first.

But Louise made no slip.

Buckingham, the mischief-maker, pressed the King hard. Madam the Queen had not recognised the little one—an insult to the beloved dead. Gently, humbly almost, Charles besought Catherine's kindness in the matter.

'Must I begin again? Again? Must I have this sly girl forever about me?' she asked Eliza, asked Frances, asked Penalva.

'It would be wise. You could keep her beneath your eye!' Eliza said.

'Can my eye follow wherever she choose to play her games? Into the King's bed, maybe?' Catherine cried out goaded.

'You will not find her there... yet,' Frances said. 'She'll not let herself go cheap.'

'The King asks in the name of his dead sister,' Penalva said.

With no sign of anger Catherine offered Louise a place among the Maids of Honour. With no sign of anger, a humble, grateful Louise accepted. The Queen had insulted her; she should have been made a lady of the Bedchamber. Well, she would bide her time. A little patience, and she would be playing her part in the Queen's bedchamber... and in the King's also. Till then her little game of hide-and-seek would hold the King secure.

Just before Christmas Charles set hand and seal to the French alliance, his *grand design*—he was at his wits' ends for money. 'This Parliament drives me; *it drives me!*' he told Catherine. 'But make no mistake. Were I free to choose, I should long ago have come into the Catholic Church.' And then he said, 'You think, maybe, I care little either way; but I care, I care very much. When I was young I gave little thought to God; but now, as I grow older, and see every day His mercies, I am drawn more and more towards Him.'

But Charles' God, she could not but think, was a God made in his own image. *God will not punish a good fellow over-much for a little pleasure taken on the side*, he told her once. She had been shocked at first. But since He was fashioned somewhat in her image, too, she had come to think He might forgive Charles anything. She was sure, also, that, give him time, he would end truly in love with God.

Louis had paid the money; now—though he had promised Charles should choose his time—he pressed for the public profession of faith. Colbert, the French ambassador, obeying instructions, drove Charles hard. Louise, disobeying instructions, made no move to bring him to God by way of her bed. She wanted more out of Charles than that! And that more she'd get if she kept him waiting. So she continued to play hide-and-seek and waited. But drive him or no, he dared not profess his faith. Of all times this was the worst. The people, already restless, might rise. It could mean—Arlington warned him, bloody revolution. It was true. Charles knew it as well as he.

Spring came in; and still Charles had made no move.

And all the time Colbert harassed and threatened; and all the time Louise drove him frantic with her pure look. She would grant him nothing—until he had proclaimed himself of the Faith. Bed with a heretic? Not to be expected!

Her refusal drove her master in France to fury. In bed a clever woman can get anything out of a man! He sent her repeated instructions. She ignored them all. Her own cool wits were a better guide.

Catherine's quiet face gave no sign of restlessness, nor of watchfulness, even. Hard-won discipline served her well; and discipline she needed now. She knew how much that chastity was worth; knew that the court laid bets—on time and price of surrender. All these months she had tried to content herself with Charles' affection; to make herself believe it was enough. But her very blood denied it. She was thirty-three; she had been married nine years... and her husband did not love her; nor was there any child to comfort her. She prayed she might not fall into the sin of melancholy.

In the autumn the duchess of York died. Catherine had not loved her—a cold woman, that without a word, made clear her joy that the Queen was barren. Never had James' wife forgotten that her daughter Mary would be Queen in her own right; nor that, by some happy accident, herself might wear the consort's crown.

Now, dying in pain and friendless, she feared lest her girl should, after all, not be Queen. She knew very well that James would leap to the opportunity of marrying again. Never, in the eleven years of their marriage, had he been faithful. Once she was underground, he'd lose no time savouring the delights of a new marriage-bed. He would beget sons... sons to put Mary from her place. She would lie there, the slow tears running down her cheeks.

One other thing troubled her; between the two she lay in torment. She had long been a secret Catholic; now she must die in the Faith she had not, living, dared acknowledge. In one person alone could she confide; one person alone trust. The Queen. The Queen must help her.

The King and Queen were on progress when Anne's message came. It was always grief for Catherine to leave Charles; to leave him with the de Kérouaille, grief most bitter. But her sister was in dire need.

Anne, once so self-sufficient, would not let Catherine out of her sight. Catherine must keep away those heretic priests that would snatch her soul from God. *Her soul and her girl.* It was pitiful, Catherine thought, and terrible that the dying woman should be as much concerned with an earthly as with a heavenly crown.

Day and night Catherine stayed with the sick woman; she knew she was adding to the nation's dislike of herself... *The foreign Queen stays by the duchess that she may not receive the rites of our English church.* They said it everywhere; they would go on saying it... and in a way it was true.

My lord bishop of Oxford came to administer the last rites; Anne shook her dying head. 'Madam,' he said, very grave, 'I trust you continue still in the truth.'

Truth? The word pricked her failing sense. *What is truth?* And her soul answering, her desperate eyes sought the Queen. Catherine understood; her priest had long been ready. Anne received the Sacrament according to the Catholic faith and died, her tired lips shaping a word—a word that living had not concerned her over much... the word *truth*.

Looking down upon the dead woman Catherine thought, She is dead and who will care? Her daughters? Maybe... a little. But not the husband that once dared the King's anger for love of her. Her pity was deep for Anne.

But at least he loved her... once. Some of her pity was for herself.

Charles burned with passion for this new love that forever promised, forever denied. He was not quite finished with *that woman*, either. She was still to be seen about the court, still to be heard. She had an ever-coarsening look; at thirty Allinda was truly growing old. Yet Charles slept with her now and then... out of kindness; the same kindness, Catherine thought, bitter, that he shows to me. Of Moll and Nell, those thorns in the flesh, she tried not to think. She missed Anne more than she would have believed possible. And Eliza was gone; wise, witty Eliza. A quarrel between her husband and the King—and that *woman* at the bottom of it. With her boundless greed my lady was coaxing the King to give her Phoenix Park; and he might have done it, too—save for Ormonde. It wasn't the King's to give, Ormonde, that had been Lord Lieutenant of Ireland, said. It belonged to Ireland; the residence of her Lord Lieutenants.

A hateful scene. *May I live to see you hanged!* she had screeched at Ormonde. And he quiet and courtly, *I desire nothing, Madam, but to see you grow old.* He was surprised to see her whiten at that. He was not to know she was remembering words spoken by other lips. Clarendon had pricked her merely—she'd been younger then. Ormonde had dealt her a mortal wound.

Catherine was troubled about the quarrel. It was not only that she missed Eliza; it was that she did not trust Arlington—he had too much influence with the King, but Ormonde was faithful and true. Melancholy settled upon her; she could not shake it off.

Charles was with the Suffolks at Audley End. Catherine went down to join him. There in that flat countryside with a hostess she could not trust, melancholy settled more heavily upon the Queen. Charles' friendship for her, his kindness—how deep did they go? She was haunted by the notion that he might, after all, listen to those that forever pressed him to put her away. And now was the time. Once he came into the Catholic Church as—sooner or later—he was sworn to do, there could be no divorce. He knew it as well as she.

XXIV

They had left Audley End to the Queen's relief and continued their progress—the King on horseback post-haste to Newmarket and his beloved horses; the Queen, more slowly, by coach to Euston, to the untrusted Lord Arlington.

A great house Euston, very lovely, its rosy stone warm with sunlight as they drove under ancient trees. There it stood amidst bright lawns, the little Ouse running blue and fountains springing crystal against the early October sky. Inside it was magnificent; the stately staircase a masterpiece, the ceilings rich and gay painted by Verrio, the fine French furnishings, the great paintings and rare statues a delight to the eye.

But always she would remember Euston with heartbreak.

A house fit for a Queen; but, in what should have been the Queen's suite, she found installed—Louise de Kérouaille.

Mary Buckingham, in the anteroom of the suite allotted to the Queen—with every intention of being overheard—made the situation clear.

'The little Louise is virgin still—so she says; and so I believe. Now the fortress is ready to yield.'

'The wonder is, it hasn't yielded already!' Kate Boynton said.

'Mademoiselle awaits the right moment.'

'The King, it seems, cannot keep from her. He's been at Newmarket these three days—and riding over here every one of them, so they say! But he doesn't stay the night.'

'He will!' There was no missing the amusement in Mary Buckingham's voice.

'But naturally; Madam the Queen is here!' Penalva's voice broke in sharp; she must just have come into the room.

'But... naturally,' Mary Buckingham agreed, very smooth; even Penalva all-but blind could not miss the malice.

From the end of the house the Queen lay awake to the distant sound of fiddle and guitar. To this revel she had not been invited—she the Queen! Insult upon insult! When the King came tomorrow she would ask permission to leave this house where, the Queen ignored, her rival reigned.

She had not been invited; but the next morning she heard all about it, Mary Buckingham hot-foot with the news.

'The King was here last night, Madam... somewhat late. He left early this morning. He would not disturb Madam the Queen; you were sleeping, Madam.'

Charles spent the night here, in this house and did not come to me. Catherine felt her heart cold as a dead child. No need to be told he had found a bed more to his liking.

'We had a wedding—oh a jest, merely, Madam!' my lady said demure and smiling. 'But nothing forgotten—prayerbook and priest and all! And we flung the stocking; and they ate the wafers and they drank the wine...'

They ate the wafers and they drank the wine. Refreshment offered to a bridal pair. No need to ask who *they* might be!

Louise de Kérouaille had slept in the King's bed; now she carried herself like a Queen.

'Would she have us think that vulgar jest was earnest?' Frances Stuart cried out in anger. 'Even she, for all her baby-face, cannot be such a fool!'

'She is no fool, that one!' Catherine said, quiet. 'She knows the wiseness... wisdom... to pretend. Of course she did think the jest was earnest—poor innocent that never heard a man cannot have two wives!'

A mock wedding; but no mock bedding.

In early July, nine months to the day, Louise de Kérouaille bore the King's son.

Catherine gave no sign of grief; she uttered no slighting word. Instead she praised the child; and, indeed, it was a lovely boy such as she would gladly have died to bear. Not even Penalva guessed at the depths of her misery.

But, at least, the Queen was troubled with *that woman* no more. Charles had endured the Castlemaine's endless infidelities, her rages and her coarse tongue; but her abuse of Louise—young mother of his child—that he would not endure. He closed her mouth with gold and with honours—she was my lady duchess of Cleveland now; he bought her a handsome house in St. James's and increased, still further, her revenues... but he refused her lodgings in Whitehall. She was no longer acceptable in the King's circle. Yet still, she came to court, brazen as she was; it was hard to escape the clack of her tongue... and the clamour of her scandals.

She had fallen lower, even, than Jacob Hall. She was sleeping with her own footman they said. True or not, the tale showed how low she had fallen. Marvell had written a lampoon, the coarsest, cruellest that ever came from even his pen.

> Paint Castlemaine in colours that will hold,
> Her, not her picture, for she now grows old.
> She, through her lackey's drawers as he ran,
> Discern'd Love's cause and a new flame began.
> Her wonted joys henceforth and court she shuns,
> But still within her mind the footman runs...

> Great Love! How dost thou triumph and how reign,
> That to a groom couldst humble her disdain.
> Stript to the skin, see how she stooping stands,
> Nor scorns to wash him down with those fair hands.
> And washing (lest the scent her crime disclose,)
> His sweaty hoof, tickles him between the toes.

The court relished every cruel word; there were few that had not suffered from *the lady*; but the Queen forbade the low rhyme. She was free of the woman; it was enough.

Beneath his smiling face Charles was playing a lonely game, a dangerous game. To please his people he must hold the Dutch alliance in open bonds of friendship; to please himself, he must hold France in secret bonds. The shame of the Medway had not yet been made good; but all foreign ships must salute the English flag in English waters. If not—*Fire upon all undipped flags!* The navy had its orders.

And still the army and the navy went unpaid. And still England and the Dutch seesawed between war and peace.

But Charles was far from despondent. He had French money in his pocket and was trying to raise more. He was refitting his ships, he was re-ordering the navy; he was conferring with his Council; he was planning campaigns with James should war break out. He snatched his pleasures where he could; his chief pleasure he found in Louise. To his wife he came to discuss his troubles; to his mistress, to forget them. She was so loving, the little Louise... and all the time playing the game of her master in France.

Three things she had been ordered to do—influence Charles to break openly his alliance with Holland; make him declare himself a Catholic; see to it that a Catholic bride was chosen for James—a bride whose interests marched with France.

She had such power, the little Louise. There was her beautiful babe; and she, herself, blooming in young motherhood.

Baby-faced Louise played her master's game; but she did not, for one moment, lose sight of her own. *Queen of England*; no less. That ceremony at Euston—it had been a promise, a betrothal; so she confided to Arlington, to Buckingham, to any that might prove useful. She knew so little of the English tongue; and less of English ways she said, eyes wide and innocent; but she trusted to the honour of England's King.

Of course, if the Queen should quietly, sensibly die, it would be best—but that thought she kept to herself. And why should the Queen not die? Of late she had not been well; she had not recovered, fully, the stupid creature, from her last miscarriage. She might, indeed, fall into a consumption; an obliging physician had given her, at most, twelve months. Let the Queen have so much as a headache and there she was, the little Louise, watching, watching.

But, if the stupid creature refused to die? Then Charles must be persuaded to put her away. A papal dispensation—and this way or that, Louise would be Queen.

Only too clearly Catherine saw the girl's game; and, for all her sore heart, laughed at it. If ever Charles should marry again, it would not be to his mistress. His regard for the high duties of a King forbade it.

But for all that the girl was dangerous. To serve Louis' interests, to make Charles believe they were his own—her constant endeavour. When Catherine tried to warn him, he laughed. Louise's little head hold such weighty matters; absurd! But even should she try, 'There's no woman, ever, shall meddle in my affairs—no woman but one; to her, only, I come for advice.' He lifted her hand and kissed it; but all the same he had uttered a clear warning—to wait with her advice until asked.

A woman of spirit, she supposed, would have snatched her hand away; but he had his own faithfulness towards her. And she loved him.

He wandered about touching this and that. He said, at last, 'If I might break my alliance with the Dutch! If I might!'

'It is not the time.'

'I know it. And Louis knows it; it would please him well to see me at odds with Holland!'

And Babyface knows it; she has her orders. Again she longed to warn him; but she had had her own warning. His anger, should she speak now, would be not for his mistress but for his wife. She must be patient, content to undermine, where she could, the influence of little-traitor Louise.

'Louis is forever at me to announce my conversion...'

And how does Louis forever get at you? She bit upon her tongue.

'It is not time for that neither,' Charles said, 'though God knows how much I desire it. But James has declared himself at last—and that is enough; it is more than enough! I implored him to wait; I commanded him! But a man must keep his own soul, he says. A King can afford no such luxury... nor a King's heir, neither. It may yet cost him the succession!'

'God will see he keeps both,' she said. And then, 'James may make yet more trouble for himself... and for you. Louis desires a Catholic wife for him. I could wish that, also; but, even more, I wish for him a bride that shall not anger your English. Watch the wife James shall choose; it will be Louis' choice... and it will be urged upon you by Mademoiselle.'

'It will be my choice; mine and mine alone! As for Mademoiselle—she's a child; innocent. But—must I say it again—I trust no mistress; least of all a mistress from France.'

'Madame Babyface is more clever than the King thinks! Oh Penalva, you should see the way his eyes follow her—as if he could eat her. And no wonder—pretty as spun sugar! Yesterday she went riding, all in cherry and silver; and the curls flowing like sunlight beneath her hat... a beaver hat with feathers, such as every woman wears; but upon her it is different. You'd swear it was new-designed for her alone. At times I could almost wish my sight as dim as yours, so I might spare myself some torment. And, with her, money runs like water. Her very drawers—the Buckingham woman spares me nothing—are of finest lutestring; and her petticoats whipped with lace—silver lace. And her garters stitched with gold and silver flowers, fastened with jewelled buckles. And her gloves! thirty-five pounds the pair, the least of them! Scented with ambergris, laced with gold, embroidered with jewels... and she thinks nothing of ordering two dozen pairs at the time! Alas that the good nuns taught me to be clean rather than fine! Sometimes I do think to order a petticoat of silk all trimmed with lace; but conscience pricks too hard. We are much in debt.'

'Were you not in debt, still you would think twice and thrice—and then you would not buy! You were bred to economies—more's the pity!'

'Pity, indeed! Economies—there are some to call it by an uglier name! But you are wrong, Penalva, my dear. Were I bred to lavish spending, still I would close my hand, even upon the price of a petticoat; the country's all but bankrupt. The King does what he can. He puts aside the best part of his own revenues to help pay the country's debts. But still there's need of money. Always the pinching and the paring... and always the debts unpaid. Shall we never lie at ease?'

Now less than ever! Unexpected disaster. The banks refused to advance more money to a government already deep in debt. The government, at its wits' ends, unable to meet the country's urgent needs, suspended payment of interest to bankers on money already lent.

'We have been near to bankruptcy, often enough,' a gloomy Charles told Catherine. 'Now it is the thing itself. The bankers mean to pass their losses on to their clients; they mean to lay hands on everything committed to their charge—gold, jewels, land, everything. They'll make payments to no-one; not even to merchants that can breed gold from gold. So we have it at last—ruin to trade; ruin to the country. And that is not the worst. What of our good name abroad? When Spain knows, when Holland knows, when France knows—most of all when France knows—we'll have a nest of hornets about our ears. Panic; and ruin at home and abroad. It must not, must not happen. Yet I see no way out. Kate, Kate, I know not what to do!'

'Could you not yourself go into the city; yourself talk to the bankers?'

'Oh Kate, must I be forever a beggar? When I was a child I would fill a hole upon the seashore. When the water ran away and lost itself in the sea, I would think, being a child, Let me pour night and day—and my hole shall be full. I know now that, let me pour forever, still the water will run to the sea and be forever lost. So it is with these debts. But, for all that I will go.'

The day he went to beg of the bankers she walked about her closet trying to warm her cold hands at the brazier... walking and wondering how it fared with him; and all the time praying. It was late when she heard his step; so light it was, she needed no word to tell of success.

'I swore to them upon my honour that—if they will meet their obligations to their clients—next year they shall be paid in full; and all back interest, besides. They believed me, Kate; thank God they believed me! And, as I have promised, so I shall do. But how it shall be done I cannot think; my lean pockets can scarce be squeezed leaner. But, though I sweat blood, they shall be paid in full.'

Dismiss your women that suck the country dry. Catherine bit back the retort. He would do without a new pair of stockings but to these women he could not say *No*. Nell Gwynn was the least demanding; but there was her boy, the little duke of Grafton, to keep in ducal estate. And *that woman*. Though she had fallen from favour she never ceased her demands. And her five bastards—dukes, earls, and countesses, all—and revenues to match.

But, worst of all, Babyface with her revenues greater than any Queen's, with her priceless jewels, her great houses, her vast estates... and like the horse-leech's daughter forever crying, *Give. Give!* Where did the money come from? Charles was, no doubt, deep in debt on her account; and then, of course, there was the money he'd had from

Louis—some of it he had surely spent upon little Miss Innocence. And, no doubt at all, Louis himself gave her money... for services rendered. And who knew how many bribes flowed through those small, greedy hands? And now she was asking for another ten thousand a year—and she'd get that, too. She had but to open great blue eyes! Only a fool like myself, Catherine thought, would trouble her head about a yard of lace upon a petticoat.

In that same month as the birth of her son, Louise was ennobled. She was the Baroness Petersfield, she was Countess of Fareham, she was my lady Duchess of Portsmouth. More lands, more gold flowing into those small, grasping hands. And not from Charles alone. To sharpen still further wits that needed no sharpening, her master in France gave her the fief of Aubigny in Berri. It had belonged to Frances' husband, part of the Richmond estates; but since Frances had no child it had lapsed to the French crown.

She was doing well for herself little-kitten-Louise; better by far than ever *that woman*, the bold-faced virago.

'It is well to be a King's mistress!' Catherine told Charles, driven beyond herself; in spite of all self-discipline the old quick spirit was not dead.

'A king's mistress—sitting pretty, some think,' he said. 'But a mistress lasts so long—and no longer! She must secure herself while she may. A man may have many mistresses; but only one wife. And she is his wife as long as she shall live. A King can have only one Queen. There's no child of mine—save it be yours—can wear the crown.'

'Not even Monmouth?' she asked quick and bitter. 'Not even handsome Jamie, the people's hero?'

'Not even Jamie. And he well deserves the name of hero! Do you forget how he fought under James at Solebay? His name, his deeds were on every tongue. I lent him to France; again he fought against the Dutch—this time on land; and with such courage—such distinguished courage—Louis made him Lieutenant-General of all his Forces; and that you know, too. It's an honour never before given to any but a Frenchman; and that, perhaps, you do not know. Distinguished by bravery on land and sea—it's enough to endear him to any English heart! Well now, we have him home again—the nation's hero, as you say.'

'The nation's hero on yet another count!' she said before she could stay her tongue. 'Young Protestant Saviour against poor middle-aged Catholic James! He's been named more than once for the succession—the whole country knows it. Buckingham sees to it...' *Buckingham that presses the King to a divorce, forever presses...*

'Monmouth shall never be named my heir; and so I have made clear!' Charles said with surprising patience, though she detected a warning note. 'Another word from Buckingham—and into the Tower he goes!'

Knowing Charles' faithfulness upon both counts—divorce and succession—she was ashamed of her peevishness. But—divorce! It was her constant nightmare from which she would wake weeping in the night. Nor was it possible to forget Monmouth because of the way he courted Louise; and the way she encouraged him. Those two were over-fond. They didn't sleep together; Louise took no lover, ever, but the King. But she bound Monmouth to her; her ally. She showed friendship still with James; it was politic. But, at any moment, the people might cast him off. And then who would step into his place; who but Monmouth, charming Monmouth?

False, vicious, unstable Monmouth—Louise had summed him up. Obstinate Monmouth; but easily worked upon... if one knew how. Louise knew how.

Everything blowing up for a second war with the Dutch; Charles made a last attempt to prevent it. In spite of the sworn alliance William, it seemed, did not trust his uncle. If Charles could bind his nephew to him? If he offered to support William in a bid for full sovereignty of the States of Holland? Surely William would think twice before leading the Dutch in a new war!

That autumn he invited the young man to England.

'Oddsfish, Kate, I can do nothing with the fellow!' Charles said half-laughing, half-vexed. 'He'll not play my game—he's too good a Dutchman; no Stuart in him at all! A dull creature; cold. Yet for all that I'll keep him in mind for James' girl; for Mary. An alliance to please the people.'

'Will it please Mary?'

'Were you asked when your match was made?'

'There was no need.'

He was, for the moment, ashamed in the face of her love.

Nothing, it seemed, could stop the war. Fight they must. And because he believed that men free to worship as they will make better fighters, he once more declared an *Indulgence for Tender Consciences*... and once more angered Parliament. Parliament, he knew well, would remember it when he needed money. Meanwhile he had three quarters of a million saved from the bankers; and the first part of Louis' subsidy had come in. He spent his windfalls strengthening the Fleet.

Now it was the Dutch that would have avoided war.

'I am, myself, a man of peace,' Charles told the Dutch ambassador, 'but my people—!' he shrugged.

Admiral Holmes brought matters to a head. He attacked Dutch cinnamon ships peacefully returning from the east. Immediately the Dutch declared war.

In May the Fleet sailed. Catherine went with Charles to wish it Godspeed. White sails crowding against blue sky; great polished cannon all-but blinding in the sunlight; men drawn up trim and ready. A glorious sight. But this time Catherine could not rejoice. So she had seen that other proud fleet sail; and against the same enemy. Would this one like that other return with torn sails and blood-washed decks... and with what ships and men missing?

It was as though, Cassandra-like, she had been granted a glimpse into the future; or as though the past had returned again. For all was as before. De Ruyter, the Dutch admiral, found the English Fleet sheltering from dense fog in Southwold Bay. Through the fog, the ships like ghosts gliding, faced each other upon the shrouded sea. And, in the ghostly silence—the sudden boom of guns, the crack of bursting shells; and flames flaring smoky red upon the reddened waters, reddened still further by the blood of the wounded.

In Whitehall Charles received the news. First it was all of victory; then, while they rejoiced—all defeat. And then, at last, the truth. Fearful loss—both sides. The *Royal James*—James' flagship, blown skyhigh. But, at once, boarding the *Royal Catherine* and fighting magnificently, James had, at last, driven the enemy back to their own doorstep. Blackened with soot, singed and scorched, he was yet unhurt; torn and burnt through a sea awash with corpses, the English crawled home.

The English and Dutch had broken each other. But France grew in strength. Louis' armies over-ran Holland; wherever they marched victory followed. But for all that the Dutch refused to surrender. William of Orange, the cold, proud young man, opened the dykes. Rather than the French—the sea; the sea!

His fine ships battered—and his money spent! Dogged, as always, by poverty, Charles asked Louis for a loan and was refused. Charles had not yet declared his faith. He was forced to ask Parliament.

'I might have saved my breath.' Beneath his smile Catherine guessed at his humiliation, his despair. 'No money—unless I withdraw my *Indulgence*. And how may I do that? To go back upon the sworn word—how may I so cover myself with shame? Men, men! They'll cut each the other's throat for the saying of a prayer or the drinking of wine and the eating of a wafer. Does God wish, do you think, a man should cut his brother's throat in such an argument?'

'A man's soul is dearer than his body.'

'He created both. God is merciful. Let a man keep a kind heart and He will forgive much. Cruelty—there's the worst sin. For that a man should burn in Hell. God, I do believe it, will not punish a man for praying this way rather than that—so he pray with an honest heart.'

'God has told you so?' It troubled her to hear him cut theology to suit himself.

He burst into laughter. 'Oh Kate, Kate, you'll be the death of me.' Suddenly he was sobered. 'If I am to patch up the cracks in this poor country I must have money. So back I go, to Parliament, cap-in-hand, to withdraw my promise of freedom. But what will men think of me hereafter?' He shrugged; a little careless shrug that went near to breaking her heart.

'They will hold me to be a weather-vane. But about those things I hold good I am constant. From that day I came home—thirteen years, Kate—I wanted freedom for men's soul. That freedom I gave; and took it back, because I must. Again I gave it; and again I take it back. But not because I've shifted; but because Parliament holds the whip.'

Parliament not only held the whip but cracked it, too. Not only was freedom to worship withdrawn; to make doubly sure, Parliament passed the Test Act.

All those that refused to take the Sacrament according to the Church of England must hold no public office. It hit at Nonconformist as well as Catholic. One yardstick to beat all.

When Charles told Catherine she went white. 'James?' her lips just formed the word.

'James, certainly. This damned act is directed chiefly against him. He loses command of the Fleet.'

'No!' she cried out. 'No!' And it was not possible such ingratitude. James to lose command, James with his courage and his victories! 'And... the succession?'

He did not answer; did not tell her that there was even more talk of Monmouth as heir to the throne. That it was not only Buckingham who pressed him now for divorce—not because of the Queen's barrenness but upon the lying grounds that Charles had married Monmouth's mother—the trollop Lucy Walter.

'I have married no wife ever but the Queen!' Charles declared it in Parliament and without. 'As for Monmouth, love him I do. But I'd rather see him with a rope round his neck than a crown on his head!'

XXV

A black summer for Charles, this Summer of 'seventy-three.

Anger against James was hardening; Monmouth's popularity ever-growing. And some breath of that secret treaty with Louis had leaked out; it followed Charles like a faint, bad odour. And still the war with Holland dragged on; but the nation that had so desired it, was weary of it to the bone. And always the long, bitter struggle with Parliament—struggle over freedom of worship for all. He had not yet admitted that he meant to give way; he had gone on hoping.

But now, now he must tell them; until then—no money. His life, it seemed, was one unending struggle.

Never had he felt so melancholy, so alone. But, for all that, he must show a cheerful face. The common people crowding into Whitehall to watch the dancing or to see their King dine with good appetite, would wonder at him. So much trouble in the country... and he so carefree!

But they did not see him in the privacy of his closet, patient upon the hopeless mass of his affairs. They knew nothing of the long hours spent with his Council, nor see him exhausted after a struggle with Parliament. But they did know that twice the King had promised freedom of worship and twice that promise had been broken. And they knew that there was some sly friendship with hated France. And they knew that the King was at odds with his Parliament so that a new party had sprung up against him—gentlemen from the country—Whigs they called themselves. And that my lord Shaftesbury—that Ashley Cooper whom the King had ennobled, and once his close friend, had gone over to lead the enemy. The wickedest of men, Charles called him; but he was merely the most expedient. But, if he had lost one old friend he had regained another. Ormonde was back again, their quarrel forgotten—trusted Ormonde with a seat in the Cabinet. And with him, to the Queen's comfort and joy, Eliza.

All about the King—disapproval, distrust. His own father, Charles thought, must have felt this same unease. Was it possible for the old, wicked tale to repeat itself?

It was a question Catherine never asked. Charles would win... in the end; in spite of everything he had the power to draw men. She was unhappy because the tide ran against him; but she was not afraid. For him, not afraid; but for herself she feared... and with some cause. False Shaftesbury playing for popularity, forever demanded the King's divorce, forever whipped the people to fear, to anger. *The Duke of York means to take a Catholic wife and a young one. A Catholic line of Kings! England beneath the heel of the Bishop of Rome! How, Englishmen, shall you endure that? The King must put away the Queen, must give the country its heir...*

Charles refused even to discuss the matter. The Queen was his wife; his wife she should remain.

There were times when she longed to leave Whitehall where the court looked and wondered how long before she was put away. Whitehall where one mistress ruled like the Queen and the other played the clown; and each inched for advantage and boasted herself to be the King's favoured bedfellow. Louise fought with her beauty and her breeding; Nell with her wit, her gutter impudence. She could plant her dart before my lady duchess could open her lovely mouth. There were smiles aplenty at Nell's impudence... but behind my lady's back; none dared offend Madam Favourite.

Louise was of the Queen's Bedchamber; it was the King's wish... and everybody knew why. It meant easier access to the King. Now, except for the King's apartments, hers were the best in the palace; they lay at the end of the Stone gallery overlooking the King's private gardens. Where others looked out upon stables and yards and huddled roofs, she looked upon green lawns, shady trees and flowing river. And, to these rooms, there was a constant coming-and-going. Catherine sitting alone save for her ladies, would hear the click of high heels passing the Queen's rooms and dying down the gallery... the world paying court to Madam Favourite.

And the rooms themselves! The Gobelin tapestries, the priceless paintings, the marble statues; the screens and hearth furniture of fine worked silver, the dishes and plates of pure gold, the goblets of glass from Venice! She had ransacked the King's choicest treasures, they said; there was nothing there but was a masterpiece and a wonder. And she, with her lovely face, her grace and her elegance was, of all masterpieces, the finest—they said that, too.

There was nothing she could not get from Charles. And what he did not give of himself she asked for; asked sweetly, asked gently. And, if it were not at once forthcoming, never a word of reproach; only tears filling the lovely eyes... a wounded dove.

'No dove that one!' old Penalva said. 'Not dove, but a bird of prey.'

None could get the better of Madam Louise save Mistress Nell. Louise could neither worst her rival nor induce Charles to send her away. 'I would as soon banish the sun!' he said; and it was true. There was no-one these dark days that could make him laugh like Nell. And, besides, he owed her something. At the height of her success she had given up the theatre for his sake. And, above all, there was her child.

For her there was no apartment at Whitehall; but she had a pretty house in the Mall, its gardens delightfully adjoining the King's.

About this house gossip was lively. Bedchamber lined—walls and ceiling—with looking-glass, they said. When Mary Buckingham repeated the gossip by her husband's orders, 'An odd taste!' the Queen said and relieved my lady from her duties.

Charles made no secret of his affair with Nell. He not only visited her in the looking-glass chamber, he would walk in St. James's; or, leaning against the wall, would chat with her—and she sitting above him on that same wall, as often as not, in nothing but her smock. There they would be, laughing and jesting for all the world to see.

He had won some popularity on Nell's account. She was of the people—and proud of it. And they, in turn, were proud of her; with her open hand and her gay impudence she had won their hearts. But for Madame Louise, when she appeared in her coach, there were hisses and catcalls; the Catholic whore, they called her, hating her alike for her faith, her foreignness and her greed. They knew all about the gold plate in daily use upon her table. She was welcome to it—molten in the fire and poured down her throat!

There was a tale about them both. There was a fine gilt coach driving down Oxford Street; and, within, a young woman alone and richly dressed. The crowd believing it was Madam from France hemmed in the coach so that it could move neither backward nor forward; the mood was ugly. Suddenly up went the window; and there was Nell Gwynn laughing and crying out, Good people let me pass. 'It's the Protestant not the Catholic whore!' So they let her pass with cheers. She was one of themselves; and honest enough to call a spade a spade.

But it's the Catholic whore they must reckon with, Catherine thought when she heard the tale. She robs the King of his treasures, she rules him with her whims, she betrays him with France, she corrupts the Council with her French bribes.

Louise could do all these things; but still she could not persuade him to dismiss Nell; he needed laughter more than ever.

She made more than the King laugh. She set the whole court laughing. When Madam the Duchess of Portsmouth walked grandly, Nell would strut behind, head wickedly held as though it carried a coronet, walking as though pages carried a ducal train.

Louise, that wounded dove, complained to Charles; but Nell, unrepentant, shook her bright curls. 'Madam from France should be ashamed to be King's whore—if she's as noble as she says. But me—' she looked him full in the eye, 'I was born in a ditch and my mother died in one—where I promise myself not to follow her. It is natural for me to find myself in a gentleman's bed. Though—' and she cocked an impudent nose, 'I had not dreamed of *such* a gentleman!'

It was a just answer; and, laughing, he was forced to admit it. After this she let no opportunity slip to make Louise appear a fool. The Prince de Rohan died. Louise appeared in mourning deep enough for a wife. She was not even a distant relative, and her degree of nobility too low to justify any mourning at all.

Next day Nell appeared before an astounded court swathed in deepest black, caged within weeds so voluminous her small figure could scarce carry the weight. Charles startled—as well he might be—asked her reason for the sable garb. She threw back the heavy veil, her mournful voice came clear. 'Sir, the great Cham of Tartary... he died yesterday!' And sobbed into her weeds.

Louise went white. She stared at Charles as though commanding him to annihilate the low creature. But he didn't even see her; he was blinded with the tears of his laughter.

The court had no little enjoyment watching the grand lady and the little girl from the gutter; but it was an enjoyment wise to hide. To offend Louise—save one were a Nell Gwynn—was to invite dire consequences. Her wealth and her influence—there seemed no bounds to either; fabulous both. Besides her income of eighteen thousand a year she had had in two years alone a present of fifty thousand pounds, together with an extra gift of sixteen thousand. She had ten thousand a year from wine licences; she had revenues from lands in Ireland to which she had no right; and, in addition, revenues sufficient to rear her son in ducal state. She had houses, she had lands; she had furnishings and jewels beyond price. And, in addition, she had gone into business; she sold places at court. There was no dishonest transaction, but her hand was in it.

She was flattered and fawned upon. None dared utter a word against her; even Nell's sallies were by innuendo. Mistress Phillis Temple, for a few light words, was banished the court; she was one of the Queen's ladies and Catherine, herself, did not escape the blame. Of such blame she was contemptuous. 'Words against Mademoiselle?' And she refused Madam Duchess her title. 'It is impossible anyone should prevent them,' she told Charles. 'She has enemies everywhere. That she makes enemies for herself—with that I have no quarrel. But she makes enemies for you, sir—and there I have great quarrel!'

It was the truth and he knew it; but, for all her kindness, a truth he did not relish. He turned upon his heel and left her. She wanted to cry after him, In all other dealings you are just and shrewd and kind. But she, your sly mistress, does what she will with you. Oh she is clever! She never raises her voice, never shows an angry face. After the loud-mouthed Castlemaine you think yourself in heaven! *She is gentle and lovely... she rests me*; you said that once. Charles, Charles, how can you be so blind? All the time she betrays you. Oh not with her body—she dare not; and she's cold, besides. But in the heart she's false. But she has given you a child... a son...

She paced the room restless, distress drove her; she was unable to sit or stand or anyway find peace.

And me? What, Charles, of me? You praise what you are pleased to call my goodness, my honesty, my commonsense. But, goodness, truth and commonsense—what comfort to a woman that loves you—and that woman your wife?

She thought she had come to terms with his lack of love for her; and with her own barrenness. Now, grief, again, overthrew her; she drowned in grief as in a sea. She flung herself before her prie-dieu and besought the Mother of God that she might bear a child. That commonsense of hers told her it was too late. She was thirty-five; she had never carried a full-term child... and her husband did not love her. But faith was stronger than commonsense. With God all things are possible. Women older than she had borne children. Physicians were but men. But God was God.

These days she was weary of the court; weary of the sight of the King's mistresses; weary of his everlasting quarrels with Parliament of which she always got the backwash; weary of the war against the Dutch, of the death and the disaster; weariest of all of the country's hatred of the Faith she loved. And, all the time, she must endure the diversions of the court—sugar coating her bitter pill. Charles needed his sugar, she knew it well; knew that, while he played, his subtle mind worked for the country's good. He needed pretty women, he needed music and dancing and the play; needed them as he needed food and sleep. But pleasure could not hold him long. There he would be, smiling, the Gwynn at his side, or the de Kérouaille; and all about him lovely women and gay gallants. And she would see the smile fade and the eyes grow sombre; and she would know his mind was back again upon his problems. She would see him leave his toying with his ladies and get up and go away. And she would follow him—the only one that dared. And he would talk and she would listen; and back he would go refreshed.

To ease his mind, to give him that comfort—it was much. But, if he might come to love her a little, only a little! She would ask no more of life.

XXVI

James had flown in the face of Parliament and people. He had married a Catholic bride. He had fallen madly in love with the picture of Maria Beatrice d'Este—and small wonder. She was so lovely a child with her great dark eyes and dark flowing curls, her skin white and faintly flushed as a magnolia blossom. A blossom of a girl; scarce that—a bud; a bud, only.

A sweet child; ignorant and innocent and bitterly unhappy. The thought of marriage disgusted her; to give herself to God her one desire. She had cried for two days and nights when they told her she must give herself to James Stuart instead.

When she reached England and saw the great sandy-haired man, she was frantic. He was old enough to be her grandfather, she cried out in fearful despair. And that, also, was not to be wondered at. He was forty to her fifteen—and an old forty at that, battered by hard and lecherous living. She was crying bitterly when they put her into his bed. Well, a crying child was nothing new to him, he said, all-impatient for the nuptials.

She lived, at first, in a state of shock; she went trembling to her husband's bed, she could not endure the touch of his hand. A wretched life for any bride; for the little nun hateful beyond enduring.

One person in this court she loved—the King. She followed him with the adoring eyes of one of his own spaniels. She might have won the Queen for friend; a good friend. Catherine welcomed the sad, pretty child of her own faith; but Madam Louise was of the Faith also; the little duchess found her a gayer companion. Louise, the sly mischief-maker, forever hinted; the Queen was sly, was cold, was mean... was not to be trusted. In spite of all the Queen's kindness to Maria Beatrice, coolness between them grew.

Not even the lovely, gentle bride could appease the people. News of her pregnancy strengthened their anger and their fear. Their anger reached out to Charles; his task was so much the harder, now. There was more talk than ever of Monmouth as heir; there was more talk of the King's divorce. Charles wished to God James had listened to his King; and, if not to him, then to Parliament and the people. But Catherine watched the girl with envy. Fifteen and pregnant.

Within six months of marriage the girl had miscarried; Catherine's envy turned to pity—she knew what it was so to lose a child. But Maria Beatrice's grief was less for her loss than for the outrage upon herself... an outrage forever to be repeated. She went about pale and heavy and frightened. To distract her, a little, Catherine, so long an onlooker, herself commanded a masque. 'It is called *The Chaste Nymph*. A rarity at this court,' she told Penalva. 'And play-acting at that!'

Afterwards they discussed the players in the Queen's closet.

'Monmouth looked handsomer than ever—the vicious creature,' Frances Stuart said. 'So charming—you'd think butter wouldn't melt in his mouth! But he treats his little wife abominably—ignores her in public; and beats her in private!'

Eliza Ormonde nodded. 'He'd sell his nearest and dearest for a groat.'

'Nearest he has; but dearest—none!' Catherine said. 'As for a groat—he'd sell his father for less.' To escape the thought of Monmouth she said, 'James' girls looked well in their parts.'

'Mary did,' Frances said. 'She's a pretty girl—those red-gold curls! But Anne. Poor little thing! She's no beauty and never will be. She takes after her mother.'

'We must give her time; she's but nine years old,' the Queen said.

'All the time there is won't take away that pale and heavy look. Her skin is well enough—her one beauty. She can thank her God the smallpox didn't mar it. Nor,' Frances sighed, 'her eyes, neither.'

Her eyes are bad enough without that; and Mary's, too—a weakness they inherit from their father,' Eliza said and did not add, a weakness held to be the result of James' lechery.

'Mary—she is a cold one,' Catherine said; 'and, I think, sly. But the little one, Anne—she has a loving heart. A loving heart but not a judging heart. Such a heart is danger.'

'A danger, indeed!' Frances said. 'She stands not far from the throne.'

'Nonsense!' The Queen's voice came out sharp. In spite of them all she would never give up hope. She was but thirty-six and looked younger—the skin as smooth, the hair as dark and free-flowing. There was a little thickening beneath the chin... true; but women older than she had borne children. 'Nonsense!' she said again.

'Nonsense, of course!' Frances misread the sharpness in the Queen's voice. 'James' wife has miscarried; what of that? There'll be more children; plenty of children—if we know James. No need to trouble our heads about the faults of Mary or Anne! Our new little duchess will have children—and to spare!'

'There can never be children to spare,' the Queen said.

Charles was listening to Moll Davies singing like an angel; but even she could not keep the King's thoughts at bay. Catherine saw heaviness close down upon his face, saw Louise put out a hand, saw that the King, unnoticing, let it lie. She was not surprised when she saw him rise abruptly and leave the room. Within a little she rose and followed him. She knocked upon his closet door but he was not there; when she went into her own rooms there he was waiting for her.

'Kate, Kate, the difficulties are too many!' He put his head into his hands and she noticed how thin they were. Yet, in spite of the lines upon his face, the black periwig, as always, gave him a youthful look. It was always something of a shock to remember that, beneath the wig, the hair had long gone grey.

'It goes on and on... and I am tired... so tired. And I must fight still—fight my Parliament, fight my people, fight the Dutch. How shall I fight—and with what weapons? The people trust me no longer—James' marriage is the last straw. They rage against Catholics more bitter than before. And Louis, that had more than a finger in the marriage, threatens to hold back the rest of the money he promised. He doesn't keep his word!'

Did you keep yours? It was a question she did not ask.

'There's none to help me. Clarendon's gone—the fault my own; a difficult man but true. And Clifford's gone, my best adviser, and others of his faith—the Test Act saw to it. And Buckingham? He's sold himself to my enemies. No great loss maybe... but once he was my friend; and without friends the wind blows cold. And Shaftesbury leads my enemies in Parliament and stirs up hatred where he can. So I must go on alone. There's work to do and I must do it. I found this country torn by quarrels; I swore to make it whole. I found it bankrupt; I swore to make it prosperous—secure in trade, its enemies broken. I swore to forgive this people everything and God knows there's enough to forgive—a father's death, a boyhood spent in wandering and fear and often enough in cold and hunger. Because they brought me home again I vowed to serve them with all my heart. But time goes by... and I am beaten.'

'There's none can beat you but yourself.'

'Oddsfish, you're right!' He squared his shoulders, a little comforted. 'The things I swore to do are right things; and, under God, I shall do them.'

He came often to her apartments but rarely to her bed. She tried to comfort herself. *Youth passes and passion passes; but friendship and the quiet heart endures.* But it was poor comfort.

Catherine disliked Whitehall more than ever. It was a poor court she held there; she knew, herself, how small, how dull. But Madam Louise? She held her court like a great Queen. In the morning her levee was crowded—Catherine heard all about it. There she would sit, Madam Babyface, fresh as a rose in a sprigged cotton peignoir—a piece of cleverness that!—looking simple and sincere and childlike... and the lovely hair flowing to the small waist; and, on each hand, a maid brushing the pale gold waves. And the room would be full of sunlight striking up from the river and quivering upon gold and silver and crystal and upon the exquisite figure they held as a casket a jewel. And the room would be full of laughter and chatter; and a guitar, maybe, playing a new song from France.

And then—Catherine knew well how it would go—Louise would dismiss the maids and dismiss the suitors and the gallants; she would dismiss the ambassadors from France—de Croissy and Courtin and Barrillon all three—and she would be alone with Charles. And then she would drop a word here and there—oh so innocent!—advising him for the good of her master in France, caring, not at all, though it should destroy Charles himself. A second St. Joan she fancied herself. She—a King's harlot! St. Joan would choose rather to burn again.

And Charles would listen and he would smile and he would say Yes or No, just as she chose. But afterwards he would come to the Queen's neglected rooms. 'She should learn to save her breath, the little Louise,' he would say. And once he said, 'I never trusted but two women in my life. Minette—' and, as always, his face fell into lines of grief when he said her name, 'and you.'

Even Minette served two kings; I serve but one...

And once he said, on a sigh, 'if we had a child! I'd name you Regent should I die. You'd rule well—your mother's daughter. And it would settle James' business.'

'A child—why not?' She looked him full in the face. 'So you do your part! And for dying—there's time enough to think of that!'

'Kings stand always close to death!' he said and she saw that the first part of her speech had made no mark; he had long given up hope. 'As for time—I am forty-four and weary to death.'

'Yet things are more good than you remember. Last year you were alone; but truly alone. Now a new party is standing by you. In the Parliament and in the Council there are men that look to the King's good before their own. Ormonde—thank God you have brought him back! And Coventry and Finch. And Osborne. I put my faith in him.'

'Osborne—there goes a brash Yorkshireman; but shrewd, shrewd. If any man can order my affairs, make economies where I see none—it's Osborne. But oh Kate, Kate! If Parliament would understand my shifts and troubles. If it would grant me something for my needs! Must want forever be my master?'

In the first week of the New Year he met his Parliament and returned blind with fury; his lips, Catherine saw, had that strange leaden colour.

'Shaftesbury rouses madness in Parliament against Catholics. And not only in Parliament. He works among the Londoners. He's got himself a house in the city and there he cozens my lord Mayor and aldermen with food and wine and lying words. He rouses their fear with lies; he tells them London is full of hidden Papists, all ripe for murder, rape and burning. He demands that every Catholic be sent from London.'

Now it was she that was grey to the lips; it was worse, worse than even she had expected.

'Not you, Kate. I'd not permit it. I could not do without you.'

'You have your... spaniels.' Even in her anger she managed to substitute the word for *women*.

'Yes,' he agreed, surprised. 'But even they—loving as they are—will turn and bite. It's going to be a hard fight with this Parliament of mine, harder than ever. I need your kindness; Kate, be kind.'

She would have given her heart's blood for him; yet now she could not take a step towards him. In spite of all his talk about freedom to worship he would allow them to be sent away—faithful servants, humble priests—those that were not essential to his needs. But herself? He needed her and so she must stay. And his Catholic mistress, would he not keep her also?

She said, cold and quiet, 'I am at the King's disposal,' and curtseyed to the ground.

February had come in with bitter winds and a flurry of snow when peace was made with Holland. Charles had broken his secret pact with Louis; he did it unwillingly and with humiliation. 'Had he opened his hand I could have stood firm. Now, like me, he must do the best he can!' Charles told a weeping Louise.

Parliament went its way enjoying its power to humiliate the King. It censured not only his Council but his friends; it impeached faithful Arlington and faithless Buckingham. The peace they, themselves, had forced upon him, became a stick with which to beat him. The cry against Papists grew louder, wilder. James must be banished from London.

'My brother!' Charles all-but choked upon his anger. 'I'd die before I agree; go, if need be, the way my father did.'

Catherine crossed herself. 'Never! Your father; he could not bend so he did break. But you; you know how to bend... and James must go.'

'A coward, then?' he broke in, bitter.

'It takes more of courage to bend than to break. And you are one to spring upright again.'

'This Parliament. It *drives* me. It hopes I'll pack and be off to France; go on my travels, again.' A sick look came into his face. 'Oddsfish; they don't know me!'

'You sit upon a throne of thorns,' she said. 'That they do not know you—it is true. You mislead them with your easy ways. But when your mind is set, they'd best take heed.'

'You know me, Kate. You know my purpose. I must say it again and yet again, lest I falter. I allow no trifling with the divine right of the Kings.'

'That is not so easy when they keep you penniless.'

'When I was a boy my tutor said a thing. *Always keep some money in your pocket.* Good advice... but I never had the chance to take it.'

Osborne gave him his chance. Osborne, the raw Yorkshireman, new-made Lord Danby, worked day and night to make his King secure. Never such a man for juggling with money. He stopped all salaries, all pensions, till the navy and the dockers were paid. He had Louise in tears. She had set her heart upon yet another diamond necklace. A bargain, never to be met with again! she wept to Charles. 'Go weep to Danby!' Charles said. And then, unable to endure the tears in those so-gentle eyes, added, 'You shall have your necklace when times mend!'

Osborne, my lord Danby, that wonder of a man, without a penny from Parliament, was setting the nation's finance upon its feet. He had paid off the troops as well as the navy; he had reduced the rate on money the government owed. Now the bankers got their two years' interest and expenses due to the Dutch were settled. Charles had money in his pocket; but he forgot his old tutor's advice. He spent it. A debt of honour came first. He that must look to a bullying Parliament for every penny had been paying off, little by little, his father's debts. Now he paid off the last of them. Thereafter the little Louise had her diamond necklace. And he was generous, also, to his old flame long burnt out. He dowered Barbara's daughters and saw them well-bestowed in marriage. They could not, in the nature of things, all be his; but he'd not humiliate any of the pretty, innocent creatures. He spent nothing on himself; but he gave Catherine a fine jewel; she put it aside in safe-keeping. Who could know what the future might bring?

Even Danby's heroic efforts could not cover everything. When Charles went to Parliament for money to meet the country's needs— the country's and not his own—he was refused; again and again refused; and sometimes there were insults—not at all veiled—concerning his mistresses.

'And not upon the score of morals. There's plenty in the House whose own morals won't bear daylight!' he told Danby and cared not at all that Buckingham was near and would make no bones repeating it. 'I have seven bastard sons—what then? They cost the country little; seven rich heiresses shall pay for them. But seven sons true-begot—royal princes all—they would indeed lighten the country's pockets.'

No wonder Parliament was bitter when they heard the King's jest. He had not even one true-born son. For a Protestant heir they would have granted him almost anything. And that he could jest about it! The gibe stung deep.

All the summer the noise of battle shook Europe; but England was at peace. The noise reached the court at quiet Windsor. But while England and its King took the rest they needed Dutch and French agents were busy—the Dutch rousing the people to demand war on France—greedy, victorious, dangerous France... *Papist France*. And the French with their corrupting gold inciting Parliament to break the new peace with Holland.

Charles refused to listen to either side. 'Let Shaftesbury do his damndest, I'll not fight France. No, nor Holland, neither. We'll have no war. Europe's in arms and the people suffer. But here—' he looked at the corn standing rich and golden, 'we reap the blessing of peace.'

In the autumn the court returned to Whitehall. Catherine was sick to the heart of the sight of Louise and Nell; sick of the sight of the King's bastards—the handsome sons, the pretty daughters; sick of the never-lessening dislike against herself because she was foreign, because she was Catholic, because she was childless. And it was the old round again—flirting and scandals... and worse; she wanted no part in it. But to be left out, to sit alone unmissed; it was melancholy. When she appeared Charles treated her with respect; and so did all that valued his good-will... but respect is cold comfort to a lonely, passionate heart. For the most part she would sit in her rooms playing at loo or basset with Frances or Eliza or one or other of her older ladies; and Penalva would sit, very quiet, listening to their chatter since she could not longer see to play. And Catherine would try to forget the laughter not far away... yet how far! And she would find her foot tapping to the sound of music and long to join the dancing. And her head would begin to ache and the pain in her eyes would grow worse so that she was forced to put by the cards and try to find peace at her prayers. But it was hard to pray; harder still to sleep. She was losing her pretty plumpness, her pretty colour; she looked ill. Charles was concerned; he sent his own physicians. But not until her heart found peace would she be well again.

It was now she began the habit of retiring to Somerset House and then, her looks unchallenged by the court beauties—in spite of Huysmans she was no Venus—and the de Kérouaille and the Gwynn at a distance, he might come again to love her a little.

But he never came. Laziness or the press of affairs prevented him... or perhaps impatience brought her back too soon. Back she would come to Whitehall; and there she would stay until she could no longer endure the coming and the going in the Stone Gallery; or Nell's too-ready laughter and her own melancholy.

Catherine was spending more and more time at Somerset House. The Queen's Side was pleasanter than at Whitehall; it was lighter, more elegant—the Queen-mother had seen to it. It was luxurious beyond anything Catherine would have asked for herself; and she found herself enjoying it. Her audience chamber was beautiful—its eight sides set with wide windows, the cornice supporting the dome carved and gilt. And her private rooms were not only beautiful, they were comfortable. There was a room all lined with marble and within it a marble bath; she could take a bath hot or cold, as she chose. Water, heated upon a great fire in the kitchens, flowed from pipes, through a silver spigot—Louise, herself, had not dreamed of this luxury. But the most treasured thing about the Queen's Side was the privacy. Her rooms could be reached only through the great ball-room, so that always she had good warning. Hidden within a panel, a small door opened onto her private staircase. She could escape whenever she pleased.

But her chiefest joy was the chapel Madam Henrietta Maria had built. Here stood the superb altar, the great paintings, the marble statues; here stood the magnificent organ and here came Matthew Locke, that fine musician, to play upon it. Here she found peace. And here, as she had promised the Queen-mother, any Catholic, however humble, was free to enter and pray. At the moment none, save secret worshippers, dared come; Catholics had been banished from London. But they would return—God looks to His own; and the chapel would be waiting.

Here, in Somerset House, though life was not joyful—joyful it could never be, lacking Charles—it was dignified and peaceful. She could live out of sight and sound of the King's women. She could attend chapel or pray in her chamber as she chose. She could walk in the garden and watch the river gay with craft. Here, in this quiet time, she set herself to perfect her English. She would read aloud; she would talk with Eliza asking her to correct the slightest fault. Painstaking she would repeat and repeat until she had the phrase correct. Though still she spoke slowly, searching for the unfamiliar word, she seldom made a mistake. In the evenings she would listen to music from Italy—she cared little for love-songs from France; or play at cards. She played always for the smallest stakes—unlike Madam Babyface who could lose a thousand in an evening... but then she knew where to get the money. If Charles had none there was always Louis to fill her hands—the little Saviour of France. Surely Charles must wonder, at times, where all the money came from!

XXVII

When Catherine looked upon Louise's boy now three years old, anguish pierced her heart. The child was his father in little. It was as though the French woman had robbed her not of husband, alone; but of child; of child, also.

And Charles treated the little boy like a royal prince. There was a governor, there were tutors, there was a chamberlain and an army of servants; there was a great house in the pretty village of Wimbledon so that the King might ride over often to see his son. The little boy was my lord duke of Richmond now. That the French woman's bastard should bear her husband's title grieved Frances; but she had no children and the title was in the King's gift. She had hoped that some kinsman of the house of Lennox might receive it; but there was no honour that Charles might bestow upon the child that he did not bestow. Little Richmond was granted the royal honour of having his train carried; of having his coach emblazoned with the royal arms. That last stung Frances, for all her gentleness, to anger. 'The brat takes the Richmond and Lennox arms—and no bend sinister! It is an insult to my dead husband and to me and to all Stuarts.'

The Queen's hand went to her head to ease the stab of pain. *No bend sinister.* Was Charles implying that he regarded the child as lawfully begot? This was worse, even, than Monmouth.

Disturbed, angry, she saw her husband grow ever more besotted, and the boy more spoiled, more insolent; in such good conceit of himself that, at times, she could scarce endure to look at him. Had he been her own she would have bred him to knowledge of his duties, small as he was, and to all princely courtesies. But still she coveted him.

Was there never to be an end to the heartbreak?

Charles said, coaxing and debonair, 'Kate, will you do your Charles a kindness?'

Your Charles. Would God it were true! But, for all that, it worked its magic.

'With all my heart.' She had made his phrase her own.

'Let your kindness reach out to a fugitive to these shores.'

His speech that could be so forthright was curiously flowery. She had heard certain rumours; she knew what to expect.

'It is the Princess Mazarin,' he said.

'You sent for her?' She kept her voice steady. All the world knew how once, driven by passion, he had offered the lady his hand; and how her uncle, Mazarin the rich cardinal, had refused him, the penniless wanderer.

'I did not send for her. She came.'

'Knowing her welcome?'

'Not unless you welcome her, also.'

Once, all ignorant, she had told the King *You lie!* She could say it now with full understanding. She said, instead, her stiffness a rebuke, 'Sir, I shall do my best.'

'That's my Kate!' and he was entirely unrepentant. 'No man ever had a kinder wife.'

'You would be the better for a shrew.'

'Well, you can play that also!' He kissed her cheek.

When he had gone her mind took her over what she had heard of Hortense, Princess Mazarin-Mancini, duchess of Meilleraye. She was a dark and dashing beauty; she was married and her reputation blown upon. She was restless, she was wild; she had left broken hearts behind in all the capitals of Europe. Charles had been infatuated with her once; when he looked upon that glowing beauty—what then?

'Madam, I have seen her!' Frances burst in upon the Queen in that impulsive way of hers; but they were old friends and Catherine loved her for it. Behind Frances, Eliza came, quiet, as befitted her years.

'She comes dressed as a gentleman of fashion; and by God it suits her!' Frances said. 'It shows off every charm. And she's brought with her half-a-dozen pretty girls dressed as pages; and there's a little blackamoor she keeps beside her to show up the whiteness of her skin.'

'Another fair and frail one!' Eliza said.

'Fair—yes. Frail?' Frances laughed. 'Tough as a riding-boot—and has need! That husband of hers—half-crazed, they say; and cold and cruel, besides. She was very young when they forced her to marry him, fourteen no more—a child, I would say, except she was never a child, that one! She's about thirty now. After the children were born—she ran away; and who can blame her?'

Catherine nodded. All Christendom knew the tale; how she had run from her husband disguised as a boy; and how she took every adventure as it came and lovers as she chose.

'She has but one philosophy,' Frances said. 'To take what she wants. She was an abominable child. That's why her uncle Mazarin—he was her guardian, married her off young; he detested her. She used to laugh at religion; she never came to mass, she was the scandal of Paris. She used to steal her uncle's purse and stand on the balcony of the Palais Cardinal and fling gold piece by piece, out of the window. The courtyard would be black with folk pushing and fighting like madmen; and cursing when a gold piece missed them; often enough someone would be badly hurt. But she didn't care; not she! There she'd stand laughing, the insolent girl. And when she tired of her fun, she'd turn her back and walk in through the window and that would be the end of her nasty game for the time being. Nasty. And costly. And she's always been the same. Fling away the gold—there's plenty more! She's rid herself of the greatest fortune in Europe. Now she has nothing but what her husband gives—and that's almost nothing. Still, she does well enough, believe it.'

'Does she come now to crawl into the King's bed and empty his pockets?' Catherine cried out, bitter.

'There's more to it than that—so my husband thinks,' Eliza told them. 'He says she's here to work against France and that Arlington brought her here.'

'Arlington may be the King's good friend; but I have never reckoned him mine—now less than ever!' Catherine sighed.

'He means her to bind the King to a Dutch alliance, so Ormonde thinks. The Dutch are paying her well. A battle royal it would seem between little spy for France and little spy for Holland.'

'The King does not take it kindly when women meddle in affairs,' the Queen said. 'She would be wise, that one, to keep her breath to cool her soup.'

Frances sighed; the sigh told Catherine how formidable the enemy.

When Catherine met Hortense Mazarin-Mancini, she hated her on sight—the woman was more beautiful than she had feared. The jet-black hair hung in shining curls; yet so white her skin, she seemed of dazzling fairness. And her eyes. Frances said they had a strange trick of changing with her mood, so that you'd swear they were black, purple, or sea-blue, even. Duels had been fought over their colour, Frances said. At this moment they were violet; violets sparkling in dew... but then the whole woman sparkled, she glittered, she flamed. Beside her Louise's baby-beauty paled.

Hortense made her curtsey with a lovely grace; she kissed the Queen's hand and turned again to Charles. They spoke together in French. The conversation must be witty... or intimate, Catherine thought, her own French not good enough to follow; for the two heads were close together behind one fan from which issued peals of laughter. And, as though the gods had not sufficiently endowed her, Catherine thought wretched, laughter and voice were music both.

For all her care in dressing the Queen was out of looks; a headache, growing steadily worse, left her pale and dim. Now and then she would venture a remark; then the glittering beauty would turn and, in her pretty, broken English, answer the Queen with respect, and so turn again to talk and laughter behind the fan.

On and on. No end to it! Catherine spared a glance for Louise; never had the Frenchwoman to face such overwhelming beauty, such elegance, such wit. Catherine trembled for the French alliance.

She might have spared her fears. Behind the babyface lay keen wits and iron discipline. Louise knew all about the newcomer, knew that Hortense was, herself, her own worst enemy; her own wild impulses could be counted upon to ruin her plans. One had but to know how to wait... Louise knew how.

The princess Mazarin was lodged handsomely at the court of the little Duchess of York. Charles was forever at St. James. He could not, it seemed, tear himself from Hortense. They flirted, they kissed openly; everyone knew they slept together. Louise remained calm above her fears. But Nell Gwynn grinned her delight—she had never expected to keep the King to herself; to see her rival's nose put out of joint was exquisite pleasure.

But not all the seductions of Hortense could move Charles from his plans. He concluded yet another secret pact with Louis—France and England to help each other at need; and signed it with his own hand.

There was a slight cooling between Charles and Hortense. Of this new secret pact she knew nothing; but she was piqued that she had not yet won him to open friendship with Holland.

'The princess. She has caught, perhaps, a whisper of the agreement with Louis?' Catherine asked anxious.

Charles permitted himself a smile. 'Impossible. Wit she has; but understanding—none! The truth is, she exhausts me. You cannot heat up an old love; twice-cooked meat—it's tough and tasteless!'

Now Catherine could afford to smile again. Louise smiled, too.

Hortense, stung, transferred her favours to a lover that had followed her to England and stayed fast at her heels. The Prince of Monaco was young and handsome; he was rich, he was devoted. Hortense, the impulsive creature, lost her head; she did nothing to hide her passion. Had she been discreet Charles would have cared little; but she offended his pride. He would be charming to her always, and generous at need; but he was finished with her forever.

'My nephew Orange asks for my niece Mary's hand,' Charles told Catherine. 'Now why? Can he be troubled about French success in Flanders?'

'I do think so. And disappointed, also, because the enchant... enchantress, the Mazarin has failed. But you; you would welcome the match?'

He nodded. 'It would strengthen me abroad and at home. It would mean peace and friendship with the Netherlands. A Protestant peace; it would please the people well. And it could call a halt to Louis' plans; he devours too much of Europe. Yes, William shall have Mary!'

'But James? He may refuse. He will want one of his own faith for his girl.'

'*Refuse?*' The dark brows lifted in the sallow face; there was a glint of anger in the pleasant eyes. 'Oddsfish, we'll have no refusal. And besides—my niece is bred to the church of England. Orange shall come.'

It was mid-October when William came; a well-looking young man but delicate; they said he had a consumption of the lungs. He was exactly as Charles remembered—proud and cold; but Catherine was sorry for the quiet stranger in the too-gay court. 'I cannot endure him nor I will not endure him,' Mary cried out to Charles; and when he smiled and refused to listen, she betook herself to the Queen. 'He is disagreeable; and he looks spiteful. Plead for me, Madam. Tell my uncle I would die, rather. Tell him, *tell* him, I beseech you, Madam!'

'If it could help you, I would do it,' Catherine said, grieved for the proud girl that had shown nothing ever, but cold courtesy to the Queen. 'But it could not help. When princes marry it is two countries that marry; my mother said this when I, myself, was wed. It is England and Holland that marry now—each for the other's good.'

'And I am the sacrifice?'

'Sacrifice,' she tried to comfort the girl. 'A well-looking young man; and virtuous, I hear.'

'Well-looking; I cannot agree—the long, pale horse-face! And virtuous? I'd give all his virtues for one spark of my uncle's kindness.'

The bride was in tears; but the country overjoyed. A Protestant match; it could mean a Protestant succession. The Duchess of York had had nothing but miscarriages or early deaths with her infants. Now she was near her time with a fifth. Miscarriage; or an infant so delicate it could not be reared—she would run true to form. The lord Mayor and his aldermen, statesmen and judges streamed towards Whitehall to express their pleasure. Every town sent its chief citizens to offer congratulation. The common people showed their delight with bonfires; Edinburgh Cross was hung with oranges and all the children had sugar-plums.

On a dark evening in early November they were married—sullen bride and cold groom. Charles did his best to lend some merriment to the occasion; even he must give it up. But when the bridal couple were bedded, he thrust his head through the bedcurtains crying out to his niece, 'Never let your step-mother be first with a boy!' And to the groom, 'Now, nephew, to your work. Hey for St. George and England!'

The Queen's birthday was kept earlier this year so that a great ball might be given before the young people left. Charles came to the Queen's Side; Catherine was dressed and her woman putting a jewelled crown upon the dark curls. 'Every inch a Queen!' Charles said. 'And a pretty one.'

And pretty she was, bright with joy of his approval... until she came into the ball-room. There stood Louise delicately, delightfully plump; there stood James' little duchess with her white-lily look and Rose de Warmestre sweet as her name. There stood my lady Southesk, my lady Chesterfield and half-a-dozen others, in the full perfection of their beauty. Women like flowers, Catherine thought. Joy went out like a candle.

Neither bride nor groom showed pleasure. Mary looked sullen and William cold. In the days before they left Catherine tried to comfort the bride. Mary took every word an insult. 'My father dislikes this match and so do I! And so we shall do—ever!'

Catherine made no answer; she had her own reasons for disliking it. James' son—if it were born and managed to survive—would be a Catholic Stuart. Mary's son—and it would inherit a double Stuart strain—would be a Protestant Stuart. No doubt at all where English eyes would wander for an heir... past James, past his child... and what of the Succession then?

While Catherine searched her mind for some comfortable answer, Mary said, quiet and bitter, 'I know how it is with you. You are glad to see the back of me; because I am no Papist, glad to be rid of me!'

'You do not believe that, child; nor you cannot believe it!' Catherine grieved for the girl; Mary, for all her commoner blood, had always held herself better than any foreign princess. Now her defences were down, her pride laid low. She looked plain and untidy, her pretty looks lost in swollen eyes and dishevelled hair, her gown thrown on anyhow. Catherine guessed she had torn herself from the hands of her maid in one of those fits of temper she had inherited from her mother.

Catherine said, gentle, 'You are a Stuart princess and you go to be first lady in a new land. You have courage and...' she rejected the word *pride*, 'dignity. And you must show both. Come dry your eyes...' and remembered how she, herself, had not shed a tear, bidding her mother Farewell, '... and let me order your hair.'

Mary pulled herself away petulant and Catherine said, gentle still, 'I do know how you feel, Mary; none better. I, too, was called to leave my home...'

Mary laughed in the Queen's face, 'But, Madam, you came to *England*!' As if that must be paradise for any foreigner on earth.

Had she known that she would return to England, its Queen, she would the sooner have dried her eyes.

XXVIII

Marry's marriage had aroused Louis' bitter anger. He withdrew his friendship... and his subsidy. Now Charles was penniless, indeed. The money Danby had saved was gone; swallowed, for the most part, in paying the country's debts. Everywhere unrest and fear. French agents spreading fear of the Dutch, Dutch agents spreading fear of the French; and Parliament's own agents spreading fear of the King—his standing army, they swore it, a tyrant's weapon to keep the people down. Fear working like yeast, risings everywhere; Yorkshire and Ireland and Scotland in arms. And everywhere preachers stirred up rebellion. In London crazy men struck fear with strange antics and dire prophecies. The mad Quaker that ran naked save for a loin-cloth, a bucket of fire upon his head, was followed by legions of madmen, all crying *Woe, woe!* Armed processions marched through London carrying torches and crying out upon the King and the bishops that had murdered Christ. Everywhere anger, hysteria and fear.

Yet still Charles held by those things he thought right. He would not disband the army; he dared not—it was needed for the country's protection. And he held still by his dream of a people free to worship as they chose. Every disturbance, every outcry, he said, did but point to the rightness of his dream. Catherine, though she could not agree—since for a good Catholic there is but one way to worship—honoured him for it.

In Whitehall Louise was brought to bed in premature labour. She lost her child; and feared to lose her looks—and that troubled her more. A child she had; and could always have another. But her looks! Lose them and she lost the King. Strangely, it was Catherine who grieved. That a child—any child Charles had fathered—should die, seemed a senseless waste. Such a child, had it been her own, must have been the brightest, the most perfect joy—and not for the succession alone.

Charles had a private passage made between his rooms and those of Louise; the court bowed lower still before her. 'What need of such a passage?' Catherine cried out, goaded. 'Is it to come at her more easily? The woman, I think, is easy enough! Is it that he may come in secret? That's a secret the whole world knows!'

'It could be for the King's convenience rather than his love,' Penalva said. 'For think, Madam my darling! He knows about her secret meetings with spies from France. He sees—like all the court—she is not unfriendly to Shaftesbury. Through that private passage he may learn much to his advantage.'

'God grant it could be so!' Catherine said; but her sigh was deep.

Everyone might bow before Louise; she had her hangers-on, she had her flatterers and her spies—but not one true friend. The old nobility were courteous but aloof; she tried to win Eliza from the Queen. Courtiers laughed behind their hands at a tale. Eliza, herself, told it to the Queen.

'She sent me a message to say she'd honour me by dining at my house—a royal command; no less! So I ordered a good dinner... and sent my grand-daughters away, Emmy and Bet, both; they were not best-pleased. And I invited no-one; no-one at all. So when Madam arrived—as for a grand occasion, and looking peaked and plain—we sat down three at table; my lady, my chaplain and myself.'

Catherine laughed outright. Company for the great Louise—one old woman and her domestic chaplain.

'It will be long, I fancy, before she invites herself again. She could scarce eat, she choked so with anger. She would, if she could, have run to the King with a tale; but, what tale? She'd invited herself and my grand-daughters were from home.'

Louise was, indeed, looking peaked and plain; she was not yet well from her confinement. Now she was for Bourbon to take the waters. It was whispered that Louis, because of Mary's marriage, had recalled her in anger. Off she went in royal state—upon that journey the Queen had never been able to afford—and Catherine prayed she would never return. 'Now please God I shall have some peace,' she told Eliza. 'Little spy for France is gone; and spy for Holland—the Mazarin is no more than a warmed-up dish. And the others—the Davies and the Gwynn and the rest—thorns in the flesh, little thorns!' And suddenly cried out, 'But thorns—even little thorns! Why must I endure them? Is there never to be an end?'

I am thirty-seven and he is forty-five. I am a woman and his wife, and love is a hunger in me, never satisfied… the passing years make more desperate my hunger. And he? He forever seeks the pleasure of the flesh and is never satisfied. Dear God, are we never free of our appetites?

Would life never go smoother, Charles wondered? He was—and he knew it—by nature a lazy, easy man, enjoying the good things of life—women and food; plays and pictures and poetry; a liberal-minded man open to the great new ideas in science, experimenting in his own small way, delighting in the meetings of his Royal Society. But there was little time for such pleasant things, he must forever tread a narrow plank. Across the precipice that yawned between Holland and France—one careless step; and disaster.

He came, as usual, seeking Catherine.

'What's a man to do? The country is mad for war with France— and Parliament whips it on. But Parliament, though it talk loud enough, wouldn't vote a penny; half of them take bribes from Louis. I do my utmost to raise forces to help the Dutch—as I am bound to do. But—' he pulled out his pockets. 'I am exactly the Dutch pictures of me—the King of England, empty pockets hanging, beseeching Parliament for money!' And could not forbid his own laughter; even in his darkest hours, laughter never failed. For pity of him and his courage she could not laugh with him; she knew well, how, beneath the laughter and lazy smiling, his wits were most desperately engaged.

Louise was still away; and he seemed to breathe the freer for her absence. Nell gave gay little parties and he enjoyed them. 'Nell helps me to laugh!' he said. 'But it isn't only that. She invites all sorts of people—some because I ask it; and sometimes we are masked. I listen, I learn... I pick up useful information.'

Catherine's heart contracted with pity. He could not go to a simple party, even, but he must take his troubles with him. She watched him with growing concern. The difficulties of his every day—the intrigue, the unending poverty, were too much. He was beginning to show signs of strain. He was too thin and more tired than he should be; now and again—and sometimes without cause—his easy temper would break into sharp anger; and that was something new. There was a strain upon herself, too. Seeing him driven and misunderstood, yet, for the most part, bearing himself with patience, she would feel her own anger rise. But, *Anger is like a good sword. Use it at need.* Her mother's warning at some childish anger. Well, there was sense in it!

Through spring and summer, the never-ending ding-dong.

'All I want is peace; peace at home and abroad. Only in peace can trade and prosperity flourish. But Parliament won't listen... little loyalty there! Those that take bribes from Louis—and that's more than half—urge me to disband the army. Disband—though they know well we're pledged to Holland. Not a penny until I disband! Louis is at the bottom of that. How he must laugh! He offered me six million livres if I'd do just that—disband. Six million in gold! Enough to settle every debt; to keep me easy for the rest of my life. But I would not do it. I dare not do it. We need the army for our protection—protection from Louis himself; protection from William, for all our friendship. Now it seems that Parliament will do it for me—and I not one penny the wiser.'

He paced restless. 'Can they not see, this Parliament of mine that, with no army we are helpless, open to every insult, every aggression? Without an army we must agree to any terms our enemies, or friends—so called—choose to offer!'

He had halted now and stood staring out of the window with unseeing eyes. She came softly and laid a hand upon his arm. 'Parliament shall see it, because it *must* see... the matter is so clear.'

He went on beseeching Parliament not to disband the army; his enemies in the House made great play of it. Why did the King need an army save as a weapon... a papist weapon to destroy good Protestants?

I seek nothing but my country's good. He said it in Parliament and without. Let Parliament withhold its gold! he'd go without bread, if he must; he'd pledge his poor credit where he could. He'd not disband.

Distrust and backbiting, pamphlet and caricature to discredit the King. Against that dark background his honesty shone clear; honesty, and good sense. At the end of the summer Parliament, for very shame, granted a small sum.

'The smallness isn't important—or scarce important!' Charles told Catherine. 'They voted the money; they showed—or were forced to show—belief in me. The rest will follow. Please God I shall yet rule this stiff-necked Parliament of mine; win my tiresome, beloved people again.'

Now he was able to send the promised help to William. At Morns the Dutch were fighting a losing battle against the French; English forces turned the tide. Now, Dutch and English victorious together, peace was made; peace upon England's terms. His prestige high in England and abroad, Charles went to Windsor a weary but happy man.

There in that quiet place he did little business; he was so tired and he had more than a touch of ague. But the summer sun warmed him to the bone and the quiet rested his tired mind; and soon he was hunting and hawking and riding and fishing, with time to remember that life was good.

In Paris Louis schemed with false Buckingham; in London Barrillon, the French ambassador, obeyed his orders—to make as much sly mischief as possible. And in Windsor Catherine, happy that Louise was still away, listened while Charles talked and planned; and closed her eyes to the pretty creatures that fluttered about him. Mayflies all; they lasted for a day. But... tomorrow? Would not tomorrow bring others in their place? Well, she would reckon with tomorrow when it came; today, in his contentment she must find her own.

It was well they had this short respite. Soon the Popish Terror would stretch out seeking to drag the Queen of England to a traitor's death.

Shaftesbury was at the bottom of that; Shaftesbury whipping into fury the long hatred against the Catholics. Once he had been the

King's man; then he had gone over to the enemy. Dismissed—and rightly—from his high office of Lord Chancellor, he came, beseeching the King he had betrayed to show favour. Charles refused. He could forgive any man anything against himself; but—urging the King's divorce—he had offended against the Queen.

Now Shaftesbury must make another bid for popularity. He would try once more to force the King's divorce. So he would please Parliament and the people; and, in spite of all protestation, he must, he was sure, please the King. Charles would be happy to indulge himself legally upon the body of some young beauty and present the country with an heir; duty and pleasure perfectly in accord.

He had not reckoned with Charles' real affection for his wife, still less with the King's principles of justice; and, least of all, with Stuart pride. That Shaftesbury should *dare*! Now, more than ever, Charles looked upon Shaftesbury as his enemy; and Shaftesbury, enflamed, went further. Now he struck not only at the Queen, but at York; at York, too. He would not rest—he swore it—until he had cut James from the succession. Monmouth should wear the crown instead of James; and, if Charles did not look to it, instead of Charles, also. Charming Monmouth; King Monmouth... that would do as he was told.

He had an unlooked-for ally. Louise was back again well, and more beautiful than ever. An unlikely ally one would have thought—herself, a hated papist. But she was Louise; and faith must wait upon ambition. She would work hand-in-glove with Shaftesbury to bring both down—the Queen and James together.

He began his campaign by whispering in the King's ear. The King's answer he knew, already; but by the King's manner he would know how to proceed.

'My lord of Monmouth is much loved; my lord your brother is not nor ever will be, Papist that he is! You, yourself, sir, of late, have come under suspicion of going some of the way—if not all the way—along with the Papists. It has made things hard for you; and may make them harder. I beseech, you, sir, please the people and your own heart... the heart of a loving father. Declare my lord of Monmouth your heir. It is all very simple. You have but to say that you married his mother...'

He had got so far only because rage had taken the King's breath.

'That strumpet!' And now his anger burst forth. 'I took her for what she was—any man's harlot. Marry her! Only a fool would expect fools to believe it! I love my son; but—I've said it before and I'll say it again— I'd rather see him hanged on Tyburn tree than wear the Stuart crown. And from you, yourself, I have endured enough. Watch your step, my lord!'

Now Shaftesbury was an enemy, indeed, his whole will set upon the Queen's disgrace. And, if with that, he might bring disgrace and death to others of her faith—so much sweeter his revenge.

From his great house in the city he bought popularity with feasts and gold; and there he entertained Monmouth as though the young man were the Prince of Wales. They called him no longer duke of Monmouth; but simply—the Duke. *The Duke*; it was James' title; but, in the eyes of the common people, it belonged to Monmouth; to Monmouth, alone.

Now when he rode through the city he was greeted like the country's heir. And he, poor, pretty fool, allowed his head to be turned. Not love for a most loving father, nor loyalty to a most generous King could stay him. Love and loyalty; he knew not the words.

Handsome and debonair, the King's eldest son—save for the unknown priest in Rome—Monmouth needed but one thing to make him the perfect heir. A lawful name. That one thing the King should provide—Shaftesbury would see to it.

The King held by that strange thing called *honour*; he would not play Shaftesbury's game. Very well, my lord thought of another—to be played without the King. A game which properly played would rid England of the King's wife, the King's brother, and all hated Papists. In this new game Shaftesbury himself would not appear. In secret he would direct his players. Already he had chosen their captain.

Titus Oates.

XXIX

Titus Oates. Catherine was never to think of him without the desire to vomit. To her dying day she would remember his face... and she was not the only one.

An extraordinary face. Loathsome. He had no neck so that the great bald head sat between his shoulders like a vast cheese. In the middle of this grey cheese—the mouth small, wet, red and mean. Above this hole of a mouth a nose, so small, so flat as scarce to be seen; and above it, the shifty, piggish eyes set in the almost non-existent brow. Beneath that dog's vent of a mouth hung the vast arc of his chin. He was less a man than a monster; there was no good man anywhere but shrank from the sight of him.

And his record was as monstrous as his face—liar and traitor that he was; and the bowels of mercy not in him. Of low birth, whose memory forever galled him, he was a continual turncoat in religion—under Cromwell an anabaptist, under Charles a Church of England clerk in holy orders. Last year a Catholic; this year returned again to the Church of England. He was lewd, he was a liar, he was a thief; twice he had been prosecuted and punished for perjury. Lewd behaviour had lost him appointment after appointment. He had wormed himself in by lies as a chaplain to the Fleet; but so vicious, so corrupting his behaviour with the young that, here too, he was thrown out, disgraced. During his flirtation with the Catholic faith he had been received into the English college of Jesuits in Valladolid; here, too, he had been cast out because of evil behaviour. This rankled more bitterly than any other insult—that despised Papists should so dare! Safe once more in the bosom of the English Church he could take revenge against the hated Papists.

Ugly his face; uglier his record. But his luck had changed at last. Shaftesbury had recognised his value as a tool; and Shaftesbury did not hesitate to use him.

It was this man that was to testify against the Queen; that, save for the King, would have brought her to the block; that was to bring so many innocents of her faith to a hideous death before his day was done.

Summer of 'seventy-eight; and the hunt was up with Oates, that mad dog, leading the hounds in chase.

...The Papists that were banished have come crawling back. They mean to fire London as they did before. The Great Fire was their work... and will be again. They will murder the King; they will put his Papist brother in his place. But the true King of the country will be the Bishop of Rome that seeks to destroy our English faith...

Mad dogs barking, filling London with the noise of their clamour. To Windsor, the noise of Oates and his hounds came faint; but, in September, when the court returned, Charles was surprised and a little bored to find that Oates was still making his 'discoveries'.

The noise of the baying grew deafening, fear of the Papists deeper, hatred more implacable. Oates had gained the ear of Parliament; and, more important, the ear of the common people. The venom of his madness exacerbated their own; they listened to him as though God Himself spoke. All his enemies they made their own; they heaped rewards upon him.

In early October, Oates appeared before the King in Council. The story he told shook them all... except the King. Once again—conspiracy to destroy the King and the Church of England. But now the plot was world-wide. The Pope at the head, the King of France at his right hand; and, at his left, the General of the Jesuits to command his Provincials in England, Spain and Ireland. A world army of Papists fanatical with hate. And the heart of the plot—the King to be poisoned and his brother set in his place.

Oates had all the details. 'Everywhere English Papists sharpen their knives to murder honest citizens while they sleep; Irish Papists will join them; the country will run with blood. From Lancashire yet more Papists will march to fire London for the second time—our fine new London. But first of all they will seize the King's majesty, to poison him.'

Yes, he could name the poisoners—Wakeman the Queen's physician for one.

'Wakeman!' the Queen cried out when Charles sought her with the news. 'Wakeman, that good man! There's none shall believe it.'

'There's plenty to believe it,' Charles said, grave. 'Oates is a liar. But hatred's a madness in the blood; it corrupts a man's whole being.'

'God help Wakeman; and God help us all!' She crossed herself. 'I think of the blood that will flow through one wicked man—and I tremble.'

But she did not, as yet, tremble for herself.

'I questioned the fellow myself,' Charles said. 'I asked him how he came to know of this conspiracy. He said—and I all-but puked—*God helped me; God and His holy angels. I went among the Jesuits that I might spy out their secrets.* So he makes good the fact that himself was a Jesuit. He has named five that are leaders—five of my peers. And it's odds they go to the Tower, all five... even Stafford, rising eighty though he is, and can scarce stand and deaf as a post! Once I should have laughed in Oates' ugly face; but it's no laughing matter—there's wickedness in it, Kate. I'm troubled... deeply troubled.'

Daily the Council sat; and the King with it. Daily the Queen grew more fearful; she feared for her priests, she feared for the helpless upon whom hatred must break. For herself she feared not at all. She was above this ugly suspicion as the sun in the sky.

She forgot that storm may put out the sun.

The accusations grew; and with it the madness. The Council had caught the foul infection. Now no nonsense was too great for it to believe. In vain Charles made clear his own disbelief. Orders were issued for the arrest of all those Oates named; every man! To the Tower went the hale and the sick, the old and the young, the high and the low.

'We haven't enough prisons to hold them all!' a sickened Charles told his Council.

'We'll empty them fast enough!' Oates' hand went up to his neck; he laughed aloud in his sovereign's face.

Daily the fear grew. And now it had something to feed upon.

Murder.

Sir Edmund Berry Godfrey, a well-liked gentleman, magistrate of London, went out one day and never came back. Five days later, his body was found in a ditch thrust through with his own sword.

'Who killed him? No need to ask,' Oates told the Council.

'But he had friends among the Papists, good Protestant though he was!' Charles reminded them all. 'Why should Papists murder so good a friend?'

'Because Papists like mad dogs know neither mercy nor fear!' Oates, himself, grinned like a mad dog.

He was murdered by you! Charles was taken by a certainty. *Your orders, to spread terror further.* Useless to speak his certainty; there was no proof.

Now the people were more than ever crazed with fear. Oates' stories grew wilder, madder... *The French fleet is sailing; the Papist armies of Christendom, marching. All over England arms lie buried. They will poison our wells. They will rape your daughters before your eyes. They will murder you as you sleep; they will entice you from your homes to murder you in secret. Remember Godfrey...* And, lest fever cool, the pitiful body of the dead man was paraded through London while the crowds wept, and burned with anger so that let any Catholic appear upon the street or his dog or his cat, even, and he or his poor creature must have been torn to pieces.

And still Oates delighted in his power, the power of his malice. And still the Council swallowed his tales—or, fearing for their skins, pretended to believe. Looking at the sly, unhealthy creature, swollen with self-righteousness and eaten by hatred, Charles felt his flesh crawl.

Oates was giving evidence against a handful of poor priests; he meant to have their blood. 'They were seduced from their loyalty to the King by Don Juan of Austria; I swear it!'

'You mean the Spanish prince?' Charles asked.

'Who else? I heard him, I swear it, with my own ears.'

'You know this Don Juan then?'

'I should! I knew him in Madrid; many's the time I've heard his wickedness from his own mouth.'

'Describe me this prince.'

'Tall and thin... and black as the devil.'

Charles surprised them all with a burst of laughter.

'This fellow here thinks all Spaniards are black! He never clapped eyes on Don Juan in his life! But I have! I know him well. He has blue eyes and reddish hair. Now!' he held Oates with a look in which there was no more laughter. 'Let us go a step further. You have told us that you saw Père Lachaise, the French King's confessor, hand over one hundred thousand pounds to one of these priests to strengthen the hand of Papists, here in London. Where did you see that?'

'In the house of the Jesuits, sir, in Paris.'

'And where may that be?'

'Hard by the Louvre, sir.'

'The Jesuits have no house within a mile of the Louvre,' Charles said and there was no more laughter in him. 'Have a care, fellow, how you wag your tongue.'

Hatred leaped, naked, into the man's eyes. Had he dared he would have accused the King himself.

Charles came storming into the Queen's closet; he had a sick look.

'Coleman's been named,' he said.

Catherine's look matched his own. Coleman! James' secretary. This might well smear James himself.

'I *told* James to rid himself of that fool. I warned him. There may well be trouble, I said. Coleman's a man that must forever make himself important. But would James listen? Not he. He knows better than us all. God alone knows where his wisdom will end!'

'But Coleman!' she said. 'A fool... yes; but a good fool.'

'A *Papist* fool. No wickedness in him, I grant you. But all the same he'll not escape.'

'But Godfrey was his friend; Godfrey warned him of danger. It doesn't make *sense*.'

'No need of sense. When Oates planned to murder Godfrey he knew what he was doing. He puts out of the way a good man that would help poor Papists; and he whips up yet more fury against the Papists themselves. Two birds killed with one stone!'

'But why Coleman?' She threw out her hands. What evidence?'

'None. And none needed. In Oates' eyes he's guilty of worse than murder—and must be got out of the way. Coleman dreams of bringing back his faith—the fool was writing to Père Lachaise on the matter. But it was talk, mere talk; a pipe-dream. And, as if the accusation isn't enough, Oates tangles it up with a tale of a bribe—one hundred thousand pounds. And that's another lie. Coleman works for his God, not for money. Oates, the filthy spider, tangles his flies with lies.' His face was sick with disgust.

'But the fly he'd most like to gobble is—myself!' Charles grinned. 'He hates me. I've proved him a liar twice at least—and that he'll never forgive. He'd kill me for it, if he could; but since he can't, he does the next best thing. I've humiliated him; now he'll humiliate me. And he's found the way—very simple.'

Stand by the truth. It was her first thought. Then, her native shrewdness showed her the clear issue. If he openly expressed disbelief, Oates would turn and accuse Charles himself; accuse him of plotting to force the Catholic faith upon England.... *Son of a Catholic mother, husband to a Catholic wife, brother to Catholic James, and to that sister he so loved. What else could you expect? The taint is in the family.* Let Oates say that long enough and the people would rise. Charles' personal popularity would go for nothing; those that loved him would be powerless.

He said, watching her face, 'Must I go wandering again? Or will they treat me as they treated my father?'

She said, shuddering upon the thought, 'You must be wise; you must watch every word. To speak too free—it can help no-one. You must sit back and let the law take its way; you have always said it.'

She was right; he knew it. But it was hard... hard.

Oates' persecutions grew louder, longer; they spread wider, reached higher. He grew yet more exalted in public esteem; already he was swollen to an extreme of vanity, of insolence. It was as though an evil spirit possessed him—a devil's familiar to do his master's work. And still his lightest, slightest word was gospel; and still he was a hero, the monstrous creature. Lest his precious skin be in danger he was given, at Parliament's entreaty, an armed bodyguard; and to keep him well-fed and snug a pension of twelve hundred pounds a year and lodgings within Whitehall.

Catherine cried out at that. 'To have him lodged within our walls; it... it vomits me like the stench of the plague.'

'Whitehall is large enough; we shall escape the stink of corruption!' But for all that the King's face was dark with anger.

Oates was actually within the palace; he had his own lodgings, his own servants; he poisoned the air for the Queen. When she could endure it no longer she would fly to the clean air of Somerset House.

And still the Terror grew.

Day after day innocent men were dragged before the courts. Coleman was found guilty; it was expected. And though he was a rash and foolish fellow, still he was innocent of Godfrey's death and of every crime—save that of loving his faith too well. He made a brave ending, thanking God that he died in the true faith. And others died as bravely. Knowing the fearful death to which he must come—the hanging, the drawing, the burning and the quartering—there was not one but, upon the gallows, prayed God's blessing upon the King and upon the country; and, especially, they prayed His mercy upon those that unjustly condemned them. Such deaths were not shameful but glorious.

Trial after trial. All over England and Wales men hanged for their belief in God. The faintest nod from Oates was a death sentence. The Queen wept for Grove and Lewis, for White and Harcourt, for Fenwick and Turner—priests she had known and respected; and for more than man can write or tongue utter.

But it was for Langhorne she wept most. They brought her his hymn written in prison, awaiting his hideous end—no hope to escape; yet still he could write.

My Jesus calls me by this sentence
   To bear his cross and follow him.
   The judge declares my death necessary.
   For the King and for the people;
   The people shout and cry out,
      Crucify, Crucify.

He who was perfect innocency,
   Hath set before me his example.
   He opened not his mouth,
   He justified not himself,
   He forgave and prayed for his enemies.
      Oh what happiness

To be dignified with so many circumstances
    Of the death of Jesus.

I am willing to die for him as he died for me.
I am willing to die,
    To see my Jesus,
    To love my Jesus,
    To bless my Jesus.
  And to sing his praises to all eternity.
Come on my soul; let us go and rejoice.

She said, and the tears poured down her face, 'Can the country afford to lose a saint?'

'We cannot afford it; yet we lose and go on losing.' Charles looked at her—she was all ignorant of her own danger; he wondered when her turn would come.

XXX

The Queen had fled to Somerset House; she could no longer endure the sight of Oates flaunting himself, nor the strange looks he sent her from beneath pale, lashless lids. And there Charles came seeking her. He was, she could see, bitterly distressed; when he tried to smile his stiff lips would not obey.

'Kate.' At his grave voice she lifted a startled head. 'The world's gone mad. There's a fellow—a common horse-thief that should have hanged long since—come before Parliament. He has, it seems, fresh "information" concerning the death of Godfrey—and how many will hang for it God knows.' He stopped; he began again. 'He swears that the murder was done here... in Somerset House.' And, at her look of utter bewilderment, said gently, 'In the Queen's Side.'

She stood and stared. She was neither angry nor surprised, nor amused. She was like a beast beneath the pole-axe; she turned a slow, stricken head.

'We do nothing,' he said. 'We take no heed... unless we must.'

A few days later he came again. It was a cold Sunday afternoon in December. She had seen him angry and very angry; but never had she seen him thus—burnt out with anger; the shell of a face.

He said, 'Kate, I hate to soil my tongue and your ears with filth, but they, Oates and the horse-thief—Bedloe's his name—have, God damn them, gone further. In the murder of Godfrey they have named... *you*.'

She could not speak; only her eyes asked her question.

'You had best hear it all!' he told her. 'The murder was done by your servants here; and you knew all about it. That's the tale! They smothered Godfrey with pillows; he names the men. The body lay on your backstairs; for two days it lay there. He saw it himself—he swears it. He swears, further, that you, with your own lips offered him two thousand guineas to remove it.'

She opened her mouth; no words came.

'Murderers leaving their handiwork for all to see!' he said. 'The thing's an arrant nonsense!'

'Yet some shall believe it.' She spoke through shaking lips.

He shrugged. 'The times are mad; but surely not *so* mad. Yet the Commons are well-pleased with the horse-thief. He's to have a free pardon for all his crimes; ay, and a pension with it! No money to spare for you or me, and none for the country's needs; but these low rascals—pensions both! And more. Bedloe—' and now he could not look at her, 'is to join Oates at Whitehall.'

She cried out at that. 'I'll not live in Whitehall while those two pollute it.'

'You must come back. I am here to fetch you!' And he was very grave. 'It must never be said that we are at odds in this, you and I. You must dearly be seen to be under the protection of your husband and your King.'

'Then I shall come; but you must let me free, at times, into clean air.'

Back again in Whitehall she could not, it seemed, escape Oates' presence. He thrust himself still further beneath her eyes; he continued to send her his troubling glances. No more than she could escape the stench of pestilence could she escape him.

Within a few days Charles came seeking her again.

'Oates cools his heels in prison, I have seen to it! It is odds, though, my precious Commons will have him out again!'

'Thank God to be free of him for this time. And the horse-thief and his tale; what of him?'

'He has altered it. Now he tells a quite different tale!'

'And still they believe him?'

He shrugged. 'He says, now, you offered him four thousand guineas if he would do the murder himself.'

'The price goes up! Four thousand guineas—I have not so much in the world! Still, it is not much to pay for such a deed. A man's soul is worth more.'

'If he have one! The new tale goes that Godfrey was tricked into the courtyard of Somerset House about five in the afternoon and there murdered. Your men strangled him with his own cravat. When he was dead they thrust him through with his own sword to make it look like suicide.'

'I might almost laugh were the thing not so foul!' she said. 'First we smother him in the passage outside my rooms and leave the body two whole days for all to see; then we alter our minds and strangle him in the open courtyard—and, in spite of the constant coming and going, no-one sees us.'

'Bedloe will have to do better than that!' Charles said. 'There's a thing he doesn't know; and you, Kate, have forgotten it. I was with you the very time of the "murder" in the courtyard. We were actually in the courtyard together. We were watching a display…'

'I remember—the army… some exercise.'

'A new exercise—secret. There were guards at every gate; and, in the courtyard itself, guards drawn up; and sentries at every door. A fine place to choose for a murder! I asked the horse-thief how they removed the body from the courtyard. He says four men carried it within. And every door guarded! He says, if you please, that Pepys lent a hand. Poor Pepys. He'll need an oiled tongue to talk himself out of this!'

'And where did they put the body?' she asked as well as she could for the sickness in her throat.

'The footman's waiting-room. Can you credit that, either?' He gave a short laugh but there was no mirth in it. 'A room where there's a constant coming and going; a room through which servants must pass to bring you your meals. Never were such murderers to catch the public eye. The thing is crazy, beyond belief.'

'Yet still it will be believed,' she said.

Charles was sickened of the bloodlust, the cruelty and the lies. Yet still he kept his easy look; and still he stood by his principles. He would allow no word against James and his succession. And he kept about him Father Hudlestone that had once saved his life and other Catholics to whom he owed a debt; and these he exempted from the penalties that darkened the lives of their brothers in the faith. Never would he forget those that, at the risk of their lives, had served a beggar-King.

When he came into the Queen's rooms in the late November twilight, she thought at first he must be ill—so leaden his look, so hollow, so burning his eye.

He said, 'Kate, I come once more with a filthy tale. Those two—the horse-thief and Oates, God damn them, have gone yet further.'

'They can go no further,' she said, weary. 'Already I am named murderer.'

'They *have* gone further. You are named in yet another "murder"; or rather plot to murder.' And he was forced to turn his sick eyes from her. 'This time to murder... *me*.'

In the silence she heard the sound of laughing—high-pitched, shrill; a laughter she did not recognise. She wondered who dared to laugh, unseemly, in the Queen's room. Now the room was beginning to move, to rock, to spin. She put out a hand to steady herself; saw Charles swaying oddly towards her. The room span more madly; the light was darkening. To the sound of ugly laughing she went down into the darkness.

She came up out of the darkness into the darkness. She was in bed. Who had put her there? She stirred upon the pillows. There was a pencil of light as the door opened. Charles came in; behind him Eliza Ormonde carried a lamp.

Charles laid a hand upon her forehead. His hand felt cold; she shivered in fever. She heard him bid Eliza set the lamp upon the table and bring a cooling drink. With his own hands he set the pillows high and raised her upon them. Eliza made up the fire and went away. Lamplight and firelight were bright in the November gloom. Charles set a stool beside the bed and took her hand. A pretty scene, cosy, domestic; but beneath it fear—fear because of the hideous crime they had laid against the Queen.

She said, at last, 'So! I have planned to murder you... *you*! Oh Charles! How—' the words died in her throat; she tried again. 'How did I set about it?'

'Poison.' He spoke so low she just caught the word.

'Well, it's a woman's weapon; more within my strength than to smother or strangle. But... poison. Where should I get it? And, having got it—how hope to cover my crime?'

'Wakeman. Wakeman is named.'

'My good physician!' She laughed again. 'Charles,' she said, 'oh Charles!' and vomited.

On the strength of Bedloe's lies three of Catherine's faithful servants were hanged. 'You could have saved them!' she cried out to Charles.

'I could do nothing save make things worse, believe it, Kate! Yes, I could have used the royal privilege, I could have stayed the sentence. And then? *To please the Papists the King turns the course of justice.* Justice, God save us! Such talk could plunge this country—mad and frightened as it is—into war; civil war; of all wars the worst. Shed so much blood for the sake of three—innocent though they were—I'd not do it. The law must always take its course.' He looked into her stricken face, his own as stricken. 'Let the blood lie upon those that shed it. Oddsfish, Kate, I'm not a man for tears; but with tears I signed those warrants. A King's tears. How little it profits them or me.'

She could say nothing. She knew him well—never a man so merciful. But his strength—she knew it also—lay in never raising his voice against the law. But who, she thought, shall weigh the value of innocent blood, be it but of three, against the blood of the many.

It was no longer fantastic that the Queen should be named in so foul a murder; no longer fantastic that she should die on the block; or by the rope even—nothing too fantastic in this nightmare England. If Charles smiled but rarely, now, he showed no sign of bitterness.

Only three knew his grief—Catherine his wife; James his brother; and Osborne, my lord Danby, that brash Yorkshireman, the King's faithful friend.

It was not only the mob that howled for fresh blood. The whole country cried aloud for the hanging of those priests chained within their prisons; and for the hanging of the five peers within the Tower. But, most bitter, its voice against James—the voice of England crying aloud that he be put from the succession.

And still the Terror grew; and every day more innocent victims went to a bloody death. In all this Charles played no part, save now and again to question an accuser; his questions showed, clearly, his disbelief in the plot against his life. Parliament, whipped on by traitor Shaftesbury, again voted him no money.

'No end to the annoyances they put upon me!' Charles went storming to Catherine. 'They leave me so poor I have not a guinea in my pocket. And now it is Danby again. The Commons impeached him once, you remember?'

She nodded; among other false accusations they had included him in the lying tale of the plot against the King.

'That impeachment I scotched before it got through the Lords. Now they've brought up the tale again; they've attainted him and he lies in the Tower—Danby my friend... perhaps my only friend. It was he that juggled gold into my pocket and they don't forget it. They mean to leave me—my precious Parliament—without a single guinea or a single friend. And it's all Shaftesbury's doing, damned Shaftesbury.'

He... and one other that plots with him, that stuffs him with her master's gold... your French harlot... She bit back the words, as from long habit she had learned.

'Shaftesbury's upon his wings once more. Now all is to do again. Now he will attack James again, James and the succession. Up again Prince of Wales' Monmouth. Jamie's a troublemaker yet in spite of it I love him... but I'll see him dead before he takes James' place.'

When he had gone, so great her need of comfort, she went seeking Penalva... a cold room, she thought, for an old woman bred in the sunshine of Portugal. Soon she must make the act of self-denial, send beloved Penalva home.

'Now Shaftesbury presses once again. Now we shall hear, once more, that the Walters-strumpet was the King's true wife.' *Now they will urge him to put me away...* She could not, for shame, speak the words; not even to Penalva. But Penalva guessed; she knew her child.

'Madam, my darling, you have nothing to fear. The King protects you...'

But he does not love me...

'He visits the French harlot by day and night!' the Queen said, stubborn to refuse comfort.

'Visits by day—there's little to fear and much to gain. Always her rooms are crowded—ambassadors, statesmen, foreign visitors. I fancy he picks up information. And, for sleeping with her, could it not be he hopes she may let fall the word to betray her mischief.'

'Send her away—and there'd be no mischief.'

'With that one—always there would be mischief. But indeed, he cannot send her away. It would make trouble; bad trouble with the King of France.'

'I am weary to the bone of the King's women; he keeps the play-actress still.'

'It is a man that needs to laugh; and you, Madam my child, have troubles enough of your own. She makes him laugh—and you should thank God for it!'

'So I do... in my right mind. Have you marked his new trick of biting upon the thumb till he winces with pain? Oh those wicked men! They have Danby in the Tower; did you know that? And Pepys; how will he talk himself out for all his innocence? And Wakeman, my good physician, that languishes still in prison till it shall please them to bring him to trial. Innocent he is; but no longer young. How shall he withstand the torments they will put upon him to make him speak the lies they mean to hear? They will keep him from his food; and worse, from his sleep. They will threaten... the rack standing by. I have heard; Oh I have heard how brave men for very misery of the flesh give way.'

'We must pray for him, Madam, for him and for all true believers.'

It was not enough to accuse the Queen of murder, brand her a traitor, make her days and nights bitter with insult of divorce, with dread of the block. But they must torment her with further insult; no end to the indignities they put upon her.

She arrived at Somerset House to find her rooms in confusion. Drawers had been ransacked and papers cast about the room; gowns, petticoats and shifts lay tumbled upon the floor. Stiff with anger she summoned her steward. 'Madam,' and he spread his hands, 'it was the officers from Parliament. I could do nothing.'

She went raging to Charles. 'I know well why it was done. It is to find evidence against me and against my good physician. Must the Queen of England stand dumb before such outrage?'

'It is best,' he said very quiet. 'I've had a visitor—a dirty harlot, one of Oates' tools. She demanded that I see Oates in private... *demanded* if you please! I told her to get out unless she chose to cool her heels in gaol; and she cried out, very insolent, *Oates has secret information against the Queen. If you don't see him you'll be sorry—and the Queen even more.* And out she went flaunting under a great dirty hat. I never laid hands on a woman in my life, but had she not gone then I swear I'd have wrung her neck! That such creature should dare! Kate, there's worse I fear to come; and for that worse we must save ourselves to fight.'

'Worse? I am insulted. I am accused of murder. My faithful servants hanged. There *can* be no worse!' But her shaking lips belied her.

He said, unwilling, 'Divorce—that old bone Parliament worries between its teeth. Well, for sheer weariness they're bound to let it drop... sooner or later. I weary of that nonsense. You're my wife, Kate; and shall be, till one or other of us die.'

Hounded on by Shaftesbury, Parliament, within a few days, brought in a bill for the Queen's divorce. Again in the House Charles swore to the Queen's innocence; swore he'd not put away his wife, swore he had no mind to take a new one. But, for all that, the bill was passed. It went to the Lords; and so did Charles. He sought out each peer, he explained, he cajoled, he threatened. What disgrace to England so to shame an innocent woman! Our name would stink in the nostrils of all good men here and abroad. *Abroad?* How would France take this? How... Portugal?

The bill was thrown out of the Lords... by the skin of its teeth.

'Eight little votes, eight only, to speak of my innocence!' Catherine shook a sad head.

'Eight or eighty... what matter?' Charles said, cheerful. 'They *have* spoken; it is enough!'

Parliament had lost... for the present. Well, it would bury the bone, till the time should come again.

The King had refused to listen to Oates' whispering against the Queen. Now Oates demanded a public enquiry before King and Council. 'I could refuse,' a troubled Charles told Catherine, 'but it would be wiser to agree.'

'Yes,' she said. 'But shall I not come also? Shall I not with my own ears hear their lies, with my own tongue deny them?'

'It is not within the dignity of the Queen. You may safely leave your defence to me.'

They were hearing the charge against her now—in Westminster Hall—the King, the Council; Oates and the accusers. She knelt before her prie-dieu; she was all alone. She could endure no-one with her, not even Penalva. God was just; she must believe it. But, for all that, the sickness of fear was upon her. She knelt, a small, still statue.

It was late when Charles returned. He was grey; he looked as though ash had settled upon his whole person. But there was triumph in his eye.

'Dear Kate, concern yourself no more. That affair is finished.' He settled himself upon a chair and laid his head upon the velvet cushions. His eyes were closed; the hand with the bitten thumb lay defenceless upon his knee. Her heart wept at the sight of it. She brought a stool and sat at his feet. She was all agony to hear; but she must wait, quiet, until he was rested.

He opened his eyes and smiled to see her there.

'Dear Kate, so quiet, so humble upon her stool; the quiet, the humility, skin deep... as I know. Well, so much the better! I like a woman of spirit; and when she hides it beneath gentleness, why then I love it!' He chuckled. 'Well, then, the examination. Almost I wish you'd been there. This Oates, this scum, came to the Bar of the House. He stood up, the gutter-rat, and, aping his betters and not knowing how, spoke in that strange fashion he conceives to be our sweet English tongue—and for that, alone he should hang—*Ay,*

Taitus Oots, dew hear accuse Queen Catherine of haigh treason! Bah, I felt my belly crawl!

'He was put upon his oath; but an oath—to him! He'd lie his own mother into the grave! He said, in that sickening speech of his, that last year—July of 'seventy-seven—he saw a letter in Wakeman's handwriting. In that letter Wakeman wrote that, the Queen, at last, had given consent to the King's murder.'

She cried out at that; Charles laid his hand upon her own and continued. 'A few weeks later, according to Oates, one, Richards, took a message from the Queen's own lips...'

'I know no Richards!' she cried out.

'... to certain Jesuits that they should wait upon you in Somerset House. Early in August, they came...'

'We were in Windsor.'

'So I told them; it didn't do his testimony much good. However; according to that testimony Oates, himself, went with them.'

'Oates at Somerset House! Is it likely?'

Charles shrugged. 'He says he was taken to the Queen's Side.'

'A lie. Who of my servants would admit him? There's no sense in the tale.'

'Sense comes not into this affair; but malice, deadly malice. These Jesuits, according to Oates, went into your private closet but the door was ajar. He heard a woman's voice cry out from within, *I will no longer suffer such injuries as a wife. I am content to join in procuring the King's death and the spread of our blessed Faith. I will help Wakeman to poison the King!*'

'I said *that*—and the door open for all to hear? I could laugh... save that I want to puke instead!'

'Oates waited, he says, till the Jesuits came out and then he asked to see the Queen. You admitted him; you smiled upon him...'

'*I* admit that vermin? *I* smile upon him? If so I did may my soul burn for ever!'

'Kate, Kate, have a patience to hear me. Never think I—or any man—believe it! However! He says he heard you ask Father Harcourt if he had received the last ten thousand pounds from France. He swears that the voice in which you spoke to Harcourt was the same voice he heard through the open door.'

She would have spoken again but he lifted a hand.

'Kate, dearest Kate; you must *listen*! I asked the fellow to describe the room—and of course he couldn't. All he could describe was one of the public rooms. If he'd ever been in your private apartments he'd know that between it and the public rooms stretches the ball-room. No voice could be heard from one to the other; not even a man shouting, still less your voice, Kate, which is gentle and low... that excellent thing in a woman. And besides, who but a lunatic would shout aloud in Somerset House—or anywhere else—his plan to murder the King?'

'When he first told the tale of Godfrey's death why did he not say all this then? Did no-one ask him?'

'He was asked. He said—Kate you must laugh!—he said he forgot. It slipped his mind!'

'He said *that*? The Queen of England plans to poison the King; and Oates knows it... and it slips his mind!'

'And now with God's good help he recalls it. He said that; actually said it, bold as brass. Then he told the court what poisons Wakeman had prepared; and how you were to give it to me!' He threw back his head and laughed.

'I cannot laugh,' she said. 'To poison anyone, anyone at all—Oates himself; even—the heart stands still at the thought. But to poison you—my husband and my King! Oh!' she was taken with sudden fury, 'that he would choke upon his lies.'

Charles said, 'I think this has cooked his goose.'

'Its neck must first be wrung,' she told him. 'I cannot think they'd touch that precious neck.'

XXXI

The whole country was set against the Queen. People—good folk in their right mind—now, in a frenzy, demanded her death. Monstrous the tale against her and those that told it, liars proved. Yet there were many to believe it; many more that pretended to believe it, lest they, also, come to the rope. Once when she walked in St. James's Park, a mad woman threw stones. 'Let her go,' the Queen said. 'She flings her stones, poor soul, because she is crazed. But there are others,' she said soft and bitter, 'that would do so also did they dare; and they are not crazed.'

Except for Charles, for Penalva and Eliza she was alone. Frances had left the court; these days, she said, she preferred cats to humans. Not one of her ladies dared the Queen trust. My lady Suffolk, aunt to *that woman*, had always been an enemy; she corrupted the others so that there was not one who would not run with a tale to Madam Louise or to Oates himself. She had, it is true, two Portuguese ladies in the Bedchamber; but she kept them at a distance lest—Papists and foreigners—they should suffer through her friendship. Charles bade her be of good courage; to show herself in no way afraid. But for all that she was afraid; she was very much afraid. Never the court so brilliant... nor the Queen so sick at heart.

Nor was she the only one. Fear. Beneath the thousand lights, behind the music and the laughter, one smelt it, touched it; the plague itself had not caused so much terror. No man knew when the sword might not fall upon his naked neck; and, lest one should be tempted to forget, one saw, always, as one went about Whitehall, the monstrous face of Oates. He walked in splendour—in a gown of fine silk and cut like a bishop's with great lawn sleeves; in rosetted shoes and a great hat hung with ribands... and all his glory making yet more hideous his hideous person.

The King had had enough of his Parliament; enough, enough! Eighteen years too much—and these last months the worst of all. They left him no peace. They were forever yapping at him to put away his wife; to cut his brother from the succession; to declare his bastard legitimate. They were forever encouraging the persecutions, rewarding his enemies, attacking his friends. Oddsfish, a man could stand so much... but no more. An end to this Parliament. Dissolve it; finish it altogether! He would call a new Parliament in March; give himself two months' grace!

In March the new Parliament met.

'Now I am worse off than before!' he told Catherine. 'The number of my friends has sunk to thirty—thirty instead of one hundred and fifty. And Shaftesbury grows yet more insolent. Again, again, he declares Monmouth true born and true heir. I have writ a paper for this stiff-necked House; copies shall go to every town, every village. My people everywhere shall see it. Does it speak plain enough, Kate?'

Her eyes all blurred with grateful tears could scarce make out the words; he took the paper again and read aloud,

'To avoid any dispute which may happen in time to come, concerning the Succession of the Crown, the King declares in the Presence of Almighty God, that he never gave nor made any contract of marriage, nor was married to any woman whatsoever but to his present wife, Queen Catherine, now living...'

'Seventeen years married,' she said, 'and it needs this to make an honest woman of me!' and tried to smile.

'Shaftesbury has pursued us both with his venom,' Charles said, 'and I have rebuked his insolence. Now my friends—my good friends—advise another course. They advise me... to admit him again to the Privy Council.'

Admit him again into the Council—the King's most bitter enemy and her own! Admit him again into the Council from which he had once been dismissed; allow him to make his mischief from that high place! The angry words crowded to her tongue.

Charles said, 'Kate, it could be worth trying; it could blunt those too-sharp claws. He's a clever fellow—you must grant it; but he's bitter, he's frustrated, and arrogant beyond belief. If I sweeten him, might he not, at least, stop his attacks? Might he not drop Monmouth, leave the succession alone; and most of all leave *you* alone? It could tie his tongue against the filthy accusation, the screaming for divorce.'

'There's a corruption of bitterness in him that nothing will stop.'

'Still I am inclined to try.'

For two months Shaftesbury had been of the Council; and in those two months more zealous than ever for Monmouth, more bitter against James, and, against the Queen, bitter beyond belief.

'You were right, Kate; how you were right! How long can I endure him?'

It was May, that sweet month; but few enjoyed its sweetness. Nine months of the Terror; and everywhere the prisons full and the gallows hung with sickening fruit.

And for Charles, himself, things were worse. This new Parliament—since it held fewer friends—was more troublesome even than the last. There were more 'discoveries', more persecutions, more besmirching of the Queen; and against James, the Commons more bitter than ever. To soften the bitterness that might cost the succession, with love and tenderness Charles sent him from the country—of all his brothers and sisters the only one left. There was grief and there were tears at the parting.

It did not help matters. Nothing short of breaking the succession could do that.

'Do what I will I cannot sweeten this sour Parliament!' Charles exclaimed to Catherine. 'I sent my brother away; and how do they repay me.'

No need to answer with the bitter truth.

They had repaid him with a bill to disinherit James; today it had passed its second reading. From the window of the Queen's closet they looked down upon a sky red with the light of bonfires and lit with falling showers of firework stars. There came up to them, very clear, the shouts, the singing, the drunken laughter from the crowds below. 'They celebrate too soon!' Charles said. 'The bill has passed its second reading, true. But let it pass a third time, let it go to the

Lords—it shall never become law. I will not allow it. I shall stop it. I shall refuse the royal assent... and the thing drops dead.'

Then, seeing anxiety in her face, he said, 'For a King to set himself against the will of the people is a dangerous thing; who should know that better than I? But when the people would filch his God-given rights, then to allow it, more dangerous still. I'll fight if I must; but first I'll show myself reasonable. Parliament shall have the right to curtail the power of a Catholic King; it may pass what act it will and I shall agree; it is their right. But the true successor must succeed; it is my right and his right; and the right we owe to God.'

And now the noise had become a clamour and a tumult. Catherine put up a hand to an aching head. 'Come within,' Charles said, very gentle; and, with his own hands, shut the window and drew the curtains against the flaming sky.

Since the Commons had not believed the lies about Catherine, Oates repeated them in the Lords. And now the Commons—thinking perhaps that the lie oft-repeated, spells truth, and believing it better to be safe that sorry—besought the King to remove her, together with all her household, from Whitehall. And now those long-ago letters written to Rome rose up to testify against her. Had she not, they demanded to know, from the first moment of her coming, written to the Pope avowing her obedience? And might not such obedience encompass the death of the King?

The clamour of hatred against the Queen and against Papists rose louder, more sickening than ever. The people screamed, with ever-growing madness, for the blood of the Queen, for the blood of Wakeman, for the blood of those five peers that still lay in the Tower. And, though the courts could not deal with the multitudes of the accused, nor the prisons enclose their number, nor gallows be erected fast enough to relieve the prisons, still the people cried out for blood. 'Let Christ Jesus come again,' Charles said, 'and they would cry for His blood—even for His, also.'

In mid-July of 'seventy-nine, Wakeman came to his trial. He was charged *that, being instigated and seduced by the Devil, he did endeavour to disturb the true worship of the country... and to put out and wholly extinguish our sovereign lord the King to death and final destruction.* Racked with nausea and fear, Catherine went down to Windsor with Charles, there in the peace of the country to await the news.

Hourly the messengers rode in. 'The witnesses confuse themselves with lies. Oates and Bedloe, the chief among them, are full of venom.'

And later, 'The prisoner is doing well. God has put it into the mouth of the innocent to defend himself.'

And, towards the end of the long and anxious day, 'My lord Chief Justice has summed up. He desires, with all his heart, to find the prisoner guilty; but he cannot, Sir George Wakeman is innocent; the summing-up shows it. Bedloe, fearing lest the prisoner go free, cried out, *The evidence is not right summed up*. And my lord Chief Justice answered, very angry, *I know not by what authority this man speaks!*'

'He should cast the creature into prison for contempt,' the Queen said.

'Madam, he would not dare. He shows much courage in that he upholds the law. He'll not anger the people more than he must.'

'Will my good physician go free?'

'Madam... who knows? The jury have retired; but my lord Chief Justice, having so far protected the innocent, has left the court—and the other judges with him. They cannot condemn a man so clearly innocent; nor dare they face the fury of the mob. They have left it to the magistrates.'

It was late at night when they heard the verdict.

Innocent.

'I thank you God!' the Queen said and held fast to her chair lest she swoon; his innocence vindicated her own.

'It was a verdict hard to come by, Madam. The jury were afraid. But at last the blessed words were spoken. Then Sir George said, *God bless the King, and this honourable bench*; and there at the Bar, fell upon his knees.'

My lord Chief Justice Scroggs had been right to fear the mob. When he went abroad foul words were cast at him and fouler objects; a dog half-hanged was thrown into his coach. And, indeed, the acquittal was something of a miracle; of all the hundreds tried by the malice of in formers and, for the most part, innocent, not above half a dozen had so far escaped with their lives.

The Queen's physician had been acquitted and the Queen should pay for it! Oates was the more bitterly resolved upon it. His agents travelled the length and breadth of the country repeating their lies so that, more than ever, the people cried out against her. Nothing, she thought, fearful, will appease them but my blood.

'I have brought these English new lands and great trade,' she told Eliza. 'I have knowingly done no man harm. I am Queen of England... and my life hangs upon a hair.'

And when Eliza, smiling, shook her head, Catherine cried out, 'But yes, yes! Two Queens of England have come to the block—and for a lesser fault than that they charge me with.'

'It was the King, not the people, brought them to their death.'

'The King does not wish me dead nor yet divorced,' she said. 'But all the same it could come to it! I am the Queen,' she said again, 'yet I am haunted by two fears—fear of divorce and fear of death. And I fear divorce more. Of death, itself, I have no great fear. I have faced it more than once with a quiet spirit. It is shameful death I fear... the people believing me willing of such wickedness.'

She thought much of her brother these days; not of Alphonso, the King—he was sick in mind, not capable of knowing right from wrong. It was of Pedro the Regent that she thought. In the old days he had loved her, made much of her. What did he think of the accusations against his sister, of the humiliations put upon her? Surely he must know; all Christendom must know. She would send to him. She would send Penalva; who better? And her two ladies of the Bedchamber were safer at home, also. They should care for Penalva on the journey. Yes, they should go all three! Penalva should feel again the sunshine of her own land upon her blind eyes; she should hear again the voices of her children, her grandchildren, her friends. She longed to go, but love and duty held her in a hostile land. She would go, persuaded that so she served her Queen; nothing else would induce her.

It was a hard parting. At the last moment Catherine must fight herself not to call Penalva back, to let another carry the message. She looked at the old face serene beneath the tears... and let Penalva go.

Never had the Queen felt so utterly alone. She missed Penalva at every turn—the love, the advice, the sweet mother-tongue; Penalva, last link with home.

She had her answer sooner than she expected.

Charles came to the Queen's Side bringing with him a gentleman.

'Kate,' he said, 'I have brought you an old friend—the Marquez d'Arouches. Your brother has sent him to watch your interests and to make full report.'

'You are very welcome, sir,' she said, 'both for your own sake and for my brother's. As for your report, you must say that the King, my husband, watches my interests as no other could. But my brother; what says he of this shameful charge against me?'

'That it *is* shameful, Madam; and the shame, he says, falls upon those that utter their lies. I am charged, Madam, to write at once, how I find you in health and spirits.'

'Sir, do so. And I shall write, also, to tell my brother that my husband's kindness never fails.'

Charles lifted her hand and kissed it. The Marquez marked the great love in her face, the great kindliness in the King's.

Later he spoke with his old friend Eliza Ormonde; he had known her and her husband, both when—during Charles' exile—he had visited the Hague.

'One hears, naturally one hears—if your ladyship will forgive me— of your King's... pleasure in women. What then of the Queen?'

'He treats her with affection and respect. He trusts her as he trusts no other, man or woman. That he has an eye for a pretty face, cannot be denied. But, in his way, he is faithful to the Queen.' And seeing d'Arouches' look of bewilderment, said, 'One might call it, perhaps, a faithfulness of the spirit. For, consider! At this moment he could rid himself of a childless queen; he could delight his people with a second marriage; he could free himself and the country of the never-ending trouble of the succession and the continuing nuisance of Monmouth. Let him but agree and Parliament would load him with money—and how badly he needs it! And the people that now murmur against him would sing his praises. But he'll not do it. Would you not call that faithfulness... and a great faithfulness?'

He nodded and she went on. 'But there's more to it than that. Madam the Queen has become a habit he cannot break. He cannot, I think, be without her. She has the listening heart. Yet, I fancy, there's more to it than faithfulness and habit—though I doubt he knows it himself. He has his mistresses as all the world knows. But when he drives with the Queen, he takes her hand and holds it fast; you may see it any day. They say here, in the court, that the wife has become the mistress. It isn't true... not yet; but one day it may be so.'

'I rejoice to hear it; and my country will rejoice. For I must tell your ladyship, we are angered at the slights put upon our princess; not the court alone, but our whole nation. We remember her with love—so good, so gentle and so pious. There is so much anger in Lisbon that, I fear, they will fall upon the English in the city and kill them all!'

'God forbid. I must go to the Queen at once—she is not one to endure the innocent to suffer. She will write to her brother at once—I know her. Pray God she be in time.'

She found Catherine at her writing-table, a finished letter before her. When she heard that innocent men might suffer on her account she cried out in distress.

'I have already written home; and I think my letter says enough to calm all anger. Listen,

> ...There is nothing that concerns me more than to tell you how
> completely the King releases me from all my troubles, and the care
> he takes to defend my innocence. Every day he shows more clearly
> his purpose and good-will towards me; and this baffles the hate of
> my enemies. I cannot cease to tell you what I owe to his kindliness
> of which every day he gives heavier proof...'

'It should cool hot heads,' Eliza said.

'D'Arouches shall take it at once!' the Queen promised. 'I bless my people for their love and trust. It comforts my heart—which God knows it needs.'

Her own people might love her, believe in her; but had she quietly broken her neck there would have been few tears in England.

That year of 'seventy-nine was, perhaps, the worst in the tale of English Catholics. Five high peers lay in the Tower; all who did not openly swear allegiance to the Church of England were not allowed to sit in either House. More than ever the prisons overflowed; there were more gallows than trees in England, they said. Men, women and children, thirty thousand of them—their faith their only crime— were driven from London leaving everything behind; many died of hunger and cold—it was death to help a hated Papist.

Beneath a still face Catherine grieved for fresh persecution fallen upon good men. It was but a preparation for her own disgrace, she knew it; her own death, maybe.

And Oates. In his silk gown with the fine bishop's sleeves, his beribanded hat and rosetted shoes he was dined and wined by high princes of the Church and State. So proud was he grown he'd not sit down with a simple gentleman. Nor did he fit his manners to his fine company; that he honoured their table was honour enough for them! He would sit gorging himself with food, his pale, flat face shining like a greasy dish; he would hiccough his drunken insults against the living and the dead—against Henrietta Maria and Minette whom the King had so loved; against James; but most of all against the Queen. And there was none that durst stay him.

They spent the summer as usual at Windsor. They lived quietly—they had need; they were very poor. Always they had enjoyed life at Windsor; now, with Oates and Bedloe out of their sight, Windsor in its summer flowering was a little heaven of peace and beauty. One other remained in Whitehall. Louise. Catherine's joy in her absence was poisoned by suspicion that the Frenchwoman stayed behind to further her intrigues.

Charles was enjoying his holiday. For a little he could put aside his cares. He rode, he fished, he walked in the Great Park with Catherine—a country gentleman with his wife. But her content was troubled; he was very thin and his face more deeply lined. The dark wig that had given him so young a look now pointed to his age. He was slower in his movements; a little, only, but enough to catch her loving eye. And he was quieter—thoughtful, perhaps, rather than melancholy; certainly he laughed less. When she remembered his jaunty step, his ready laughter, she felt like a mother whose child is threatened. She longed to take him in her arms and give him whatever toy he fancied.

But when he had his toy again—one not of her giving—she was far from pleased. Louise came down to Windsor—uninvited it was true, but Charles did not send her away. He was, it appeared, more enamoured than ever.

'She is glove... glove... on hand with Shaftesbury; the King must surely know it!' the Queen cried out to Eliza, the only friend now she could trust. 'Yet here she is back once more to betray him and to plague me. I hate her, I despise her... but dear God, how I envy her!'

Louise went back to Whitehall—to spin her spider-threads Catherine said; and not without disturbing Charles' peace. She left him restless; he could not, it seemed, rest until he was worn out; and not always then. He would exhaust himself with too-long rides, too-long walks, too-strenuous games. 'He forgets he is no longer young,' Catherine said; and then, at the look in Eliza's eyes, 'Perhaps he does not forget... perhaps she has been reminding him—the French harlot. Perhaps that is why—to show himself, and her, and all the world, that what a young man can do, he can do also.'

She missed him one day; he had gone out after dinner and had not returned for their usual walk. She thought, maybe, the heat had kept him within; yet, when she enquired, she was told he was playing tennis. Tennis; in this heat! Later, in the full glare of the afternoon, she asked after him again; and still he played. Two or three times she went out, large shading-fan held above her head, to see if the game were done. And each time there he was, running and catching the ball upon his racquet; and returning it—she must admit—with all the vigour of a young man. It was past supper-time when the game was ended at last. But he had no mind to eat; he would walk a little first. She tried to dissuade him—he had played all afternoon; he was heated and had no coat...

'A coat—in high summer? What need of coat?'

'The dew is falling and you are tired.' *And oh my love you are not as young as once...* She said no more; he was in one of his obstinate moods.

Next day he went down with fever.

Once, only—when he had cast his wig aside on board ship—had she known him sick; it had been a light sickness and long ago. Now he was sick, indeed. He shivered with ague, he burnt with fever, he had a continual, raging thirst. At times he lay and babbled and knew not what he said. She would sit by his bed hollow with fear. Sometimes he would open his eyes and know her and be glad to see here there. Other times he though she was Barbara, or Charlotte his daughter, or Louise or Nell. And once he thought she was dead Minette. That day the doctors despaired; she had a foretaste of life without him. It was as though they had plucked out her living heart by the roots.

Charles opened his eyes; he was alone in the room with the Queen. He was very weak but his mind was clear. He began to speak; she rose from her stool and bent to hear.

'Send for Halifax...'

'Yes,' she said. 'Yes.' Of all his Council he trusted Halifax most.

'Tell him... send for James. In Brussels. James must come... at once. Tell Halifax... very secret. Till James come... I cannot die in peace.'

Voice steady, eyes dry, she promised; and, on that promise he fell asleep. He awoke to find her still by his bed. Dear Kate. Of all women—and men, too—he trusted her most; Louise, least. A well man could take Louise as she was; even, laugh a little. A sick man—no! He could not laugh now.

He began slowly to mend. He was a sick man still; but neither pain nor fever nor tormenting treatment called forth a murmur. He submitted with a most sweet patience to the continual cupping, the tearing plasters, the nauseous drafts. When James arrived he found Charles on the mend; he was weak still; but he had a good appetite and a fund of new and bawdy stories.

For joy in the King's recovery no-one questioned James' return.

'Is it that they question the succession no longer?' Catherine asked, watching with joy the colour returning to Charles' cheeks. 'Do they accept James as heir?'

'Oddsfish, I trust so! But Kate, I am much troubled by Monmouth.' And he did not, she noted, call him Jamie. 'Shaftesbury forever pricks him on. More than ever he gives himself the airs of a Prince of Wales—he's assumed the Feathers, so I hear; actually added them to his arms... or something so like, that ignorant folk—and some not so ignorant—believe he does, indeed, bear the arms of the heir to the throne.'

'Then we must undeceive them!' she said with a cheerfulness she did not feel. No need to remind him that, wherever Monmouth walked, crowds followed calling down blessings on his head; nor that everywhere his health was drunk openly as Prince of Wales—he knew it perfectly. But did he know, also, that Louise slyly encouraged Monmouth—Louise with an eye on her own son's chance of a crown? *If one bastard might inherit, why not another?* She knew Louise's thoughts. They called Louise subtle—and so she was, when subtlety wasn't blinded by mother-love. Richmond was a lovely child and Charles doted on him... but Richmond was the son of a foreigner and a Papist. Monmouth's mother had come of good Welsh stock; he was the white hope of the Protestants.

'You should send him out of the country,' Catherine said. Charles nodded. Catherine was right. Monmouth must go.

Monmouth made straight for Holland where he might, more easily, intrigue with William of Orange. Charles was disturbed when he heard it; to hold the balance even he gave his brother permission to live in Scotland.

And now it was open, deadly warfare between Shaftesbury and the King.

To strike at the King he struck again at the Queen. The King had refused to rid the country of her by divorce. Well, there was still another way—the block. True that way had failed once; but it would not fail again. He would proclaim her once more a would-be murderess—all set to murder the King. A new story... and a good one. And plenty to lie their souls away bearing false witness. And plenty to believe it; and plenty to pretend they did—she was a Papist. This second charge could not fail.

Before my lord Shaftesbury in secret Council appeared a man called Buss; he was one of Monmouth's cooks and he told a strange tale.

'October of last year I was at Windsor; and there I overheard talk between the Queen's priest and the Queen's confessor.'

'Their names?' Oates asked.

'Antonio is the confessor.'

Oates nodded.

'The priest is Hankinson.'

'There's no Hankinson among the Queen's priests. Do you, perhaps, mean... Hudlestone?' Shaftesbury asked, sly.

And Buss accepting the correction and so bringing in another victim, Shaftesbury said, 'Continue with your evidence.'

'The priest told the confessor that four men had been brought from Ireland to do their business for them...'

'What business?' Oates interrupted.

'Why, sir, to murder the King!'

Shaftesbury shrugged. 'I do not believe this tale!' and, indeed, he did not! But that it should be spread far and wide and he, himself, not be held responsible, added, 'It is not within our sphere to deal with this. You must lay your charge before a magistrate!'

'Again, again, my good priests are named, again they will come to a shameful, hideous death!' Catherine wrung her hands. 'Again I am named in a plot to murder my husband and my King. Everywhere my name is held in hatred. The fellow Marvell writes his filthy verses.' She thrust a paper in Charles' hand. Two lines leaped to his eye.

> With one consent let all her death desire,
> Who durst her husband's and her King's conspire.

'You should read your Dryden!' Charles dropped the paper in disgust. 'He answered the foul thing at once. He says the charge is false, wicked and cruel. He says you're the best of Queens, the most loving of wives; he says my life is—how does it go?

> ... the theme of her eternal prayer,
> 'Tis scarce as much his guardian angel's care.

'And that's the truth, Kate... and Dryden's the better poet.'

'Yes,' she said, 'but how if they shall believe this Marvell?'

God, Catherine knew, must be watching over her. Bedloe died; and the air was sweeter for his passing.

Charles, himself, came with the news. 'He confessed; on his death-bed he confessed that all the accusations against you are lies!'

'God be thanked!' she cried out. And then, 'But they will see to it, my enemies, that it is not known.'

'It cannot help but be known. Bedloe sent for my lord Chief Justice and cleared your name. In the fear and agony of death he gasped out, *The Queen was not in it, nor was ever in it... The Queen is innocent...* Not even Shaftesbury would dare now. This clears your name for ever.'

'Thank God!' she said it again and went to her chapel to thank Him in a more fitting manner.

XXXII

The King had recovered from his sickness; but—Catherine saw it with grief—he was less strong than in the summer when she had fretted at his lessened vigour. But his mind was as clear, as quick, as shrewd as ever. She trusted that time would restore him fully. She herself, worn with worry on his account and with fear on her own, was unwell. It seemed to her that her innocent servants reproached her from the grave with their bitter dying. Nor did she feel herself safe. Twice the fearful accusation had been spoken against her. It had been spoken in vain; but would the words of a dying man end it for ever? Would it not be spoken yet again and again until it came to be believed? *Divorce; or the block.* One only thing stood between her and the horror of her fate—the King. During the daytime she contrived to show herself cheerful; but at night she lay sleepless; and, in the small hours, fallen asleep at last, would awake weeping from nightmare dreaming to nightmare living.

She had reason enough to fear.

In October the King met a Parliament more bitter than before against the Queen. In the Lords and from his high place in the Council, Shaftesbury was more vindictive, more dangerous than ever. But Charles had had enough... enough! By the second week in October Shaftesbury had been dismissed; for the second time dismissed.

His long hatred of the King swelled like a poisoned boil. Crippled now with gout, wretched with pain, restless, frustrated, humiliated, his hatred of the King came near to madness. From his great house in Aldersgate street he set about further mischief. He stirred up the Londoners to urge the King to recall their idol; and, when Charles refused, they prayed publicly for handsome Jamie in all the churches of London. And all the time Shaftesbury wined and dined and made much of the King's enemies. He encouraged every tale of Papist plot; Oates rose still higher upon his wings. Once there had been, at least, some charge against those accused, some travesty of a trial; now good men came to the rope or rotted in prison... and no charge, no trial; no reason, even, save that they had spoken with insufficient respect of Mr. Oates and his toadies.

Charles could no longer work with this obstructive Parliament that hindered his every step. He would prorogue it till January; and, in answer to the uproar, declared that it should not meet for three months at the least; nor for six, nor for a year, if necessary. A man must have some peace; given a little peace a man might work for the country's good.

He had played into the enemy's hands. Yellow with gall Shaftesbury made the most of it. He sent his agents the length and breadth of the country to incite the people; to urge them to sign his petition that the King call Parliament again. The voice of the country should force the King.

And everywhere angry men signed or made their mark. And in London, also, in Whitehall itself, his voice was heard. *You have no meat; you have no money because there's no Parliament to protect you. The King must call his Parliament—and there'll be cakes and ale for all!*

And everywhere the people cried out against the King.

In the midst of the seething discontent, Charles stood firm. 'I stand by my word,' he told Catherine. 'Parliament shall not meet for three months at the least; more, if needful. Shaftesbury means it to meet now, while heads are hot—that's his strength. I mean to wait till heads are cool—that's mine. He means the bill against my brother to have its third reading; I mean it shall not. If Parliament meet now, with the mob screaming for Monmouth, it will bring the bill in again; its first business. Then I'd be faced with a choice of three things. To agree. To abdicate. Or Civil War. And rather than let any one of these things befall the country—I'd die. Well, I don't mean to die; it's more pleasant to keep Parliament from its business.'

'No Parliament; no money!' she said. And must it go on for ever, the dreary, grinding poverty?'

'We've managed before; we'll manage again. Oddsfish, I have the right wife!'

On Ascension Day, in hideous mockery, the trouble-makers marched through London carrying images of pope and devil obscenely embraced; and, before the hideous couple, an effigy of murdered Godfrey.

At Somerset House yet another effigy lay before the Queen's door. Catherine went white when she heard of it. And well she might! The dumb, lying witness had been placed there further to inflame the mob; and inflame them it did!

And that was only the beginning. Pamphlets—clever, wicked, lying—were circulating north, south, east and west. The country was a vast tinder-box.

Charles came to the Queen's side holding a pamphlet; his face was dark as the November sky without. 'It says... it says...' he looked at the paper with disgust, 'that my brother was responsible for the Fire—James that, with his own hands, beat out the flames, that stood nightlong passing buckets in his blistered hands. It tells the people that, unless James be removed, London will go up in flames a second time. It says that Papist troops, all fully-armed, will burst upon London to murder the men; to rape the women, and to dash their infants' brains against the wall—and all before their very eyes. This thing—' and he cast the paper across the room, 'is meant to strike terror; and it does. One thing only, it seems, can avert the tragedy...'

I can guess.

'Monmouth. Monmouth alone, can prevent this burning, this killing, this outrage.' His lip twisted. 'Monmouth must come home again. Monmouth must be named successor. *Monmouth, Monmouth,*

Monmouth... They cry out his name as though he were Christ Himself!'

He stopped short. The sound of joybells broke sharp upon the ear; and, with it, a more distant sound that, coming nearer, resolved itself into cheers.

Joybells and cheers. While they looked from one to the other, Sunderland, the King's friend, came hurrying. He said, without awaiting permission, 'Sir... sir...' and though he was elegant as ever, he had lost something of his famous drawl. 'Monmouth. He's back again!'

They saw the King's face go grey. He opened his mouth; no words came through the stiffness of his lips.

'They've taken him from his coach, they carry him shoulder-high. They press to kiss his hands, the hem of his coat, his shoes even. Never such joy in the streets!' Catherine thought Sunderland a trifle malicious; she had never quite trusted him. He stopped. 'Sir, he's below. He demands to see you!'

'*Demands!*' The words tore through the King's lips; almost she expected to see the wound-marks there. 'He dares... he *dares!*' He choked upon the words. 'Tell him to leave Whitehall at once. Tell him I'll strip him of his honours. Tell him I'll not answer for myself! If he values his life he'll go at once!'

When Sunderland had gone, Charles said, harsh and hard, 'Monmouth, to do *this!*' And then more gentle, 'Jamie... my son!' And they remembered both of them that other King wailing *My son, my son!*

Monmouth had been commanded to leave Whitehall; but not London. He rode into the city; and there, Shaftesbury, setting the example, went upon his knees to kiss his hand.

'The people follow him wherever he goes; they cheer him as though he were the King himself!' Sunderland said; and did not tell Charles that Nell Gwynn went nightly to sup with Monmouth— Nell that London loved, setting the seal upon his popularity.

But for all that Charles heard it; Shaftesbury saw to it.

It hit him hard that Nell had turned traitor. Ah well! He tried to ease his hurt, a whore's a whore; and a whore she is—herself has said it. And, if I read the signs aright, Louise betrays me, too. But Kate, where least I deserve it, Kate is steel-true.

And then, being Charles that so loved women, he must find excuses for those two... Nell betrays me without thinking; it's scarce betrayal. She thinks it no harm to smile on Monmouth—she's no statesman. To smile on all—it is her trade. Too late now to unlearn her tricks. But for Louise? No excuse; try as he might—no excuse at all.

But still he used the private passage—Louise was in his blood. But it had other uses; for all her blindness Penalva had seen that clearly. Why did Louise smile upon Monmouth; what secret there? Did she do more than smile? In the flesh she was faithful enough... but, in the spirit? Did her sly fingers dabble in some plot? What did that subtle mind hope to gain? Chiffinch, listening outside the private door, could mark who went in at the other and how long the caller stayed. And Charles, himself, might come, unexpected, into the room. Then a conversation might be stopped at once; but even while they made their salutations, a word, a look, a breath, even, flashed knowledge to his mind. So he kissed and fondled Louise and enjoyed it; he let her babble and pout... and waited his moment.

Monmouth judged it wise to return to Holland. He feared the loss of his honours and the pensions that went with them. For his life he did not fear; he knew the loving-kindness of his father. So back he went leaving Shaftesbury to do his work for him.

Pain and disappointment and anger had curdled within Shaftesbury; he was pure wickedness these days. Already he had lured Louise to his side; now he would blind her with fear.

'If the bill to exclude York doesn't go through, the people will turn yet more bitter against the Papists. Not one will escape. Do not think the King will be able to save you, Madam. On the contrary. You have earned their especial hatred. They will brand you—a common nuisance.'

He was lying; but she was not to know that. He was watching her; she gave no sign. But he guessed how, behind that smooth brow, the wild thoughts ran... *Brand me with an iron ... my lady duchess of Portsmouth! Whip me at the cart's tail, like the lowest, the vilest of whores...*

He turned the screw a little. 'They will send you out of the country... when they have done with you. And not a penny of all you have gained! And where shall you go then, you and the child! Back to France, perhaps?'

Back to France shamed, branded, destitute. Let her so return and Louis would turn his back. Nor—lacking gold—would a convent open to her; not even the cold convent. They knew it, both of them.

And still not a flicker in that still face; but he knew of the terror beneath—he was as subtle as she. Now, having shaken her with bitter fear, he offered a little hope.

'You can save yourself, Madam. Take your stand with Monmouth. Stand with him and there's naught to fear.'

'Fear?' She said as if the word made no sense.

'Fear, Madam. And—it you are not wise, there is, believe it, very much to fear. But if you are wise... ah then!' And he played upon her hope—the secret hope he knew so well.

'Help England and you help yourself. Use your power with the King to break the succession. And once it is broken, your son, the little Richmond shall succeed. It is a promise, Madam. Oh the mob screams out for Monmouth. But the mob! How quickly it will change its tune! Against the voice of Parliament the mob is dumb. And Parliament shall name your son. I swear it, Madam.'

And still she gave no sign that she all-but swooned because joy could tread so hard upon the heels of fear.

He said, 'It is not unknown in this country for the King to choose his successor; and the King loves little Richmond above all his sons. Once it was Monmouth; but not now, nor ever again. So you must smile yet more upon Monmouth—you are good friends, are you not? And you must coax the King to forgive him... a little. And while Monmouth pulls your chestnuts from the fire you must persuade the King to let the bill go through. Madam, you can do it. And when York is out then your son is in—the next King, I swear it!'

She wished Charles no harm nor Monmouth any good. But in her position she must look to herself. If her choice lay between being branded harlot and sent penniless from the country; or remaining, lifted to the peak of glory—mother to the King's heir—only a mad-woman would hesitate. But...

Her cool brain once more took command.

...if they would not accept James, a true-born Stuart because of his Faith, would they accept her son, a Catholic also—and a bastard? She had only Shaftesbury's word for it—a man not to be trusted. She'd get something more substantial while she could.

She said, 'I will go with you in this. But, my lord, there's been little enough money coming in of late; and, with no Parliament sitting, less is likely. It ill befits a King's mother to go barefoot. Would you say... a little sum... eight hundred thousand pounds perhaps?'

'A large sum for a pair of shoes,' he said sour; but for all that he admired her impudence. 'Still you shall have the money.'

'And who shall give it me?'

'Who but Parliament... when it meets?'

'By that time my toes will be through.'

'Do your part, and the King will sign long before that! As for the shoes—you shall have them at once!'

And have them she did. He sent her a dozen pairs. And she had the money, too—though she must wait longer than either of them thought. Parliament did not meet in January and she must wait till October; and then it voted the eight hundred thousand pounds—this Parliament that had no money for the country's urgent needs.

Charles said never a word on the subject. But the lines were scored deeper about his mouth. It gave him a grim look that was the kindest of man. And still he let Louise babble and smile; and still he went on watching.

His mistresses have sold him, both. Madam Playactress in her small way, Madam French Spy in her great one... and James is in far Scotland and can do nothing. How long may a man stand alone? Catherine asked herself the question everyone asked. But they—and she, for all her love and admiration—had underestimated him. He had learned to stand alone; he had learned to wait—smilingly, patiently, to wait.

All about him his enemies waiting... in Parliament, in the Council; and in London and beyond, the common people Monmouth and Shaftesbury had seduced from their loyalty, waiting, all waiting for his foot to slip. But he was cheerful, still. *Give them enough rope and they'll hang themselves* he told Catherine more than once. But still she fretted, wondering how, with all their numbers, all their cunning, all their wealth, he could keep himself free of their snares.

The year wore to its close. And still Charles called no Parliament; and still he held himself quiet and said nothing.

His enemies began to lose their heads. In the Council Russell, together with two others, threatened to resign unless the King called Parliament. To their astonishment the resignations were accepted.

'My waiting policy has served me well,' Charles said, come as usual to Catherine; beneath his quiet face she caught the glint of laughter. 'Three empty places. Now I shall put in Councillors of my own. Good friends, young and wise, all three. First Lory Hyde—faithful son of a faithful father; but the old man looked backwards, Lory looks forwards.'

She nodded her approval.

'And Godolphin; a wise fellow, tactful. He sees far and deep.'

Again he had her nod.

'And the third...' he hesitated. 'What do you say to... Sunderland?'

'I am not sure that I trust him.'

'Your reason, Kate?'

She could find none. Too young? Too elegant? She could scarce admit a fault there. He was clever; beneath that drawling manner a quick brain worked... too clever? She could not say. She would look at the handsome dandy, hear the charming drawl Oates tried, so ludicrously, to copy; she would listen to his protestation of love, of loyalty. *How long will he be faithful?* she would wonder. And always the same answer. *As long as he gets his price.*

The new year came in; the year of Grace sixteen-hundred and eighty. Twenty years since Charles had come home... twenty stormy years; and now the sun was rising for him again. They were so pleasant, Charles' new young men in the Council, so discreet, so willing to listen, so willing—if you could believe them—to play their part in ridding the country of Papists. The King's enemies could find no fault with him or them. And London, even London that remembered Monmouth with love and hated York, even London cheered when the King rode through; and, seeing his kindliness and the charm he had, they forgot Monmouth... all-but.

Shaftesbury watched in ever-growing dismay.

'Shaftesbury doesn't know what to make of it!' Charles told Catherine, told Lory Hyde, told Godolphin and Sunderland, taking tea, all of them in the Queen's closet. He had got back some of his gaiety, though the lines in his face must stay graven for ever. 'The country's sick of sedition, sick of tales of Papist plotting; sickest of all of the hangings, the dreadful hangings—and no man knowing when his own turn may come. All over the country they're signing petitions—thousands upon thousands of signatures; and those that cannot write, putting their crosses. And all petitioning me to stop the bloodshed, to give the country peace. But Shaftesbury doesn't see it, doesn't seem to *understand*…'

'Never count on Shaftesbury's lack of understanding,' Sunderland drawled. 'Nor on the country's wisdom; nor yet that it will stand firm by its own petitions. As for Shaftesbury—he has no intention that rage against Papists should die; still less intention that you continue to stand firm in the people's love. He, I do think it, sir, prepares some fresh surprise.'

It was springtime when Shaftesbury first whispered about a black box. Soon all England was whispering. The whisper reached Catherine walking white and silent in Whitehall. She caught its echo in Eliza's troubled glance, in Louise's air of triumph.

Charles came to the Queen's Side and he was actually laughing.

'A black box. A most mysterious box. And what do you think it holds? Marriage lines. My marriage lines with Lucy Walter.'

And what does this make me? Neither wife nor maid nor Queen. Intruder in the King's bed and upon the throne! She said no word; only her great dark eyes asked the question.

He said, and now he laughed no longer, 'There's no marriage-lines of mine anywhere, save yours and mine. As for the box—Shaftesbury never set eyes on it—and so he admits. He swears the bishop of Durham told him about it. He chose his bishop well! Durham cannot ram the lies down the fool's throat; the good man's dead.'

'Lies, yes.' And she was pale still. 'But not a fool's lies. The people will believe it. They will believe it because they want to believe it. They want Monmouth to be named heir… handsome, worthless Monmouth, *Protestant* Monmouth!'

'Oh Kate, how I am punished for that youthful folly! A moment's pleasure—scarce that, she was no sweetmeat, Lucy—and then, unending trouble.' Black anger shook him. 'This tale—it makes me a worthless villain. And what, my poor girl, does it make you? By God, Shaftesbury shall pay for this!'

He strode over to her writing-table; she saw the quill tremble in his clenched hand. She came to look over his shoulder.

> On the word of a King and the faith of a Christian, The King was never married to Lucy Barlow alias Walter, the Duke of Monmouth's mother; nor to any woman whatsoever except the now Queen...

'This shall go to my damned Parliament at once!' he cried out and signed his name with such violence that the quill dug into the paper. 'It shall be printed in its thousands. Oddsfish, I'll have it nailed to every church door!' And he trembled still with his fury.

No more talk about the black box. Shaftesbury could show no proof; the King's declaration had killed the tale. No black box. But those that wanted to believe—the legions that cried out for handsome Jamie—went on believing or professed to believe in the King's marriage to Lucy Walter.

That Summer they went to Windsor earlier than usual. It was May, that sweet month, with the river running clear and the hawthorn out and the birds singing with full throat. 'So we escape the noise of Whitehall, and the sight of Oates' monstrous face,' Catherine said. At Windsor it costs less to live, she might have added, for they were still very poor; poorer than many of their subjects. Parliament had been prorogued until Autumn; but had it been called, there would have been no money so long as the King refused to come to heel.

'Louis offers me untold gold, to keep this damned Parliament from meeting for three years. I can name my price—in millions. Dissolve or prorogue, he cares not which. But I'll not do it, Kate!'

She thought of the houses falling into disrepair, of servants and tradesmen unpaid; of the army and the navy she dared not think. She said now, '*Must* you call Parliament? You manage without it very well; you and the Council. Slowly things come into order.'

'Yes.' He sighed. 'Yet a country should not be too long without its government. I have said October and October it must be. If it again prove impossible I shall dissolve it; but only because it pleases me—me and not Louis. It shall be for England's good and not for France... but, oddsfish, I could do with the money.'

May slipped into June. Charles walked, he rode, he swam, he played his games... but always with diminished vigour. He would rise from his warm bed in the cold dawn and go down to the river—no coat, nor hat, nor periwig, even. Then tired and heated from sharp walking, he would seat himself upon a log, the dew still falling and everything glittering and wet. He was, she thought, inviting trouble. He had forgotten the sickness of last year; he forced himself, she thought, to exercise; he would not allow himself to believe he was growing old.

'You get over-tired,' she told him once, 'overheated... and the weather is treacherous.'

'English weather. It's like a woman—blow-hot, blow-cold. A man grows used to it,' he said. And then, 'You are like your own country, Kate, warm and steady... not but what you cannot blow cold, also, when conscience drives. With you a man knows where he is!'

'Is that a good thing?' She wondered if he had found her capricious might he not have taken pains to woo her.

'It is a good thing. It rests a man.'

But he did not alter his ways. It was his way of refusing to grow old. Distressed she was but not surprised when he fell sick again. He shook with ague, he burned with fever, he trembled with rigors. She wondered how long even that strong frame could endure it. He was thinner than ever; there was an outbreak upon his lip; a cold sore so that he could not smile but with pain... and yet he smiled. The thing would soon be gone, he said. But it did not go. It lent him a piteous look. When she remembered his gay and dashing manhood she could have wept.

July passed and August. The warm sun cured his ague and the sore place on his lip. He was less restless; he was, she thought, happier. He smiled more often; it was not the gay smile she had loved but a wiser one. She would, God preserve him to her, learn to love it better than the old. Always she had guessed at the hidden wisdom; now gaiety worn thin, wisdom showed clear.

That Summer of sixteen-eighty he summoned his Council to Windsor. He came from that first meeting, that new, wise smile upon his lips. He said, 'Kate, goodness and commonsense grow apace. Pepys is released. His butler that accused him, upon his dying bed, declared his master's innocent. *And is believed...* that's the thing, Kate. Once Oates would have dragged Pepys through a lying trial; now he dare not. The people are sick of blood. Nor is it any longer a miracle for an accused man to be fairly heard, and the innocent acquitted. Even a short time since it was not so. When by a miracle the innocent was acquitted there were insults for the judge. Remember the hanged dog? Now when a man's found innocent the courts applaud and my judges are no longer afraid. One day there'll be justice in all my courts; I pray God for it, for the sake of my poor people that suffer. And for myself, also I give thanks. To have the law free and uncorrupt, strengthens my hand.'

Day by day the acquittals grew. Shaftesbury had no intention of letting it last. He needed no telling that law and justice strengthens the King's hand... and he was never at a loss for a trick.

He set out to pack the juries; it was as simple as that. He knew well how to plant his bribes. Soon, all over England, mayors, sheriffs and corporations fed at his hands; and, in London, with his wining and dining, with his favours and his promises, magistrates were bribed, witnesses suborned, evidence suppressed and, once again, the innocent brought to a shameful death.

Sweet Saint Catherine, how long? Catherine would kneel importuning the ear of her saint. Once, seeing Charles paler and more tired than usual, she said, 'Let time be weary and wicked, in the end He speaks.'

'But... He is a long time speaking,' Charles sighed.

XXXIII

Charles and Catherine sat in the Queen's closet this cold November day. So they had sat since early morning, the long hours dragging. James' succession was being decided now—once and for all. Ever since Parliament had met in October it had been inimical. 'I wish I had never called it; I wish it with all my heart!' Charles said. 'I could have kept the succession safe, I could have pocketed Louis' gold; I could have made my own life easy. This Parliament of mine! I appealed to it, I implored that the country should be at peace within itself. I spoke with all my heart; I swore to do whatever the House should ask—except one thing. I cannot break the succession—that is in God's Hands, not mine. But short of that, they could make what safeguards they chose to limit the powers of a Catholic King. But there they sat, obstinate and cold. I might have saved my breath.'

He brought his thumb to his lip and bit upon the nail.

'They proceeded with the Bill as though I had not spoken. They rushed it through—three readings in one week! And scarce a voice against it. Now, at this very moment it lies before the Lords. If it should pass...'

If it should pass... Charles leaned forward and held his cold hands to the fire. 'It means the end of peace.' And did not tell her that already Shaftesbury's mob was ready to march on Whitehall. 'I should use my royal veto—and then? Civil war... again. God forbid!'

She rose and knelt before her prie-dieu. Within another room in the palace Louise, that devout Catholic knelt, too. *If the Bill passes!* she might yet be the mother of a King.

Daylight lengthened and waned. Chiffinch came bringing wine and cold meat; he took it away untouched.

At midnight Lord Conway brought them the news.

The Bill had been thrown out.

'God be praised!' Charles said. And then, 'Now my precious Commons will find a victim—they must feed their anger somehow. I know them. Whoever it be, God help him!'

Certainly Charles knew his Commons. They had found the victim. And, since this time they must be sure of success, they had picked one of the five peers still in the Tower—the old man Stafford; his Catholic blood should, a little, allay their thirst. They meant to have the blood of all five; and they'd start with the oldest, the weakest, the most friendless. As Charles had prayed, God help him!

The King could neither sleep nor eat; he was not truly well. Since his illness he had, when disturbed, a light but recurrent fever—and the fever was on him now. At such times he had little use for Louise or any other. Only to Catherine could he speak his heart.

'Stafford will die, Stafford that once served me well. A difficult man but honest; and in this—blameless. You think, Kate—and others think—I should exercise my prerogative; but it wouldn't do. Justice is what Stafford demands; not the King's mercy. Such mercy brands a man as long as he lives... and after. No. The law must take its course. True justice comes only from the law.'

'But if it be injustice that comes; grave injustice?'

'Justice will right herself in the end. She'll not wreck though she be coasted upon a sea of blood.'

She sighed from her heart for old Stafford. Yet Charles, she knew, spoke not from a cold heart but from a heart passionate for justice. For the King to break through a judgment in law with his prerogative could only mar its course.

And now, to add to their troubles, Monmouth was back again—and no permission. He had made an almost royal progress in the west; and now, in London, he was being received—and not by the rabble alone—with royal honours.

Mr. Pepys came hot-foot with the news.

'Things go Shaftesbury's way. He throws his gold about and all London knows him for a good fellow!' Pepys all-but spat. 'He goes about, his arm loving about Monmouth; *my dear son*, he calls him. He stirs up yet more hatred against the Papists. He's got Cornish and Bethell in his pocket; they'll see—those two honest sheriffs—that every jury's packed with party men.'

'Justice may yet wreck upon a sea of blood,' Catherine said.

'She'll outride the storm,' Charles said. 'Believe it!'

About Monmouth, himself, Charles would not ask; no need—Mr. Pepys could not be stayed.

'Monmouth is London's god. Wherever he goes they flock to kiss his hand. They cry out, *God bless the Duke; the Protestant Duke! Down York. Up Monmouth, up!* And, sir—you should know it—they walk backwards before him... even the peers.'

'I made a rod for my own back, Pepys!' Charles said and his smile was wry.

Five innocent men awaiting trial for high treason—and no reason save that they held by the faith. Four were vigorous men with friends. Bring them first to trial and they could defend themselves; they might, even, as Wakeman had done escape the rope. But the fifth... the fifth! Close upon eighty; a man frail in health as in temper; querulous with age; a man to raise against himself many enemies. Choose that man, choose Stafford, mark out the path with his death and the others could not hope to escape. The tormented and quartered bodies of all five should hang in the winds of heaven.

On the last day of November, the old man came to his trial in Westminster Hall. It was no ordinary trial; it was an impeachment by the full House of Commons. Upon the dais, on either side of my lord High Steward of the Court, places stood ready for the King and Queen. Catherine dreaded the occasion; but a fearful fascination drew her—she herself might have stood in the prisoner's place... and might yet stand. Who knew the depths of Shaftesbury's wickedness?

When the King and Queen came to their places, the Commons were already seated. The galleries above were crowded, bright with the robes of foreign guests, of men and women of high fashion. The gentlemen waved their muffs in greeting, the ladies flirted with their fans... and all laughing and chatting as at the play. Moving towards her place, Catherine caught sight of a head dressed as for a ball; it moved from side to side, greeting, laughing, gossiping. It belonged to Louise. She carried upon her lap a small gold box of sugared almonds; now and again she would nibble, laughing still. The chair beneath the canopy, piled high with woolsacks was, for the moment, empty; on either side stretched rows of empty seats awaiting my lords the peers of England.

At a table near the Bar a woman sat with papers and pens before her. Catherine knew her—Stafford's daughter, my lady Winchelsea, come, since other help there was none, to set down with truth, all that was said today, so that her father might know how the case stood.

Catherine felt the heart sicken in her breast. What work was this for a daughter to set down each word that must hang her father? Yet the lady's face though marble-pale, was composed, unstained by tears.

And now came the great procession. First the clerks that were to transcribe the trial, in black gowns and white bands; and, following them, the Clerk to the Court walking together with the Clerk to Parliament; and thereafter the Masters-in-Chancery, walking two-by-two. Then, walking alone, the King's Attorney-General; and, at his heels, those other attorneys that were to press the charge with him. And now came the judges walking slow and solemn, two-by-two in their great robes of black and red. *Black for death; red for blood.* Catherine could not drive the thought from her head. Behind the judges four serjeants-at-arms carried maces; and, ending the procession, walking with Black Rod, Garter, carrying the white wand of my lord Steward's office.

When all these had come to stand before their places, came those that were to pronounce upon the prisoner this day—my lords the peers of England, each his hat upon his head, and walking according to his degree. And now, all standing, the great officers—my lord Privy Seal and my Lord President of the Council. And then, walking alone, great train upborne by four pages, the Great Seal carried before him—Heneage Finch, my lord Daventry, lord High Steward of the court.

All this splendour to hang one innocent man! Catherine's heart played coward; she wished herself any place but here.

My lord High Steward seated himself upon the Woolsack; and now the court might sit, also. He took the white wand from Garter that offered it, kneeling, and handed it to Black Rod that, kneeling, took it.

And now the voice of the crier ringing through the silence. 'Lieutenant of the Tower, bring forth your prisoner, William, Viscount Stafford. God save the King!'

In he came, slow, the frail old man white as a bone and paper-thin; but he walked upright and proud to his shameful place. 'My lord Stafford must kneel,' Black Rod said; so the prisoner went painfully upon his knees and there knelt till my lord Steward gave him permission to rise.

My lord Steward leaned forward in his chair.

'My lord Stafford, the Commons of England here assembled in Parliament, have impeached you of High Treason; and you are brought to the Bar this day to be tried upon that charge. You are not to be judged by any jury but by the whole body of the House of Lords—the highest and noblest court of this or any Christian land. Here no false weight nor measure will ever be found. The balance will be exactly kept and every grain of allowance your case will bear will certainly be put to the scales.'

Dear God, the hypocrisy of men! Catherine caught Charles' eye; it was his thought also.

'As it is impossible for my lords to condemn the innocent, so it is equally impossible they should clear the guilty. Therefore hear with patience what shall be said against you. When you come to your defence you shall have a fair and equal hearing.'

God grant it! Catherine prayed.

The old man bowed and put a hand to the Bar as though to keep himself from falling. My lord Steward said, 'If your lordship find yourself infirm, you may have a chair while they read the charges.'

'I thank your lordship.' The prisoner seated himself. He sat, one hand cupped to his ear that he might hear better; his fine wig slipped a little with the movement, so that the scant silver hair showed; and very old and pitiful he looked.

'William, Viscount Stafford,' the voice of the Clerk to the Court came clear, impersonal, 'you are charged this day that you did most wickedly conspire against his sacred majesty the King, to rob him of his royal state, crown and dignity; and, further, to murder him by poisoning, shooting or stabbing; and that you offered rewards to several persons to execute the same.

'And you are charged further that you conspired to extirpate the Protestant religion, to subvert the lawful government, and subject it to the tyranny of the Pope.

'How say you; are you guilty of these charges or no?'

And he, in his thin old voice, declaring his innocence, and being asked how he would be tried, answered, 'By God and my peers.'

Mr. Serjeant Maynard, the King's Attorney, rose in his place to speak and the old man at the Bar must rise to listen.

'May it please your lordships, I am here by command of the House of Commons to prosecute this great charge against the prisoner. There are two parts to his charge—the general; that is the subversion of the whole nation—the King to be murdered, and the Protestant religion to be suppressed. And there is the particular—this lord's part in that plot.

'It is my part to urge the general. When Oates first made his discovery it had not the weight we think now it clearly has. We were, as it might be, asleep. The murder of Sir Edmund Berry Godfrey awakened us.'

The murder of Godfrey. Catherine's hands twisted in her lap. *What has it to do with Stafford, save to whip the court into a rage? They cast their looks of hatred upon him… and upon me, upon me, also. God help the prisoner; and God help me!*

He proceeded to whip them further.

'The design was not to destroy this man or that; but the whole body of Protestants here in England. Not a murder but a massacre. Not to destroy the King alone—though that is the greatest offence in our law; but to destroy our religion, to destroy *us* because of our religion.

'It is strange, my lords, that Englishmen should contrive to make an invasion of strangers upon their own country. Yet, let us not wonder at it. For Papists say it is lawful to kill a heretic King; nay more—it is a holy service to God for which they may be canonised as saints…'

Catherine took in her breath at this piece of wickedness. Now he was telling the court that Papists know no law of nature. A Papist would murder his own children and put them in the fire should they turn Protestant.

'I come now to the murder of Sir Edmund Berry Godfrey...' and he proceeded to tell the court how an upright magistrate had been foully murdered by Papists; and how these same Papists had tried to tempt Bedloe to do the deed with rich rewards.

But you do not say how the Protestants, the great lords, bribed the horse-thief with money and with honours and with lodgings in the King's palace... nor how he died denying the lies he told about me, your Queen...

'So my lords, Sir Edmund was brutally murdered that the discovery of Papist treason might go no further.'

Lies. She saw Charles bite upon his sore thumb. *But if it were true, what has Godfrey's murder to do with Stafford? He was never charged with it.*

And now Maynard having seated himself, Sir Francis Winnington rose in his place.

'My lords, Mr. Serjeant Maynard has dealt with the general; so now I deal with the particular. I look upon the cause this day to be the cause of the Protestant religion.'

It is not that cause you are here to try; but the guilt of this one man. She looked at my lord Steward; it was clear he saw nothing wrong in this. She looked across at Charles; he was frowning and biting upon his thumb.

But worse was to come.

'The religion of Papists countenances and encourages the murder of princes; and the massacre of those they miscall heretics.'

The murder of princes. Did you not seek to murder me? And massacre. Are you not guilty of that, also? Beneath her still face Catherine heard her thoughts cry so loud she wondered he did not turn to look at her.

'What, my lords, gave these Papists the greatest encouragement to enter into this detestable conspiracy was that they had—to the great unhappiness of the Kingdom—the expectation of a papist successor.'

Charles sat unmoving; within him anger burned at this crooked dragging-in of his brother. From her place in the fore-front of the gallery Louise sat smiling... and did not hide her smiles behind her fan. Her eyes were on the Queen; it was as though she whispered, *York's turn will come; and your turn will come... and then... and then...*

And now Winnington was dealing with the evidence in the trials that had followed Godfrey's murder.

He drags in Coleman as if hanging proves his guilt; it proves nothing but their wish to find him guilty. He drags in my good Wakeman that the court found innocent. But guilty or innocent, when those two were tried there was no mention, ever, of Stafford. What have they to do with the old man at the Bar?

'And so I come to the heart of the matter. My lords, the prisoner offered five hundred pounds to any that should kill the King. Now we shall produce our witnesses.'

He sat down; but the old man at the Bar that had stood long must stand till evening. And now another rose to take up the long tale.

At the name of the first witness the prisoner objected.

'I do not know his name. I humbly beseech your lordship that this witness and all the rest that bear witness against me, look me face-to-face according to the law.'

My lord High Steward answered neither *yea* nor *nay*; but only, 'You shall have all fair proceedings that may be.'

But, knowing the malice against him, the prisoner was not satisfied. He said, 'The law says that my accusers must look upon me face-to-face.'

'You may see him where he stands,' my lord Steward said.

So the prisoner straining his weak old eyes said, 'I do see him and I know him not!'

Then the witness told a tale that did but damn himself, for he was a reneged Jesuit—a priest—that, for the offer of free pardon, was content to betray his friends.

'The Jesuits of France had great hope of their religion in England. The duke of York had great hope of it and the Queen, also.'

Her own name flung suddenly, unexpectedly, hit her with the full force of a blow. She managed to sit upright still; but the room swam about her. Through the dizziness she heard the witness say, 'They said, these same Jesuits of France, that *one* stood in the way.'

'The one that stood in the way—they named him?'

'Sir, they did.'

'And that name?'

'The King.'

Catherine took that—her second shock. When she had righted her mind, they were questioning the man about the Fire of London.

'It is known everywhere that the Papists fired it. Of course they deny it. They say it was an accident. But they say also—' and each word came poisonous and slow, 'it were no great matter if all had been burnt.'

'How long since this man has been a priest?' The old man at the Bar shot his sudden question.

'No man is bound to answer a question that shall accuse himself!' my lord Steward said, very quick.

Protected, bribed and pardoned to betray his God; what truth in him? Catherine sent out her question into an uncaring court.

And now this witness being gone—having said nothing to damn the prisoner, but casting deeper suspicion upon the King's brother and the King's wife, there came a Mr. Dugdale. Another Jesuit to betray his God and his friends!

He was going further than that other; not only did he betray those friends already named, but others not yet accused or even thought of... soon, soon they would be both.

'I saw a letter from Boscabel to Harcourt. It said there was no better way to forward the work than by the sudden death of the King. They said that whosoever took part in the killing should have pardon for all his sins. They said the King was a heretic; and it was lawful to kill him. It was no more than killing a dog.'

Looking across at Charles, Catherine saw that he believed not a word. But for all that, anger stiffened his body, flamed in his eye. That such words should be spoken of a Stuart King! It was an anger shared by all; the hissing breath proclaimed it.

'Call Doctor Oates.'

A sigh went through the great room as of acclamation; it was as if the whole court should rise and applaud. He came mincing in his silken gown with the make-believe bishop sleeves. His greasy dish-face glistened with sweat; the tongue licking at the small mean mouth made it wetter, redder... the mouth that looked like a dog's vent.

Catherine tasted hatred like a sickness in her throat. Never, in her whole life, had she hated anyone; hatred—it was violation of her whole nature. But this monster. He stank of innocent blood; he was corruption to spread corruption. She looked about to see who shared her disgust; if any did, he dared not show it. And the creature, besides, had a fascination—a perverse fascination—especially for women. She saw Louise kiss her finger-tips towards him.

The court hung upon his words. He had a gift for words though he mangled them with his drawling parody of the good English tongue.

He had never been a Jesuit, not he! Yes, he had been in Jesuit colleges in France and in Spain. He had gone to spy—though he put it more prettily. He had gone, he said, to find out what he could to protect the Protestant cause.

You were thrown out of both colleges; you were thrown out of the navy for corrupting young boys—you, a chaplain, making corruption more vile. You know it; and the court knows it. Yet there you stand, liar that you are, swearing away the life of an innocent man. In her mind she addressed Oates with passion. She looked across at Charles; again he had brought the injured thumb to his mouth.

Oates bowed himself out; and now, one after another, reneged Papists betrayed Christ and their fellow-men.

On and on; old tales raked up. And now, to frighten the prisoner, the judgment against Coleman was read out; the fearful punishment. But the indomitable old man, so far from being frightened, cried out in his querulous old voice, 'I do not hear one word he says!' And my lord Steward, pitying him, perhaps, answered, 'This does not concern your lordship.'

It was growing late; and the air in the court foul with the stink of people and the cloying perfume of the ladies. Attorney Sir William Jones rose and, addressing himself to my lord High Steward, asked whether he would hear the case today or wait till tomorrow.

'There is much more to come; it were better to wait till tomorrow,' my lord said; and Mr. Attorney then addressing the question to the peers received his answer with one voice, *Ay.*

XXXIV

They came out into the dark November evening with a fog rising from the river. They sat side by side in the coach, and, for awhile, neither spoke. She was crying softly into the darkness; he came out of his own melancholy to comfort her.

'Not men but wolves,' he said. 'A savage pack that lusts for blood. You do well to cry for the cruelties of men!'

'That old man... his eyes fail; and his hearing, also.'

'But not his heart; his spirit's great. He'll not bend his neck and so they'll break it. But—' and he shrugged, 'he'll not, I think, mind dying. A martyr's death; it may even please him.'

'*That* death... a traitor's death...?'

'Not that death; I swear it!'

'Such a death!' she said. 'Not man nor beast deserves it; not Oates, himself!' She was shivering and he put his cloak about her. He said, and she caught in the sudden flare of a linkboy's torch, his grim face, 'Nothing's so cruel as these "lovers of God!" I have striven for tolerance but none will have it so. No! For a word in a prayer they inflict upon their brothers the torments of Hell. And it goes on—turn and turn about. Once it was *your* turn...'

She looked at him bewildered.

'Not your own; you were never cruel in your life, Kate. But—your Inquisition; have you forgot? And here, in this very England, the torments and the burnings. The people don't forget our good Catholic Bloody Mary. It frightens them still; and frightened men are cruel. But turn and turn about—as I said. Now good Protestants hold the whip!'

'It is different!' she said. 'Here they torment Catholics from hatred; with us it is to save a man's soul.'

'May you not care too much for his soul and too little for his body?'

'We cannot care too much for a man's soul; so we make him safe in God.'

'I think,' he said, very slow, 'we must learn to love man before we can love God.'

'God comes first!' she said obstinate and shocked.

'The more we love our brother, the closer we come to the mind of God—the Scriptures put it plain.'

She looked at him, this heretic she so loved. She said, 'You translate the Scriptures to please yourself; and that's a heresy—a heresy you are pleased to call tolerance. This tolerance of yours—Charles, I must speak; it is nothing but a weighing of this and that to avoid inconvenience... which inconvenience includes a too-kind heart. Such tolerance God does not require of us; he requires a whole heart and not a half. I think...' she sent him a long look, 'you care for no church at all.'

'I am not free to choose; but were I free—' he shrugged lightly, 'why then, the Catholic faith is the only faith for a gentleman. I have said it before!'

'Oh,' she cried out, 'must you forever hide behind a jest? Do you believe in anything; anything at all?'

'I believe in God and His goodness. I believe that He likes us to laugh a little—if our laughter be not cruel. I think He will not punish a man unduly for taking a little pleasure—as it were—on the side. I think He hates nothing more than lies—unless it be cruelty or betrayal.'

She said, sorrowful, 'You make God in your own image; which image is good enough for a man. But to speak for God! Such talk is heresy. I know it, here.' Her hand went up to her head. 'But here—' and she laid a hand upon her heart, 'I am no longer sure. Living among heretics I am grown weak.'

'You have grown up,' he said. 'And you have learnt something of compassion.' He turned her face and kissed her; but even in that sweet moment her heart cried because it was upon the cheek his kiss fell and not upon the mouth.

That night she could not sleep for thinking of the old man—the prisoner. Charles had come to her bed; and though he, too, had been restless, he slept now, one hand flung out towards her. In the moonlight, his face all silvered, the grey of his hair was not to be seen; he looked as he must have looked in the first glory of his manhood. She was taken with so great a love, her heart, it seemed, must break. She came softly from the bed to kneel before her prie-dieu. She prayed, first of all, for Stafford; and for his judges that God might put justice into their hearts. She prayed for Charles that he might be given grace openly to avow his faith. Last of all she prayed for herself that Charles might come to love her a little, and that she might not love him so much that she should stray from God. She was shaking with cold when she crept back into bed.

Next morning, sick with headache and lack of sleep, she could not attend the trial; but she prayed for the prisoner and for the pale lady, his daughter. And all the time two thoughts pierced like nails. *But for the King I, myself, would stand at the Bar.* And, *If they murder Stafford we must all share in the guilt, all, from the King down to the youngest child that runs screaming with the mob.*

It was late evening before Charles returned; he sat in the great chair too weary even to pull off his gloves. He said, 'The trial goes as we might expect. Lies; and great mischief done—not to the prisoner alone; but to us all. We cannot so injure a fellow man and not injure ourselves.'

She said nothing. She bent to pull off his gloves and brought him a cup of the sweet Portugal wine he loved. Presently a little colour came into his face. 'Stafford bore himself manfully,' he said. 'He questioned false statements, he caused witnesses to stumble, he showed, clearly, that they lied. But the court didn't care; it made no difference save to anger them. The fellow, Dugdale, gave a false date—three years out. Three years! Yet when the old man protested, my lord Steward told him not to make a strain of the matter. Stafford cried out, Three years; is that a strain? They should have saved him, those three years... but it was not allowed.

'They had Oates up again, the obscene animal, swearing away a man's life; swearing he'd met Stafford here, there and everywhere. Stafford declared on oath he'd never set eyes on the fellow until this trial. And that's true enough; the old man's been away from London till they clapped him in the Tower. Pray my lords, he said, give me leave to ask whether Doctor Oates has not said several times since I was first imprisoned, that he never saw me in his life.

'Oates denied it; naturally he denied it. He was lying; you could see how his pig's eyes would not meet the old man's; and the way he kept licking that obscene mouth of his. Stafford said, If ever I saw this doctor in my life, I'll willingly die. Well die he will; they mean to have his blood.'

Third day. Fourth day. Fifth day.

'Your own name came into it,' Charles said, eyes haggard in their sockets. She put a hand before her as though, blind, she must feel her way; he took the hand in his. 'There's none to believe it—not Oates himself,' he said, 'pretend how they will! Stafford, his own life at stake, defended you.'

'The *brave* old man!' she said.

'He was not afraid to attack Oates—though he knows it must prejudice yet further his case. He said, When Oates first made his deposition, he was asked if he had anyone else to accuse. He said he had not. But afterwards he accused—he dared to accuse—the Queen.

'Oates did not answer; he could not. But Mr. Attorney-General answered for him. Dr. Oates did not know at that time whether it was lawful to accuse the Queen! Stafford's courage is great; but it won't help him. Nothing will help him. Now all is said; tomorrow—the judgment.'

On the last day of the trial Catherine was present. She must see for herself how the thing ended—she that had so nearly stood in the prisoner's place... and might yet stand.

It was eleven o'clock; and, save for the peers and the officers of the law, the court was full. The Commons sat gossiping; Stafford's daughter sat white as the paper before her; if you pricked her, Catherine thought, she would bleed not blood but tears. And still the ladies of the Court behaved as though all were set for the play; especially Louise flirting her fan and bestowing her smiles, and nibbling at a comfit from her little box.

Now the Clerk of the Court cried out for silence and the great procession entered. My lord High Steward settled himself beneath the canopy; the peers, wearing each his hat, seated themselves. And still the Bar remained empty. Catherine thought of the old man waiting alone; and could not bear to look upon his daughter.

In the silence my lord High Steward spoke.

'My lords, I beg that I may take your votes as I sit; I am not well enough to stand.' And this being granted, he addressed the least of the peers.

'My lord Butler of Weston, is my lord Stafford guilty of the treason whereof he is impeached, or not guilty?' And he, standing, put his hat from his head and said 'Not guilty, upon my honour,' and seated himself.

Catherine's hand went to her heart. Maybe there was hope.

One after another, standing, each man recorded his judgment. She tried to keep count but the numbers escaped her. Charles, she could see, kept count also; she saw his face settle into a mask of grief and knew the sentence before a word was said.

My lord High Steward said, 'My lords, I find there are thirty-one that hold by the prisoner's innocence; and fifty-five that hold by his guilt. Mr. Serjeant-Crier, make proclamation to bring the prisoner to the Bar.'

Catherine could not bear to look where the old man stood. She heard my lord Steward address him. 'My lord Stafford. I have heavy news for you. My lords the peers do find you guilty!'

And the old man clasping his hands, as in prayer, said, 'God's holy Name be praised!'

It was a martyr's acceptance; simple and infinitely moving. It should have cried out the truth; but the court was beyond caring.

'What can your lordship say why judgment of death should not be given you according to the law?'

'I am surprised, for I did not expect it.' And the old voice came out strong; no fretfulness in it. He had taken on a further measure of dignity. 'But God's Will be done. I will not murmur at it. God forgive those that have sworn falsely, against me.'

My lord Steward said, 'I never yet gave sentence of death; it goes hard that I must begin with your lordship. My lord—and this is the last time I can call you so; for the next words I am to speak shall attaint you. The judgment of the law is this...

'... *hanged by the neck... cut down alive... entrails burnt before your eyes... head to be severed... body divided...*'

There was a long sigh; Stafford's daughter had slipped sideways in her chair.

Catherine had tried not to listen; but for all that she lost nothing of the hateful words that were to echo and re-echo in her ears.

But the prisoner who must no more be called *my lord* listened with courtesy; and with courtesy thanked their lordships for their patient hearing.

'Here in the presence of God Almighty, I declare I have no malice in my heart towards those that have condemned me; and I beseech you all to pray for me. I have but one request—that, in the little short time I have to live, my wife and children, and my friends, also, may come to me.'

My lord High Steward nodded; then he said, 'I believe I may tell you one thing more. My lords will be humble suitors to the King that he will remit all punishment but the taking of your head.'

For the first time the prisoner broke down.

'My lords—' and he was all shaken with his tears, 'it is not your justice makes me cry but your goodness.'

Then my lord Steward broke the white staff; and the prisoner, an axe-edge turned towards him, was led away. As the King and Queen left the court, there came clear the noise of the rabble insulting the old man soon to die. As she went, Catherine looked for Stafford's daughter; she was nowhere to be seen. She was in an inner room crying her heart out that she had heard words no Christian ear should hear... and a daughter's ear least of all.

Within the coach Charles said, 'The lords will ask me to give him a clean death and that I shall do. But there'll be trouble. The mob, sicked on by the good sheriffs of London—Shaftesbury's creatures—will demand the full penalty.'

'*That* death... they *want* it; the full sentence?'

He nodded. 'But I'll not have it; of that be sure. As for the old man, grieve no more; he'll die gladly—so it be by the axe.'

Charles, that shrewd judge of men, was right on both counts.

The sheriffs, Bethell and Cornish, were not willing for the old man to die a clean death. They petitioned the Lords that the full sentence be carried out. But the Lords had heard enough; many believed in Stafford's innocence and more than half had declared it in court. The King must be obeyed.

On Wednesday, the twenty-ninth of December, the prisoner went to his death. Mr. Pepys that missed nothing, brought the story to the King.

'The scaffold was hung with black; and the coffin, God save us, stood ready. The executioner brought up the block and covered it with black woollen stuff. Then the old man climbed the scaffold. He had a thin, fragile look, like fine china; but he was strong and steady. He asked the executioner if he had been paid for the black stuff; those of us that stood near the scaffold heard him plain. It went to my heart to see a man so thoughtful for others in such an hour. The fellow said *No*; and Stafford took four guineas from his pocket and put it in the man's hand. Then he took a paper from his bosom and began to read. I have it here, sir; he requested it to be brought to you.'

'Read it,' Charles said.

Mr. Pepys took his spectacles from his nose and wiped them upon a handkerchief of fine lawn. 'It is the heat in the room, after the cold without, mists them,' he said and began to read.

'... I do most truly, in the presence of the eternal, omnipotent and all-knowing God, protest upon my salvation that I am innocent...'

Mr. Pepys turned the pages with a plump, white hand.

'There is much in his defence, sir; and that you have heard in the court. And, indeed, you may believe him. You know, sir, how many innocents have come to their death on a false charge. I, myself, as you know, lay in prison on just such a charge; and save for the good-ness of God that saw fit to make my innocence known or ever I came to trial—my man that laid it making his dying confession—I should, myself, have come to a traitor's end.' And shuddered; plain Mr. Pepys must have suffered the full rigours of that death. Voice a little unsteady, he began to read again.

'I do beseech God bless his Majesty who is my lawful King, whom I was always by all laws human and divine to obey... I do hold that the constitution of the government of this Kingdom is the only way to continue peace—which God long continue.

Next to treason I hold murder in abhorrence. I so much abhor to be the cause of any man's death, how much the less would I endeavour the assassination of his majesty whom I hold to be as gracious a King as this or any nation ever had.

...I do desire that all people will forgive me any injury I have done them in anything, either wilfully or by chance. And I do heartily forgive all those that have injured me. I forgive even those that so falsely brought me hither by their perjuries... God forgive them.

...I beseech God not to avenge my innocent death upon the nation or upon those that were the cause of it. I do, with my last breath, assert my innocence.'

Mr. Pepys stopped reading and unashamedly wiped his eyes upon the fine handkerchief. 'When, sir, he had made an end of reading he knelt to pray. He prayed alone; for there was no priest of his faith allowed him. Then he cried out in his thin old voice, *God bless his majesty that is as good a prince as ever governed. Obey him faithfully as I have done; God bless you, gentlemen, all.*

'He was about to kneel for the strike when some fellow in orders—a rat of a man—thrust his way to the front shouting, *Do you disown the indulgences of the Romish Church?* And he cried out, the old fighting spirit with him still, *The Church of Rome allows no indulgence for murder; or for lying. What I have said is true.*

'Then sir,—the first strange thing! The crowd that had come to curse, blessed him instead; they cried out, *We believe you; God bless you!* Then he turned to his friends and gave them such trinkets as he had upon him—his watch and the ring from his finger, and the crucifix from his neck. Then, with his own hands he took off his coat and, folding it quietly as though he went to his bed, he gave it to his man who took it weeping. Then the servant took off the peruke; and there he stood an old, old man with thin white hair and the pink scalp showing through; older, even, than I had truly understood. His man folded the white hair beneath a black silk cap; and, as though it were a pillow, he laid his head upon the block.

'And now, sir, the second strange thing. The executioner lifted his arm with the axe... and it fell to his side. Three times he lifted his arm; and three times it fell to his side. The fourth time he brought it down upon the neck. There was a long groan from the crowd.'

'The crowd... it *groaned*?' Catherine lifted wet eyes.

'Madam, it did. The tide was turned. The executioner held up the head and proclaimed, according to his duty, *Here is the head of a traitor!* But his voice was drowned in the sobbing of the crowd.

For the first time the King spoke. 'His death was murder!'

'And sir, he was brave, not only upon the scaffold but before. They say he asked for a cloak. He said, *I may shake with the cold, but, not with fear. I trust in God.*' Charles looked as if he were about to weep; it was like an echo of a ghost. With just such words his own father had gone to just such a death.

'Well, sir, there's the end. The crowd went home very quiet; and some were weeping still. I believe, with all my heart, they are sick to the guts of the lying trials and the horrible cruelties. The human heart can endure so much—and no more. Pray God this trial may be the last.'

'Amen!' Charles said; but there was no cheerfulness in his face.

XXXV

On the night of Stafford's death Catherine awoke in the dark hours to find the room painted with red light. Her heart went small with fear. What Catholic heart could forget that those of her faith had been accused of firing London... and of meaning to fire it again?

She came quietly from the bed and Charles stirred. 'What ails you, Kate?' he asked with quick kindness.

She was kneeling upon the window-seat, staring up at the sky. There, in the darkness, blazed a crimson-tailed star.

'A judgment on us all for Stafford's death; and for all innocent deaths!' she said through chattering teeth.

He came from the bed and made up the fire; for still he suffered now and then from ague. He came to join her at the window.

'Oh Kate, my foolish Kate. It's a comet. You have seen one before; you looked at it through my spy-glass.'

'It was not the colour of blood.'

'My Royal Society shall explain the colour... and the explanation will have nothing to do with blood and vengeance.'

He brought her back to bed and lay warming her cold hands in his own; but still she lay and shivered.

'Your Royal Society can explain much; but there are things beyond their explainings. *There are more things than are dreamed of...* What does your Shakespeare say?'

'...than are dreamed of in our philosophy. Truer for him than for us today. Newton or Wren or Evelyn would want a last word there.'

'There are things beyond even *their* philosophy,' she said obstinate.

The bad year that had seen Stafford's death was ended; she prayed the new one would prove better. It looked as though her prayers might be answered.

The people were sickened of the smell of blood. Now, every death, whether by axe or rope, chilled their anger to a mortal disgust. And the judges, for the most part, sickened, too, so that the number of hangings grew less... but still there were hangings enough.

Eaten by spite Shaftesbury whispered in the ear of his friends in the Commons. *Whoever shall give the King money is the nation's enemy*; in the House the resolution was passed. Louise, though hand-in-glove with Shaftesbury, was not best-pleased; this hit her, too! But Charles grinned. I am no worse off he said, but his smile was wry.

Catherine did not smile; she found it hard to smile these days. She was sleeping badly and the old headaches were back; they would never be less until her troubles were less. And troubles she had, God knew—the pressure upon the King for divorce; and the never quite-stilled whisper that she had agreed to the King's death. And she was troubled, too, for Charles, surrounded by enemies and not knowing which way to turn for money, yet carrying himself with courtesy towards all. She was haunted by fear of disaster so that she would awake weeping from short, troubled sleep.

For some little time there had been a new face about the court; a handsome face. Its owner, a young man of elegance and breeding, might be seen, at any time, walking along the Stone gallery towards Louise's rooms. Yet for all his gallant air he was shabby—the cloth of his coat shiny with wear, the ruffles, though clean, not so fine as should be; and his shoes, mute testimony to a man's poverty, scuffed heel and toe.

Once when Catherine met him in the gallery he started, the colour suddenly pale in his cheeks. He made her his courtier's bow; and, though it was deeply respectful, she fancied a shifty look in his eye. When she mentioned the new-comer to Charles, he laughed. 'It's Fitzharris, the Irishman. I've had my eye on him since first he came. Chiffinch watches for me—the secret door to Louise's rooms is useful. How long he stays we know; what they say we cannot know—they keep their voices low; but I can make a guess.'

'Her lover?'

He burst into laughter. 'Your kind heart misleads you, Kate. *She* take so needy a lover? She needs money—her gambling debts, alone, are ruinous. I fancy that, through this shabby gentleman money, will flow.' And at her puzzled look, laughed again. 'She lies close to Shaftesbury as his glove. Mistake me not! She lies not in his bed... she'd not dare; and he's too racked with gout to take his pleasure. But he, it seems, holds the purse-strings... and my purse is empty. She works with Shaftesbury; Fitzharris, I fancy, is the go-between.'

'Send them away!' Catherine cried out. 'Send them away—the Frenchwoman and the Irishman, both!'

'They are safer where they are—under my eye.'

She tried to forget Fitzharris so poor, so debonair, so disturbing. With increasing headache, increasing heartache, she was to remember him again.

Charles came over to the Queen's Side; he was disturbed. She could see it by the way he played with his watch, swinging it this way and that; and by the way he carried it over to match the time by her clock; and by the way he wandered about the room and could not meet her eye.

'No good beating about the bush!' he said, at last. 'Kate—it's the old nonsense again! Fitzharris tells a tale; he's told it in the Council already. He says you mean to poison me still; he says James stands with you in this. He says de Mello has proof and will provide it.'

'My... *godfather*?' She tried to laugh but her lips refused.

'Fitzharris is a liar—bold and unashamed. But, repeat a lie often enough—and there's plenty will take it for gospel. So much so—' and he was gloomy, 'Parliament declares if I come to a violent end, every Papist—yourself included—shall suffer for it.'

'My poor people!'

He said, gloomy still, 'They bring it upon themselves—running to betray each other at a price! Nor is this the end of it. In addition to this little plot, he swears there's another. Irish Papists, it seems, are also out to murder me. Mark it, Kate; the fellow's an Irishman, himself; a double traitor to his own. All the names at a price! And the price? His life pardoned in advance and his mouth stuffed with gold... so he thinks; and so Shaftesbury thinks. But I'll not have it. I'll have no more ratting, no more pardons in advance, If a man come with his "discoveries" he'll speak—we'll find the way to make him. And, if he's guilty—he'll hang!'

Catherine said, 'I know not whether to be more sorry for myself that I am so besmirched with lies; or for my poor friends in the Faith; or for the wretch himself, that barters his soul, betraying not only his friends but his God, also.'

'He's up to his neck in trouble... to the neck, indeed!' Charles said. 'He lies in the Tower; and the charge? High treason. We haven't examined the evidence yet; but, I fancy, there's enough to hang him. He thinks Shaftesbury will save him; but the old fox lies low. This tale of poison; he'll stick to it now, if only to save his neck. Poor devil, he never thought to find himself in such a pickle. He thought, at first, merely, to turn a dishonest penny with the tale; and needs it. Married; and with a brood of brats... and not one ha'penny to rub against another.'

'It's a hard thing when children cry for bread,' she said.

'It's not your concern!' he told her, very sharp. 'Oh Kate, I know you—your heart betrays your wits! Help them—and then? *The Queen bribes him to keep his mouth shut!* There'd be no stopping evil tongues.'

'Will it help me if his children starve?'

'They are not your concern,' he said again. 'To make them so may damn you in the eyes of many. Kate, remember, I implore you, the foul charge he lays against you.'

'What must I do? What must I *do*?' She beat her hands one against the other.

He took the frantic hands in his. 'Nothing.' A smile lifted that grim mouth of his. 'Before we hang a man we must find the rope!'

'We have found the rope!' Charles flung a paper upon the table. 'Treason and sedition; and all writ with the fellow's own hand. And every word enough to hang him!'

She picked up the paper; and, since reading of English did not come easy to her, read slowly,

The True Englishman speaking Plain English

I thank you for your character of a popish successor which you sent me, wherein our fears—and the grounds thereof—are justly set out.

She lifted puzzled eyes. 'But the man's of my faith; why should he fear a catholic successor?'

'Read on.'

She read on, repeating the words aloud to make sense. She said, bewildered still, 'I thought he was to accuse his own; but it is the Protestants he accuses, *the Protestants*!'

Charles said, that grim smile lifting his lips, 'He's a double-tongued serpent, this Irishman. He tells his lies—and Protestants will hang. But mark me well! If he be a liar proved, in hope to save his skin—or even if there be profit in it—then he'll turn himself about. He'll swear the Papists were at the bottom of it; that his friends lied to him. So he hangs them all—Protestants and Catholics alike. A pretty plot!'

She put a hand to her throat lest she vomit; she said, when she could speak at last, 'Too deep a plot for so humble a fellow!'

'But not too deep for Shaftesbury! For the present I stand by and say nothing; meanwhile this precious Fitzharris cools his heels in the Tower. Thence to the gallows is a short step.'

When he had gone she picked up the paper again.

I am in greater fear of the present possessor of the throne. Why do we frighten ourselves about the evil that is to come, not looking at

that which is at hand? We would cut off the budding weeds and let
the poisonous roots lie still...

It was clear incitement to murder the King.

If James be guilty, Charles is so, too. Believe me these two brethren
in iniquity are in confederacy with the Pope and with the French to
introduce Popery and arbitrary government...

Oh, it was clever! Who could doubt that this vile thing had been
written by Protestants? High Treason. And Protestant necks would
be stretched.

She went on reading.

Let the English rise and fling off their intolerable riders. Blow the
trumpets, stand on your guard, withstand them as bears and tigers.
Trust in your sword in defence of your lives, laws, religion and properties...

The wretch; the perjured wretch that stirred the people to murder
their king, that did not fear before God to bring innocent men to
their death—Protestant and Catholic alike.

She read on, unable to take away her fascinated eyes.

Charles obstructs justice. He is joined in will and deed to James'
villainies. He is afraid to be discovered a Papist and a betrayer both of
his people and the Protestant religion. If he were heartily concerned
for our religion would he not oppose a Popish successor?

Shaftesbury's lickspittle, whipping the people on to James' exclusion and bloody revolution. Civil war; brother slaying brother.

Has he not turned out of his Council the most zealous Protestants
such as Shaftesbury?

Clever, clever! Who would suspect a Catholic here? There was
more, much more.

James and Charles... are corrupt both in root and branch. They study to enslave England to a French and Romish yoke. Have you not eyes, sense of feeling? Where is the old English noble spirit? Are you become French asses to suffer any load to be laid upon you?

And now incitement became exact and pointed; time and place set.

If you can get no remedy from his next Parliament—as certainly you will not—then up, all as one man! Oh brave Englishmen look to your own defence ere it be too late.

Now there was mention of Richard II and Henry VI. She knew nothing of them; but clearly each had lost his crown and his life... again the clear incitement to put Charles from the throne. Thence, like those other kings his journey would be short; from the cell to the scaffold.

She put her head in her hands; she was overcome with shame, with sorrow, that her fellow-worshippers in God should so serve the devil.

'Fitzharris must hang; his own words betray him!' Charles told Catherine. 'Shaftesbury cannot help him... if he would.'

'Shaftesbury can make trouble for us all!' she said, grave.

And make trouble he did.

'It is not proper,' he told both Houses, 'to bring Fitzharris to trial in the common courts. For such an offence he must be impeached before the Lords.'

'A man must be judged by his equals. This fellow is a commoner,' my lords the peers replied. 'It cannot be done!'

'First set-back to Shaftesbury!' Charles said. 'Impeachment is private; evidence may be twisted this way or that. Now Fitzharris must stand in the cold light of common day... and Shaftesbury trembles for what that day may bring.'

Before the trial, the Council met to examine the witnesses; it was usual in cases of treason. And since the King's wife and the King's brother had been accused, Charles sat with the Council. He had studied the documents; and now, so penetrating were his questions and so keen his eye, few liars could outface him.

Before ever Fitzharris came to his trial, his lies had been confounded. He had, indeed, done the Queen some service. Not only did her godfather de Mello deny the whole tale; he took the chance to dwell upon Catherine's character and her deep love for the King. He had killed the poisonous lie forever. Back went Fitzharris to the Tower, there to remain until he faced the charge of high treason.

Second set-back. Anger, pain and bitter frustration drove Shaftesbury beyond endurance. For the first time he began to talk too much; and he was not always wise in his choice of listeners. There was Mr. Justice Warcup, sheriff of London, whom Shaftesbury considered a friend; and so he had been... once. But Shaftesbury's spite and the King's courtesy had turned him about. And he was not the only one. Daily he came to Whitehall and brought his news with him.

'Shaftesbury swears he'll draw a line about Whitehall. He says, sir, you're to meet the same death as your father—which God forbid!'

'He'll draw a line about his own neck, if he isn't careful!' Charles said. 'The tide is on the turn. The people begin to look to me—their King. But Shaftesbury's so blind with hate he cannot see it. I've had as much from him as I intend to stomach. I mean to muzzle him and Parliament together.'

Someone had carried the news—Louise, perhaps; she had enough spies in Whitehall. When Charles went down to the House the Commons had already declared that whosoever should advise the King to prorogue Parliament was an enemy to the country and a lover of papacy. Charles said nothing; the resolution had been passed. He turned his attention to the Lords.

He found a scurrilous Shaftesbury dealing with the same matter.

'I am no promoter of papacy, and certainly I am no traitor,' Charles, very pleasant, broke in upon the tirade. 'And I need no advice. I do here and now prorogue Parliament.'

A week later he dissolved it. What use to prorogue? He'd get no good of this House, ever. Writs were issued for a new Parliament to meet in March. Maybe both Houses, then, would hold more of his friends; it could scarce hold less.

The election results showed two things. The tide was certainly turning towards the King... but turning slowly. In this new Parliament he would not have enough friends.

'They mean to have another try at the Exclusion Bill; and, Kate, they mean to go further. This time they mean to exclude not only James; but Mary, Mary also! They mean to name Monmouth. Monmouth!' His mouth twisted. 'Never—save over my dead body!'

'Dead bodies!' Catherine crossed herself. 'There'll be plenty of those! Riots in the streets; they'll see to it, Shaftesbury and his London mob.'

'Kate; you've put your finger on a point! I'll not allow this new Parliament to meet in London. Oxford. Oxford's the place. Oxford's loyal. He'll raise no mobs in Oxford! And more! Shaftesbury and Monmouth may rouse the riff-raff but the solid citizens of London and good folk everywhere are with me. By the time we get home again London will be quiet.'

Catherine made no answer. She prayed it would be as simple as that. In mid-March they set out for Oxford; it was cold and clear with buds breaking and birds singing; and in the coppices pale primroses and violets. The line of coaches stumbled over the soft dirt roads. When they stopped to change horses Catherine caught sight of Nell Gwynn roguish as a boy in a great caped coat of man's cut and a tricorne perched upon her red curls. Louise, too, was in the height of fashion with a top-coat of gallant cut but she had gone further; she had perched a tricorne upon a curled periwig. Nell looked a saucy stripling. Louise, a court gallant.

Catherine's spirits were not lightened by the sight of either. Nell she could accept... if she must. But Louise was a traitor—and not less a traitor because Charles knew it. He knew it and dared not offend her; for the sake of his friendship with France he must tread softly. But he kept a close eye on her; and, if keeping a close eye meant a night in her bed, he'd not, Catherine thought, sighing, find that too hard a duty.

Wrapped in her furs against the cold, she considered the nature of Louise... A cold woman. Ambition forever drove her. She was the King's mistress; she had immense power, immense wealth; yet she was always short of money. A lavish spender and a reckless gambler, she could not, in spite of all her wealth, refuse a bribe. She disposed of high places, she made her recommendations... at a price; she coined her influence into gold. She dipped her fingers in high policies—both here and abroad. She held the secret threads that bound

England and France—and always she served France first. That she was well-paid for her services made her no less a good Frenchwoman. A good Frenchwoman... yet she had given up her nationality to become an English duchess. She had climbed high; once she had hoped to climb into the highest place of all; yet it could have been no more than a hope. She must have known that Charles would never make her his Queen. She cared for him as much as she could care for anyone—save herself and her son. She wished him no harm... if it could be avoided. Of James she was not so tender. He stood, she believed, between her son and the throne.

She wished Charles no harm ... if it could be avoided. But... if it could not be avoided? Catherine's mind took a leap, pounced upon a sentence in Fitzharris' traitorous libel.

> James and Charles study to enslave England to a French and Romish yoke...

A *French* yoke. A humble foreigner new-come to court, how did the Irishman know that? Louise. Louise had told him; told him not only what she knew but what she guessed—the last secret pact with Louis, the promise to enter the true Church. Oh that Charles had got rid of her, long ago—when first he'd found out what she was! To send her away now... dangerous. She could make plenty of trouble; and already Charles had enough on his plate! That he would be allowed to meet this new Parliament in peace, Catherine could not believe. Any moment might find Monmouth and his mob at their heels. Charles, she fancied, thought so, too—they were travelling as fast as they could go, driving late into the night so that torches flaring in the darkness enclosed them into a small and private world.

It was cold within the coach and wrapped in her furs Catherine shivered. She suffered, always in the damp English weather; but now her heart was warm because of Charles' care for her. He came riding up with an extra rug and laughing all over that grim face of his. 'They tell me, Kate, that yesterday, high in the sky, over Oxford's towers, there shone a golden crown. The good folk of Oxford take it for a sign!'

'Amen to that! And—' she laughed with him, 'how shall your famous Society explain that?'

'My famous Society concerns itself with things in nature you may hear and touch and see. And I? I like to think these crown-seers are loyal folk whose eyes see what their heart desires.'

'Amen to that, also!' *You'll need all the good-will you can get. Your enemies will leave no trick unplayed, no game too low.* And she remembered their pamphlets falling thick and fast like dirty snow to enrage the mob with lies.

He saw which way her thoughts ran and said, 'Do not trouble your heart. The King I am; and the King I stay.'

Now as they drove along the quiet roads, the tide, it seemed, was running more swiftly towards him. For the people, both gentle and simple, stood bareheaded in the cold to greet him. And, when in the bright frost of the morning they reached Oxford, though no crown shone in the city, the city turned out in full splendour of civic robes and holiday clothes. And there were speeches that warmed his heart; for they hailed him as protector of their rights; and as saviour and father of the country.

He took praise as quietly as he had taken insult. But, for all that, he was deeply touched. It gave him courage to meet this new Parliament of his. There was villainy afoot and he had few friends there. But oddsfish, come foul or fair, he'd weather it!

XXXVI

The Parliament men came riding into town—and their armed retainers with them. An army invading Oxford; and everyone wearing his colours—a blue riband in his coat; and on his hatband a writing, *No Popery*.

Charles was actually opening his obstinate, inimical Parliament when, from her window, Catherine heard the noise—hooves striking upon cobbles, wild voices screaming their *huzzas*. She looked out into the street and could scarce believe her eyes.

Who was it came riding between my lord Grey and Sir Thomas Armstrong, an army streaming behind them—disaffected peers carrying each his sword, rebellious commons each with his cudgel? And for whom did the crowd cheer as the army rode, so that the narrow streets shook with the sound? For whom but Monmouth, handsome Jamie!

Catherine's hand went to her mouth to keep back the cry.

Charles, dealing with the succession, heard the clatter and wondered at it. Unmoved, it would seem, he went on addressing both Houses.

'Neither your liberties nor your properties can exist when the just rights of the Crown are invaded; or the honour of the government laid low. The established law of the land cannot be departed from save by act of Parliament. I require you to make the laws of the land your rule, because I am resolved they shall be mine.'

Parliament listened coldly; it waited for Shaftesbury to show his hand. And show it he did—and in no uncertain terms.

Monmouth must be named—the next King. That, or Civil War.

It was not unexpected. But that Monmouth should be so foolish, so ungrateful, so treacherous—Charles' hurt was none the less.

'I will never yield and I am not to be intimidated!' he cried out to Parliament. 'I have right and law on my side, and all good people stand with me. And above all—' and he was fine and proud—'the Church stands with me. She and I are not to be divided.'

That night he spoke to Catherine on the matter.

'My friends in Parliament advise me to come to terms. And the terms? James to be deprived of the throne; and more—to be sent from England, for ever; for ever, Kate! If he will swear to bring up any son he may have in the Protestant Faith—then the eldest shall succeed. In that case Mary shall act as Regent till the boy come of age. But—' he shrugged. 'Bring up his son as Protestant! James would never agree. And, banish my brother for life—I could not agree, either. I cannot and will not do it!'

'Let him stay where he is at present—in Scotland. We must wait for better times.'

'There'll be no better times with this Parliament; each day sees it stiffer in obstinacy.'

Things were, indeed, hardening—each side. Now Charles and his Parliament could expect nothing from each other. Yet though he was thoughtful, he was cheerful; it surprised Catherine to hear, now and then, a gay little tune escape his lips.

Today the Commons were to bring in the bill that named Monmouth successor. They would brook no interference from the King! Let him but show his face and the door would be locked against him. Let him be warned!

But for all that Charles sang as he dressed. He watched his valet Toby Rustat arrange the curls of his wig, himself he settled the ruffles and cravat; he took his hat and cane... a gentleman about to saunter the streets of Oxford.

But first he paid a little visit to the Queen. He found her looking drawn and anxious. 'All's well, sweetheart—' and he was very gay. 'I have found a way to deal with this rebellious Parliament. Never ask me how! A little patience and you shall see!'

He returned within the hour—and better pleased than ever.

'No more Parliament!' he said; and while she stared amazed—two Parliaments dissolved in so short a time, he told his tale.

'I went down to the Lords and slipped in the back way. There's an ante-room leads to the meeting-chamber and there my good Toby was waiting with my robe and crown. I could hear Shaftesbury speaking; he was stirring them up well. I wouldn't have given sixpence for James' chance. They were just about to vote—to make Monmouth the successor—when in I went, robes and crown and all; and sat myself in my place. I sent Blackrod for the Commons and in they came all agrin.

'They were going to get their way—they were sure of it. Soon they were smiling wrong side of their faces. I dissolved the House. You should have seen their faces then!' His own face creased into a smile.

'And then?'

'Nothing. What could they do? I dissolved it—and it was dissolved. Now we're off to Windsor to escape the hubbub! Chiffinch has everything ready. No more Parliament for me; I'm sick to death of it! My grandfather did well enough without it. My father tried to deal with it—and lost his head. These Parliaments of mine have worked to one end—to show the people I'm a man of straw. Now, I also, shall work to one end—to show them their King's a King!'

'God save the King!' she dropped a little curtsey. And then, 'The old story. No Parliament—no money. Without money how shall you manage?'

He bent and whispered in her ear.

He had made a new pact with Louis. In the secrecy of the Queen's chamber it was made; no-one but he and she and the French ambassador present. A treaty so secret that Louise was not to catch breath of it—Barrillon, the new ambassador, had insisted upon it; he had long taken Louise's measure.

A simple treaty. Friendship between the two Kings... and Charles undertaking to withdraw little by little from his alliance with Holland. For this he was to receive four hundred thousand pounds. He had meant to do it—French gold or not.

'I don't want our armies in Holland,' Charles told Catherine. 'And I don't want war. Peace—it's what the country needs and what she shall have. And I have, besides, another reason. I don't trust my nephew of Orange. He stands behind Monmouth—Monmouth shall pull William's chestnuts out of the fire. William works, very sly, to break the succession; he bribes my Parliament more heavily than Louis, even—and good reason. For, break the succession, and who more fitted to be named than my niece's husband, himself a Stuart—my sister's son; and a Protestant to boot?

'If Louis likes to pay me for what I believe to be right—and meant to do in any case—I'll not say *No*! I'd not sell England for any man's gold—nor never have. Once Louis would have paid me for disbanding the army and I refused. I refused; and Parliament did it for me—and never a penny in my pocket! He would have paid me to prorogue Parliament for three years—it's not so long since. And I refused. Now I have done that same thing—and no payment. Well, Kate, let us forget our troubles; Windsor is the place for peace.'

Here at Windsor, though he kept his finger on the pulse of the times, he was able to take his ease. Buoyed by his recent victory, some of the weariness was ironed from his face..

'Here we shall stay summer-long and grow young again!' And then, with that charm of his, 'But you, Kate, need nothing to bring back your youth. You are that same young Kate that came to me from Portugal—and not a new line on your face!'

It's not for want of troubles! She bit back the words. What if she did look younger than her years—though there were still lines enough? Let one look never so young, one cannot put back the clock. Never, now, could she have a child; through her, Charles, her dear love, was involved in a death-struggle about the succession. Parliament or no Parliament—the throne was trembling.

Charles had struck a quick, stout blow—a completely unexpected blow and his people liked him the better for it. He had another adviser now—the best of men, Lord North, soon to become my lord Chief Justice. Scroggs, himself attainted, lay in prison awaiting his own trial; and the charge? Browbeating those two liars Oates and Bedloe; and never was charge more unjust. He had fawned before them, till Justice had thundered too loud to be ignored.

Windsor was more than ever peaceful. Monmouth was still in England; but Jamie had learnt his lesson, Charles thought, love blinding his clear sight. And Louise was not there. She had not endeared herself to Charles by her behaviour at Stafford's trial; and, feeling a touch of frost in the air, had retired to the Sunderlands at Althorpe till her sun should shine again. Nell Gwynn was at Windsor, but, as ever, she kept out of the Queen's way; and since she had not lost her power to make Charles, for a little, forget his troubles, she was welcome... more or less. He slept but little these nights. He would rise from his bed in the small hours and go across to his own rooms... and it was not for Nell that he went.

He would sit through the small hours bent upon his problems... *Shaftesbury can no longer work through Parliament, since Parliament there's none; yet he'll spit his venom still. And Jamie. Will he keep the peace? If not—the Tower. I'll not leave him at large to make his mischief. I'll not let him to Holland, neither, to plot with my nephew; watch William. And watch Louise. She knows more than somewhat about Fitzharris; Shaftesbury's the link, I fancy. Soon he comes to trial, the lying Irishman; but liars sometimes speak truth. How will Louise come out of that? She's deep in every sly business, the pretty traitor. I'm a fool about women... but not such a fool! Watch, watch Louise.*

So much upon his heart. He would sit pondering till daylight came and brought North with it. A good friend, Frank North; clever and honest and wise. Kate liked him and showed it. When they sat together in her closet, she would, with her own hands, pour his wine; or, an especial treat, his dish of tea. Her spirits were higher these days, her headaches less; the poisonous lies about her had been forever stilled; and together with North, Charles was straightening out his difficulties.

They were, all three, in the Queen's closet; Charles sat carelessly stroking the silken head of the spaniel curled in his lap.

'Sir,' North said, 'you are winning the people; but too slowly. And you will not keep those you have won...'

Catherine lifted a startled head.

'... while your enemies print their vile pamphlets unchallenged. You must, sir, beat them at their own game. You must answer the libels; show them to be the work of liars. You must tell the people your plans—what you mean to do for the good of the country; build up trust...'

Charles got up so suddenly that the little creature upon his lap yelped. He placed it gently upon a chair and stood stroking its head. 'There, there!' he apologised.

'Yes,' he said, 'with all my heart. We'll put out a newsheet; it shall appear every week.'

The King's newsheet was clear and forceful. It fastened the blame where it belonged—upon the King's enemies. It was new, it was exciting; it spoke with their King's unmistakable voice. Week by week, it won him friends.

To take the people into his confidence had been a master-stroke. He followed it with a *Declaration* in which he dealt with the bitter question of the succession. He set forth the traitorous designs of his enemies; he desired, he said, nothing so much as to serve his people—a people united in the blessings of peace. He told how he had sworn to accept any safeguard Parliament should propose for the safety of the Protestant religion—so long as it was consistent with the succession of the crown in true and legal descent. James must come to the throne.

It was read aloud in every church throughout the land; it was nailed to every church door. It was truthful; it was sensible; it was clear—even a man that could not read could understand and remember. It was reassuring. This was how it was to be—old customs, old laws respected; with new ones added to guard the people's rights. It hit the English taste perfectly; it won him many friends.

He had put his trust in the people; and with trust they repaid him. The tide that had been on the turn but slowly, now came racing in, to lift him upon a triumphal sea. To Windsor came not only princes of the Church and State, but country clergy and country gentry and the common people; loyal subjects all, to kiss his hand and swear faith with him. And he received them all, the least and the greatest, with his kindliness and his warm interest in them and their families—which was not the least part of him charm—so that they went away well-pleased with him and themselves.

'Oddsfish!' he would say, 'how I love this England and these English!' And Catherine, seeing the grey of exhaustion upon him, could wish he might love them a little less strenuously.

It was full June when Fitzharris came to his trial. From the beginning there was no hope.

The poor wretch fought hard for his life. He had not drawn the vile libel inciting the people to murder the King—he swore it upon his hope of salvation. It had already been drawn by one Everard...

But Everard was too ignorant a man—that was well seen. And Everard had two witnesses to swear that Fitzharris had brought him the libel already set out. And Everard had, at once, informed the justices. And, above all, the document was in the handwriting of the prisoner, was it not?

Yes, it was in his own hand—he must confess it. But he had *copied* Everard's paper at my lord Shaftesbury's request. No, he had not seen my lord himself; my lady had told him so... my lady duchess of Portsmouth.

At the sound of that exalted name a long breath went through the court—surprise, enjoyment, anticipation.

It must be copied, my lady said, that the King might see for himself the wickedness of Papists. Yes, they had paid him for copying it. No, he had not received the money from my lord's own hand, nor yet from my lady's. It had been given him by Mistress Wall, my lady's gentlewoman...

That my lady had had a hand in the matter, Mr. Attorney appeared to find difficult to believe—though all Whitehall had known the prisoner's frequent journeying to her lodgings; there had been others, besides the Queen, to fancy he might be the lady's lover—the debonair young man.

In vain the poor wretch fought for his life. Those that had used him had more wits than he. One by one the witnesses spoke, and each word a strand in the rope to hang him.

Terrified he changed his tale. It was exactly as Charles had foreseen.

The whole thing was a Protestant plot to bring death to the Catholics. He had lost his wits altogether when he asked that Oates be called—Oates that scourge of Catholics. Outraged that he should be called to testify for a Papist, Oates said, 'I can do nothing to help.' And, since the stink of the court was overmuch for his daintiness, asked leave to retire; and off he went mincing.

What now, oh God, what now? Desperate, lost, he remembered one that had played her part in this sorry tale, that had smiled upon him once; surely she would smile still. He requested that Mistress Wall be called.

It was no welcoming waiting-woman that faced him now. Nor— leaning upon the Bar, sweat glistening upon his green face—was he the well-looking young man for whom she had been willing with her favours. He was *the prisoner*. He might well—she had been warned—draw her own neck with his into the noose.

If she will but answer me with truth, there might be hope... some hope yet. He sent out his whole soul towards her.

'Was it not I, myself, myself, and none other that, in the first place, brought the libel to the King?'

'No!' The word struck sharp from her lips.

'Did I not promise to bring supporters to the King? Did I not, indeed, bring in my lord Howard of Escrick?' Too late he knew he had done better to forget Howard of Escrick—a man whose honour stank.

He hurried on to this next question.

Did I not... Did I not?

And *No*, she answered each time. *No* and *No* and *No*.

He was driven by his agony when he cried out, 'I pray you speak the truth!' And she, very fierce as such liars are, 'I defy you and all mankind to say I do otherwise!'

She was gone. And now, one after another, the rest of the witnesses—some bought, some threatened, some truthful; and all, all denying him.

No-one to help him... no-one at all. What of the lady that had led him on; that had flattered and made much of him; that had hinted at no favour denied? It was a small favour he asked now—to her, small; to him, life itself.

He said, 'I pray the court that the lady be sent for—Madam, the duchess of Portsmouth.'

At the request a gasp went through the court. My lord Chief Justice Pemberton was so taken aback he had no words. 'We cannot send for her,' he said when he could speak at last. 'If she choose to come—good; if not we have no occasion to make her!'

And still the poor wretch urged; and a footman was sent to summon her.

He had driven the last nail into his coffin. She had no mind to help this intriguing fool, she that had laughed and nibbled at her comfits while they swore innocent Stafford's life away. This fellow had done those things of which he stood accused—no matter who had set him on. She'd lift no finger to help this liar, this rash meddler whose word, were she not careful now, might bring herself to a traitor's death.

The court awaiting my lady, another witness was brought—the prisoner's wife; a poor wretched thing whose gentle breeding showed still. She had been pretty once; now, near her time and sick with fear and grief, she looked as though she had neither slept nor eaten for days. But still she had some spirit left. She stood up and questioned the witnesses that had testified against her husband. But it could not help; nor did my lord Chief Justice intend that it should. He put an end to her questions.

As she went out, poor and shabby, a thin hand upon her great belly as though to quiet the child she carried, in came my lady duchess in her silks and laces and her proud, sleek air. The two met face-to-face; and, as my lady passed, she drew her skirts away. She did not know who the poor creature might be; but she guessed... she guessed.

And now there was one to hurry with a chair and one with a footstool; and yet another to carry a cushion. She sat down, pomander held to her nose, against the stink of the court, and disdainful of those that craned to see her.

It was little good the prisoner got from her, though he grovelled abject, imploring pardon that he had incommoded her. 'I am sorry to see your grace come upon my account; I hope your grace will excuse me. It is for my life!' But her grace would excuse him nothing; rather he should pay for dragging her into the rabble of the court.

'I desire your grace to tell the court whether I was not employed by you to copy the libel concerning the King? And whether I was not also employed by you to bring it to the King? And did not your grace say it was a great piece of service? And did not your grace encourage me in the whole matter? And did I not do it by your grace's direction?'

It was sailing too near the wind. Anger threatened to choke the words in my lady's throat. She took in her breath; she said, very languid, 'When must I speak?'

'Now, Madam,' my lord Chief Justice told her. 'Will your grace be pleased to take the stand?'

And she with her French accent and every word stone-cold, 'I have nothing to say to Mr. Fitzharris. I was not concerned in any sort of business with him.' And then, remembering that all the world had seen him hastening to her lodgings in Whitehall, added, 'He did desire me to give his petition to the King that he might get back his lands in Ireland. And I did speak to the King about it. But never did I speak to the prisoner about anything but that. Never, never!'

And he, the words grating against a dry throat, 'Does not your grace remember...?'

And my lord Chief Justice, anxious lest he offend the great lady that had won her greatness through whoring, 'If you will ask any question of my lady, do so; but do not make a long discourse.' And the prisoner, all lost in his fear and his need, wailing out, 'My lord, she may forget... she may *forget*!'

Once more he set his soul to make her speak, knowing it his last chance.

'Upon what account had I the money you gave me?'

'For charity.' And her scorn was searing.

And now he must throw away his life with both hands.

'I am sorry your grace is under the influence of Mistress Wall.' And, indeed, it was clear that those two had hatched their tale between them.

Her nostrils flared. That he should dare proclaim her, the great duchess, under the influence of her waiting-woman! She said, 'I did not come to wrangle with you. I came to say what I know; and not one word more will I say.'

And to all his frantic beseeching she had but one word. *No*. At last, she said, lying—for never would she help him, that had dragged her into this stinking court, 'If I could do you any good I would do it. But I cannot. And I do not see how I am in any way useful here.' And, having killed him with her tongue as surely as if she had pulled upon the hangman's rope, she swept away like a Queen... save that the Queen had never moved so queenly.

On and on; and every witness denying him; and, though for the most part they lied, still his guilt was clear.

And now all was done; and he must listen to the dread sentence; prepare himself for a hideous death. He was half-fainting as they carried him away.

Eliza said, 'Fitzharris' wife, the poor creature! She was faithful while there was hope. Now they have bought her with promise of a pension to make good their lies, to testify against her husband. She cannot save him... and she has five little ones; and a sixth on the way.'

'But to blacken his name—her husband's name!' Catherine said.

'She can make it no whiter. Who could blame her, seeing her despair? Madam, it was for the children; the children, crying and pulling at her skirts.

'Yes... the children,' Catherine said. And for the first time in her life deceived Charles. She sent money and food to the prisoner's wife; Eliza, that discreet woman, took the matter in hand.

The day Fitzharris died, died yet another man he had entangled by his lies—a man innocent and upright. Brought from Ireland by guile, and for no cause save that he was head of the Irish Catholic Church—and against Irish Papists Fitzharris had spoken. Tried by a jury that knew nothing of his quality and cared less; the witnesses those that sold blood for money, and denied time to defend himself, Oliver Plunket was condemned to that same cruel death as traitor Fitzharris.

Essex that had been Lord Lieutenant of Ireland and knew the man kept silence until it could no longer be borne; he besought the King to save an innocent man... a good man, loyal to the bone.

'Then his blood lies upon your head. You might have saved him. I cannot pardon him now, because I dare not. Rivers of blood would flow. God knows I sign his warrant with tears.'

They met on the way to the scaffold—lying accuser, innocent accused—each in his shameful sledge.

'I pity Fitzharris more,' the Queen said, 'because he is guilty and because he is afraid to die. But the other is innocent and unafraid. His death is not shameful but glorious. He dies a martyr. Pray God his death win him a martyr's crown.'

'Pray God,' Charles said, 'that after him no Catholic in this country of mine be put to death on a false charge; that he be the last to die because of his faith.'

'So good a man does not die for nothing!' she said. 'God will hear our prayers—both yours and mine!'

'I wish I could believe it!' Charles said, gloomy. 'God has all eternity; but for us whose life is short, His patience, at times, seems overlong!'

'Yet He will answer... and soon. I believe it!'

XXXVII

Fitzharris had cooked his goose; and with it Shaftesbury's goose and Louise's also. She was out of favour and would so remain till she died.

For the sake of friendship with Louis, he was, as ever, courteous. The apartments at Whitehall were hers still; he continued her allowance, he visited her daily, he saw that she was treated with respect. But between them—nothing. Now no word of the King's secrets reached her ears; that was the bitterest blow. She trembled lest Louis hear of her failure. She set her spies everywhere in Whitehall but she gleaned nothing. Secrets were discussed no longer in the Queen's closet; they were discussed in the ruelle of her bedroom—the guards posted without. And much was settled at Windsor; and there she came no more.

'She has ventured overmuch with my enemies,' Charles told Catherine, told North, walking all three in the summer gardens of Windsor. 'That she sold my secrets I knew; but that she should bespatter me with dirt, lend herself to a plot to put me from the throne—put an end to life itself—that I did not believe.

'Fitzharris was a liar, true; but even liars are driven sometimes to the truth. His trial has put a weapon into my hands—a weapon to make an end of Shaftesbury. There was to have been an armed rising in Oxford; Shaftesbury was deep in that! We know it beyond question.'

'Knowing is one thing,' Catherine said. 'Proof, quite another.'

'Proof will not be hard to come by,' North promised. 'He has suborned witnesses with bribes and threats—the trial has hammered that home! Those witnesses we shall make speak.'

'Howard of Escrick is safe in the Tower. It'll not be long before Shaftesbury joins him,' Charles said.

'Have a care, Charles; have a care!' Catherine cried out. 'If the proof fail, you are worse off than before.'

'I shall take all care, never fear!' He reached up and pulled a rose; he handed it to her and she received it as though it were a jewel of price.

It was late and Charles had not yet come to his bed. Catherine looked at her clock before which a lamp forever burned. Two o'clock. She was disturbed; he needed all the rest he could get. The late trials had taken their toll—Stafford's because the man was innocent; Fitzharris' because of his guilt.

She came from her bed and threw her bedgown about her. In the King's chamber she found Charles and Rustat dressed for a journey. The valet knelt pulling on his master's boots; cloaks and gloves lay upon the table.

Charles smiled his welcome. 'I'm for Whitehall, Kate. I did not come to say Goodbye; I thought you would be sleeping.'

She asked no question save, 'Who rides with you?'

'Enough for my protection; my good Toby, here, Frank North left directly after supper. I go to get the proofs; yourself advised it.'

He returned to Windsor that same night, weary but satisfied.

'Before six this morning we had Shaftesbury from his bed and into the Tower. We've had his house searched. There's papers enough to hang him. Fitzharris didn't die in vain.'

'I doubt he'd agree with you!' she said drily; and then, 'But if it be true that he helped you somewhat, could you not, a little, help his widow? The pension she was promised—has she had it? She paid for it in tears of blood.'

'Is there no end to your compassion?' He was half-admiring, half irritable. 'Well, but I love you for it, Kate!'

Shaftesbury was safe in the Tower till he should come to trial; now the King could sit back and rest a little. He spent the whole of the summer at Windsor. Together with North he studied the documents in the Shaftesbury case; he met his Council; and there was no Parliament to plague him.

For the first time Catherine's heart was at rest. For the first time she had nothing to fear from any woman—not from Barbara Castlemaine, her beauty forgotten, her greed and violence alone remaining; not from Hortense Mazarin-Mancini, throwing her beauty to a score of young lovers, as she had once thrown her uncle's gold. And now, no longer from Louise. Once it had seemed that her innocent looks and her sweet deceitful tears must hold Charles for ever. Now he had discovered her fangs—the plump, poisonous, little snake, and she was finished.

There was still Nell Gwynn. When she boasted that the King slept oftener with her than with Louise she was telling the truth. He slept with her seldom; with Louise, never. His taste for women was lessening; he was less vigorous. It was clear when he came in from exercise. He tired more quickly, recovered more slowly; affairs of State took increasing toll. He had left his fiftieth birthday behind; but he was still a fine figure of a man—to Catherine, the finest in the world. True the recent trial had scored yet deeper lines about his mouth; but when he smiled... when he smiled he was still that same man she had at first sight loved then, and forever. But her love was different now from the love she had known then. Once it had been a passion in her young blood. She had longed for him; she had wept, she had stood by *the right*... and it had all been tangled up with her own rights, now her love was deeper, more tender. She longed for him still but she could—God forgive her— sacrifice both rights and right for his happiness. She had his trust, his tenderness; it must suffice.

That year Gascar painted her portrait. She was unwilling. Forty-three; the time for portraits was passed. But Charles would have his way. 'You wear well, Kate—your eyes as lovely as ever. They'll not change though you live to be a hundred.'

'And the wrinkles?'

'Every woman, as she grows older, bears her character clear—writ in her face. To some it's no advantage. To you, Kate, it does good service.'

When the picture was finished she looked at the little plump lady with the dark, pretty curls and the soft dark eyes in the round still-young face. 'It flatters me!' she sighed.

'All true women plump a little—though it's well to have a care. There's Barbara now...' And she, remembering the voluptuous beauty that had once caused such heart-break, could not forbear the smile— the woman was a mountain! Did he think of Louise, also; Louise that could not deny herself the sweetmeats she loved? Soon Louise would not be plump but downright fat.

'Should you doubt time's kindness for you, here's a tribute from your devoted admirer—Waller!' He brought a paper from his pocket. '*How are we changed since first we saw the Queen*...And changed, indeed!' He pushed the dark wig awry and began again.

'How are we changed since first we saw the Queen!
She, like the sun, does still the same appear,
Bright as she was at her arrival here.
Time has commission, mortals to impair,
But things celestial is obliged to spare.
May every new year find her still the same,
In health and beauty as she hither came.'

He looked at her and twinkled. 'Court painters and poets may flatter somewhat—we expect it. But there's little flattery here! A far cry this, from the wicked lines of Marvell!'

That summer they had an unexpected visitor. It was William of Orange. Catherine had never cared for William. That he had breeding, brains and courage she was forced to admit; but for all that she distrusted his sick, calculating face. He had his eye on the throne. He meant—and did not trouble to hide it—that James should be excluded. He meant Mary to be named in her father's place; and he was not the man to play second fiddle. He was full a royal Stuart as Mary herself. If she were named heir, her husband should be named, equally, with her; he'd see to it!

Mary had wept leaving England; and well she might, Catherine thought, looking at the cold shut face. And now Mary was happy—if you could believe William. Catherine was inclined, rather, to believe the tales she'd heard of his unkindness—his lack of love and the way he humiliated his wife. There were no babies as yet. Five years married—and no sign of a child. There never would be; he was impotent, Catherine thought. And, besides, he preferred boys to women, so they said. She grieved for Mary.

William wanted to talk in privacy; he cast a doubtful look upon Catherine but Charles said, very gay, 'You may speak in front of Kate; she's my good counsellor.'

William, not best-pleased, began. 'It's France...'

So that was it! He'd come to make mischief between Charles and Louis! That there was a secret alliance between those two, he could not know; but he was shrewd enough to guess. Catherine looked at Charles; she could see by the smiling attention he paid to William, that Charles' thought was her own.

'Louis,' William said, careful, 'is forcing the Rhine States into union with him—and some of them are over-near for my liking. We must keep Louis *here*!' And he pressed a pale spatulate thumb upon the table. 'His armies are everywhere—a danger not only to me but to you, Uncle; to you, also!'

'To me? No danger at all! One knows where one stands with him!' And then, very softly, 'Does one know that with you, nephew?'

William's cold face didn't change.

'You see,' Charles said quiet and pleasant, 'I know your sly bargains with my enemies in Parliament—both Houses, William. The Exclusion Bill must have cost you a pretty penny. And money down the drain! That bill's not passed—nor never will be!'

Not even the faintest colour stained William's long face.

'Ah well, nephew, it's every man for himself—in your philoso-phy—though loyalty's a word to be remembered. But nephew, were I minded—which I am not—that England should run with blood, war costs money. And where should I find that? I should have to call Parliament—my Parliament you have so judiciously bribed. And that I don't intend to do. I've no intention of fighting the Exclusion Bill all over again—which is what you want. But—*no Parliament, no money*! I don't need you to tell me that. Well, I haven't much in my pocket; but, money at a pinch I can do without! I have, instead, the growing good-will of my people, and that—though you cover me with gold, head-to-foot—I cannot do without. So, no war, no Parliament—and no Exclusion Bill!

'And now, William, that we understand each other, let us talk of pleasanter things. You've said little of my niece. We've not seen her since the wedding; when does she come to us again?'

When we come as King and Queen. The cold insolence in William's eye spoke plain. Charles gave no sign of the anger that boiled within him—this was after all no surprise. He said, 'There's an old saying; it concerns counting one's chickens. Maybe you never heard of it; and Mary has forgotten. You would do well to keep it in mind, both of you. James is England's next King. Remember it.'

William said sour and insolent, 'You may get him on the throne—though that I doubt. But, believe me, you'll not keep him there!'

'Is Saul also among the prophets?' Charles asked smiling; but his eyes were bitter.

William did not stay long. It was neither expected nor desired. 'His face turns the sweets of life sour,' Charles said. 'Poor Mary, she's no sweetmeat herself. Well, let's gather our honey while we may; let's to sea, Kate!'

It was the first time he had invited her aboard his yacht for other than a day. Such an invitation was a privilege reserved, till now, for his most intimate friends—a man's life, Charles had always said; no woman had ever been asked.

The summer days were all delight. How could it be otherwise for her, loving the man and loving the sea? And for him it was delight, also. 'I grow young again! he would cry out, his hands busy about the ropes. And once, when she stood watching, he cried out, 'Why, Madam Queen, come help. You grow too fat!' And, laughing, she would learn some of his sailor's tricks. She had known his kindness always; now she saw how it reached out to the least of those that served him—sailors, cabin-boys and especially the young pages. He would stand and watch them at their play, he would warn or applaud; but he watched not the play so much as themselves, judging which one he should advance—and which pass by.

She would remember, always, how she and he had come upon young Bruce deep in a game of chess. The boy was puzzled as to the next move; and Charles, with plenty to puzzle out upon his own account, stood patient, watching. Young Bruce lifted his hand and Charles put out his own—his long fine hand—to stop him. 'Guard the Queen, Tom. She's the King's strongest, quickest defender. Once the Queen's lost—the King's lost, too!' And, in front of them all, kissed her upon both cheeks. So he had kissed *that woman*; so he had kissed Frances Stuart and the de Kérouaille. Now it was his wife, his wife that took the salute. Yet, she must not allow herself too much hope; it was his charming way.

It was not all holiday for Charles. There were some to say he put his pleasures first, being a man of no endurance; and of these, Shaftesbury was not the least. Never was there a greater nonsense. Charles was a subtle man hiding his thoughts and biding his time. Even now, in the midst of his summer sailing, he was at the Nore inspecting the Fleet; he was at Chatham calculating what ships might be sent against the pirates that threatened Tangier; he was at Southampton, he was at Portsmouth. Lazy they called him, this man that, beneath his easy ways, was steel tempered by adversity.

And now he was reaping some of his reward. Scotland had accepted the succession. When, at Sheerness, they brought him the news, he hastened below lest he disgrace himself with tears. And there Catherine found him.

'It's the first step. Now England will accept James, also. It's his right; his divine right. I'll call no more Parliament to make its trouble. Parliament's corrupt, as well we know! Corrupted by friend Louis on the one hand and by nephew William on the other; and in between— the few that stand by me. Well, Parliament matters nothing. The people begin to trust me; I have, I believe, their growing good-will. A little good-will leavens the lump.'

Growing good-will. He had described it exactly. Those that had given him an indulgent kindness, and those that had given contempt and worse—friend and enemy alike undervaluing his guts—were beginning to learn his quality.

Even in the Tower Shaftesbury felt the changing mood. He wrote imploring that he might be allowed to leave England; he would not, he swore it, set foot in Europe. He would go to the far Indies, to distant Carolina, to wherever the King commanded.

'I command nothing!' Charles said. 'Tell my lord that the law must take its course. I never interfered with the law, nor never shall.'

That autumn he took Catherine to Newmarket, she all amazed to find herself there. Newmarket was his innermost shelter from the troubled world. Here he lived a simple life, with his own hands grooming his beloved horses, giving himself up to the good fellowship of the grooms and sharing the pleasures of the little town. No woman, till now, had ever lived with him in this house; not even the Frenchwoman, not even at his most besotted. He had slept with Louise at Euston, never at Newmarket; he had brought her over to see the racing; but never had he allowed her to share his man's world. Now Catherine was there... *I am here because he needs me. He needs me because he is growing old. I see, already, the look he will wear as an old man... no longer eager; quiet—not yet serene. But give him time it will come, serenity, and happiness with it* ...And she remembered how once he had said, *You are my harbour and my home. And once, A man sickens of sweetmeats; but good bread's the staff of life. You are that staff, Kate...*

Shaftesbury's trial was fixed for the Old Bailey; the last week in November. Tensions ran high. For a word, friend would turn against friend, old enemies embrace; and, friend and foe alike, so much tinder. A spark, by bad luck—and conflagration. Conflagration and Civil war.

Charles, as always, appeared calm; but Catherine saw that he had gone back to the old trick of biting upon his thumb. She saw, with pity, how the nail bitten to the quick, the thumb grew red and angry; it was beginning to fester. No use her talking to him; he'd brush it away as nonsense. She spoke to Toby Rustat instead. Toby would keep an eye on him; to Toby he might even listen.

A week before the trial there was an ugly incident.

Murdered Godfrey was never, it seemed, to rest in his grave. Torches flaring against the Winter sky, Shaftesbury's party marched through the packed streets of London. First in procession came the effigy of the murdered man, carried high upon a cart where all might see his bloody wounds. And, lest not enough hatred he stirred, an effigy of the Pope followed, to be burnt in the fire; and about it, obscenely dancing, attendant devils shook horned heads and brandished pitchforks. Behind them followed mock priests clad all in black; and cardinals in scarlet red as blood. Now came those dressed as cavaliers, lovelocks flowing beneath feathered hats; and, about their necks—halters. Last and alone—the shameful sledge that carried criminals to the gallows; and, riding, therein, a fine gentleman, wearing, also, his halter.

At this, the crowd roared its hatred; though for whom it roared it did not know. It was the monster, Louis of France. No, it was the scarce less-hated monster, James. And now the cry went up *The King; the King himself!* The crowd bellowed its anger; the sky rang with the sound. Yet it was not the King they hated; not, in this moment, James or Louis. It was the unknown figure in the sledge that drew their hatred, focused it, released it in wild screaming to the reddened sky.

From the leads of Whitehall, Charles and Catherine watched. Charles said—and she saw how he bit upon his thumb, 'It's well that's an image in the sledge. The mob's so mad with hatred that—alive or not—it's Smithfield for him and the burning.'

She turned her white sick face. *They will burn the thing in the sledge since they cannot burn you!* He said, since he had the same thought, 'This affair has its uses. By tomorrow hatred will have burnt itself out. Today, being stirred by my enemies, the mob hates me. Tomorrow, being stirred by myself, it will love me; tomorrow they'll not hurt a hair of my head. There's no purpose in a mob—save at the moment of hating. Then, if they can lay hands upon their victim—' He whistled. 'Such a victim I don't intend to be!' Then seeing the sickness still in her face, added, 'This mob; it's nothing but prentice boys led by the riff-raff. London's loyal—I'll wager my head. And the number of my friends grows daily. Tomorrow the Londoners will cry out their blessing and all the prentice boys will cheer for me. So who's the worse?'

'For such a show of hatred we are all the worse!'

In the last week of November Shaftesbury came to his trial. 'If ever a man deserved to suffer the full beastliness of a traitor's death—it's Shaftesbury,' Charles told North. 'Not the poor fool Fitzharris but Shaftesbury—Shaftesbury all the time.'

North nodded. 'The papers we took from his house are enough to hang him; him and others. We have the names of those traitors that would keep my lord, your brother, from the succession.'

'And two lists, besides. Let us not forget them!' Charles' grin was twisted. Those to be loaded with honours; and those for the gallows. The first, names himself and his friends—it goes without saying. And the second? I and my friends—in which you, Frank, stand high. All, all of us to be hanged—with the possible exception of myself. For me, with luck, the honour of the block.'

'Shaftesbury will never hang!' Catherine spoke suddenly. 'His lies and his money will breed mischief still. It will be—how do you say?—a picked... a packed jury.'

'You may call it both,' Charles said.

'You were right, Kate!' Charles strode grey and furious about the Queen's closet. Her nod dismissed her women. When they were alone, he said, 'The grand jury—picked and packed by those precious sheriffs Bethell and Cornish—declare there's no case to answer. *No case to answer*—the traitor that would murder his King and plunge his country into Civil war! And more. I am advised to withdraw the charge against Howard of Escrick.'

'No!' she cried out. 'No!'

'Yes. Even North advises it. He says any grand jury, at this moment, will declare no case against Howard, also.'

'Two wicked men to work their mischief!'

'But not for long!' He bit upon his thumb wincing with pain. 'I'll have justice in this land if I die for it... and that I may well do before I clean the whole of this filthy stable.'

She said, 'God will give you health and strength.' And went across to the window that he might not see her grief for his lean looks and his poor bitten thumb.

Shaftesbury, liar and traitor, went a free man to his great house in Aldersgate. But, though he set once again about his bribes and his promises, few joined him now. The day of his glory was gone. But for the King—though full day was yet to come—his sun was shining. Bethell and Cornish might take Shaftesbury's bribes and bribed juries serve his purpose; but London's new lord Mayor was the King's man. He made a great banquet for Charles; and the King rode through the city that had shouted for Monmouth and now shouted for him, crying out its loyalty and love.

'No mob this time, Kate, but the sober citizens of London. I reined in and I spoke to them. I said, *As long as London is faithful, I fear nothing!* You should have heard them then! Your St. Catherine must have heard them in heaven! London's with me—and Shaftesbury knows it. He's sold his house in the city; no-one trusts him any more. For the first time I feel my throne safe beneath me.'

Discredited and idle—he who had directed Parliaments, whose hands had pulled so many strings—Shaftesbury took ship for Holland.

'The sea's drowned many this wild weather,' Charles said, 'I am not unhopeful.' And, a little later, 'Oh Kate, the devil most truly looks to his own. Shaftesbury's safe; and all the heads of the Dutch States ran out to meet him. And, first and foremost—who? Who but my nephew! It's a thing to be remembered.'

William gave Shaftesbury a fine house in Amsterdam.

'Shaftesbury knows some secrets worth buying,' Charles said, troubled. 'And William—mean though he is—is willing to pay for them. My nephew cannot hide his itch for my brother's shoes.'

'Do not trouble your heart,' Catherine said. 'William is not God's choice.'

In the spring Shaftesbury went down under the attack of his old enemy—gout; and the gout, according to his physicians, entered his stomach and killed him.

'I remember his treachery against you, and how he brought good men to their death,' Catherine told Charles. 'I cannot, God forgive me, pray for his soul!' Instead she thanked Him that had removed the King's enemy from him.

XXXVIII

'No Parliament and no Shaftesbury with his never-ending mischief... and no more plots against the King!' Charles said. 'Now we shall have peace at Whitehall as well as Windsor! *Peace!*' In his mouth the word was a benediction.

She looked at him, so tired, so grey; so unquenchably cheerful.

No Parliament; no trouble... and no money. Charles dismissed yet more of his household; he made it the opportunity to turn Oates out of Whitehall... and no pension.

'And no voice raised in protest!' he told Catherine. 'That snake is scotched; its back broken.'

'The air is sweet again,' she said.

Life in Whitehall was not only peaceful; it was gayer, richer than it had ever been. Embassies came from distant lands, embassies never before seen in England; exotic dress and strange speech added interest, added dignity. 'Many embassies—' Charles said, gratified. 'A sure sign of the respect in which the crown is held.'

Morocco sent ambassadors to discuss peace for Tangier so long overrun by their own pirates; never before had Morocco so much as noted England's protests. Catherine received them with especial joy; Tangier was her own city and there had never been money to protect it. Nothing like these men had ever been seen—so handsome, so barbaric in great circular cloaks of white wool and the bright silk of their jewelled turbans, and the high socks of gay, soft leather.

They had brought with them as gifts, two lions. 'I christen them Charles and Kate!' the King said. 'But which is which it were best not to enquire too close.' They had brought, also, thirty ostriches. 'To make fair return I should send a gaggle of geese!' Charles' eye was sardonic upon the assembled court. But Catherine pitied the poor creatures brought from the Moroccan sun into this cold country.

There were balls for the visitors, there were feasts, there was horse-racing. In Hyde Park Londoners stared open-mouthed at the visitors' cloaks flying, galloping upright in shortened stirrups. Louise gave a great entertainment; the tables were set with gold plate, the couches were piled with silken cushions. On each couch a gentleman reclined between two ladies—the ladies, though first in beauty not first in virtue.

The visitors had gone home and Charles took Catherine to Newmarket to rest. James came from Scotland to join them; he came quietly—a test to see how he would be received. He was accepted, if not with pleasure, with no sign of dislike; it was better than either of them could have hoped. Charles had arranged a round of simple pleasures. There was horse-racing, of course—though Charles no longer took part he enjoyed the excitement and the fine points of a race. There was cockfighting; and wrestling. There were plays acted in the barn by strolling players—poor plays and poorer players—but a play was a play! And some of the players were pretty wenches; Charles liked to see them about the little town. 'The best holiday of my life!' he said. 'So long since I have been a little free from care; so long since James and I were together. I feel a boy again.'

And, indeed, Catherine thought, in spite of grey hair and heavy lines, his grin held something of the boy. She said, 'James says you mix too free with the people; a stranger, he says, would not know which was the King.'

'And you?'

She looked with love at his noble height and bearing; she said, 'Even a child would know the King!'

'James is too stiff in his ways. He's twice as able as I am; and he has a great sense of duty. But there's no ease to him; that's his weakness—though he thinks it strength. The people can't see through his stiffness to the real goodness beneath; they make overmuch of his faults.'

It was the third week in March—and a week of their holiday still to come. Charles, strolling about the courtyard, came to a halt... the *smell of burning*? He could be mistaken; since the Great Fire he did, at times, fancy the acrid smell. Troubled, he followed his nose.

Even before he reached the spot he knew he was right. The stables were afire. Heavy smoke lit with firework sparks floated heavily upwards to stain the clear sky. In the smoke and the heat and the roar of flames, the horses, mad with terror, gave voice, stampeding. Hopeless, the grooms were trying to deal with the flames. The wind was against them; the wooden buildings caught one from another; flames like banners streamed upwards to the sky.

Blackened wood, scorched trees and withered grass—a groom, carelessly smoking, the cause. The holiday was over and Charles was glad to go—to leave behind the smell of charred horseflesh; and the sight of those poor creatures he had ordered to be shot. They rode to Windsor a week before their time.

And thereby saved their lives.

It was not until June that they knew how close the escape. It was then that one, Joseph Keeling, oil-merchant of London, came to the Secretary of State with a tale; a tale of murder simple and certain; and in its simplicity, its certainty—terrifying.

'Four of them in it; Sir Robert West that's a lawyer in the Temple leads them. I have the names, sir.'

Mr. Secretary cast his eye upon the list... West, Rumbold, Wildman and Ferguson; they'd been Shaftesbury's creatures, all!

'They meant to murder the King. And not the King, alone; but his brother, too... yes, sir, both. *Lopping* they call it; the word regicide having too wicked a sound for their liking. Lord Howard of Escrick's in it, too; he hates the King. He wanted the *lopping*, God save us, done at the playhouse. Very proper, he says, to strike the King down in the midst of his pleasures. But—strike the blow in public! Not one of them dare take the risk!

'Well, sir, they talked and they talked and they got the plan perfect. Rumbold—he's got a house at Hodden; it lies between Newmarket and Windsor.'

He stopped to let that fact sink in.

'They call it the *Rye House*. It's a tall house deep in the country; but the main road runs near. Now, sir, between the road and the house there's a ditch where men could lie hid—forty, if need be; but a handful could do their business.

'Now, sir, all the world knows the King takes pleasure in a hard gallop. And, if he rides in a coach, it's much the same—he liked to be well ahead. Well then. The plan was to block the road with bales of straw. The coach or the horse, whichever it was that carried the King, would have to halt. Then those that were hid in the ditch would take the King together with his brother—it was a sure bet they'd ride together—and kill them both. And no man able to say who'd done the bloody deed. And so, sir, it would have turned out. But the Lord in His goodness sent the fire to Newmarket... and there was an end put to that!'

'Why should I believe this wild tale? And how did it come to your knowledge? And why, though the King should have been murdered, did you say no word till now? And do you come now in hope of reward?'

'You should believe it, sir, because it is true. Nor is it a wild tale but a true one. I had it of one that was drawn into the affair and now repents, and him I am sworn not to name. I did not tell the tale before because I did not know it till now. As for reward—I want none save to know the King is safe.'

'I spoke too soon of peace!' Charles said with a wry face. 'All the time they were plotting to take my life. Keeling's tale is true. Well, we have the ringleaders in prison; and Howard of Escrick's back in the Tower. The man's a rat. He was found hidden within the wide chimney of his dining-parlour, the brave fellow! They say he whined like a dog when they took him. Now he's busy swearing away better lives in hopes to save his own.'

Howard's confession revealed two plots. One to kill the King—the Rye House Plot; the other to surprise Whitehall. Then the King and his brother being dead, and Whitehall in the regicide's hands, they planned to put an eager Monmouth at the head of the State. Not as King, no more Kings; a Republic once more; but this time, an aristocratic republic. And aristocratic, indeed! Not a few peers were involved; among them the names of Monmouth, Essex and Russell stood first.

At the sight of Monmouth's name Charles' face set like stone. He was not surprised. '... not surprised. But, oh Kate, Kate, the words of that other father comes to me—that father in like case; the King with the beloved son turned traitor. *Oh Absalom, my son... my son...* But unlike that other King—' and his mouth twisted into the sardonic grin that showed the measure of his hurt—'I don't intend to die for mine.'

When he saw the name of Essex, his face went grey. 'Essex' father died for mine on the scaffold.'

'Can such a man be a traitor?' she said, knowing, like all the world, Essex to be an upright man.

'His words could stretch to it. Yet, Essex, I swear it, would not willingly harm a hair of my head. And *murder*—it is not in his book. It is all a matter of philosophy with him. He thinks there's a contract between King and people. If either side break that contract, any way, then the wronged partner is free to break it utterly. That contract he says I have broken. Russell, also, it would seem, shares his nonsense. Nonsense; but dangerous. Sedition. High Treason. Warrants are out for their arrest... and for Jamie's arrest.... for Jamie's arrest, also.'

Charles might not be willing to die for a treacherous son; but he'd save him if he could. In the dark of the night he went, himself, to warn Monmouth; but Monmouth needed no warning—he knew well how to take care of himself. Monmouth was gone.

Essex and Russell might have escaped; both. The warrants were out; but there was time and time enough. They were, perhaps, *meant* to escape. Russell's house, though guarded in front, was left free at the back. And about Essex' house—both in town and country—no guard at all. But they were proud men both; and, in their own eyes, innocent.

They had not taken freedom while they might; now it was too late.

Russell was taken first. Day by day Charles sat with his Council, listening to the accused, listening to the witnesses; and unfailing in courtesy.

'I have never,' Russell swore it, 'conspired against the King. I have never desired the King's death.'

'*If the King step outside the law, the people have a right to stop him by any means they may...* Did you not write that?'

'Yes, I wrote it and believe it. But that our present King has stepped outside the law—that I never said nor yet believed. He is as good a prince as ever lived...'

He had spoken against the Divine Right of Kings—in these troubled times a dangerous proceeding. And there was information concerning more dangerous proceedings on his part. To the Tower he must go till he came to his trial.

Essex was in the country. So easy he seemed, even his so-loved wife that shared his thoughts had no notion of his danger. Perhaps he did not fully realise it himself—he could easily have escaped abroad. When he heard that Russell lay in prison, then he began to understand something of his own danger; and it was more than ever too late. Till his friend was free, Essex would not seek his own freedom.

When Essex appeared before the King and Council, he was troubled and confused. For the first time he understood what he had done. He had made of himself a traitor; he, whose father had died for the King's.

He, too, went to the Tower; he took imprisonment badly.

'There are natures,' Charles said, 'that can support the loneliness, the confinement and the darkness; such a one is Russell. Others—like Essex—sink to the ground. And, besides, they have put him in that same cell from which his father went out to die.'

Catherine's brows went up.

'An unnecessary cruelty, I agree,' Charles said. 'And that his father died for mine, you need not remind me. I think of it always. He should have escaped while he could... I can do nothing, now.'

Essex could neither eat nor sleep. In this cell, from which his father had been led to die for faithfulness to his King, knowledge of his own guilt came, relentless, home. Now he wrote to the wife he loved, admitting his crime and asking pardon for the ruin he had brought to her and to their children. Loving and distracted, she yet wrote he must not trouble about her or the children. They would manage well enough.

After that he appeared calmer, more reconciled to his prison. He asked for books and for pens and paper, and these were granted. He asked for a penknife to pare his nails and this was refused. He asked for a razor to trim his beard and this was not refused... with that same razor he cut his throat.

'I did not want him to die, Kate!' Charles lifted a stricken face. 'I owed him a life for his father's sake; and that debt I meant to repay. I could not stay the trial; the law must take its course. But the King's prerogative stands in law—and this time I meant to use it. The pity of it, Kate, the *pity*... good son of a good father... and did good work for me in Ireland.'

'To die by his own hand. God have mercy on him! A good Christian take his own life—why?'

'I asked myself that question, too. A throat cut with a razor is no more pleasant than cut with an axe... and death by the axe is a proud death; and, moreover—the punishment accepted—it brings divine forgiveness. Not so self-murder; for that a man's twice-damned—a double crime. Well, I have my answer now. Had he come to trial they must have found him guilty; and, having found him so, must declare him corrupt in blood... his honours and his estates forfeit. This way he saves his children from shame and poverty... if I make no claim. That claim I shall not make.'

The death of Essex carved yet deeper lines in Charles' face.

The day Essex died Russell came to his trial.

'Another good man misled!' Charles said. 'Such men the country needs. But for all that he must die.'

It was late when Charles returned from the trial. 'It goes against him. There's some to murmur that the trial's unjust; witness after witness perjured. There's plenty of false-swearing, that's true... too many frightened for their skin; Howard was actually giving evidence when the news came of Essex' death. He stood there and wept; then he wiped his tears... and went on swearing Russell's life away. But it's all one, Kate. It's no false—swearing sends Russell to his death, it's his own written word; enough there to hang him and to spare. And so he must die. He knows it. And she knows it, also, the young wife that sits sad and patient, and makes her notes of the trial. I pity her with all my heart; and him, I pity, too. But I'd not save him if I could. Men like him lift no sword; yet their words drive home not one sword but many...'

He stopped speaking; Mr. Pepys had come with news.

'Mr. Solicitor General sums up with malice; but Pemberton's been just throughout—thank God for a Chief Justice that's not afraid of justice. The jury is out now.'

'Russell's a dead man,' Charles said grey and grim. 'And I'll thank my lord Chief Justice not to be over-tender. For all his high-thinking

Russell would have had my life. To Essex I owed a life; to Russell I owe nothing. I am satisfied he should die.'

Russell took his appalling sentence with calm; and, in the Tower, remained calm still. Bedford, crazed with grief, ran this way and that, seeking to buy off the sentence against his son and heir—his brilliant so-loved son. To Louise he offered a hundred thousand pounds if she would obtain the King's pardon. She refused—so she said—to interfere with justice.

'Refuse. Louise refuse a hundred thousand pounds!' Charles' smile was mocking. 'Of course she asked; asked till I was sick of the sound of her voice. *A good man... a good man*, she kept saying. Well, but these good men; the mischief they make! Untold. A sort of innocence they have... childlike... to drown the country in blood.'

Catherine sighed. Russell did have a certain childlike innocence; she pitied him. She looked at Charles as though her eyes would plead for him.

'I'll not interfere with the process of the law; I'm tired of saying it... yet I'll say it as long as need be. But Kate, you cannot imagine the weariness... yet take this for your comfort. He'll not suffer the full rigours of the law. He shall die by the axe; a quick death and not dishonoured.'

If Russell could have his way, so you would die, also! She smiled that he could so temper justice with mercy.

Bishop Burnet—a man of better heart than his tongue would suggest—was with the prisoner the night before he died.

'I have no fear,' the young man said. 'A little pain—less than the drawing of a tooth; and then, arms of a loving God. I pray my death shall serve my country better than my life.'

'As indeed it shall!' Charles burst out when Burnet told him. 'For he lived a traitor; dying he may serve to warn other traitors. Be sure, Burnet, he would have killed me. He is safer dead.'

That same night Russell wrote to the King, declaring, on the word of a dying man, his innocence. He implored the King's mercy towards his wife and little ones; for, unlike Essex, he had not forestalled death. His honours and his estates, alike, had fallen forfeit.

And, the writings being done, there came into his cell his wife and little ones. The children, too little to understand, yet felt death in the air and fell aweeping. But Rachel, his wife, listened very quiet, to his last wishes. She showed no sign of her anguish until Lord Cavendish, that loved him well, offered his own cloak for escape; he would, himself remain in the dark cell until his friend was safe. It was then that her eyes lit with hope; and that was the only thing to show her anguish.

But Russell said, 'How should we live, my love, if my friend should suffer and, perhaps, die in my place? But, let me face death unflinching and I may, perhaps, clear my honour.'

She said no word; only the hope died from her eyes as she looked at him so young, so perfect in health… and yet a dying man. She put a hand to her mouth to hold back the weeping. She held up her face for his last kiss.

When she had gone and the children with her, Russell said, 'This parting is worse than death.' And, in a little, he said, 'The bitterness of death is passed.' And he jested a little with Burnet that was to stay with him till the end. He wound his watch smiling that the habit had so firm a hold. 'I am done with time,' he said. He went to the window, the small barred window from which he would never see another night sky stitched with stars. Tonight he saw no stars, either; from the dark sky rain fell. He smiled. 'I trust the rain will stop; if not, it will spoil tomorrow's show.' Thereafter he went into the inner cell to pray; and so continued till sleep took him kneeling.

It was Pepys, as usual, that brought news of the execution.

'It's a tidy step from the Tower to Lincoln's Inn Fields, as you, sir, know; and all the streets were crowded. As the procession passed, some called out their insults; but most wept and gave Russell kind words. To all their insults he was deaf; but the kindness touched him to the quick. He smiled his thanks; speak he could not, for he was singing psalms all the way. Once he did stop singing to speak to Burnet; I was walking with the procession and I heard him plain. He said, *I shall sing better soon.*

'So we came to the scaffold; and there he turned and spoke in a clear voice. *On the word of a dying man I know of no plot against the King's life nor against the government. I pray for them both—King and government. And I pray, also, that God continue the Protestant religion as long as the sun and moon shall stand. And then he said, I die in charity with all men.*

'Then he knelt and prayed; and, that being done, he stood up and pulled off his periwig—and very young he looked with his short bright curls; indeed, sir, I had not known him to be so young. He took off his cravat and his coat; he gave the executioner both gold and forgiveness. He knelt and laid his head upon the block... When the executioner held up the head, a sigh went through the crowd, so innocent the face, so very young...'

'But for all that a traitor,' Charles said.

When Pepys had gone he took up the letter Russell had written the night before he died. Catherine came to lean upon his shoulder; they read it together.

...I have always loved my country more than my life. I would have suffered any extremity rather than have consented to any design against the King's life. I pray for him with all my heart, and for the nation that peace be preserved and that he may be happy here and hereafter.

'A good man but dangerous.' Charles' face was gentle.

He read further and his face darkened.

'He confesses that he tried with all his might to exclude James. A Papist King, he says, must always be bound by limitations; and therefore such a King is no King. And more; a Papist King must always breed jealousies and plots. But a Protestant King, his preroga-tive untouched, may rule a happy and a safe nation. This fellow—' he struck, contemptuous, at the paper, 'blinds himself and others... others also. And he thinks, he actually thinks his sentence a hard one! Oddsfish, I have been too easy in the manner of his death. He should have suffered the full sentence according to the law.'

She looked at him startled. It was unlike Charles, good easy man. He said, already ashamed of the outburst, 'I'm tired, Kate, tired to the bone. This is the most uneasy throne in Christendom. I fight for James; and so for God that put Stuarts upon the throne. I wear out my life in the cause—if I am not cut off before that! And James. How long will he keep the crown when I am dead?'

'As long as God shall choose. As for dying—it's equal chance James will die first.'

'Yet still I must fight. It is the principle!' He lifted his face; it was a mask of stubborn pain, harsh and hard. She thought how happy he had been born a simple gentleman, to enjoy his simple pleasures—to go to the playhouse, to work in his laboratory, and to have no arguments heavier than those of his Royal Society... a simple gentleman against whom no man plots, nor he himself causes any man's death.

Charles said, 'The throne of Kings is built upon blood; the blood of good men as well as bad. And no King can stay the bloodshed save through peace. Please God I may bring peace to this stubborn people.'

'You will do it!' she said.

'If I live so long.'

'God measures the days and the work... and you will do it.'

'Your faith is strong, Kate.'

'In God... and in you.'

'You give me faith, too.' He took her hand and kissed it.

XXXIX

No more hangings in the name of God; no more plots against the King, nor rumours of plots. Oates' hideous face sickened the Queen no more. Fitzharris was dead; dead, Essex and Russell—and rightly dead; though for Essex Charles grieved for the debt unpaid.

In these quiet days he and his people were growing to know each other, to trust each other. He came to the Queen's Side, one day, bright with happiness; he had, for the moment, the eager look of a young man.

'London!' he cried out, 'I have won London; truly won her at last! The city has written a new charter—of its own free will, written it. And that charter acknowledges my right—the King's right—to veto the election of all its officers, my lord Mayor, sheriffs, magistrates, all!'

'Oh,' she said, 'I am glad; how I am glad!' *And it is time... time! Twenty-three years to recognise his simple right!*

'Be glad,' he said. 'And not only for me. This means so much... so very much, Kate. It means that honest men alone shall take office—so far as it be in my power to judge. I'll have no more packed juries; no more liars and toadies like Bethell and Cornish. No more innocent men sent to the gallows—deliberately sent—nor criminals allowed to go free.'

'And so it shall be all over the country. London sets the example!' she said.

London had, indeed, set an example. Now, one-by-one, all over the country, towns laid their charters at the King's feet.

'I am well-pleased with my loyal cities,' Charles said. 'I begin to wonder whether, in truth, authority does not come from the people, rather than from the King.'

'What becomes of divine right, then?'

Oxford answered that question. Oxford made a bonfire of every book that questioned his authority. To question the King was to question God—destructive alike to Church and State. Obedience to the King. Only so could Englishmen live the good life.

'Oxford was always loving, she speaks for herself!' Charles said. 'But for the rest—we must be content to hasten slowly. The way is still long and it is still hard.'

Not too long, not too hard, she prayed, watching him with anxious eyes. She had accepted that he should be slower in body, more easily fatigued. But now he would fall asleep in his chair after dinner—and that was a new thing; it plucked at her heart. And yet he enjoyed a brisk walk, still; but he rode little and swam not at all—the water was too cold and he too breathless. Sometimes, watching him asleep in his chair, she would remember the days when she had first come into this country; when Charles and James—the strong young men— had raced each other, swimming from Whitehall to Hammersmith. Well, that was all of twenty years ago; he was fifty-three now; and she had little cause to complain. His wits were keen as ever; and his kindness, constant. His temper was even—upon the whole. He could flare into sudden anger; but he showed less of the irritability men of his age—and younger men, even James—showed.

Yet, looking at the sleeping face, she found it hard to endure the thought that he, who had outstripped all men—on horseback, at the dance, at the hunt—was growing old. She would scold herself, at times, for an ungrateful heart. God had kept them both in good health. And what could she ask for more in this world—and the next—than to live in quiet and kindness with him whom every day she loved more dearly? And then she must remember that each precious day stole from the future... one day there would be none left.

The end of July brought a wedding and she put away sorrowful thoughts. Plump Prince George of Denmark had come to marry James' daughter Anne.

'A good marriage—if Anne could bring herself to make it so,' Catherine told Eliza Ormonde. 'A pleasant young man.'

'She doesn't care for men; maybe because men don't care for her. She's plain and she's shy. And those peering, anxious eyes don't add to her beauty.'

'She's well enough when she takes the trouble,' Catherine said. 'Her hair is pretty and her complexion perfect; she can thank her God the small-pox left it untouched. And her voice... so sweet; a voice to melt the heart.'

'When she chooses—which isn't often. She's obstinate.'

'She's gentle—when you know her,' Catherine said. 'And humble where she loves.'

'At this moment her heart's given to Sarah Jennings. A thousand pities!'

Anne had no intention of making the best of the marriage. The very idea of marriage frightened her; she hated the notion of sharing her bed with fat George. She wanted nothing but to be allowed to love the fascinating Sarah, to share her secrets, to giggle with her in corners. A little weary of Anne's adoration Sarah urged her to take what came... while yet it was there.

'The little Jennings talks good sense!' Charles said. 'I would my niece had half as much.'

'Never trust her!' Catherine said. 'I caught her once poking fun at the groom; and Anne stood head hanging and a tear running from her poor eyes.'

And once Charles, himself caught Sarah at her game.

'Why, child,' he told his drooping niece, 'there's a certain cure for George's figure.'

'Please to tell us, sir.' Sarah rose from her curtsey. 'I grow a little plump, myself.'

'My cure is for gentlemen, only. He has but to walk with me, to hunt with my brother, and do justice upon my niece.'

'Fie, sir!' Sarah covered her carnation cheeks; but her laughing eyes that peeped between her fingers belied her modesty. Anne had no notion what it was all about. 'Of course my husband will do me justice; I shall see to it!' And tossed her head.

Sarah went into peals of laughter; when Anne pressed her she refused to share the joke.

Louise, so circumspect till now, was making a scandal with young Vendôme, new-come from Paris. He was handsome and gay; and, for the first time, the calculating Louise looked like losing head as well as heart. The court was amused, the French ambassador disturbed, the Queen well-pleased—save for Charles' humiliation; and Charles himself? Black with anger. Louise was young enough to enjoy sleeping with a man—for that he could scarce blame her; but she should have made a show of faithfulness, she should have preserved the King's dignity. He sent the young man packing back to France, whither—if she were not more careful in future—Louise should follow him.

But his chief anger was for himself because he no longer cared in the old way, for women. He wanted nothing from them now but to pass a jest, to drop a light kiss, to hold a pretty hand. He wanted no woman in his bed—the good days were gone. He preferred to sleep alone; or, with Kate, kind, comfortable Kate. He grieved at this clear sign of growing old. The little Jennings—his blood quickened at the sight of her; but, had she offered to sleep with him, he would have found his excuses.

Charles is growing old and I am growing old, and the whole world is growing old Catherine thought, not yet passed her forty-fifth birthday. But her brother Alphonso had just died; and she felt death, a cold wind upon her neck. For twenty years she had not seen him nor yet written to him; he would not have understood her letters. She grieved, not because he was dead, but because his life had been to him a sick and useless burden.

'What happiness did he ever know?' she wept when Charles tried to comfort her. 'Not even a happy childhood. A little boy, when the sickness fell and left him crippled—body and mind. A slow little boy dragging a painful leg. I was younger; but I'd cradle him in my arms like a baby. He was called to the throne—a young man; yes, but for all that a slow little boy full of pain. Pain he knew always but pleasure—none. He sought it in vices he was too sick to understand... or even to enjoy.

'My mother took his place—the Regent; and, thereafter, Pedro. He wouldn't take the name of King—that was Alphonso's. But he took his brother's throne and he took his brother's wife. And Alphonso. Poor little boy; poor witless King. Health gone, wits gone, throne and wife gone... all gone. This past eight years... the dark cell; an animal, chained.'

Charles said, gentle, 'Be glad he has left it all behind. He is in Heaven—you must believe it; his vices forgiven. Already he has served his purgatory. God is compassionate; he knows peace at last.'

'Yes,' she said. 'Yes. But still I must weep remembering him... and remembering my childhood. So long I have forgotten; and now it all comes back... the flowering trees and the pomegranates, and the citrons that smell like heaven. And the camellias that grow five times the height of a man—not the poor things you grow under glass and consider a miracle; and so they are, growing at all in this grey, wet England. And the oleanders and the mimosa and the magnolias; and everywhere sun and blue sky.'

'One of these days you shall go back,' he said.

'Not without you!' And it was as though someone had walked upon her grave.

Peaceful days. A King growing steadily in the love of his people; and the country growing steadily into prosperity. One thing grieved Charles. Monmouth. And the grief was not anger but love.

'I long for the sight of him. I long for him... and I fear for him. A man grows no younger, Kate; and I've lived hard all my life. A little fever or a chill; or a stumble, maybe... and the end for me; the end for Jamie. James will not forgive him. James was never one to forget or forgive; constant in hate as in love... and he hates Jamie. Oh Kate, Kate, what shall become of this Absalom of mine? Shall I not call him home?'

'You cannot trust him.'

'He would be safer under my eye.'

He was eating his heart out for his son. 'Then you must send for him!' she said.

'Louise will fight me over this!'

She nodded. Louise would certainly fight. These days she displayed great affection for James; she was his champion, his friend, his sister. James was her insurance for the future; her only insurance and she knew it. She had given up her cherished hope. The succession was no longer in question. It could not be broken; there was no Parliament to break it.

Charles said, 'If I might have Jamie home, my heart would be at peace.'

'Then you must send for him,' she said again; but, *As long as Monmouth lives, you'll know no peace!*

It was late in November when Monmouth came home. Mr. Secretary came hastening with the news. My lord duke of Monmouth had arrived and given himself up; he humbly besought that he might see the King. He waited, under guard, below.

For Charles it was as though the sun had burst through the winter sky. He longed to run to meet this so-loved son, to take him by the hand; but Jamie must be received coldly; he must be made to understand, once and for all, that his capers were at an end; one other would cost him his head.

Charles and James sat alone in the presence-chamber. Monmouth, debonair head low, knelt at their feet.

'I do beg forgiveness of you both—of you, sir, my King and father; of you, sir, my uncle and future King. I do confess I knew of the plot to exclude you, Uncle, from the throne. For this I am most heartily sorry.'

James, pinched mouth and cold eyes, froze the fount of eloquence; no hope there! Monmouth turned again to his father. 'As for the plot, sir, against your life, before God, I am innocent. What man would take it upon his soul to slay his own father?'

'It has been known,' James said cold and bitter.

But Charles could endure it no longer. He rose and took Monmouth in his arms and their tears mingled.

'The tears were running down his cheeks, Kate,' Charles said later.

He was ever an easy weeper… an easier breaker of the given word… She said nothing. She had no wish to spoil his happiness; but, stronger than ever, she felt that bringing home Monmouth was a mistake.

Charles said, glum, 'You and Louise appear to be at one in this! Yet be glad for me; he is truly contrite.'

I wonder. And for how long?

'He has written his confession; he has, with his own hand, signed it. Kate, be content; my son is home again.'

Handsome Jamie throwing his sunshine about the court; and in that sunshine, Charles basking, though the King's Council sat with dark faces; darker the face of Louise; darkest of all—James.

Never a man so capricious as Monmouth, so swayed by those he called friends, so swayed by his own desires. When his confession was published those friends came flocking. He had betrayed them and himself—they swore it. They would be hanged, all of them. Nor need he think himself would escape. When he knelt to the block he would rue the day he had submitted to his father's blandishments—he that might have been King.

Monmouth denied his confession; denied, even, that he had made it, denied it long and loud. Never had he confessed; never! Nor would he ever—an innocent man. Catherine had never seen Charles so stricken. His face went stiff and grey as lead; the eyes blazed in stained sockets. 'Tell him to get out of the country!' he commanded James. 'Tell him to go—to Hell, if he choose. Soon or late that's his destination. If he's not away within twelve hours—the Tower!'

He meant it; even Monmouth knew it. Out he flung—back to Brussels and his mistress. But he was not unduly cast down. He'd be coming back again; the King would send for him. The King could not long sustain the agony of his absence.

Charles was the worse for the brief reconciliation. He ate his heart out for his son. 'You were right, Kate, I know; I know. He must come home no more—for my brother's sake; and for the country's sake; and most of all for his own sake. For let him come home again, he must lose his life.' Of his own unappeasable longing, he said no word. She was to think, afterwards, that it had helped to shorten his life.

The new year of 'eighty-four came in. It had been a harsh winter; now it was more bitter than ever. The year of the Great Freeze they called it. The Thames was frozen, the ice like iron; the river had become a wider, grander highway. Shops were set up, fires leaped upon the ice; dark ice below, dark sky above borrowed rosy light. Whole oxen turned upon the spits, chestnuts and potatoes roasting in the ashes flung their warmth upon the bitter air.

Charles and Catherine stood at a window looking down upon the gay scene. Charles said, 'A merry winter—for those that can afford it. But there are others that huddle in hovels and alleys; this cold will kill them.' It was because he felt the cold, himself, she thought, that he was troubled for others; more than once he had opened his lean purse to buy them meat and bread. So he had done during the Plague and after the Fire; so he would do whenever he knew people were in want.

It was hard to get him from the fire these days; sometimes she would coax him down upon the ice. Wrapped about in the sables the ambassadors had brought from Muscovy, they would skate together hand-in-hand; he with something of his old grace, she plump and pretty and smiling. And the people would raise a cheer; but it was for him, for him alone. Though she lived in this country a hundred years, she would still be *the foreigner*. Well, if it was him they greeted with kindness, she was content. She would cast a glance at him from time to time; when the colour died in his face, she would see with anguish, how thin he looked, how *old*. Now and again he would mention—casually as was his way—a pain in his side. He never complained; it was nothing, he said. But now and again she caught his look of pain and wished she might take it upon herself. And he had his moods. Sometimes he was melancholy, when forgetting all he had done, he could remember only all there was yet to do. Sometimes he was his old happy-go-lucky self, enjoying the play—though no longer the players; and listening to the singers from France—their light, lewd love-songs, for a little, gave him back his youth.

Three years since he had called a Parliament. 'I am well enough without it!' he would say, laughing, to those that besought him to call it again. 'I am at peace from those talkers; I, and the country together.'

And peace the country had, sailing upon the course he had charted. But... when he should be no longer there to guide them? Again and again his Council urged him. 'It is time we had a government once more. Sir, you must call a Parliament.'

'I'll think on it!' he would promise. But the more he thought, the less he liked the notion. A new Parliament would start once more upon an exclusion bill. Though the country had more or less accepted him, James' crown would be once more in danger. Again there would spring up the old misery of plots and rebellion; the whole peaceful country once more in a ferment... perhaps revolution. He would never, God helping him, call Parliament again.

'What can a Parliament do better than you and I together?' he asked his Council. 'Here in England we are at peace; but Spain and France and Holland lay Europe waste with their wars.' He eyed Halifax, eyed Sunderland and Ormonde, eyed them all one by one. 'When I came home this poor country was bankrupt. Now we grow rich. We send our wool, our leather and our iron all over the world. Our ships return from the East laden with silks and jewels, with spices and essences. We sail the Indian Ocean; and the South Seas. What more do you want?'

Give his country a government to keep an even course when the pilot is gone. One after another they fell silent. Looking into the worn face they had grown to love, they could not endure the thought.

XL

Bitter Winter gave way to a cold and leafless spring. Save that the days were longer it was hard to believe that spring had come. Looking at Charles so peaked and pale, Catherine would think again of spring in Lisbon—sun and warmth and blossom. Since her brother's death the thought of home continually drew her. She longed to go back to the land of her birth and the places she had known as a child; but more than that, she longed to take Charles from this cruel weather that he might grow strong again.

He had lost most of his gaiety, though his wit could sparkle still. He was brooding more deeply upon the things he had left undone. At heart so modest a man, he did not realise all he had managed to do. That he had done greatly—he would have laughed at the notion, thinking rather upon the follies of his youth and the work yet to do.

This year the trouble in Europe grew more than ever pressing and a frightened Spain declared war on France. William of Orange saw his opportunity; he urged Charles to stand with Spain and Holland against France. Charles refused—though it would have pleased his people well; but Spain was his old enemy, France his old friend; and Holland—Holland the old untrusted. And, he doubted besides, whether all three could stand against the ever-growing might of France.

'I'll not do it!' he told his urgent Council. 'I know my nephew of Orange. If things go well—which I doubt—he'll have feathered his nest with secret treaties. And, if they go ill—as I fancy they will—then he'll turn his back and leave us to hold his baby. This country prospers now; I'll not drown it in a bath of blood!' And when Halifax, speaking for the whole Council, urged him further, Charles refused still. 'A man can see no further than he can. I'll not fight France. You say that war is bound to come. Well, if it must—it must. Till then—no war. The longer we stave it off, the stronger we'll be, if the time comes.'

'*When* the time comes!' Halifax corrected.

'That time is not now.'

And it was not only his perfect certainty that peace was a gift from God not lightly to be thrown away... there was also that little matter of his secret understandings with Louis—those subsidies, those promises to enter the Catholic Church.

The weather was still unseasonable and the trees leafless when, late in Spring, they went to Newmarket. The house had been rebuilt; it was more spacious, more comfortable. And life there was different from before. Once it had been a man's world; then Charles had brought the Queen; now he had Louise with him and Nell also. For, since he rode so little and raced not at all and must be content to sit at ease and watch, time hung heavy on his hands. Nell he had brought because still she could make him laugh. Once when Nell sang, Catherine had left Charles to enjoy the jigs, the naughty jests, alone; now she would stay for the pleasure of hearing him laugh. Louise he had brought because he had forgiven her. A little since she had been very ill; until she was out of danger he had—himself surprised—slept ill, not enjoyed his food, not been able sufficiently to attend to the business of State. With him old ties of affection must always hold; and, besides, they were bound together by their son—little Richmond. In Louise Catherine found no pleasure at all; and the little boy reminded her, all too often, of those other handsome sons and pretty daughters, so that she found it hard, even now, not to weep that she, alone, had not given her husband the joy that the least of his lights o' love had given.

But it was a mood that never lasted long. She had her husband's deep affection; more than he gave to any woman nowadays. And this happiness was enriched by seeing the real love his people gave him; a love different from that they had shown him at first. Then it had been a high tide of pleasure in a romantic young man; pleasure with an undertone of distrust. That tide had receded leaving him alone upon a lonely beach. Then, slowly, the tide had turned again. Now it bore him high upon the considered love of his people. Wherever he went crowds gathered to cry out their blessings; when he touched for King's Evil the crowds were so dense that a man must have a care lest he be pressed to death. That he had given the country solid blessings it was, as yet, too early for them to understand. It was the man himself that had won them—adversity had shaped him to a gentle courtesy; when he must chide he would pleasantly, reasonably, set the fault right so that no bitterness was left behind. And he had, within himself, a true humility before God and man.

Summer came in; a hateful summer. After the bare winter and leafless spring, it now lacked rain. The roads were thick with dust as they took the way to Windsor, the leaves too-soon yellow, the blossom pinched. Charles had been putting aside money from his scant store to buy grain—if he could find a seller; Europe was suffering from the same bad weather. 'Like Joseph in the Scriptures I should have guarded against the lean years,' Charles said, '... but there was never any money.'

'You shall have the grain,' she said, 'I have written to my brother.'

Here in Windsor, the gardens were green so that it was possible to forget, at times, the parched countryside; and, besides, God would send the rain... and her brother the grain. It was for her a summer of rare content and it was well she should have it—the last true happiness she should ever know.

She was always to remember one drowsy afternoon. Charles was sitting in his great chair, eyes half-closed. He was speaking—thinking aloud, a habit that had grown upon him.

'There are travellers that come with their tales of this wonder and that... but home is good enough for me. When I was a boy I wandered... too much. Never—of my own will—shall I leave home again. But James.' His voice sharpened a little. 'What becomes or James when I am gone?'

It was a question he so often asked himself these days; and always she met it with the same response—a hand put out to hush him; she could not endure the thought of his dying. He touched it lightly with his own. 'Death comes for all; if you have a good wish for me, Kate, wish me to die before you. You are my comfort and my strength; without you I would not wish to live.'

If this be his true wish, grant it, God! But grant, also, that I follow fast upon his heels. She thrust down the desolation in her heart.

'When I am dead and gone what shall my brother do? I am troubled about James; so stubborn he is—always in the right! He sets men against him. Now he is back again on the Council, he is forever in bitter dispute. And, that he is often, truly, in the right, makes dispute no less bitter. I fear for him; I fear that, when he comes to wear the crown, he'll be obliged to travel again.'

He was silent, musing behind closed eyes.

'I have fought for James, fought how long, how wearily! On his account I all-but lost the love of my people. What happens after death no man can say. But this I know—let James lose the crown and I shall weep there in my grave.'

At this desolate picture she lifted a hand to her eyes; and since he had made her weep, it must be sunshine again to make her laugh. 'Oh Kate, I have made you melancholic. Let's have the fiddlers.' And, within a little, there were a dozen couples dancing the country tunes he loved so well; and there he sat, laughing and clapping out the rhythm so that it was hard to believe that a short time ago they had been melancholy, both.

In the late summer they went to Winchester. Charles had fallen in love with the city and the love was mutual. Wren was building him a great house there and Charles longed to see it finished.

'Sir,' Wren said, himself not so young as once, 'a house must have time to grow. Give me a full year at the least; and, after that, maybe another year. The longer your house takes a-growing, the longer shall be your pleasure when it is done.'

'A year; and then a year! Too large a slice of a man's life!' And it was as though he said, *I have so few years left... in the grave what pleasure?*

He could not, it seemed, let himself rest. Save for that short time at Newmarket, he had not allowed himself to relax. At Windsor he had been constant with his Council over affairs of state—foreign policies and the prospect of war; the shortage of grain and the price of food. All summer he had been making his journeys—to Chatham, to Rochester, to Portsmouth, to Southampton to look at the Fleet; to Hounslow, to Salisbury to review what Parliament had left him of the army... slowly, quietly, he was strengthening his regiments. So much to do... and so little time to do it. Yesterday he had been a young man quick and strong; today... He did not like to think of today; of tomorrow still less.

The dry summer passed. And now that it was too late autumn came in with driving rain and heavy storm. The scant grain that had survived lay beaten to the ground. Charles tried to buy wheat from France, from Spain, from Italy; there was none to spare. For the sake of his sister, Pedro spared what he could; it was little enough; for the most part the people must go hungry.

And now it was November again and Catherine was forty-six. 'Your birthday, Kate. Let us celebrate it beyond the ordinary. Let us make for ourselves some cheerfulness.'

She looked her surprise. For several years now they had kept it quietly. There had been, indeed, little money and much unrest.

'The years go by,' he said, 'and who knows how many may be left? You have been so true a wife; the world should know how much I treasure you. It has not always been so, I know it; and the world knows it. Now let it see how dear I hold you.'

Dear as a sister? Not that, neither. He loved Minette with something of passion. But I must make myself content. He needs me; it is enough.

Towards the end of November they came from Windsor to keep her birthday in splendour. There was a great ball, there were mock seafights on the Thames, there were fireworks.

They stood together on the balcony of the great ballroom and watched the brilliant lights shoot through the sky, to blossom and fall; great glittering castles sprang up against the dark sky; fiery ships sailed the seas of heaven. And when, at last, her coat of arms entwined with his shone high above London, they took hands and went within.

The great ball-room was brighter than day so that they must blink, a little, coming in from the night without. A thousand candles shone upon silks and orders and great jewels. Charles gave her his hand to open the ball; and, as they danced, she thought of the changes the years had brought—herself, forty-six, fat and middle-aged, but pretty still, Charles said. And Charles looking old... too old. And Eliza come from middle-age into old age; handsome still, but old... old. And dear Penalva lying in the earth of her own land. And all the laughing girls—gay Frances Jennings and sweet Rose Warmestre, and the Hobart girl, that strange boyish beauty that loved girls only, so that they whispered she was no woman at all. And loveliest of them all—Frances Stuart. They were scattered—married or widowed or retired from the court; or, like Frances... dead. And there were no more great beauties like the beauties of old. Gone... all gone. And there were none to take their place. James' young wife touched the heart with her pregnant prettiness; but it was prettiness, prettiness only. And Sarah Jennings was scarce pretty; she deceived you with a sparkle and a liveliness. No more beauties; and no more bitterness. Nothing to fear from these pretty young things. The years that had taken her own youth had brought her the greatest gift of all—the undying tenderness of her husband.

She gave him her hand in the dance... *the years give; but the years take till they take the greatest gift of all...* The hand tightened upon his arm.

And so her last birthday of Charles' life came to its sweet and bitter close; and back they went to the cheap and simple life at Windsor.

It was more bitter than sweet. For now Charles was walking less and less—and always with difficulty; there was a sore place upon his foot that would not heal. But, wet or fine, he visited his horses every day—the horses he could no longer ride; he talked to them, Catherine said, with that same courtesy as they might be Christians.

Now that he went abroad less, he spent more time in his laboratory. He had never had time enough; now he worked long and patiently. He would come into Catherine's closet eager as a boy for all his limp, to talk about his experiments. He was trying to fix mercury; but why, she could not understand.

'Fix it—and there'll be a new metal for our use!' he said. But there were metals enough already and she could not see the need of it.

He was fifty-four and weary beyond his years. James, but a few years younger, florid and well-fed, looked scarce middle-aged.

Fifty-four; and still no rest from the constant rub of poverty. But... *no Parliament, no money!* They lived as best they might upon their modest revenues—and even those they did not entirely spend; all the time Charles was putting guinea to guinea. *I must pay my debts.* He kept saying it. It was as though time pressed him hard.

'Your father's debts you paid long since,' Catherine said. 'And the most part of your own, also—we have lived so simply. Time, now, to indulge yourself a little.'

'A man must leave a clean slate. If I could pay the last penny I owe, I'd die in peace.'

But his private debts were the least of his troubles; they were, indeed, all-but paid. More than ever—under the continuing threat of war—money was needed for the army and the navy. 'Let me show too open a friendship towards Louis or towards William, let me but make the slightest gesture too much—and the threat will break into war itself, If you want peace, you must be prepared for war.'

He came, as always, with his troubles to Catherine.

'Halifax is forever at me to call a Parliament; and the Council supports him. And, I begin to think, maybe I should. I fancy we might agree together, a new Parliament and I; the old faction is gone. But James is dead against it—I think with little need. The country accepts—more or less—the notion that he shall be King. But call a Parliament—and it could mean war; war with France. Louis swallows up all Europe; he'd swallow us too—if he could. Not the land beneath our feet; but our prestige, our trade, our life-blood. The country knows it; and the country ettles for war. But I'll not have it!' His sombre eyes flashed. 'I'll have no war! So—call a Parliament? Kate, I think and think again; and always I come back to one thought—one man at the helm; that's dangerous... and I grow old. And, if the people cry out for war, would my two hands hold them back? I doubt it. But Parliament could—if it had the mind; Parliament could hold them back.'

'But it has not the mind? If Parliament, itself, wanted war? It could happen; you have said it!'

'That's a risk I'd have to take, *must* take! I see it plain. That single pair of hands upon the wheel... suppose they drop altogether? A settled government—the country must have it. Or else, chaos. And, maybe, the risk is not so great. Things have changed. I could, I fancy, persuade a Parliament to peace.'

'You must persuade it!' *Not for the country's sake alone but for your own. What of the secret understandings with France? the secret moneys? What of that treaty at Dover when you swore to change your Faith? It stands, that treaty, a damning witness against you!*

She was pricked with anger against long-dead Minette that had tied him hand-and-foot. Was there never a woman, save herself, to stand for Charles; for him and him alone?

'I think I shall persuade it. These last few years I have kept the country in peace and we have prospered. Prosperity—it speaks with a louder voice than mine.'

'And if the voice of anger speak louder?'

'I should be sorry. But now I see my duty plain.'

'Then call your Parliament—if you must. But first send James away. Give him Scotland to play with. Then, and not till then, you may call it!'

'My best counsellor!' He bent and kissed her hand.

XLI

One thing above all troubled the King's heart. He was so tender a father; and Jamie tore at his heartstrings. He knew well the young man's worthlessness; knew him to be unstable, false. Yet he had almost brought himself to believe that this treacherous son could be shaped by love into honesty. Or, perhaps in his heart, he did not believe it, but yearned so for his Absalom that, without sight of his face, life lost its savour.

'I do long and long to see him again! But for James' sake I must not bring Jamie home... must not, at least, countenance it. I pray, at times, he'll come back in secret.'

'Defy you—and he must go to the Tower; yourself did say it!' Catherine reminded him. 'And, indeed, the Tower is where he should be! Have you forgot? How long since he made his confession and signed it with his own hand? And when you forgive... forgave him, he turned about and denied he had ever confessed, denied his own signature! To recant—it would be bad enough; but to deny, to brand you liar and forger—you and James, both! He's best away. For, however he return, openly or in secret, with permission or without—he'll set the country by the ears. Again, again, the plotting and the accusations and the dreadful shedding of blood.' *And you may lose your crown, my love; crown and life together. The people have come to trust you—yes! But who can answer for the madness of a mob? And what of James?* 'James,' she said, 'will certainly lose the succession—if he doesn't lose his head first!'

'Yet Jamie must not stay where he is—overnear my nephew for my liking. William treats him as though he were royal; James is fierce upon that matter. He has writ from Scotland taxing William. But, if I might bring Jamie back, keep him beneath my eye...'

'You tried it once before! I beseech you, Charles, never deceive yourself! Here or there, he'll make his mischief. But to keep him from this country and those that would put him in James' place—'tis the better of two evils.'

Since he must not ease his heart with the sight of his son, Charles sent him gold and gifts and loving messages. And then, surprising Catherine and all his Council, he ordered that all matters standing in the records against Monmouth be cut out. Nothing left to testify against his son when James should be King. A clean slate... if Jamie could keep it clean.

Late in November Monmouth came home. My lord of Sunderland—faithless friend—had his hand in this. It was to advance Monmouth and to pleasure William, rather than the King. Louise, too, had played her part—James, out of the way in Scotland, was no longer, perhaps, so safe an insurance. It was well to have a foot in both camps!

Charles did not receive his son openly, but happiness shone in his face. Nor is a man like Monmouth easily hid, even if he desire it. Monmouth did not desire it. He paraded himself and his handsome mistress; and Charles himself made much of the ill-used young wife and the two pretty children.

To James in Scotland came rumours of favour shown. Disturbed and angry he wrote to Charles and did not mince matters.

Rid yourself and the country of Monmouth. Charles heard it—and not from James alone; he heard it in the Council, he heard it from his friends; and, most of all, he heard it from his wife. And, indeed, he recognised the wisdom of it himself. So back to Flanders went Monmouth carrying with him the secret hope that soon he would be home again openly and for good.

Charles missed his son and he missed the children; and he was far from well. The sore place on his foot troubled him so that he could scarce walk; and he had grown obstinate in the matter. He would take no advice from his physicians; instead he concocted his own cures in his laboratory, which only inflamed the sore place and made him sick. 'You are more set upon the nonsense of fixing mercury than in curing your ulcer!' Catherine cried out once. It was after she had come upon him leaning against a wall his face drawn with pain. When he saw her he began to walk to show all was well; but she could see how painfully he limped. Shaken with grief and fear she did what she had never thought to do—she went to Louise to beseech her entreat the King to have better care of himself.

Louise shrugged. 'Once, Madam, the King said he had no concern with the souls of ladies but only with their bodies. I reverse the order. My concern is no longer with his body but with his soul.' And then she said very earnest—and not only because she obeyed the French King's order, 'The days go by and we grow no younger. Madam the Queen knows that, in his secret heart, the King holds by the true Faith but dare not say so. Always he means to speak out; and always he leaves such speaking... I fear he may leave it too late. Speak to him, Madam; remind him of his eternal soul.'

Catherine said, 'Before I came into this country, it was sworn for me—a condition—that I should meddle, never, in the religion of this country. I would give my life that the King should declare himself... but I must not do it. And he? However he yearn to come into the true Church, for the sake of the country, he'll not do it.'

'And shall he barter the Kingdom of God for this miserable Kingdom on earth? The eternal kingdom for a few hours here?'

You would have bartered your own soul for this kingdom—miserable as it is, for your son. And still would—If you could! She bit upon her tongue. She said, instead, 'If Madam the duchess can persuade the King as to his faith, she would find mine a grateful heart. But, first of all, persuade him as to his foot. Bid him obey his physicians.'

'That is a wife's part, not mine!' The depth of Louise's curtsey did not cover the depths of her insolence. She did not add that, since her first safety lay with the King, she had already advised him in the matter of his foot; nor did she say that, though he had laughed, the set of his jaw had advised her to say no more.

In spite of the pain Charles was serene. Soon his beloved son would be home again—for good; he and his wife and the two small children. He had said nothing to Catherine; he would wait until the thing was full-planned. Sunderland was working in the matter now.

December was going by; soon it would be January. *A new year... a new beginning for Jamie.*

The new year had come and gone. January had moved to its end. Monmouth would come any day now; but still Charles had issued no writ for a new Parliament. Soon he would do it; soon! He was so weary a man and he savoured his peace.

The first day of February, in the year of grace sixteen-hundred and eighty-five... a day Catherine would never forget.

It was a Sunday and the air full of the clash and peal of bells—a sound she loved; it lifted her soul on wings, she said.

Charles had attended church; and, her own chapel ended, came seeking her. She saw that he limped more than usual; and was, more than ever, restless. He wandered touching this thing and that; she felt her heart dissolve seeing with what pain he walked. He caught her look and said, 'I am better, Kate; the discharge has stopped. As for the pain—I make nothing of it!'

'Thank God!' she said; and neither knew that, of all signs, this stopping of the discharge was the worst.

He wanted to talk and she knew it. She sent away her woman; and, as was her way, brought him a chair. And when, with difficulty, he had settled himself, she brought a cushion and set it beneath his foot. And since she might not offer him wine lest it fire the humour in his foot, she brought a dish of sugared fruits new-come from Portugal and seated herself upon a stool at his feet.

He stretched out his hand for a comfit. 'You're a comfit, yourself, Kate,' he said. 'Comfit and comfort... and comfort I need. I need it greatly. I have wasted too much time. I am close upon fifty-five—and what to show for it?'

'You have turned all to blessing,' she said.

'It is your good heart speaks.'

''Tis your good work.' She went across to the window where, upon the river, she could see his ships crowding, rich in merchandise. 'Trade is the life-blood of a people—you have always said it; our trade prospers as never before. Your ships sail to every quarter of the globe. To India and the Indies...'

'It was in your gift, Kate; your dowry.'

'I brought you one talent; you multiplied it fourscore. You send our ships to find new trade-routes; even now they seek a passage to India through the frozen north.'

'They have not found it yet.'

'They may, or they may not; but the thought, the... the con... ception, is great. And you have made the navy strong—the good God knows how! You need fear no enemy by sea. Yet you work not for war, but for peace... all the time for peace.' She went across to the window. 'You love a fine builder like a brother; and stone-masons, also, and carvers in stone. From this window I see new churches rise into the sky—Wren's churches. I see the scaffolding of St. Paul's and I know that, day by day, it rises higher; and that it will be a glory to London... London... the fine houses of brick and stone. You love a good house, Charles. Almost I forget how the old wooden houses leaned one to another to shut out the sun. And there are wide streets where once the stinking kennels ran. London; your London, it rises like the phoenix-bird from the fire.'

'My London!' And now he was smiling. 'The fire we thought so great an evil has turned to blessing. Here, at least, I leave some memorial behind.'

'Over-soon to talk of memorials!' she was sharp with her fear. At once she regretted her sharpness; she came from the window. 'There's your Society,' she said. 'Your Royal Society... a toy, some think. But it has made new discoveries in Nature... wonderful, to touch the lives of us all. With your building and your Society, you show the world a way to live; a new way, more clean, more healthy. Where's the plague, now? Where's the scurvy?'

'But still the poor suffer enough. To them, life's a long, hard dying—Nell says that and she should know! Well, God give me time and I'll alter that. Every man to sit beneath his own fig-tree—or rather, apple-tree. Every man, however humble, shall be aware of his own human dignity, aware and worthy. This I set above all things. If I might help to bring that about—oddsfish, I'd ask no better!'

You shall! She looked into his weary face and the words died in her throat. She had never lied to him; she would not begin now. She said, instead, 'Be content. You found a bankrupt country and you made it prosperous. You found it torn by quarrels—Catholics, Protestants, Dissenters—all, all at each other's throat. You have drawn their fangs; you have broken the wicked persecutions; you have brought the country into some sort of... of....' she paused for the word, 'togetherness? oneness? You are a good King, Charles; maybe... a great one.'

'Am I, indeed?' His smile was wry. 'You think it because you love me.'

'Because I know you.'

'A good King—I strive to be. But a good man; a good husband?'

'I desire no better.'

And when he pressed her to make plain his faults, she said, 'A most beloved husband; is it not enough?'

'It is not enough; I am not worthy to husband you... my little funny Kate that came to me with her old-fashioned farthingales and her ridiculous curls and her sweet face. Yes, and with her high spirit and her strong will and her pure soul. But I do thank God for you; and I ask His pardon and yours for all I have done amiss. Have I your pardon, Kate?'

She brought her hands to her face that he might not see the tears running down her cheeks. 'You have made my life glorious,' she said, her face hidden still. 'As for God; we are all His sinners. Can you doubt His mercy?'

She longed, in this moment, to speak of his need to worship as his soul demanded; but he looked unutterably weary; she would not add to his burdens. She said, instead, 'You should rest now. Shall I call Rustat to help you?'

'No. I am well enough.' He bent to kiss her cheek and went limping to the door. When she heard his uneven steps die along the gallery, she flung herself upon her bed and wept. Afterwards, even in the first shock of her grief, she was able to thank God for these last sweet days; and, above all, for this last afternoon.

That evening she went seeking him. It was late and she doubted he had supped. He had no great appetite these days; and did not others think for him, he would—often as not—forget his meals. And, besides, she could not long be from him. It was not that she feared he might die; for all his worn looks his time was not yet. If she might carry him to Bath or to Tonbridge he would do well enough! God would not let him die—he was too-much needed, his work but half-done... and she forgot those others whose half-finished work had not stood in the way of their death.

She found him in a sheltered alcove in the Stone gallery and he was not alone. At either side sat a lady; at his feet, a third. She saw—and could scarce believe her eyes—that the two were Barbara Castlemaine and Hortense Mancini. It was Louise that sat at his feet. That the first two should be there shocked and amazed her. Neither had been seen for months; and then they had come to beg some charity knowing that he would never refuse a kindness to an old love.

The three loveliest women in Christendom... once. Now, like Catherine herself, they were middle-aged, though indeed, Louise was scarce that; in her mid-thirties, only. She, at least, was comely still... comely but no more. She was as plump as a partridge; fatter than the Queen by far. And Hortense. They'd said, once, she had the most beautiful bosom in Europe—and that, Europe might have judged for itself. Now there was too much bosom, too much hips, too much everything... and no waist at all. And Barbara, that mountain of fat! Through the ravaged remnants of her beauty, the ugliness of her nature showed clear. Of all three she had been, perhaps, the most beautiful... and she had worn worst.

Catherine's eyes went to Charles. A couple of braziers burned near his chair and he had a rug across his knees—he felt the cold these days. He lay back, eyes closed, against the cushions. She stood watching him. Now he toyed with the fair curls of Louise, or the dyed red hair of Barbara; now he fingered the fat white shoulder of Hortense.

In Catherine the old anger flared.

Now she saw him bring his hand back to the spaniel upon his knees. Women and dogs, he loved them both. Now, it seemed, they were equal in his love, for he touched them both—women and dogs—with the same gentle, indifferent hand.

Anger died as suddenly as it had flared; she was about to go quietly away when he opened his eyes. 'Why, Kate!' and he was smiling. 'A little gathering to give us back our youth!'

Their youth! So old, so worn, all four of them; so utterly removed from the appetites, the hungers that drive the young; at peace, one with another, these women, in the sisterhood of faded, jaded charms.

Quite suddenly she pitied them. She herself had never been a beauty; it had cost her enough tears. But she had come to her middle years as a woman should, Charles said; losing the charms of youth but gaining other, better charms—charity, compassion, gentleness. She prayed it might be so. Certainly there was no more anger in her nor jealousy as she looked upon the quartette of old lovers.

'Have you heard my new singer, young Deperrier, new-come from Paris? Boy! A song for the Queen.'

She had rather he did not sing for her today; it was the Lord's day. But to please Charles she smiled and nodded.

The boy came forward, made a leg to the Queen and went to lean against a pillar. His hand fell gently upon the guitar, his young voice lifted. It was a love-song, somewhat lewd. Charles, she saw, had turned his face to listen; and, unable to endure the sight of the old tired lovers and the fresh young singer whose voice seemed to mock them all, she went softly away.

She passed the gaming table piled high with golden guineas where courtiers pressed laughing and staking their gold; and so came face-to-face with Mr. Evelyn come to visit the King. He said, cold and severe, 'It is not golden guineas they cast away but golden hours. Guineas one may, with luck, find again; but the lost hours—never.' He looked across to Charles and his ladies; and it was as though he said, *These have cast away their golden hours; they will find it never again.* She wanted to cry out, *You are old and we are all old… be generous.* But so severe his face the words died in her throat.

When she came back to her closet she thought of the players at their careless gaming; and it seemed to her that Mr. Evelyn was right. It was not their guineas they threw away but the hours of their life. Well, by God's mercy they might yet have time to repent of their foolishness… but those four, their faces turned to a lewd song; for them, how much time? Three of them were none of her business; but the fourth? The fourth was her passionate concern. Charles' face in all its ageing weariness rose before her. *He may have little time left.* For the first time she consciously accepted the fact. *If he should die, he loses the most precious thing of all—his soul.*

She was resolved to speak with him come what might that, before it was too late, he should declare his Faith and his God.

XLII

She had made up her mind. But she could not rest. She had admitted into consciousness the thought that he might die; now she could not, for one moment, escape it. Not another night should pass; she would speak to him when he came to say Goodnight; God had been patient long enough. Between the stirrup and the ground a man could save his soul... or lose it.

She knelt to pray for wisdom to find the right words and set herself to wait. Finger between the pages of her missal, for it was still Sunday, she found herself listening for the sound of his coming; but there was nothing save the clear ticking of the clock and the murmur of her ladies in the room beyond.

She must have fallen asleep in her chair for she started suddenly at a small, sharp sound; it was Eliza gently putting seacoal upon the fire. The little clock by her bedside struck ten.

Eliza said, 'Madam, the King came; but you were asleep and he went away again.'

'You should have awakened me!' Catherine cried out.

'He would not allow it. It was his command.'

'I think he has not eaten.' Over and above her distress she was further troubled, remembering how she had gone to fetch him for supper and, finding him among his ladies, had gone away again.

'He has supped, Madam. Young Bruce is in the ante-room; he'll tell you so.

'Yes, Madam, the King has supped,' Tom Bruce said. 'He came first to you; but you were asleep, so he went to Madam the duchess of Portsmouth. She gave him a porringer of spoon-meat but he could not take it; too strong, he said. So they brought him a pot of chocolate and that he did drink—and enjoyed it, too. He went back to his own rooms early; he was tired and we made him ready for bed. But, Madam, he's himself again. He laughed and he chatted and

353

he made his jests—good jests, too. He's been talking about his new house abuilding at Winchester; it has a fine lead roof, it seems. He's so happy, Madam, that the house will soon be finished. Soon I shall lie in my new house covered with lead, he said.'

She nodded, troubled by she knew not what.

'I must go now, if Madam the Queen will pardon me. The King sleeps; I share the night watch with Harry Killigrew.'

The young men lay before the fire in the King's bedchamber, listening to any sound from the bed. It was not easy to hear. All through the night the King's clocks—many and curious—struck the hour, the half and the quarter—and not always together. Harry Killigrew was for stopping them; but Tom Bruce that knew his master better, said 'No. He will wake missing the sound.' Twice the Queen stole in, looked down at the sleeping face and crept out again. 'He'll be well tomorrow, Madam,' Killigrew said; but the dogs were restless, whimpering in their sleep, so that Bruce wondered whether they knew by instinct those things that come to humans by the cold light of reason.

She awoke from short and troubled sleep; and the tears were pouring down her cheeks. Waking and sleeping, she had been haunted by the King's words. *Soon I shall lie in my new house covered with lead.* By sane morning-light she knew it meant nothing but what Charles himself had meant; yet, might not God have meant it for a warning? She came from her bed early as it was, to pray for his good health, and more especially, that he might save his soul this day.

There was no more sleep for her nor did she wish it. Eliza, sleeping lightly as the old do, heard the Queen astir and came hastening. She made up the fire and rang for the Queen's women. They had tied the ribands of her morning wrapper and were brushing the still-dark curls when Sir Edmund King, Charles' chief physician, asked that he might speak with her.

'Madam, the King is not well; not well at all!' and he was very grave. 'When I went to dress the sore place on his heel he spoke to me; but, Madam… his speech was not clear. I think he had no pain; he was drowsy, half-asleep. And, indeed, before I had made an end of dressing the place, he was fast asleep. He slept a short time, only;

and when I asked him how he did, Madam, he answered me... in French. He knew not where he might be!'

'I stayed while they dressed him; and all the time he muttered, speaking to himself. But he answered never a question. He would begin to speak and stop in the middle forgetting what he meant to say. I would have him in bed, Madam; but he makes it clear he must be dressed. The levee is crowded...'

'Oh!' she cried out. 'Can they not leave him in peace?'

'Madam the Queen knows better than that! I have no power to turn the gentlemen away. And if I had, I'd not use it. Madam, you know well the tales they'd put about. *Poison*. It is always so when a prince is sick.'

'Yes,' she said and remembered that such tales did not always wait upon sickness. And then, 'But *how* sick? How sick is he?'

'Madam, I cannot say as yet. But this for your comfort. In a little, he seemed a trifle better. He knew what he would say; he would have spoken, could he find the words.'

Above her fear rode grief for him. How he must suffer, he, to whom words had always come quick as his own quicksilver.

'He groped his way to the chair where he always sits to be shaved. I think, Madam, he could not see plain. And he could not sit upright. He laid his head down on his breast... and then, Madam, I think, he did have pain... He gave a groan and fell back against the cushions.'

Charles groaning! Charles that would bite his tongue in two before he gave a sign! She turned away her face.

'Pain, that's a good sign, Madam; it shows his senses are returning. I knew he must be bled at once and someone went to find the Duke.'

She nodded. It was high treason to bleed the King without permission from the Council.

'While we were waiting, I saw the King's face go black. A congestion of blood. I dared wait no longer. I took out my pocket-knife and opened a vein in his left arm.'

'You put your life in danger,' she said. 'The King will not forget; nor the Council, neither.'

'The blood-letting relieved him. By the time the Duke came—one slipper on and one off, so great his haste—the King was a little better. He can move... a little; he speaks, Madam; he asks for you.'

'You should have called me sooner.' She wrung her hands.

'To what end, Madam? He would not have known you; and you—you need your rest to gather strength. The human frame can endure so much—and then, no more. Now you shall see the King while he knows you and needs you. You are the first and only one for whom he asks.'

When she came into the sickroom she fell back a step. The stench of burning flesh and stale blood all-but overthrew her. They had been putting pans of coal upon the flesh to bring him from his fit. She sickened at the smell, the sight of his agony. As she came in at the door, his eyes, those dark eyes of his, opened and closed again. He had asked for her; but he did not know her... or anyone.

She knelt by his bedside praying God would ease his pain and bless her with some of his agony. Still kneeling, she rubbed his feet that seemed already cold with the coldness of death. 'It is but the cold-ness after the seizure,' Sir Edmund said. 'It will mend. And, indeed, Madam, you may take comfort. He bleeds freely; it's a good sign.'

She said nothing; only her eyes asked her question.

'He is in God's Hands. Pray, Madam; and hope.'

Dear her love's body and most precious; dearer yet and precious beyond compare, his soul. And, if he died now, what hope to save him?

She looked about her. James sat, florid face patched red and white. At the head of the bed Mary, his young wife, knelt; she was pray-ing. Louise was not there; it was fitting. But the words she had said concerning the King's soul came winging, to batter with the Queen's own thoughts, against her heart. She sat and most desperately prayed that wandering soul to return, that Charles might, in time, remember his God. And if not...? *Sweet Saint Catherine intervene that God Himself shall stoop to gather his soul.*

She went on praying; and all the time she rubbed the King's feet as she prayed. Her arms were growing heavy, growing hard to lift. She forced them to their task. Her head was heavy; her whole body heavy and cold. There was a darkness before her eyes. She lifted her hands to push the darkness away; her hands dropped.

She came to herself and she was lying upon her own bed. How had she got here? She must, she supposed, have fainted, kneeling there by the bed. Charles' bed. Charles. She must go to him. She tried to rise; fell back upon the pillows. Lying there, helpless, she asked herself with anguish, whether Charles had been able to speak, to sign perhaps, to make James understand his desire concerning his soul. And so wondering, remembered Louise; Louise that had not been allowed into the King's room nor ever would be. Louise that would never see him again. For the first time she truly pitied Louise.

All day long, the coming and going in the sick man's room; churchmen and statesmen, courtiers and friends... and James, his heavy face hanging in folds of grief. Catherine sat in the stale air of the bedchamber—air staled by sickness and by heat, and by the breath and bodies of so many people.

The heat was affecting herself; she felt light and empty, so that she must hold herself to the chair lest she float about the room. She went slowly across to the window to put her cheek against its coldness. Below a great crowd stood, every face like one face lifted towards this room. The river was crowded, also; she could hear a man calling from one boat to another, asking how it was with the King. And the voice that asked and the voice that answered, was the voice of lamentation.

James sat, as for hours he had sat, torn between his brother and his new responsibilities. Already he had consulted with the Council; together they had taken measures for the peace of the country. All ports had been closed—across the sea Monmouth waited, Monmouth the people's darling, the Protestant Saviour. If Monmouth knew the King was dying, he'd be back in England and leading a rising before the breath was out of his father's body. Monmouth should know when all Christendom knew and not before. Now no ship could go out with the news, no port open to receive him. Before he could set foot in England James, the new King, would have been proclaimed. Such a proclamation might bring his brother's bastard to a halt. Insurrection against a proclaimed King has an ugly sound.

Monmouth must be kept out; not only for England's sake, nor yet for James, but for Charles', for Charles', also. His last hours must not be troubled. For, though his mind wandered now and then, home it would come; and, let a thing threaten his England, his spirit would know and be troubled.

In spite of perplexities, difficulties, responsibilities, James, also, was concerned first and always with his brother's soul. Charles, if he knew anything at all, must agonise in his heart, to be received into Holy Church. James must not, he knew, leave this room where the church-men waited, all of them, to snatch his brother's soul from salvation. Whatever other duty might call, here he must wait until this so-loved brother was able to speak, to make his desire for salvation known.

No end to the torment in the sick room. Daylong the bleeding, the blistering, the burning. Catherine bit upon her lips lest she cry out *Enough. Let him rest. Give him quiet and clean air. Turn out these intruders upon his sickness.* And remembered how, long ago, when she herself had been sick he had, with his own hands, turned away the crowds and let in sweet air and peace. But he was the King; such peace is not in the King's grace. In the public eye he must die; he may hide nowhere but in the dark earth.

And now it was evening; and still the hideous nightmare. Catherine felt herself torn by anguish. While Charles suffered he was alive; *alive...* and she could hope. But, so terrible that suffering she found herself praying, there by his bedside, that God would take His tor-mented servant unto Himself.

The dark of night gave way to the dark of morning. The anguished eyes had closed; Charles slept a little. In the midst of thanking God for this respite, her own eyes closed. She awoke at once to the small sound that escaped his lips. They were tearing off the plasters. She raised her stricken face and Sir Edmund said, 'Madam, you should rejoice rather. While the King feels pain, there's hope.' And then he said, 'The King must sleep again. Madam the Queen should sleep also... while she may.'

Back in her own room she prayed that God do whatsoever He would with her dear love. One only thing, she implored—that he might be received into the Faith; only so could he find peace to die.

Not surprisingly she fell asleep where she knelt.

She was awakened when her women undressed her and struggled against them. *I must go to the King... I must go to the King!* She kept saying it.

Eliza Ormonde came into the room. She said, 'All day long, in every church they pray for the King—Protestants and Catholics,

Dissenters of every creed—even in their synagogue, the handful of Jews. All, all pray for him. There's no man, woman or child old enough, but weeps and prays.'

'The prayers of good people and their tears would comfort him—did he but know. But they cannot speed his soul to God.'

'That, Madam, we do not know,' Eliza said.

When Eliza came later, she said, 'Madam, the King is better for the people's prayers. His speech has returned. And indeed, Madam, imagine it! The physicians have forbidden him to talk! Ormonde told me that the King smiled at that—as doubting his ability to hold his tongue.'

'Dear God be thanked!' the Queen said. 'But the pain... the *pain*. What of that?'

Eliza said, gentle, 'Not more than he can bear; he has a kingly courage.'

When Catherine went again into the King's room he was propped high upon pillows. He knew her and put out a thin hand; she took it gently within her own. Once he had said, *A mistress is a sugar-plum; a wife's the bread of life*. She thought again of Louise and pitied her—a sister in sorrow yet an outcast.

It was night again. In the sick room the crowd had thinned; the physicians remained and several of the Council, together with my lord Bishop of Wells watching his opportunity to administer the last rites... and James equally watchful that he should never do it.

Again the long night made hideous with their remedies. With morning light Charles seemed a little better still. His speech was clear; he knew perfectly what he said and what others said to him. 'By God's Grace he is out of danger,' Sir Edmund said.

In streets and churches, the people wept and prayed still; but now it was in thankfulness and joy. In the dark afternoon of the winter's day the glow of their bonfires fell upon the pale cheeks of the sick man. But before news of his recovery had spread far beyond London, the King's eye had clouded again; he lay cold and shaking in his bed. But his mind was clear; with a cheerful face he thanked them all for their care of him.

When he slept at last Catherine was persuaded, herself, to rest. He was still clear in his mind and she allowed herself some hope.

Monday, Tuesday, Wednesday... and now Thursday.

When Catherine went into the King's room she could see, without telling, that hope was gone. 'He cannot live the night,' Sir Edmund said. Tom Bruce came and put his arm about her as though she were not his Queen but his mother. He said, 'There was never a King so loved. Men and women of all degree leave their affairs to weep and to pray. London is a city of mourning.'

The short winter daylight faded; the clock struck seven... the dark night seemed endless.

And now came the bishops again, good men, to do their duty by the King's soul; but to James and Catherine they were birds of prey snatching at that same soul. They spoke to him of his immortal part; and how, soon, he must stand before God. He listened; he made no answer. Then my lord bishop of London spoke less gently and more urgently; and, after him, the archbishop of Canterbury putting aside his wonted gentleness and speaking, very clear, of salvation.

But the King, it seemed, was too weary to listen; or, maybe, he listened to another voice—the voice of his own soul. So when they offered him Communion, he said *Not yet*. Then, my lord bishop of Wells whom the King loved, reminding him again of this last journey he must soon take, said, 'Sir, do you repent of your sins?'

'God knows I do!' The King's voice was, for the moment, strong with truth. 'With grief I do repent.' So the good bishop read the absolution for the dying and said, 'Sir, will you take Communion now?'

The dying man made no answer. He wanted no prayer but the prayers of that Faith he had in his heart so long embraced. He was—Catherine could see it—in agony of soul lest his life depart and he make no confession. She could endure it no longer. She went, quietly, from the room. If by some blessed miracle he should ask for a priest, all must be prepared. Already the Holy Sacrament from her chapel at Somerset House stood waiting—the wafer and the wine. *Sweet Jesus let it not wait too long!*

Shut in alone with her grief Louise made that same prayer. She wept now for Charles—she that had always wept for herself. He had been generous and loving; and she had paid him ill. She had sold his secrets, she had conspired with his enemies—good Frenchwoman, she could do no other. She stood greatly in his debt. Maybe, at this last, that debt she could cancel. If through her he partook of the true

Body and Blood of his Saviour and so won his immortal life, it was he that would stand in her debt to all eternity.

But she must not go near the King; a man must not have his sweet sin before him in the hour of his death. She understood that very well; she was a good Catholic—and, because of that, she must save him from the ever-lasting fire.

She must see the Queen again... but would the Queen see her? Luck was with her; in the Queen's anteroom she found Barrillon waiting. There was little love between herself and him; but, for all that, he carried her request to the Queen. 'Madam,' he said, 'the duchess of Portsmouth desires, humbly, to speak with you.' And then, lest the walls should hear, said in so low a voice she must strain to listen, 'It is of the King's soul she would speak.'

'Let her come in,' the Queen said.

When Louise came into the room, Catherine, in that first moment, scarce knew her. The pretty plumpness had fallen into folds of grief; between swollen lids, the blue eyes that had taken the King's heart, peered small and red. Again Catherine was moved with pity that Louise could not, in decency, go near the King to take her last Farewell. She took Louise by the hand—and it was the first time in all these years she had done that—and led her to a chair. But Louise would, by no means, sit in the Queen's presence. She said, 'Madam, nothing but the King's most bitter need forces me upon you at such a time. I beg you will find some way that he may take the Blood and Body of Christ and so save his soul.'

They call you grasping... and so you are. Yet, when your need is greatest you think only of him... of yourself not at all.

Louise said, and now she knelt to the Queen, 'Madam, the King lies surrounded by heretics—and no-one to give him the last rites. He lies there tormented lest he be made to receive those rites his soul cannot accept; for that would be blasphemy. It is we that must think for him, we two alone. Madam, do something, I implore you, before it is too late.'

'We wait our chance. All is ready. Monsieur l'Ambassadeur, will you go to the King's room? When you catch the Duke's eye, take him aside and tell him our purpose. Tell him he must clear the room. Only he can do it—he is master here.' *As he will be master everywhere...* Catherine closed her mind against the thought.

'May heaven bless you,' Louise said.

When Louise had gone Catherine wandered restless. Did Charles want to be received into Holy Church? He was in his right mind; he knew he was dying. Why had he not, of himself, asked for a priest? Did he fear for the succession, lest this be the last straw upon the camel's back, Charles guarding the divine right of Kings to the end?

Barrillon came back. 'The duke is with us in this. *I'd lose all rather than my brother should lose his soul*, he said. But I fancy he'll not lose anything. All's quiet in the city. Without a doubt they'll proclaim him when...' He could not finish the sentence.

XLIII

In the sick room Charles lay infinitely weary, infinitely patient, infinitely sad. James bent to whisper in his ear. 'Sir, you have refused the Sacrament of the Church of England; will you accept that of the Church of Rome?'

'With... all... my... heart.' The familiar words came low and slow.

'I go to bring you a priest,' James whispered.

'Thank God. Then—' and James could see the effort with which he gathered his failing strength, 'There... must... be... no... danger... to you.'

'Though it cost me my life I'll do it!' James said, very low. He turned to those staling the air of the King's room—the five-and-twenty peers and all the Council; and the foreign ambassadors waiting, waiting till the King should die. And, more important than them all, the five bishops, ready to catch the King's soul for their God.

'I must speak with my brother in private,' James said. 'I must ask his wishes about those things that touch him and me alone. Go now, all of you. When we have made an end of talking I shall call you again.'

They thought it a strange request; he could see it in their faces and could not blame them. It was their right to be here. They looked at the King; and he, faintly nodding, they must obey. But, as they went James held back my lords of Bath and Feversham—Protestants both; but hearts more loyal nowhere to be found. 'Keep guard; let no-one enter while I am gone!' he commanded.

Catherine's clock chimed nine as James came into the room. The waiting had seemed endless and she had almost given up hope.

James said, 'He thanks God that, at this late hour, his soul may be saved. *With all my heart*, he said.' They smiled one at the other at the words so perfectly Charles. 'And yet he begged me to do nothing to bring myself into danger. That a dying man should so think of others!' There were tears in the cold blue eyes she had never seen there before; not when his first wife had died, nor her infant sons, nor those babes his second wife had lost.

'All is ready!' the Queen said. 'But—' and in her distress she had actually forgotten the matter, 'the priest... my priest has no English.'

'The Lord has provided. Father Hudlestone is here. I saw him praying as I passed his room.'

'God be praised. Good deeds come home to roost,' she said and remembered that Charles, though it angered many, kept the good priest with him—Father Hudlestone had once saved his life. Now the priest should save his life again—life eternal. She stopped on a thought; she said, 'The good Father risks his life in this. He'd not care overmuch. But Charles would care; and I should care!'

James nodded. 'Charles would bring no man to his death—not though he save his own soul.'

Despairing, they looked at each other. In agony of spirit the dying man waited; the priest stood ready. But, between the King and salvation, a man's life stood.

She said, at last, 'Let the priest borrow cassock and wig; no-one, I think, will know him.'

He nodded. 'I will go at once to Hudlestone and then to my brother. Madam, will you come with me?'

By the private stair that led to the head of the King's bed—that stair by which he had led many a gay lady—Chiffinch, a ravaged creature, led the good Father. The curled wig upon his old tonsured head was so effective a disguise that the Queen must look twice to know him.

'Sir,' James said in the silent room where only my lords of Bath and Feversham kept guard, 'here is the priest that once saved your life. Now he is come to save your soul.'

The King's lips moved in thanks.

Hudlestone knelt beside the bed. 'Sir, are you prepared to be received into the Catholic Church?'

Charles' lips moved again. Catherine thought God Himself gave strength. He said, very slow, 'I die in the Faith of the Cath... o... lic Church. I am sorry for my sins... sorry so long com... ing ... into the true Church. Jesus is... merc... i... ful. Hope... hope for sal... va... tion. Die in... char... it... y... all... the world. Par... don, en... e... mies. Ask par... don all... all I have off-end... ed.'

His eyes closed; sweat poured down the grey face. Hudlestone waited; Catherine wiped the wet face with a napkin.

'Sir, will you make confession now?' the priest asked; and Charles nodding, James went with Catherine to the window, where the fainting voice could not be heard. At the door Bath and Feversham kept watch.

When the Act of Contrition had been made, Charles said the prayer very slowly after the priest; thereafter he lifted weak hands and, by himself, said *Mercy... sweet... Jesus.*

'Now your majesty shall make ready to receive the precious Body and Blood of our dear Saviour,' the priest said.

Charles tried to lift himself in the bed. 'Meet... my Lord... not... not... lying in my bed.'

'Sir, lie still. God understands.'

Father Hudlestone put the wafer on the sick man's tongue; he could not swallow it. James went to the door and called for water. Now Charles could swallow the wafer; he lay back quiet.

Father Hudlestone left the way he had come and the company returned. Now the bishops came again to their duty. When once more they offered the Sacrament Charles shook his head. 'I... have... made... my peace... with... God.'

It was ten of the clock now. Charles lay back upon the pillow, his eyes closed; a look of peace upon his tormented face. Catherine sat looking down upon him. Let her eyes behold him while they might. Sir Edmund King saw how she swayed in her chair, one hand to her head. Yesterday she had fainted. He said, 'Madam, it grows late and you must rest. I must bleed you a little, or I cannot answer for the consequences.'

In the Queen's room he bled her in the arm; and, though relieved of the drumming of her blood and worn with grief of this long day, she could not sleep.

All through the night the brothers talked—the one that was King and the one soon to be King. His confession of Faith, his reception into the Church of his heart, had given Charles strength to say all that must be said. He bade Chiffinch bring his keys. When he tried to take them, they were too heavy. It was Chiffinch that put them into James' hands. 'I... give... them... to... you... with... great... joy!' Charles said.

James knelt; the tears poured down his rigid mouth.

Charles said, slow and very clear, 'I... pray... God... to... bless...the... count... ry...in... you, and... you... in... it.' A spasm of pain—the only sign he gave of agony—twisted his face. Sir Edmund begged that he should take a little rest; but he smiled as who should say Soon there will be time enough to rest.

So the brothers talked; for the first time, perhaps, telling of the love in their hearts one for the other. And, in spite of the King's weakness and pain, it was harder for James, the cold man that had never opened his heart.

It was midnight when Eliza Ormonde came for the Queen. She found Catherine full-dressed and kneeling—as these long hours she had knelt—before her prie-dieu. That Christ, all-loving, would accept her dear love's soul she could no longer doubt; she prayed only that the passing be gentle. As she went through the gallery to the King's rooms, she saw Louise standing grey as a ghost and could yet spare pity that this woman could not come to the man she had, in her fashion, loved, to look upon him for the last time.

When she came into the room Charles sent her a smile of great sweetness; she knelt beside the bed and he put out a hand and laid it upon her head. *It has no weight nor substance; it lies like the hand of a ghost.*

He said, 'Kate...' and there was so much tenderness in the word that her heart all-but broke. She knew that he wanted to ask her pardon and could not bear he should ask it. She knew that he wanted to say his thanks for long friendship, long kindness; she could not endure these things to be said. They must remain secret between her heart and his. She laid a finger upon his lips; they moved under it in the ghost of a kiss. She smiled at him; then, seeing how he lay there so tormented and so good, bearing all with a most patient courage, found herself praying that he might rest now without further torment; that God would call him now... now.

The room began to spin about her. The tormented figure in the bed and the bed with him, was moving slowly... slowly; and now in ever widening, ever quickening circles. There was a blackness rising before her eyes; a weight as of the whole world pressed her down. She put out her hands to thrust away the weight, to break through the darkness, that she might once more set eyes upon her dear love. She was pushing at the darkness with her two hands; she heard a voice speaking... *Forgive me... I am not well.* She did not know the voice was her own.

She opened her eyes upon the darkness; and it was not the darkness of night. Through the curtains a shaft of daylight came slanting... an infinity of motes dancing. The blackness, she saw now, was the blackness of mourning... black curtains about her bed, and at the windows, and upon the walls. They had been busy about that business while she slept. She understood the meaning. She fell back upon the bed.

Charles is dead. He died today. She sought carefully in her mind. *Friday, the sixth day of February in the year of grace sixteen-hundred and eighty-five. Charles is dead. He died today. Friday the sixth day of February...* over and over again.

James came into the darkened room. He was the King now and she must rise. She struggled upwards but he put out a hand. 'Sister, lie still.' And it was long since he had called her *sister* and not Madam. But still she struggled to lift herself.

'I must see him!' she cried out. 'I must *see* him!'

'No.' And he remembered the dark agony imprinted upon the dying face. 'He would not wish it.' And since she struggled still, '*I* do not wish it!' There was new authority in his voice; voice of a King.

He seated himself; a thing he had never done without her permission; but now it was right he should do so.

He said, 'You would wish to know... everything. When they carried you away you were crying out he should forgive your weakness. You remember?'

She nodded.

'He said—and the tears ran down his wasted cheeks, *She ask my pardon? It's I should ask hers. And I do it with all my heart. Yet, no need; no need. She forgave me long ago. Yet I am sorry. Tell her... tell her so...*'

He stopped; for the first time since Charles' illness, she was weeping.

'Then he said Goodbye to me.' James' face was drawn with grief. 'He said he had always loved me. He said he had sent me away because a King, at times, is forced to act against his heart... as I, myself, should find. And then he spoke of you...'

She was glad of the darkness that he could not see her tears.

'The kindest wife, he said; the best, the most loving...'

But not most loved; he never said that; he never said it.

'He bade me cherish you.' He stopped; he said, unwilling, 'He asked for his sons.'

No son of mine to bless his dying eyes. She lay there desolate, seeing them, the handsome boys, kneeling to take his blessing.

'It was Bishop Ken admitted them. There's some to censure him that he admitted the King's bastards—fruits of his sin—to his dying bed.'

'I cannot think God will take it amiss,' she said; and it was as though Charles himself spoke there in the room.

'Young Richmond was crying; at thirteen a boy should discipline his tears. I saw my brother's head turn this way and that seeking... seeking; but he could no longer see. And if he could have seen? He'd not have found the thing he sought.' James' voice was bitter; blunt honesty drove him on. 'His lips were moving; there was no sound in his voice. *Jamie*, he was saying, *Jamie*... he kept saying it. In all the world he loved his Absalom best.'

She was weeping now so that her whole body shook and trembled. He said, 'Enough for now.'

She cried out at that. Every word, every last thought—though not for her—was precious.

'When his sons were gone,' James told her, 'he spoke of... others.'

'You may name them,' she said.

'His children are provided for, he said; and his French mistress, also. But he asked me to guard her dignity that the wind blow not too cold when he was gone. And he remembered the playactress, also. *Let not poor Nelly starve*, he said.'

'It does him honour.' But for all that there was bitterness in her mouth.

'And then—it was growing towards morning—he spoke no more of those that were dear, but of that which was dearest of all—this land and this people; he blessed them both together. And we fell on our knees all of us within the room—and we prayed with him. Then he prayed that his people, everyone, would forgive him if he had done amiss or neglected anything that might have done them good. His voice was faint but by God's miracle it was clear. And all the time he lifted his hands to God.

'And then the pain took him...' James' face twisted. 'It was very bad. Yet he thanked God that gave him strength to bear it; and he thanked those that had cared for him in his sickness. And then—had he not been dying, I had thought he jested—he said, *Gentlemen, forgive me. I have been long a-dying.*'

'It was no jest,' she said. 'Never a man more perfect in courtesy.'

James nodded. 'And now it was morning. He had not slept all night. He asked the time. Six o'clock, Tom Bruce told him; and never have I seen a young face so stricken. It is a good young man. I shall remember him.

'*Draw the curtains* my brother said. *Let me see the light... for the last time.* So Tom drew the curtains; but it was not yet light. And had it been light... he had not seen it. And then... a little thing; yet it was perfect Charles. He whispered about a clock that must be wound. Tom Bruce said it must be his eight-day clock and I went and wound it. He could not see nor hear; but somehow he knew it ticked again, for he lay and smiled.'

Catherine, herself, could not forbear the smile; it was as James had said, perfect Charles.

'He lay murmuring a little... of his children; of this one and that. But mostly of you. *Kate*, he kept saying, *Kate*... I think he wandered then, for he said something about a harbour and a home.'

She held her lips with her two hands lest the cry break forth.

'After that he spoke no more save to say the name of God. And then he plucked a little upon the sheet and he sighed gently, and—very quiet—was gone. It was between eleven and noon.'

'Life has stopped for him. And for me... for me, too. Stop the clocks; stop all the clocks!' she cried out, her voice thin and high with grief.

'Life begins for him—we must believe it!' James said. 'After all the agony—a gentle falling asleep. He died as Christian a gentleman as ever lived; he died the name of God upon his lips; he died in the true Faith. How should a man die better?' And then he said, 'Never such sorrow at the death of any King. Everywhere the people weep as for a child or a father, or a lover or husband. Pray God I die as godly as he; and that I be so good a King, so greatly loved.'

'Amen to that.'

He was dead. She had been his wife, his counsellor, his friend... but never his love. Now she was nothing, nothing at all. And there was no child to comfort her. Those women had their children; but she had no child to bless her with his likeness. Her grief was so bitter, so dire, so eviscerating, it was as though she mourned husband and children together.

When James had gone she dragged herself from the bed, and prayed for the soul of Charles. And, having prayed, stretched herself upon her widow's bed. She looked about the darkened room, lit only by the one lamp that burned before her clock and thought, All that is left... a perpetual darkness.

Epilogue

An old woman sat at her writing-table. She was small and plump yet of immense dignity; and her brown and wrinkled face wore the wise and patient look of a monkey. Catherine of Braganza, Queen-dowager of England—though by that land forgot, her name gathering dust on old documents. Catherine of Braganza, Queen-regent of Portugal—like her mother before her; and, like her mother, accounted the wisest ruler in Europe.

Today was her birthday; and she had a rare hour of leisure. A fitting moment to take stock, to think back.

She dipped her quill into the inkhorn, and began to write.

Twenty-fifth day of November, in the year of Grace, 1705

Today I am sixty-seven. And it is twenty years since my dear love died. Twenty long and lonely years. At first I would not accept that he should be dead and I live on. But the years go by; and the galled neck accepts the yoke. These last years it has been easier for me; for I am come home again to my own land.

I could never have endured those first years after Charles' death, in that cold, grey England, had I not always the dream to come home. For nigh on eight years I fought the English Parliament that, for some reason of its own, would not let me go. But how that dream should, at the last, be fulfilled, I never in my wildest thoughts imagined.

That she should be welcomed by her brother she had hoped; but the joy that shook the whole country had gone beyond all imagining.

Thirteen years ago. And even now astonishment and gratitude moved her still. And this last year had brought the most amazing change of all.

Who could have imagined that I should sit here in the King's place, and with my Council, order all things? But my brother is a sick man and his wife dead; and he, himself, besought me take his place till his son be of age. His one comfort in sickness and sorrow he says, that I hold the reins in my strong hands. Yet I rule not by his wish alone, but by the will of all Portugal. Truth and Justice in my hands they say—and I do pray for it. And I think that, with God's help I do not too ill.

These few months of my Regency I have prosecuted war against the armies of France and Spain; and sent them packing. Philip of Anjou claimed Spain; and to Spain he is welcome—more or less; though I prefer not to have him on my doorstep. But when he threatened to enter my house, also; when he laid claim to this land that my father freed from the Spanish yoke—that was not to be endured. Our victories-in-arms speak of God's Mercy and the rightness of our cause.

The clock struck the hour; the eight-day clock young Bruce had wound for the dying King. She looked at it, never, without remembering Charles. Now, as ever, her thoughts turned to him.

It is not enough to love peace, Charles always said. One must seek peace and pursue it even to the bloody heart of war. To win peace one must be ready to strike first. From Charles I learned, too, something of the art of Kingship. And the first lesson was to keep my own counsel beneath a still face. How often, when I was young, did my tears or tongue betray me? He taught me, also, to let the law, for good or ill, take its course. Never to interfere but to alter, if it may be done, such laws as are unjust or over-hard. Such little wisdom as I may have, I have learned from him.

The steady ticking of the clock reminded her that when next it struck the hour, she must leave this quiet room to meet her Council. She moved her shoulders as though to ease them of a burden. Yet it was precisely this burden that gave her courage to live.

That morning James came to tell me Charles was dead, I cried out my life was ended, too. If I had guessed at the years ahead—the bitter years in England—despised, too poor to live in royal estate, would my heart have not died, too, so that they must bury me with my dear love? But God gives us neither foreknowledge nor choice. It is He that decides if He has work for us or no.

There in the quiet close, the small bare room that had been her mother's, her thoughts went back over her long life, its beginnings so far away yet so clear—as though one looked through the lenses of a diminishing glass.

Her first pilgrimage on her return had been to the Convent of the Sacred Heart. The same old walls, the same chapel—on the altar the same flowers, you might think. The same nuns—fat ones and thin; melancholy and merry. And the children, too, the same.

Here time stands still; unaltered—save for me, standing old and wrinkled among the timeless children.

Joyous days in the convent, innocent and gay; yet her schooling had been a mistake.

A Queen should be bred to queenship; but I went into England so unqueenly that, for all my three-and-twenty years they laughed at my innocence—or ignorance, according to the kindness of their tongues. Yes, in this same England, with tears and with anger, I learned my first hard lessons in queenship; and the hardest—to curb my high anger.

Her passions and her tears... the clock struck the quarter unheard. On this, her birthday, the years drew her back.

Queen-regent of Portugal, signing her royal decrees. Did *she* know that—the woman who had once cost the young Queen of England so many tears. Barbara Castlemaine—poor, wretched woman; it was her turn to weep now. Fortune had turned her back for ever.

This same year that saw me Regent, she married again—and at once regretted it. Yet here, Fortune a little relented; for, the handsome young bully had a wife already and so my lady was free of him; free to live in poverty, robbed for the most part of her wealth—the Beau had seen to it. Barbara, duchess of Cleveland; high-sounding name... dishonoured name. Raddled, fat and dropsical, she lives her lonely life, at odds with her children, despised for her poverty, ridiculed for her marriage-venture and hated for her vile temper. And once she had the King of England's heart beneath her heel. I never thought the day would come when I must pity her...

By a natural step Catherine's mind moved on to *that woman's* rival.

The little Stuart. Frances. Frances living alone and dying alone with her cats; naming them for friends long-dead; talking to them as though they were, indeed, those friends... She died two years since, Frances, lovely and childlike to the end.

Barbara. Frances. And then, Louise. Louise had shaken the dust of England off her feet. She hadn't been satisfied with the allowance James had made her, though—five thousand a year—it was generous enough. She'd wanted the fifty thousand she'd been getting—more than half of it in Irish taxes. But she'd been a rich woman without it; she had her prudent investments in France as well as in England; she'd had her lands, her houses, her jewels. Back she'd gone to France—and a fleet of ships to carry her plunder—to look to her interests there and to flaunt herself in Paris and Versailles.

And flaunt herself she did! But, alas, a great personage no longer; her day of usefulness was over. She lived at first in more than royal splendour. Her clothes, her households, her coaches, her horses, her entertainments—never such extravagance even in the court of France. And her gambling debts! Her fat purse had grown lean; and there was no good-natured Charles to fill it again. Still, the French King had been kind; to her at least! And no cost to himself. He had forbidden her tradesmen to sue her for debt... and many an honest family he'd ruined.

Poor Louise. That debauched boy her son had run from her, no-one knew whither; to England it was thought. So to England she had planned to return to look to her affairs—her money; and that which she loved even more—her son. But William had forbidden her to set foot on English soil ever again... William, his life's ambition realised—William King of England; sly William, mean William denying every penny James had given. William-with-the-crown, William refusing Louise. If Charles could know! Mouth twisted in pain she thrust William from her mind; but still he hovered, waiting his admittance; she could not keep him out for long. Resolute, she turned her mind to Louise.

But Louise had done well enough; her French investments were excellent; there'd been a shrewd sale of property and, in addition, Louis had doubled her allowance. But she, to whom all English backs had once bent, counted for nothing now; that her pride could not endure. She'd done the wisest thing; retired to the country where she could play the great lady. She lived in Aubigny now, her estate that had once belonged to Frances and her husband Richmond. She devoted herself to good works; she'd founded a convent with a hospital. Who would have thought it of Louise, good Catholic though she was?

Catherine took up her pen.

She made my life bitter. I was jealous and with reason. And, had I not been jealous, I must still have hated her because again and again she betrayed Charles to her master in France. Yet, through her he made a good ending; through her he saved his soul. I forgive her everything.

And then Hortense. Hortense Mazarin-Mancini de Meilleraye. The last rival; her own and Louise's. Clever Louise; she'd made a parade of sisterhood—Louise's wits ruling her heart. But Hortense had a wild, wild heart; a heart to run away with her wits. All, all lost for love. And, in the end, love, itself, lost.

So lonely, so poor her dying, broken in means as in health... drinking herself to death. So dreadful an end to all her glory. She never left England... alive. Always she had loved travelling; dead, she went her travels again. Her crazy husband claimed her body and dragged it with him wherever he went; fantastic ending to a fantastic life. And then, tiring—not unnaturally—of his grotesque burden, he'd left it behind in some French village where the country-folk treated it like the relic of a saint, Louise a living saint; Hortense a dead one! I think Charles would have smiled at that! And there Hortense stayed until her children took her away. She lies now, at rest, next to her uncle the Cardinal. I trust she disturbs his peace less than when a wayward, troublesome girl...

Wayward; a troublemaker wherever she went and now she was dead. And that other wayward creature, dead, also—Charles' pretty, witty Nelly. Her story a short one. She'd been in debt when Charles died—her own kindness the chief cause; open heart, open hand. James had paid her debts and given her many a present, besides. And when she died two years after Charles—and never the same gay Nell—James had paid for her funeral.

Let not poor Nelly starve. Charles had asked it, dying. There were some to doubt it, Louise, not least. But James vouched for it. And it was right and proper. In his dark hours she made Charles laugh; and, in his darkest hour, he remembered her. Nell had the wit to die betimes. So she is remembered with love by the common people of England; and especially by those that keep old bones warm on her charity. *Whore-with-a-halo*—there her epitaph.

The clock struck the second quarter. But she did not hear it. She was lost in the past remembering those long dead—Falmouth for whose death she had first seen Charles weep; and Buckingham hateful and debauched and dead these many years... dead long before death took him at last, ruined—health, wealth and wits. These two had sought her downfall; but Clarendon had stood her friend—though she hadn't known it then. Dear Clarendon, kind heart, true friend. And how could she forget Shaftesbury that Charles had called the basest of men? Shaftesbury... and Monmouth. Of Jamie she could not bear to think.

But it was not only people that were gone. Whitehall was gone, too. Gone the room where Charles had died and the room where she had been told of his death. Gone Louise's lodgings that had been the wonder of the world. Gone the Stone gallery where the musicians sang; and where Charles had sat among his ladies that last Sunday of his life... the Stone gallery where all the world went visiting Louise. Gone up in flames because of a tipsy maidservant careless of her candles. Gone. All gone except the Banqueting Hall; the noble room where all England came to see the King at meat... the room from which the first Charles went out to die.

Whose ghost walks there? The first Charles stepping out in the cold of that Winter's morning? Or my own Charles, laughing and gay?

Ah well, if Whitehall was gone, another new landmark had risen, the landmark she had watched growing.

St. Paul's. The great church Charles planned with Wren, there in my quiet room, and I pouring the sweet Portugal wine and listening while they talked... talked of the noble dome at whose very thought people once laughed. They laugh no longer, seeing it rise high against the sky lifting men's hearts to God. Charles never saw it finished; it was William that had it consecrated.

She sat, her small wrinkled face a mask of grief. For, after all, William had taken the crown. James had come to the throne and all set fair... at the first. But James was James—obstinate, blunt, not clever with people. And Monmouth...

And no longer could she escape the thought of him.

...Monmouth was Monmouth—handsome, worthless, false and charming. Dear God, how charming! So Jamie led his doomed rebellion; and, being taken, crawled before James, grovelling for his life.

He wrote to me from his prison cell; and since Charles would have wished it and because, in spite of all his faults I loved him once, I tried to save him. But it was useless... useless. So, in his dying, proud as any King of them all, Jamie laid down his handsome head upon the block.

A tear rolled down her cheeks. For Jamie? For Charles? For the sorrow of life?

It was justice and it was sense—James could do no other. But I wept in a black gown remembering Charles that had so loved his Absalom.

But for all that James did not keep the crown. Four years, four little years and the crown was lost; the crown Charles had risked his own to save. So James went his travels again; and with him his wife and little son, a slur cast upon his birth—the son for whom he had agonised and prayed.

The clock struck the three-quarters; but chin cupped in her hand she did not hear it. All that talk about a babe smuggled into the Queen's bed in a warming-pan. Such nonsense! The boy was James' true son. She, herself, had actually seen the child delivered. It was a thing to set on record.

I was within the Queen's bedchamber from the beginning of her travail until the boy was born. I did not stir from her bedside until I saw him delivered. The midwife brought him first to me and put him in my hands. A lusty child—and his birthright writ clear upon him—the handsome Stuart.

But for all that—or because of it—since the people had no desire for a second Catholic King, the English were finished with James. He fled to France with his wife and little son. And Mary—selfish Mary that had behaved so ill to a most loving father—was Queen. And whey-faced William—and now he could no longer be kept from her thoughts—whey-faced William wore an equal crown.

Surely Charles had turned in his grave the day of their crowning. He had never trusted William... and good reason; all his suspicions had proved themselves true. William had used every means to discredit James, to bar him from the succession. It was William that had been behind Shaftesbury and Monmouth; yes and behind Oates, too, paying him well for his bloody persecutions of good Catholics. Events had made it plain.

Shortly after Charles died James brought a libel suit against Oates; and the creature—being no longer the public idol and no jury fearing him—was found guilty and fined one hundred thousand pounds which he could no more pay than the man in the moon. So he was cast into prison—the object, maybe, of so great a fine. His luck was gone, it seemed, for good. Two years later he was convicted of perjury—and rightly convicted. His punishment was horrible.

Even I that hated him that had brought so many good men to torment and to death, even I sickened of its savagery. They stripped him of the once-fine bishop's robes soiled now with the grime of his prison; and they put a writing upon his head setting forth his crimes; and they stood him half-naked in the pillory of Palace Yard. And there did not lack those he had injured to take their advantage. Thereafter they marched him, all foul with their filth, through the streets to the tune of their catcalling—proud Oates that had once but to look at a man to spell his death. And that done, he was whipped from Aldgate to Newgate; and the next day from Newgate to Tyburn; seventeen hundred strokes they gave him so that he fainted beneath them and was dragged half-dead back to prison.

No punishment she had thought once, too great for him that had brought innocent men to a tormented, shameful death. Yet Christians should remember that God is a God of mercy... but mercy James lacked; singularly lacked. So the punishment was to end only with Oates' life. That men should not forget his wickedness he was to be pilloried five times a year as long as he should live; and each time in a different place. And so it fell out during the four years of James' reign.

And then, when William came with Mary a strange thing happened; yet not so strange if you knew the truth.

She lifted her pen and wrote,

William repealed the punishment. Well, a merciful man might well do that—though William, no more than James, was known for mercy. *But William released Oates from prison... and William gave Oates a very comfortable pension...* and William was not one to pay save for value received. It is not hard to believe that William—that cold and rigid Protestant—had set the creature on to swear against the innocent; or that William knew more than a little about the Rye House Plot... William with both eyes on the succession. And certainly he did not disapprove of attacks upon me... *I, Titus Oates, do accuse Queen Catherine...*

The mincing, poisonous voice rang in her ears. Even now she sickened, remembering; even now she would awake in the dark night crying out against the monstrous charge. And, on her death-bed, also, must remember...

But, this for her comfort. In England bloody persecution had come to an end; for over twenty years no Catholic had died for his Faith—his Faith alone.

She stopped suddenly on a thought.

The day Plunket died, Charles had said, *I pray he be the last to die for his Faith.* And she—*Pray God death bring him a martyr's crown.* And then she had said, *God will hear us both.* Charles' prayer, it seemed, was answered... twenty years is a long time. And for her own prayer— maybe she'd made a prophecy there, also. In His own time God would speak.

William and Mary. With all their faults, this, at least, they had done—given peace to those of the true Faith. Maybe they hadn't cared enough, either of them, for God or their own faith. Maybe this was God's inscrutable way. Turning Catholic James from the throne, He had preserved the lives of Good Catholics.

William and Mary. But Mary had not enjoyed her crown for long. Five years—and she was dead; dead of the little pox that spared neither prince nor pauper nor Queen nor whore. And there was William crying his grief aloud so that the sound of his mourning reached across the sea to Lisbon.

It was the year I came home to my own land; the year of grace sixteen-hundred and ninety-three. How should I forget it? William had a cold heart; he had treated her ill and all Christendom knew it. Thereafter he reigned alone. Eight years alone. Unwilling to share his greatness with another. Reigning alone, living alone; unloved, yet oddly respected, the dour Dutchman that was, for all that, true Stuart. So Anne came to the throne. Two of Lawyer Hyde's grand-daughters to wear the crown of England. Had he ever, in his wildest, maddest moments imagined two Queens sprung from his seed?

Head between her hands she considered Anne.

Anne fat and foolish with her poor peering eyes and her loving heart; her very kindness a stumbling-block. For Anne, too, had her mistress; a mistress more mischievous than any mistress of Charles—he had known how to circumvent those that meddled in his affairs. But Sarah Jennings—that same pretty Sarah that had teased and tormented Anne's girlhood—now teased and tormented the Queen. She wielded power, she dictated policies, she furthered all to serve her own ambition; and the ambition of her husband Marlborough—that same John Churchill Charles had surprised in bed with *that woman*—her paid lover. For that betrayal of his king and friend she had paid him well... but William a had paid great deal better for an even greater betrayal. It might truly he said that the Churchill fortune was based upon betrayals.

But that was long and long ago... sixteen years since Churchill had been translated into my lord duke of Marlborough, twenty, almost, since he'd started his intrigues with William; and longer still since he'd crept into *that woman's* bed... when the Queen was young and Charles, for a little, had loved her.

She sat there grieving for days that were gone; and because love had lasted so short a time.

She shrugged, impatient. To grieve was foolish. For, if there had been sorrow, there had been happiness, also; such happiness as is given to few. And if that happiness had not lasted, yet it had shed joy enough to light a lifetime. And afterwards, when his passion was spent, and she was sick or with child, he showed such tenderness as he had shown no woman, ever... she was his wife.

How should she complain? Some wives had neither love nor a husband's kindness. Minette, so enchanting, what kindness from her vicious husband, ever? Or, if there's still loving between husband and wife—how if it come to a bloody end? How had Madam Queen Henrietta-Maria endured to live after the head she loved had fallen to the axe? Yet, with the most of men and women love goes over; and even Madam Henrietta that had so tenderly loved her husband, yet lived to love again.

She took up her pen and wrote,

But I am one to love but once and for ever. And Charles—though his dying was hard—died a good death. For he died in suffering, sent by God and nobly home; a long suffering by God's Mercy that gave him time to make his peace with Him. And for that mercy I do thank Him. For be the time long or short—and time though it seem eternal here, is yet but a moment in the face of eternity—we shall meet again. Flawed we are—it is our human condition; but in the end we shall surely win to God that is All-mercy.

Charles used to say—and how it troubled me once—*God will not be too harsh if we take a little pleasure on the side.* And I think, perhaps he was right. Charles is safe in his hope of heaven... and surely heaven would be a sad place lacking him...

She considered this last thought a little shocked. Yet he was safe in his hope of heaven—she could not but think it. So kindly a man that would give freedom to each man to seek God in his own way; that had set his face against persecution in the name of God, and so brought upon his head the anger of all men—Catholic to Quaker. So patient a man, seeking always the good of his people. Yet Parliament had accused him that he took money from Louis—Parliament that had cheated him to the tune of four-and-a-half million pounds... and he so poor, at times he lacked a cravat. Yet, patient and wise, he never threw their cheating in their face. He did take gold from France; but he never sold his country. It was a thing his enemies never understood. It was a thing to be written down, to be made known and never forgotten.

He never did one thing Louis asked unless himself desired it also; desired it for the good of the country. Louis wanted him to disband the army and offered enough to pay every debt. Charles refused. But Parliament disbanded it; and Louis got his way... and Charles never a penny the better. And the most part of the moneys he received from

France he spent upon the country's needs. Had Parliament paid him his rightful English gold, there had been no need of gold from France. Had Parliament not cheated...

How easy to cheat that generous heart! Through herself he had been cheated—but without her knowledge. Her dowry was never paid; yet, save for that one time they'd quarrelled over *that woman* he'd never cast it up to her.

They made over-much of his witty tongue and his light pleasures; they made over-little of the great wisdom in him, the gentleness, the kindliness. Because of these things Charles is bound for heaven; and I, maybe, may climb at his heels.

She rose and went to the window and so stood, looking over the bay where she had sailed to England more than forty years ago. She heard her thoughts clear in the quiet room.

How often did I trouble God with my complaints that Charles whom I loved with all my heart, loved not me? I forgot what Minette said to me all those years ago; but now, now I remember it. *To be allowed to love—it is the reason for living.* So young she was for such wisdom. But I? I needed a long life to learn that truth. To be allowed to love; to keep that love faithful as long as one shall live—heaven's best gift. Such a gift God gave me. For Charles was my dear love and I was his wife. Charles made glorious my life and for that I thank Him that knows all and orders all.

The clock struck the hour; the Council waited.

She squared her weary shoulders; she turned to the door.

Some Books Consulted

Bryant, Sir Arthur, *King Charles II*.

Burnet, Gilbert, *History of His Own Times*.

Chamberlayne, Edward, *Angliae Notitiae*.

Charles II, Five Letters. Camden Misc. 5.

Clarendon, 1st Earl of, *Life*, in which is included a continuation of his history of the Grand Rebellion.

Clark, John S., *Life of James II, from original manuscript*.

Cominges, Comte de, *A French Ambassador at the Court of Charles II*, ed. by A.J. Jusserand.

Cunningham, Peter, *Life of Nell Gwynn*.

Davidson, Lillias C., *Catherine of Braganza*.

Dictionary of National Biography.

Ellis, Sir Henry, ed., Original letters. Camden Soc. Orig. Series. 23.

Evelyn, John, Diaries.

Fornéron, Henri, *Louise de Kéroualle*. Trans. C.M. Crawford.

Hamilton, Anthony, *Memoirs of the Comte de Grammont*.

Howell, Thomas B., *State Trials*. Vols. 7 and 8.

Hudleston, John, *A brief account of the happy death of our late sovereign lord King Charles II*.

Jamieson, Anna A., *Memoirs of the beauties of the Court of Charles II*.

Newton, Lady Evelyn, *Lyme Letters, 1660-1760*.

Oman, Carola M.A., *Mary of Modena*.

Pepys, Samuel, Diaries.

Romney, Earl of, *Diary of the times of Charles II*, ed. Robert Blencowe.

Somers, John, Baron, *A collection of scarce and valuable tracts*, ed. Sir W. Scott. Vols. 7-8.

State Papers Domestic.

Steinman, George S., *A Memoir of Barbara, Duchess of Cleveland*.

Strickland, Agnes, *Lives of the Queens of England*. Vols. IV and V.

TORC, an imprint of TEMPUS

We Speak No Treason
The Flowering of the Rose
ROSEMARY HAWLEY JARMAN

'Superb' *The Sunday Mirror*
'Brilliant' *The Sunday Express*
'Outstanding' *The Guardian*
THE NUMBER ONE BESTSELLER

£6.99   0 7524 3941 3

We Speak No Treason
The White Rose Turned to Blood
ROSEMARY HAWLEY JARMAN

'A superb novel' *The Sunday Express*
'I could not put it down' *The Sunday Mirror*
'Ablaze with colour, smell and sound, for lovers
of the historical novel, this is a feast' *Vogue*
THE NUMBER ONE BESTSELLER

£6.99   0 7524 3942 1

Wife to the Bastard
HILDA LEWIS

'A spankingly good story about Matilda'
The Spectator
'Well documented historical fiction'
The Observer
'A work of quiet distinction' *The Sunday Times*

£6.99   0 7524 3945 6

Wife to Charles II
HILDA LEWIS

'A lively story, full of plots and trials and
executions... Fragrant is the word the tale brings
to mind' *The Observer*
'Filled with splendour, intrigue, violence and
tragedy' *The Yorkshire Post*

£6.99   0 7524 3948 0

Eleanor the Queen
NORAH LOFTS

'One of the most distinguished of English
women novelists'
The Daily Telegraph

£6.99   0 7524 3944 8

The King's Pleasure
NORAH LOFTS

'This is everything that a good historic novel
should be'
The Guardian

£6.99   0 7524 3946 4

Harlot Queen
HILDA LEWIS

'Hilda Lewis is not only mistress of her subject, but
has the power to vitalise it'
The Daily Telegraph

£6.99   0 7524 3947 2

The Concubine
NORAH LOFTS

'Fascinating'
The Sunday Times
THE INTERNATIONAL BESTSELLER

£6.99   0 7524 3943 X

If you are interested in purchasing other books published by Tempus, or in case you have difficulty finding any
Tempus books in your local bookshop, you can also place orders directly through our website

www.tempus-publishing.com